PENGUIN BOOKS

SAMANTHA SMYTHE'S MODERN FAMILY JOURNAL

'An addictive concoction of humour and calamity that you'll read in one sitting' *OK!*

'Revel in someone else's domestic hell – or simply enjoy the reminder that you are not alone' *She*

'A surprisingly accomplished comedy of modern manners' *Daily Mail*

'An amusing, uplifting read' *Heat*

'Funny but also charmingly touching' *Woman*

'A very witty read' *Closer*

'A lightly amusing chick-lit number about the trials of mummyhood' *Tatler*

ABOUT THE AUTHOR

Lucy Cavendish has spent most of her life working in journalism for the *Evening Standard*, the *Sunday Telegraph*, the *Observer* and the *Guardian*. She lives in Oxfordshire with her husband Michael and their four children. This is her first novel.

Samantha Smythe's Modern Family Journal

LUCY CAVENDISH

PENGUIN BOOKS

PENGUIN BOOKS

Published by the Penguin Group
Penguin Books Ltd, 80 Strand, London WC2R ORL, England
Penguin Group (USA), Inc., 375 Hudson Street, New York, New York 10014, USA
Penguin Group (Canada), 90 Eglinton Avenue East, Suite 700, Toronto, Ontario, Canada M4P 2Y3
(a division of Pearson Penguin Canada Inc.)
Penguin Ireland, 25 St Stephen's Green, Dublin 2, Ireland
(a division of Penguin Books Ltd)
Penguin Group (Australia), 250 Camberwell Road, Camberwell, Victoria 3124, Australia
(a division of Pearson Australia Group Pty Ltd)
Penguin Books India Pvt Ltd, 11 Community Centre, Panchsheel Park,
New Delhi – 110 017, India
Penguin Group (NZ), 67 Apollo Drive, Rosedale, North Shore 0632, New Zealand
(a division of Pearson New Zealand Ltd)
Penguin Books (South Africa) (Pty) Ltd, 24 Sturdee Avenue, Rosebank,
Johannesburg 2196, South Africa

Penguin Books Ltd, Registered Offices: 80 Strand, London WC2R ORL, England

www.penguin.com

First published by Michael Joseph as *The Invisible Woman* 2007
Published in Penguin Books as *Samantha Smythe's Modern Family Journal* 2008

1

Set in Dante MT
Typeset by Palimpsest Book Production Limited, Grangemouth, Stirlingshire

Printed in England by Clays Ltd, St Ives plc

ISBN: 978-0-141-02729-6

www.greenpenguin.co.uk

Penguin Books is committed to a sustainable future
for our business, our readers and our planet.
The book in your hands is made from paper
certified by the Forest Stewardship Council.

For Raymond

My name is Edward, I am eight years old and I live in a house with my mummy Samantha, my daddy John (the Second) and my little brothers Bennie, who is two – who is a bit annoying and poos everywhere – and Jamie, who is eight months and only eats butternut squash. I love watching the telly, particularly Open University and Scooby Doo videos, and I think stew is disgusting. I have a best friend called Stanley whose mummy doesn't let him eat sweets or tell lies or draw snake pictures on his willy.

My real father is also called John (the First) and has come to visit his mummy who is in the hospital near our house, so he's staying with us. I like him because he calls me Eddie and he's a bit like a pirate, although I don't think Mummy is that keen . . .

Dear Reader,

I thought I'd just give you a quick note on how to navigate/read this book. For those who love detail, like me (even though I seem so scatty and disorganized, underneath that exterior lurks a deeply organized woman), there are endless descriptions of domestic bits and pieces *all in this typeface*, which you will hopefully love and enjoy. There are bits on What the Children Like to Eat and the Politics of Television and How Much Laundry I Do in a Week and everything to make a domestic, or even undomestic, goddess smile with contentment. However, for those of you who find the intricate details of everyday life a total and utter bore, skip these and read on and miss out with impunity on why Edward won't eat John the Second's favourite beef stew and the definitive guide to going for a walk with two children still in nappies . . . for all will be revealed in the end!

I hope you enjoy it. I really do.

Samantha Smythe (mother of Edward, Bennie and Jamie)

Prologue

Someone once told me that being happy is not wanting what you haven't got but wanting what you already have. I think about this often. I am a married mother of three boys. I live a pretty nice life in the countryside. I like the peace and the quiet. I like the animals and the trees and the flowers and the fields. It reminds me of when I was a child and I learnt about everything. I spent my days watching things hatch and emerge and mate and move and die. My mother taught me about flowers and fruit and how to make a kitchen garden. My father taught me about life.

Sometimes he would take me and my older sister, Julia, walking through the crop fields around our house. We'd wander down dusty paths and watch the crows and the jays tearing around and flapping about overhead, dive-bombing the red kites that flew in soaring circles on the thermals way above us, up and over the Chiltern hills and valleys. We'd find used and abandoned birds' eggs along the way and my father would bend down and pick them up and caress them in his hand as if they still had poor broken babies inside them. But the fledglings were long gone – either eaten or hatched, I never knew which. Then my father would show me the colourings on the speckled shells and me and my sister would go home and find his bird book and look up all the eggs in it. One of us would then run and show him and he'd peruse the page a bit and nod his head and say, 'I thought as much.'

Before my father died, before everything turned black and dark for him, I think his mind went back to his time in the countryside when all was light and easy. Once he asked me how I knew the difference between all those ruined egg shells and I told him that it was he who had told me. Couldn't he remember that? It turned out that he couldn't. I think it was one of the last conversations we ever had.

Now I know many things. I know how birds' eggs crush and crumble and what ripe crops taste of. I know how cornflowers and speedwell spread and gallop like wildfire through the fields. I know how dragonfly pupae creep to the top of the rushes in the pond and then break out and fly off with their glittering wings. I know about frogspawn and tadpoles and pond snails and water boatmen. I know about life and death and love and hate and many of the grey areas in between. And I know what it is for a child to grow inside my body and be there, safe and warm and cocooned by me.

So here I am, me and my life. It is chaotic but sometimes, most times, it functions. Sometimes it does not. Sometimes I go around shouting and screaming and then my second John (I had Edward with my first John but we parted) will take me upstairs to our bedroom and lie with me and calm me down, and our children will line up along the wall like little silent ghosts watching a real-life enactment of Bedlam. I will then feel dreadful about my lack of self-control and spend an hour apologizing to them, which makes them think I am even more mad.

I wonder where my time has gone. It seems such an

age since John and I had some freedom. Life has been taken over by the clock. Get up time. Breakfast time. Playgroup time. Lunch time. Walk the dog time. Feed the dog time. Supper time. Bath time. Bedtime. Clean the house. Do the laundry. Go to the shops. Make the food. Throw the uneaten food away.

How has this happened? How have John and I become so weighed down in domesticity? We need some more spontaneity, me and John, I think. And now I want to find him somewhere in this tip that we call home. I want to dig under the toys and the milk-sodden cot sheets and the *Postman Pat* annuals and find him and hold him and tell him that I love him and that I'm sorry that I can be bad-tempered and scratchy and overcritical. I want to tell him how happy I am that he found me and Edward and scooped us up and balanced us all back out again. After all, where would we be without him?

As the sun drifts over the hill and disappears behind the front of our house and the dusk comes in, I sit in my garden, in my fragrant beautiful garden that I have watched grow and blossom, and I think, suddenly, about how insecure this all could be. Maybe John will have enough and leave. Maybe something catastrophic will happen and we'll end up separated and hurt and lonely. I know what it is to be unhappy, to be let down. But my second John came and now my first John is just a memory. I must live in the here and now for it is the here and now that I trust. This I do know.

And so I thought I kind of knew everything pretty much until one week, one summer, when everything changed.

1. Saturday

It's Saturday afternoon and a man I have never met before is driving me too fast down the M4. We are in his Vauxhall Vectra. His mobile phone rings constantly, every five minutes. It has an annoying bouncy ring tone. When the man is not on his phone – ''enley. I'm in 'enley!' he yells incredibly loudly down the receiver – he's telling me how fast, quick, speedy he is in his Vauxhall Vectra. 'I've been up since four o'clock this mornin',' he tells me proudly. 'I've done five jobs so far. And now I'm with you in 'enley going to 'ampshire.' He seems very pleased about this. For a while I wonder why. Four o'clock this morning. I look at his speedometer: 92 mph. Reading flashes past in a haze. Junction 10. And it suddenly occurs to me, as his phone rings again – ''enley. I'm in 'enley!' – that I'm going to die.

I'm on my way to interview a famous, super-skinny television presenter. It's what I do for a living. I'm a freelance food and health writer. I used to write about important things like 'Can superfoods keep you healthy?' and 'Ten top food sources to help minimize the risk of Alzheimer's' but now, since I've had children, my brain doesn't seem to be able to concentrate on anything very much. Consequently, I have now limited my journalistic prowess to sneaking into people's fridges and analysing their dietary habits. I do one a week for a glossy, mid-market women's magazine. It's not exactly what I set out to do with my life but it can actually be quite fun. One film director's fridge was stocked full of champagne; an American pop star didn't have an egg in sight, and a former glamour model had caviar in hers, expensive and Russian. But this famous, super-skinny television presenter is so tricky to pin down that it's taken me a week to sort it out. I've been through hoops; we started off agreeing on a Thursday and then it went to a Friday, a Sunday and, finally, this Saturday afternoon.

'Well, that's great,' she said delightedly over the telephone. 'Saturday afternoon at my house in Hampshire.'

Only it wasn't great for me. 'I have three children and no child care on this particular Saturday. My husband is working on Saturday this week,' I told her. I'd suggested the Sunday when he wasn't going to work. I'd suggested any other day when I could get help, but Saturday . . . Saturdays are bad.

This is what happens on most Saturdays: 7 a.m. kids get up. Edward gets up first. He then wakes up Bennie, for no apparent reason other than that Edward thinks that is fun. Bennie then careers into our bedroom screaming, 'Mulk, mulk,' and then John and I have one of those just-roused-from-sleep vague bickers.

Me: Darling, are you going to get Bennie some milk?

Him: Erggh, erggh.

Me: You haven't seen him for three days and I'm sure he'd really like you to get him some.

Him: Erggh, erggh, erggh.

I then get up, pad down the stairs and get Bennie his milk. Back upstairs John seems dead to the world. Bennie tears off downstairs to watch something violent and unsavoury with his brother. In about half an hour, one of them will burst into tears – usually Bennie – and come upstairs wailing. Edward will then run upstairs and hotly deny having done anything. The baby, Jamie, will wake up and start crying and the whole 'who's going to get the bottle' conversation will start up again.

Between 7.15 and 7.45, there is usually a brief half-hour respite. During this tiny quiet window of opportunity, this is, on this particular Saturday, what I am thinking about: what footwear should Edward wear for his 15-km school's sponsored walk? Did I wash his soft jeans that I want him to wear so that his thighs don't chap? Oh thank goodness I remembered to buy some bottled water, crisps, chocolate, sandwich loaf, cheese and Nutrigrains for his packed lunch. Will I let him take the dog? Probably, but where will she be able to get water from? Bound to be troughs on the way. Shall I take Bennie too? Maybe for the first 4 km in his all-terrain buggy. But what if I get a puncture? Nothing much I can do about that. God, what time's my mother coming to take care of the baby? What's the time now? Nearly a quarter to eight. Better get up. There's the washing from last night to hang out and a white wash to go on and the pets to feed and two picnics to be made and I need to get them all changed – Bennie's nappy is soaking and Jamie's smells – and fed and watered and ready to get going.

I roll towards John who smells sweetly sweaty and is still sleepy. 'What are you thinking about?' I ask him.

'Sex,' he says and grabs my bottom.

On this Saturday morning, John leaves for work. He grabs a slice of toast and a coffee, shoves a bottle in the baby's mouth and swings Bennie up and kisses him and winks at Edward, remembers to kiss me and says, 'Love you, Samantha,' then slings his leather bag over his shoulder, finds his sunglasses that Bennie has tried to put on the cat, retrieves the car keys from the dog basket where I had seen them last night but was too tired to remember to pick them up, and sweeps out of the house. All in the space of a few seconds.

I am left here, mouth agape, kitchen a mess, three children to clothe and feed, and all before my weekend starts too. Damn him, I think irritably. Sometimes, quite a lot of the time actually, I wish I were him. I wish I could have a bath on my own without some mad child getting in it, and then have the time to choose what to wear. I wish I could leave the kitchen in a disgusting state, milk and eggs everywhere, and all the utensils out of the drawers because that's what the baby likes to do all day every day. He takes all the pans and cake tins out and then solemnly puts them all in his mouth, but he doesn't know how to put them back. No one in this house seems to know how to put anything back into any drawer, bar me.

Today Santa has agreed to come in and help. Santa is my part-time au pair. She will come in at eleven to take over from my mother. My mother doesn't really approve of Santa. It's not Santa as a person she doesn't approve of but the whole concept that anyone can't run everything in the world by themselves.

'But why do you need help?' she'll say when I say oh-I-hope-you-don't-mind-but-Santa-is-coming-to-take-over-later-on. 'I never had help,' she'll say. 'I did all the cooking and the cleaning and looking after of you two girls and I always had your father's dinner ready for him when he came in,' and then she'll go on to tell me how my sister

Julia, with her six children and her perfect marriage, doesn't have help either. 'Julia's house is spotless!' my mother will say and I'll see her mentally noting the yoghurt spilled all over our kitchen table and the dried patches of milkshake on the windows where Bennie threw it yesterday when he and Edward were playing a game known as 'milk attack' (variations on this game: broom attack, stick attack, Winnie-the-Pooh hot-water-bottle attack).

In reply I usually say, 'But you didn't work and neither does Julia!' and then she will get a bit cross and huffy and will say that a) what I do for work isn't really work either ('Celebrity fridges?' she'll say with a snort), and that b) bringing up children full-time, like she and Julia have done, is far harder work than doing the odd bit of journalism. Then she'll say that it wasn't that she didn't want to work but that once you got married and started a family you were expected to stay at home and be a housewife.

'I made a lovely home for your father,' she'll say.

That makes me sigh in exasperation and say, 'I'm only gone for a few hours a week!'

The upshot of it all is that my mother has made me feel so guilty about having an au pair that I now lie about it.

Today I can see there is potential for a mother–Santa run-in. My mother is mashing up some butternut squash. Santa doesn't think the baby should have butternut squash alone as she says a baby of Jamie's age needs to experience lots of new tastes. She will find a potato and a carrot. My mother will sulk about this but Santa, who is Hungarian and tends to say 'blaady hell' a lot, won't really pick up on it.

★

I get back from the walk with Bennie at one. At 1.30 p.m. the Vauxhall Vectra appears. My mother has gone home but is coming back at five to take over from Santa, who has to go to a previously arranged babysitting job. I have told my mother that there is a chicken casserole in the fridge. I made it for the babies, which is what I sometimes call Bennie and Jamie, after the health visitor, who came on Thursday and made me cry, told me they weren't eating enough meat. Edward is not having casserole because he doesn't like 'wet food'. That's what he calls it. But my mother has said she won't make a different meal for Edward. Jamie is not having casserole because he only likes butternut squash.

The telephone rings. It's the skinny celebrity's agent. The skinny celebrity doesn't want to show me her fridge today. I tell the agent I am going to cry. I tell her she doesn't understand what I've been through to get these few hours on a Saturday. I tell her I'm coming anyway.

Halfway down the motorway, past junction 10, I realize I'm going to die in a seven-car pile-up because Vauxhall Vectra man is bound to fall asleep and plough across four lanes, leaving blood and guts and broken hearts in his wake. I try to call my husband. I want to tell him that I love him. I want to say that I'm sorry I didn't have sex with him this morning and that I wish I'd told him I loved him more often. I want him to tell the children that the sacrifices I have made for them haven't really been sacrifices at all and that I'm sorry for shouting and being bad-tempered and saying 'no don't do that' all the time and that I'm sorry for smacking Bennie's bum about the pooing thing. But when I look at my phone it's dead. No battery. No signal. No chance to say anything at all.

2. Saturday continued . . .

If John was not working on this Saturday, he'd stay home and cook. In fact, he's recently become obsessed with cooking. A few days before he is intending to cook, when he has what he calls a 'window of opportunity', which makes Edward's eyes goggle as he always takes things very literally, he'll go and buy the meat from the butcher. He'll go off in the car, saying he'll be out for ooh, maybe half an hour, and then not reappear for ages. He'll spend at least an hour at the butcher's, discussing cuts and where the meat has come from and if it is organic or locally produced and that type of thing, and then he'll go off to the greengrocer's and buy fresh vegetables. He'll ask the grocer if they are also organic and when they were picked and whether or not they have been sprayed and will they last until the weekend, and then, finally, he will actually buy some carrots and potatoes, leeks and celery.

So on a non-working Saturday, he'll don his apron and he'll set up for his cooking day. He'll get out all the utensils, virtually every single one, and place them nice and neatly in a row on the surface next to the cooker. He'll then get out his ingredients. If he is making his favourite recipe, beef stew, which is what he makes just about every Saturday, his routine is simple: he just needs the beef and then the onions studded with cloves, garlic, some orange peel, retsina, carrots, celery, stock and a tin of tomatoes. He's got so enraptured with this recipe that he'll even make his own stock. John is very protective of his stew. He'll insist that no one can eat it before Monday so that the flavours can 'seep', as he puts it. So we all have to sit there and watch it mature in the fridge. If he hears so much as a tiny little clang of the lid, he'll leap up and run into the kitchen to make sure no one is sneaking a quick spoonful.

Edward hates Mondays because Edward hates wet food. At first, I used to spoon the meat onto Edward's plate having drained off all the stew bit but Edward soon became suspicious.

'What is Bennie having?' he asked one day when he saw meat and vegetables and gravy slopping round Bennie's plate.

'He's having something different to you,' I said.

'Is he?' said Edward, his eyes widening. 'It doesn't look different. It looks just the same.'

'How can you say it's the same, Edward? Bennie's has gravy and carrots and celery. Yours is just dry cooked meat.'

'It is not, though, is it? It's stew without the stew bit. I know it is.'

From that day forth he has refused to take part in Monday dinner. Instead he puts a bagel in the toaster, lets it burn a bit, and sits watching the television, munching it.

So, to vary his menu, and to make Edward happy, John will sometimes cook fish. Edward and Bennie like baked cod with cheese on it. Sometimes, on a Saturday morning, John and Bennie will go to the fishmonger's because Bennie is mad on seeing all the slippery bodies lying at the counter. He'll gape at them and try to stroke them through the glass counter. Often, if you buy a trout, say, Bennie will pick it up and put its dead fishy nose right up close to his.

''ello,' he'll say to the fish. 'Is dead?'

'Yes, it's dead, Bennie,' John will say.

Bennie will then make a face like a monkey's bottom. 'Poor fishy.'

Other times, when it's the shooting season, John will perch Bennie up on the window sill of the sitting room so that Bennie can see far into the fields beyond.

'Look, Bennie,' he'll say, 'those people out there are shooting pheasants.'

'Bang bang?'

'Yes, all bang-bang dead,' John will reply. Then he'll tell Bennie all about how, when the pheasants have been shot and strung up for a while, we will eat them. 'I'll cut them up and put them in a pie!'

Bennie will dance around excitedly, chanting, 'Cut 'em up! Put in pie! Cut 'em up! Put in pie!'

If Edward happens to be in the vicinity, he'll say, 'Cut what up, Bennie?'

'The peasants!'

Edward will then pull a face and say, 'We don't eat peasants here, do we, Mum?'

'No, darling, we don't, because we're not cannibals.'

And he'll say, 'What does canni-whatsit mean?'

This is how we fell in love, me and John. We met one night at a party. He had just finished designing the set for a play – a truly magnificent ensemble with revolving doors and hidden surprises and an end scene in which a life-size and fully moving animatronic dragon crept out from under the stage and unfurled itself, scale after scale, in front of the audience's eyes – and I had interviewed the director about what he had in his fridge. I don't know why I went to the party really. I had avoided parties for a good long while, partly because it was a trial to arrange babysitting for Edward and partly because I felt so out of place. I was a single mother of thirty. For some reason, I seemed to be the only person of my age group who had a child. My friends all thought it was mad. While they went to art galleries and the theatre and the cinema and dinner parties and cocktail parties and just parties in general, I spent most of my time dragging a truculent three-year-old round the supermarket and trying to resist letting him eat endless packets of gummi bears. By the time I'd got Edward to bed – too late, too often – I was so tired I'd just collapse. So when people asked me out, I invariably didn't go.

Anyway, there I was, at this party. Edward had gone for a rare sleep-over to my mother's. I had arranged it two weeks previously but, the day before, my mother had called up to say she'd absolutely forgotten but she was part of a local community bridge team and they had a very important tournament that evening and could I please make it another night? I said that no I couldn't possibly make it another night as I didn't think the director of this very successful play with the life-size moving dragon that came out of the floor would move his launch party *just for me*.

'Oh you're going out for the night, are you?' she said in a rather accusatory fashion.

'I am going to a party. I may well stay out the night in London or I may well come back and get some sleep.'

'I never got to stay out the night when you and your sister were little.'

'Well, you weren't a single parent,' I replied.

The party was at a very grand London hotel. I knew

no one, bar the director, who was busy talking to everyone else. So I was sitting at a table surrounded by people I didn't know when John the Second sat next to me. He was tall with dark hair and blue eyes. We started chatting about work and soon he was nearly falling off his chair laughing when I told him what I did.

'I write features about food and health,' I said, 'and every week I do this article called "What's In Your Fridge?" I go and meet celebrities and look inside their fridges.'

'You can't be serious!' he said, but I told him I was, in fact, perfectly serious.

'You just list what people have inside their fridges, then, do you?' He smiled at me and I remember thinking how much I liked his smile. It looked warm, kind, genuine and very sexy. 'Shall I tell you what's in my fridge?'

I nodded.

He then screwed up his face in a most endearing way and said, 'An onion, three eggs, a carrot, a chicken, some Thai green curry paste that I made yesterday for a meal I'm cooking a friend tomorrow night . . .'

'Oh are you cooking a meal for your girlfriend?'

'I don't have a girlfriend,' he said, winking at me. 'A pint of milk, half a lemon, an avocado, a bottle of Prosecco and some beer! What does that make me?'

'Hmm,' I said, 'quite sophisticated.'

'*Quite* sophisticated! I'll obviously have to try harder!'

Then we talked about where we grew up. He told me that he'd spent his life in Elstree, Hertfordshire – 'near the film studios' – but that he used to go on holiday every year near the sea in Donegal. As he talked about these long summers spent birdwatching and fishing and sailing and swimming until all hours, I watched and took him in. I saw how wide and strong his hands were and that made me like him immediately. His hands looked like practical hands, hands that could make things work and fix things like small and irritating children's toys (well, that's what I thought then; now I know that, for a set designer, he's the world's most impractical man). I liked the fact that he was big, not just physically tall but also round like a teddy bear. John the First, mal-humoured John the First, was as skinny as a rake, but this John looked warm and lovable and trustworthy, and yet, as we talked, I realized he was even more than that. He was interesting. He was interested. Soon I realized that he was actually rather interested in me and that felt great.

And so on we talked; about how we loved watching the seasons change from the harshness of winter to the hopefulness of spring and then the leaden heat of summer. We talked about our families and I told him about Edward, so then we talked about Edward. Then we kissed a bit and afterwards he asked me how I felt about being a single mother and I told him. I said that sometimes I found it tiring and confusing, and he held my hand then and kissed me on the top of my head and said, 'Poor you.' And that was it for me really.

John and I ended our evening, which was probably actually at about three in the morning, talking about Edward and drinking wine in the Honesty bar of the hotel, and I got the giggles because by then we were being terribly dishonest.

'I'm charging the drinks to the theatre company,' John told me. 'They've had their pound of flesh from me!'

I thought he was making a pun so I laughed and he didn't get it for a while but, when he did, he thought it was very funny so we made up a mad game where everything we said had to have some reference to a play. So he'd say something like, 'Tell me about your sister,' and I'd say, '"Tis pity she's a whore,' and we thought this was very witty.

Then he said, 'Where does your father live?'

'Full fathom five my father lies,' I said, which is not strictly true because my father is cremated not lying dead under the sea.

Anyway, at the end of the night he told me that he had a room at the hotel and I stayed with him. And jolly nice it was too.

The first time John came down to mine, I hadn't told Edward about him so I got ready secretly in my bathroom. When I put Edward to bed he said, 'You look pretty, Mummy,' and he looked at me very suspiciously.

And, at 8 p.m., John knocked on my front door, armed with chicken, a Thai green curry sauce he'd prepared the night before and a bottle of Prosecco.

Later on, we went up to my room and made love and then lay on the bed looking at the moon and looking at each other and quietly talking and drinking the Prosecco. Eventually, we got dozy but, before I fell asleep, John kissed me goodnight and crept into the spare room.

'I don't want Edward to find me in your bed,' he said and I nearly cried with joy and relief for I didn't want Edward to find him in my bed either but hadn't known how to tell him that.

Then, in the morning, when Edward bounced into my room and sat on my head and tickled me and told me I was 'stinky', I told him I had someone I wanted him to meet.

'Who is it?' said Edward.

'A surprise.'

'Is it Father Christmas?'

'No, it's not Father Christmas because we don't have Christmas in June, do we?'

'Oh no,' said Edward.

We crept along the landing towards the spare room and . . . there was no one there. The bed was made. The curtains were open.

'There's no one here!' said Edward.

'No,' I said, feeling disappointed. But then I went back to my bedroom and laid my head on the pillows and took a long deep breath in. There. I could smell him. I could smell him! He had been here!

At that moment Edward walked back into the bedroom. 'I think Father Christmas was here,' he said, 'but he had to go and get ready for Christmas.'

'Edward, I think you're probably right.'

John looks older now. He still looks handsome, maybe more so. His hair is streaked with silver grey. His face has filled out. He looks a bit careworn, though; not as care-free as that morning when he crept out. He loves to tell me that story, about when he woke up feeling so joyous that he just wanted to shout, 'I LOVE HER!' across the valley and up the hills, but he dared not so he walked out into a midsummer's morning with the sky all pink and the birds all singing and he got in his car and drove back to London, laughing all the way. Oh he was so carefree then.

Now he looks tired, not all the time, just some of the time. And he claims this tiredness has given him a stomach ulcer. Maybe once a week he rather dramatically retches into the loo. When he is very tired, after a long week's work, he tends to shout at the children in the morning. I hear him say, 'Bennie, what the bloody hell are you doing!' and 'Edward, put your clothes on RIGHT NOW!' and I think to myself, 'I bet that man rarely shouted until he moved in with me and we had all these children.' But when I tell him that he always laughs and says, 'But, Samantha, you know I am devoted to our children!' and I do know that, deep down inside.

But maybe when he walked into my back garden again five years ago, to meet Edward for the first time – maybe then he wished he could run out. But he couldn't, for I had finally told Edward about him and, once he had coaxed Edward out from behind my legs by offering him chocolate, the deal was done. He walked off into the gathering twilight, with Edward on his shoulders, clutching a box of Quality Street. By the time they came back it was dark and I was worried, but Edward was so happy, chatting away as if he had known John all his life, and three months later we all moved into a bigger house together. After a couple of years, Bennie was born and fairly soon after that, I felt sick in the mornings and my breasts went all tender and we all knew what that meant.

As for Edward, well, we lie about Edward. It is the easiest way forward. When people see me and John the Second and our three boys together, they assume we are an entire family. They don't know about John the First. Sometimes, though, I think, 'What does family mean? Are we a family?' We look like a family but at times I am not so sure. Occasionally, when Edward looks at his little curly-haired blondy brothers, I think he feels different to them.

Bennie and Jamie flit back and forth from their father to me. They have no idea how people can separate and relationships rupture but I think Edward does know this, deep down. I think it sets him apart.

Sometimes I wake up in a sweat having dreamt that everything has collapsed on top of me due to something I have done – but I can never quite remember what that thing is.

What the Children Like to Eat

Edward

Edward is a fussy pain in the neck. He is your archetypal meat-and-two-veg bloke. He likes roasts – chicken, beef (but not too rare), pork. He doesn't like any form of cooked ham, gammon, bacon. He doesn't like game. But he will eat lamb chops, pork chops and burgers in a bun as long as the bun is white, soft and unhealthy. He will not eat chicken drumsticks. He particularly likes sausages and mash but he hates gravy. In fact, he hates all wet foods so casseroles, risottos, stews and soups are out. He will not eat offal.

Edward loves chips – all chips, be they oven ones or French fries. He likes all potato in pretty much any form, bar sweet potato. He doesn't like parsnips, turnips, swedes or squash. He loves cucumber and raw carrots but hates cooked carrots. He likes green beans, fresh or frozen, but hates all other beans, especially if they are tinned – chickpeas, black-eye beans, haricot, butter, kidney, cannellini – but he adores baked beans. He hates tinned sweetcorn but will eat, at a push, frozen sweetcorn. He loathes mushrooms and tomatoes.

He adores chocolate, crisps, Nutrigrains, Babybel cheese, juices in cartons, breakfast cereals, fizzy drinks and fruit – but only grapes, apples, bananas and strawberries, and only if you cut them into small bite-size chunks for him, and ice cream – but only strawberry, vanilla, mint or chocolate.

He has the same thing in his lunch box every day: Marmite sandwich on wholegrain bread, apple Nutrigrain, Babybel cheese, two Frubes (one purple, one orange), a packet of Hula Hoops, a carton of apple juice and a packet of raisins.

Here is a good suggested dinner menu for Edward:

Monday: sausages and mash (no gravy) with broccoli
Tuesday: pasta and pesto – green not red
Wednesday: breaded cod with chips and peas
Thursday: baked potato with baked beans and cheese and
    cucumber and raw carrots
Friday: burger and chips and frozen sweetcorn
Saturday: hot dogs and baked beans
Sunday: roast meat, roast potato, peas and broccoli and
    NO GRAVY!

Bennie

Bennie is of a Mediterranean disposition when it comes to food. He likes to eat on the move. He loves food he can pick up and put down and dip into and rub all over the furniture and/or give to the dog. He pretends he likes everything Edward has but he doesn't. He just can't bear Edward to have food that he hasn't got. This means you have to cook Bennie something entirely different to Edward but put some of Edward's food on his plate, or else all hell breaks loose.

Bennie likes everything Edward does not. He loves quiche, eggs, fish, vegetables, salad, tomatoes, peppers, smoked salmon, cream cheese, taramasalata, quails' eggs, stinky cheese such as Camembert, hummus, pitta bread, olives, sun-dried tomatoes, couscous, tabbouleh, pasta with arrabiata sauce, anchovies, wild mushroom risotto, my home-made onion tart, lentil and squash stew, sweet potato. He loves exotic fruits such as paw-paw and mango, and also melon, pineapple, blackberries, raspberries, peaches and pears. He loves avocado, prawns, lemons, black pepper, garlic.

Bennie does not particularly like meat, apart from rabbit stew, John's beef stew and chicken drumsticks. He especially dislikes sausages. He often spits them out. Sometimes he chews them into a disgusting pulp, which he then deposits on my hand when he can't be bothered to swallow it. He thinks he likes chocolate, chocolate biscuits, sweets and toffees, but he doesn't. He also often puts these in his mouth and chews them into a pulp, which he then spits out onto the sofa. Do not be fooled by his wails. I've never known Bennie finish a biscuit, ice cream or chunk of chocolate – ever. The only sweets he ever actually eats are Smarties. He calls them 'pops'.

He quite likes crisps.

Here is a good suggested dinner menu for Bennie:

Monday: John's beef stew with sweet potato, squash, watercress and dill

Tuesday: prawns, pak choi and asparagus stir-fry with noodles

Wednesday: Mediterranean platter – hummus, tzatziki, olives, pitta bread and swordfish-and-pepper kebabs

Thursday: baked potato with tuna, cucumber, cherry tomatoes and sweetcorn

Friday: chicken casserole with carrots, shallots, celery and button mushrooms

> Saturday: roasted peppers stuffed with feta cheese and pine
> nuts
> Sunday: the roast – you never know, he may eat it if it's
> got gravy on!

Jamie

Jamie likes nothing but butternut squash. Read this and be warned . . .

3. Sunday

Sundays are my day for a lie-in. John normally gets a Monday because he doesn't tend to work on Mondays. As the rest of the house gets up and starts the day – Edward clothed in his school uniform, packed lunch ready, tie tied, Bennie fed, Jamie still in his Babygro, with a bottle of milk stuck in his mouth before we all set off in the car to drop Edward at school – John snores away oblivious to the rush and noise. On a Sunday, however, things are different. Sunday is my morning.

The lie-in must be one of the most contentious issues in a relationship. This is what should happen: Edward will get up ridiculously early, as per usual, and creep downstairs to sneakily watch something like *Super Mario* or *Power Rangers* on the television. Bennie, who has the ears of a bat, will then immediately wake up and scream his head off. The correct response to this, on my Sunday lie-in day, is for John to get up, lift Bennie out of his cot, take him downstairs, fix him breakfast and then play with him. He should also very carefully listen out for the baby, who will probably not wake up for another hour but, when he does, should not be left screaming rather loudly in his cot. John should hear the sobbing baby and run upstairs and get him up, then take him downstairs and stick a bottle of milk in his mouth. This way happiness and contentment lies.

Only that never happens. What actually happens is that Edward gets Bennie up and brings him into our bedroom, saying, 'Bennie's done a poo in his nappy.' Bennie then careers round our bed, leaping on us and bouncing around on my stomach and generally behaving like a loony until someone – oh let's think who that person might be, might it be ME? – has to get up and find some wipes and a nappy and enough hand–eye coordination in a state of semi-sleep to hold down a slithering elver-child long enough to change the aforementioned offending nappy. That person then slides back down into the warmth of the bed and sneaks her hand over to her husband and instead of slapping him rather sharpishly on the head, which she really wants to do but doesn't because it will not have the desired effect, strokes his back in a tender fashion.

'Mmm,' murmurs John, rolling towards me.

'Darling, Bennie and Edward are up.'

'Mmm,' says John, snuggling into me in a hopeful fashion.

'I think Jamie might be awake. I can hear him rolling around his cot. Maybe he's stuck.' There's more mmm-ing. 'It's my morning for a lie-in,' I say, desperately. 'And now I can't hear Jamie. Maybe he's got his head under the covers.'

'Oh mmmm.'

I want to say, rather loudly, 'BUT THIS DOES NOT CONSTITUTE A LIE-IN, YOU MISERABLE LAZY BASTARD.' Instead I sigh and rub his back a bit harder and then, with no resources left, I motion to Bennie, now wandering around with my earplugs sticking out of his mouth, that he should leap on his father. This usually does the trick.

But even now it's not all over. For John, who will then get up looking as though someone has smashed into his face, will, most Sundays, bring the baby into bed. He'll tell Bennie to go downstairs and get Edward to give him some milk, then roll over and go back to sleep, leaving me to play with Jamie, who is fascinated by my nipples. 'Erggh, blerp, ga,' says Jamie, tugging at them. At last, after much rubbing of backs and persuading the baby to kick him and grab his hair, John will get up. He's never very happy about it but he will do it eventually. Of course, by this time, I am totally awake. I then lie there and try to get back to sleep but I can't because of the noise. I reach for my earplugs. They are not there because Bennie has taken them downstairs clamped in his mouth. For twenty minutes I lie in the bed, scrunching my eyes shut and trying to think of something really dull – even my poor dead dad's game of counting sheep backwards as they leap over a stile doesn't work. I told my mum that the other day.

'Mum,' I said, when she was telling me how I should try to count sheep backwards because that will always work, 'it doesn't work for me.'

'Of course it works,' she said crossly. 'It always worked for your father.'

I then pointed out that maybe it wasn't the sheep thing that worked for my father but the fact that he drank over a bottle of vodka a day. 'That's why he DIED,' I said to my mother.

'I'm not getting back into this,' she said.

So by 8.30 a.m. on this particular Sunday, I am downstairs.

'What are you doing down here?' says John cheerily,

27

now wide awake and cracking eggs into a pan. 'It's all under control.'

But it isn't because it never is. Bennie has made a Rice Krispie mountain on the floor and is solemnly putting trains in and out of a pretend tunnel. The baby has got stuck in the fireplace, which no one has cleaned out in weeks, and is covered in ash.

Edward, who is picking his toenails, looks down happily at Bennie and says, 'I remember when I used to do that!'

'Don't stress, dearest,' says John when he sees the look of horror on my face. 'You're not supposed to be here. Go back to bed, darling. Have a rest.'

Now I really want to murder him. It'll all backfire on him, though, which is something he hasn't worked out. For the war of the lie-in is a silent and deadly one. Tomorrow I shall be just like him. I shall pretend to be dead when Bennie comes in with his smelly nappy. I shall lie like a log when Jamie starts crying. I shall not make the packed lunch or iron Edward's school uniform or shine his shoes. And, when I eventually do get up far too late, I shall take all the bread and milk and eggs and cereals and throw them around the kitchen.

For now, though, I shall be gracious.

On Sundays, we usually go for a walk. I think that's what all families do. We look at the weather and we ho and hum and discuss at great length whether it will rain or whether it will clear and then we decide, whatever we think of the rain situation, that we'd better go anyway because the dog needs a walk. This Sunday, however, it's different. I agreed to go to the private view of my friend

Genevieve who is doing an art degree. I met her a few months ago when I started taking Bennie and a very tiny Jamie, only weeks old and furled all round himself like a rose petal, to playgroup. I only started going to playgroup because my health visitor, who can be rather bossy, told me that Bennie needed to get out more.

'That child's bored!' she said one morning when she came to see how me and the newborn were doing. 'Look at him!'

I looked at Bennie. He did, it has to be said, look immensely bored. He was piling little bricks on top of each other and then knocking them down, piling them up, knocking them down.

I pull up at the local village hall with Bennie.

Genevieve comes to the door. She is tall and slim and wearing her usual uniform of superior-casual clothes – long, floaty, white palazzo pants and clean, white, cotton shirts. Sometimes she'll wear jeans with an embroidered top or a little kaftan or a paisley wrap dress. Genevieve always looks good, with her clean skin and her long brown hair neatly tied back. She is attractive but not pretty. She is also one of the most focused women I have ever met. Twice a week she goes to Oxford Brookes to do a master's degree in art history. I see her, sometimes, staggering out from the local library weighed down with books. As one of her modules she has chosen to take a ceramics course and her first-ever show is today.

As we walk through the door Bennie dashes off and immediately careers into Jessamy, who bangs him over the head with a metal truck.

'Waa!' he yells.

'Jessamy!' says Genevieve, shooing her daughter off into

the small garden in the back, closely followed by Bennie, who has a strange attraction to Jessamy.

I turn around and there, right in front of me, is a vase. It is huge. It dominates the room. At first I can barely make out the image painted on it. It seems to be covered in dark swirls and great nodules of oils.

'You need to step back a bit from that one,' Genevieve calls out to me. 'It's not really a big enough space.'

I step back into the hallway and, suddenly, I see it. Etched onto the side of the vase is a tree. A huge tree, an oak maybe. It has big, heavy leaden boughs, and pinned between two of the snakier branches, held stretched against the trunk, is a woman. Her head has dropped forward. Her body is weighed down. I look at the picture more intensely. What are those things crawling along the branches, falling off the tree as if larger versions of leaves? There are quite a few of them, all dark, almost black. I can barely make out what they are. Oh my God. I see it now. They're babies, all of them, and they are heading, unmistakably, towards the woman.

Genevieve dashes over. 'What do you think?' She is looking anguished.

I am stuck for words.

'It's very . . . erm . . . very maternal,' I say finally.

'Oh.' Genevieve now looks relieved. 'I'm so glad you think that. Nicholas thinks it's about sex! But it's not,' she continues happily. 'It's about nature! Mind you, after they saw this, my examiners told me I should go and see a psychiatrist!'

Nicholas, Genevieve's husband, is big in the world of oil. He obviously earns a fortune and travels abroad all the time, which I think Genevieve finds frustrating.

Genevieve used to travel the world too when she was in the import–export business. She specialized in native African arts and crafts. Once, when I was at her house, she showed me the most amazing statue of a heavily pregnant African woman carved out of wood and inlaid with beads. With her long neck and hair piled on her head and then this wonderful, round, extended belly, I found the statue absolutely mesmerizing.

'Where is that from?' I asked her.

'It's from Nigeria. It's a Yoruba beaded figure.'

It turns out that Genevieve particularly specialized in the arts and crafts of the Yoruba tribe. Genevieve told me how she used to go to Ibadan – the biggest town in that tribal area – and, from there, into the villages, and buy up just about everything and anything. She would then box it all up and ship it back here and sell it through exclusive shops in London. She told me the mark-up was amazing. Soon Genevieve had almost twenty people working for her.

'I actually felt like a major player,' she said once when I was asking her about it at playgroup. 'I felt what I did was useful. I employed local people to source goods for me. At least I put a lot of my money back into the business to pay people's wages. I think it transformed their lives.'

But then, one day, while on a flight back from Lagos, she met Nicholas. He'd just been over to have a meeting with the bigwigs of a major oil company and had, apparently, taken them to task over their poor ecological record. Genevieve liked the fact that he wasn't just about earning money but that he also had a social conscience. 'We cannot treat the land and the people like this and expect to survive,' Nicholas told her. Genevieve looked at him and saw herself

– intelligent, motivated, driven, but, at heart, a true liberal.

Travelling became impossible once she had children, so she gave up work to look after Phillippa, now eight, and Jessamy, three. She thought she would find fulfilment in being a mother but her self-esteem began to crumble. Life in London proved too tricky and so Genevieve and Nicholas left their city life and all their sophisticated friends and moved out here. The day after the move, Genevieve wrote some little notelets and pushed them through all her neighbours' doors. On them she'd written; 'I am new in the area and would like to make some friends so I am wondering if you would all like to come to our house for tea this Sunday at 4 p.m., Genevieve Sinclair.' She made cranberry and orange muffins and showed everyone her Yoruba statues.

What Our Family Usually Does on a Sunday

On a Sunday, John likes to drive to the garage to fill the car up with petrol.

'What is that about?' I ask him virtually every weekend as he picks up the car keys and waves me goodbye. 'What kind of a person makes a date with a petrol pump?'

But John always just smiles and says that if he doesn't go now, he never will. He says that it is his job to make sure the car is in full working order for the following week. It is my job, apparently, to get the children ready.

'Come on, children,' I say as the first few drops of rain inevitably start appearing on the windows. 'It's a lovely day. Let's go out for a walk!'

Edward then usually quietly and casually disappears upstairs. Bennie, who realizes something is up but doesn't know quite what, exactly, runs around screaming. It is almost impossible to get him dressed. He has his hands clasped firmly over his buttocks as I threaten him with a smack since he has just pooed behind the television again. The dog is whining and pawing the back door with excitement, scratching all the paint off.

I normally dress Jamie first because he is the one who moves the slowest. Jamie hates getting dressed. When he sees me coming with his vest and dungarees he goes into fast-slugging mode and shoots off out of the kitchen and into the hall and then pretends to hide under the stairs. By the time I catch him, he looks like a piece of fuzzy felt. The faster he goes, the more black dog hairs attach to him. I pin him down and, against much protestation, I get his vest, dungarees and a jumper on him.

I then find Bennie, who is still under the table. I tempt him out with a ramekin full of 'pops'.

'POPS!' he yells when he sees them. He runs out to grab his little bowl but I am too quick for him. I then have to sit on him while he squeals and shouts, 'Bad Mummy!' and then bursts into tears.

I shove him in some trousers, force on his welly boots and put a coat on him. Just then, Edward mooches down the stairs, still clad in his pyjamas.

'Get dressed!' I hiss at him.

'Oh why?' says Edward. 'It's raining. Can't you see that it's raining or are you blind? B-L-I-N-D. You know . . . blind like a bat.'

I then lose my temper and shout and scream and tell him he'll never watch television again and that I'll sell the computer and give the dog away to a more deserving home. He sits there and picks his toes.

Once I have stopped hating him, which takes two hugs and three kisses, Edward and I agree that I will go upstairs and find his clothes for him because he can't possibly be bothered to find his own clothes for himself. By the time I come back downstairs, Jamie looks like a piece of fuzzy felt again, only a wet one as he's now upset the dog's water bowl and crawled his way through it. Bennie has taken off all his clothes apart from his socks and his nappy.

'I dun poo!' he says happily.

Jamie flails his arms around again.

'He says he's done a poo as well,' says Edward, who has now turned the television back on and is watching Spiderman the Movie.

'How do you know that?' I ask him.

'I understand babies,' he says, his eyes not swerving from the screen.

By the time John gets home, it's pretty much the same as when he left. We then go through the tried and tested Get Out of the House routine. John takes over capturing and dressing the babies. I pack the bag. This is what I pack: nappies – three nappies, size 3, for Jamie; three nappies, two size 5 and one pair of pull-ups, for Bennie. Johnson's aloe vera baby wipes because all the others give Bennie a rash. Nappy bags, which can also be used to clear up the dog's mess. Two plastic bags, which are better for picking up the dog's mess and are handy for wet clothes / soiled knickers / half-eaten food. One pot of Sudocream. One tube of Bonjela for Jamie's gums. One tube of suntan lotion. One small bottle of Calpol for babies and young children. Waspeze. A comb. A lighter, just in case John wants to smoke and has, as per usual, forgotten to bring his. Three packets of raisins. One packet of Babybels. Two packets of crisps. Frubes. Two cartons of apple juice. Two Avent bottles of milk; a pre-warmed one for Jamie, a cold one for Bennie. Organix baby breadsticks. One rattle. One

34

*cuddly bear. Three cars and a toy tractor. I also take Edward's
waterproof and wellies. Bennie's raincoat that he hates but is,
at least, waterproof. Three woolly hats in three different sizes.
Two sets of gloves and one pair of mittens for the baby. A towel.
Two umbrellas. The double, all-terrain buggy. The double, all-
terrain buggy waterproof rain sheet. One blanket. One picnic
blanket. The dog lead. The dog. A change of clothes for both
Bennie and Jamie. A spare pair of socks for Edward. A road
map of the UK. My mobile telephone and my telephone book.
Money. A large bottle of water.*

Later on, when it is night time and the children have gone
to bed and our dog Beady, named for her beady brown
eyes, is floppy and exhausted, I look at John. We are lying
in bed. I came home from Genevieve's art viewing in a
state of strange emotional discomfort. John kept looking
at me queerly and asking what the matter was, but I did
that thing people often do. I waved him away.

'Nothing is wrong,' I said.

Then John rolled over and said to me, 'What is it you
want, Samantha?'

I said, 'I want to lie naked on the bed as the sun comes
through the window in the early morning. I want to stretch
out like a cat and fall into one of those ear-twitching sleeps
when you're not quite awake and not quite asleep. I want
to doze and wake and doze some more and then, when
I wake, I want to drink chilled white wine and read my
book and, later on when the sun is fading, I want you to
come to bed and we can make love and lie and hold each
other while we talk about the day. I want to feel comfort-
ably lethargic rather than exhausted. I don't want to be
heavy-limbed and tired all the time, for I am so tired. My

children will grow up and when people ask them what their mother was like they'll say, "She was tired." I want to smell of new-mown hay. I want to be lithe and tanned. I suppose, essentially, I want to be twenty-five again. Have we become overrun with babies?' I ask John.

'No, Samantha. We love our babies.'

'What about us?'

'We love us too,' he says simply. Then he kisses me and holds me tightly and, eventually, we fall asleep just in that way.

4. Monday

Today is Monday and I have woken up from a terrible dream. In it, John the First had come back and I told him I still loved him, and I ended up going off with him. I was on an aeroplane with him and it was about to take off and all these fireworks were exploding. I turned my head to look out of the window, then suddenly I saw John the Second and Edward standing on the runway, their faces blotched with tears. I was trying to scream to them that I had made a dreadful, ridiculous mistake and that I loved them more than anything in the world but they couldn't hear me above the blasted fireworks that kept going off.

Bang! Bang! Bang!

Suddenly, I started wondering where on earth these fireworks were coming from.

Bang! Bang! Bang!

I reluctantly open my eyes to find Bennie smashing a hammer into the bedroom walls. The plaster is going everywhere.

'Whooeeh!' goes Bennie.

'Bennie!' yells John the Second, abruptly coming out from his own secret dream land. 'I am trying to sleep!'

Bang!

John leaps out of bed and grabs Bennie's hand. 'BENNIE! Be quiet!'

''orry, Dada,' says Bennie and then he quickly slips his hand from John's grasp and tears off down the stairs.

John groans and gets back into bed.

I sidle over to him. 'John,' I say, resting my hand on his chest, 'I had a terrible dream last night.'

'Mmm,' he says, arching his back into me like a cat. 'What was it about?'

I tell him and add that in the dream I had real feelings of love for John the First, and now I'm upset about it.

'Oh dear,' says John, 'that sounds terrible,' but I can see that he is smiling at me.

'But it is terrible!'

'Oh Samantha.' John looks beseechingly at me. 'It's a dream.'

'It felt real. I left you and then you and Edward came to the airport to find me and you were crying.' Suddenly, oddly, I feel as if I am about to cry.

'Samantha!' says John, seeing my eyes well up a bit. 'What's the matter? Are you pre-menstrual?'

'No, I'm not. But aren't dreams supposed to mean something?'

'Yes, but I'm not sure what. I mean, how far did you go with your first John in this dream? Did you have sex with him?'

'No!' I say, a bit shocked.

'Did you snog him?'

I am about to say no again when I see his face. 'You're teasing me.'

'Oh no, I'm not,' he says, tickling me. 'I'm just saying that if you ever go near that man again I'll . . .' and he reaches out of the sheets and mimes a punch.

Now I start giggling. 'I'd like to see you try. He's taller than you!'

'Oh my Samantha, come over here and snog a real man.'

Just as I am about to take him in my arms under the warmth of the sheets and hold him and kiss him we hear a huge bang downstairs and then 'Waaa!'

'Jesus Christ!' says John. 'What is going on?'

Bennie suddenly comes flying into the bedroom. He is wailing like a banshee. Edward follows behind.

'Bennie hit his thumb with a hammer,' says Edward, 'and I need someone to take me to school.'

'It's my turn,' I say to John.

'No, it's all right.' He yawns and kisses me on my forehead. 'I'm up now. I'll do Edward. You do Bennie and Jamie.'

'Great,' I say sarcastically.

When John gets back we go into the garden to 'consult our diaries'.

'I thought you were taking Edward to school on Friday,' John says, flicking through his pages.

'I can't take him on Friday. I have to go and see some rock star's fridge,' I say, flicking through mine.

John sighs. Bennie comes out to the garden and positions himself under the table, looking rather sleepy. He was up half the night. John looks down at him crossly. 'Do you really have to do that on Friday?'

'Yes,' I say, a touch defensively. 'I work too, you know.'

'Oh great,' says John, looking fed up.

Later, I am in my study, when the phone rings. A few seconds later John appears. 'It's your sister,' he says meaningfully.

'Ah well, right,' I say as he passes me the receiver.

'Hello!' I hear my sister's voice virtually before I put my ear near the telephone. 'Is that you? Are you there?'

'Julia,' I say. 'Right, well, hi.'

'How are you?' she enthuses.

'Well, I . . .'

'Are you working?'

'Well, I . . .'

'Poor you! How dreadful to have to work.'

'Well, it's just that I . . .'

'And your poor children. They must miss you!'

'Well, John's here and Santa's here and . . .'

'Well, it's not the same as having mummy, is it?'

'God,' I say, 'you're sounding just like Mum now.'

'Am I?'

'Yes. Mum keeps going on about having an au pair but, Julia, I work, as you well know, so I think it's basically OK.'

'Of course we all know you work. I just wonder . . .'

'Wonder what?'

'I just wonder if you do think everything's fine? I mean, I'm sure it is fine,' she says in this rather irritatingly over-concerned voice.

'Yes, I think they're all fine really.'

At this point Bennie wakes up and, finding himself abandoned in the garden, starts screaming his head off.

'Is that little Bennie?' asks my sister.

'No.'

'Yes, it is. He's screaming!'

'No, he isn't. It's not Bennie. It's the next-door-neighbour's child.'

'The next-door-neighbour's child? But you must go and comfort it!'

'Julia, it's not my child. I really don't see why . . .'

'You don't see why you shouldn't go and comfort a screaming child?' she says accusingly.

'I can't just walk into someone else's house.' I am getting a bit annoyed.

'Why not? If you thought that child was being abused wouldn't you go and do something?'

'Yes, but that child isn't being abused.'

'How do you know that?'

'Because it's bloody Bennie!' I yell.

There is a silence.

'I knew it was,' she says. 'You'd better go, then.'

'Yes. Well, bye, then.'

'Good luck with your work,' she says and puts the phone down.

When John comes back into the study he finds me in tears.

'I can't carry on like this,' I say.

Julia always manages to make me feel guilty about my children. She doesn't mean to, I know that, but she's got six children and she's never had a nanny or a cleaner or an au pair or a babysitter. She's never sat there moaning down the telephone about how tired she is, how difficult she finds it, how tedious it all is sometimes. She radiates happiness and wholesomeness. God, she's even going to do a course in child psychology! She called me up and said, 'I'm thinking of enrolling in a part-time degree course at Birmingham university,' and I was so gob-smacked I didn't say anything. How on earth is she going to find the time? Then again, she's an immensely practical woman.

She met her husband, Joe – who is partial to the odd glass or two of wine whereas she never touches a drop and is always going on at me about my overt wine consumption – when she was in her very early twenties. They bumped into each other in the sociology department at Exeter university, found they had a lot in common and the next thing we all knew they were married. Pretty soon after that they had their first child, then they bought a dog. Then they had their second child, rescued a cat and bought another dog. After they had their third child, and the rescue cat had had her second set of kittens, all five of which they kept, they bought some chickens. Two years later, they had their fourth child and invested in a farmhouse, some land, a goat and another dog, and on it went until they found themselves with lots of kids, lots of farm animals, countless cats and an over-worked Aga.

Despite all this, I have never seen my sister and Uncle Joe argue. I argue with everyone. I argue with people even when they don't want to argue.

But I don't really want an argument with John. Hours have gone by since we last spoke. I told him I couldn't cope and he just looked at me so I have spent most of the day writing copy about the skinny celebrity's fridge – 'She keeps popcorn in salad trays!' – and generally overseeing the increasingly fractious children. I have cooked lunch and tea and now dinner. I have given Edward Marmite sandwiches and made Bennie honey ones. I have mashed up more butternut squash and fed mucky little Jamie. I have cleared up the garden – sunloungers and toys and the mildewed paddling pool have all been hosed down and tidied up. John sloped out and took the dog for a walk. And now it is early evening and there are shades of dusk creeping up onto the brick and flint wall out in the garden. I can smell the jasmine and see the pipistrelles whirring around the garden, fast and dark, picking off the dozy evening insects. The patio still smells of the heat of the day. When John comes back in the dog's black fur is still warm.

I look at John and try to read his face. Jamie is in bed. Edward is reading with Bennie in his bedroom and they are engrossed in Edward's old *Thomas the Tank* books. I can hear Edward reading in his usual monotone to Bennie. I go for the door, thinking I might disappear upstairs and inveigle my way into telling the story, but John cuts me off. He looks very serious.

'I've been doing some thinking,' he says.

'Ooh don't do that too much,' I joke.

'We need to change things. I can't sit back and watch you become this stressed-out and unhappy.'

'Oh I'll be OK. I'll survive and I'm not unhappy really. I'm just tired.'

'I don't want you to just survive. I don't want you to feel so tired. I want you to be happy. I want you to enjoy your life. I need to know what you need to do this.'

'I don't need anything.'

John sighs. 'You can be difficult to help sometimes.'

'I know,' I say, and we go upstairs to see the children.

5. Tuesday

My mother is supposed to pick Edward up on Tuesday nights. It is supposed to be their bonding session, but today she rings and says that she can't possibly pick him up tonight because her car is going in for a service.

'I would, darling,' she says, 'but I can't.'

I then think about it and remember that she told me she couldn't do it last week either because her car was going in for a service. I call her back. 'Didn't your car go in for a service last week?'

'Did it?' she says, sounding all surprised.

'Yes. That's why you couldn't collect Edward for me last Tuesday, remember?'

'Oh yes. Silly me, I must've got my dates wrong. Well, let me see . . . Oh you mean today Tuesday?'

'Yes.'

'Oh well, yes, I think that I can.'

'Great.'

Then she tells me that, actually, she can't pick Edward up the following Tuesday as she is off on a cruise.

'Off on a cruise? You never told me.'

'I'm telling you now. I'm going down the Nile and then I'm spending a while relaxing in Luxor.'

'Relaxing from what?'

'Bye bye, darling,' she says and rings off.

So, no help from that quarter, then. Great.

*

Then, just as I am about to wake Jamie, who is fast asleep in his cot, the phone rings again. It's my best friend Dougie. I haven't seen or heard from him for a couple of weeks but Dougie always does that. He's either around all the time or so off-message that you wonder if he's even alive.

'Have you been in London?' I ask him.

He, however, in his particularly airy-fairy faux-mysterious way, won't tell me where he's been. 'It doesn't matter where I've been,' he says. 'It doesn't matter where I am now. I just need to make a quick arrangement with you.'

Twenty minutes later, after lots of me saying, 'Yes, I'll be in on Friday evening but only after I've come back from meeting this rock star to look in his fridge but no that won't mean late in the evening but maybe around six,' we establish that he wants to come down on Friday night.

'Is that OK?' he says.

'Absolutely, but only if you tell me where you've been.'

'London. I've rented a flat there.' And he rings off.

Before I wake Jamie up to feed him breakfast before we all go to playgroup, I have one of those rare moments of silence. Bennie is in the sandpit in the garden. The peace is so unexpected that, for a minute or so, I'm not sure what it is. I am boiling the kettle and looking out of the window when I have the most unbelievable sense of déjà vu. I remember when I saw this house and this valley for the first time ever all those years ago. It was a sunny day then too. We drove down from London in my Mini, just Edward and me. John the First said he was going to come with us but, at the last moment, he changed his mind. I left him in London strumming his guitar. But this move to the countryside felt like a new beginning. The air was fresh and clean and there was no traffic and I could see the deer on the hill and I showed them to Edward, who was then two, and he waggled his head at them. A girl trotted past on a horse and Edward waggled his head again and then he sat in the damp grass in the field opposite the house and played with the grass as he always did. I saw a future for us all then – me and Edward and John the First. I called the agent and told him I'd rent the house for a few months before deciding whether to stay in the countryside or not. I thought that we would be happy, that we would survive. Now, as I smell the dampness of the grass from the heavy dew of the night before and I feel the slight coolness of the summer morning on my skin, I gaze out at those selfsame deer grazing on the hill and that pied wagtail bobbing up and down on top of the mossy garden wall and I think about how we didn't survive.

For the first few months, me and John the First were too busy either arguing or not talking to properly understand what was really going on. Once, after a particularly ferocious row, I flew out of the door and ran across the lane and up the steep hill in front of the house and, when I'd got to the top, I looked back down onto the valley. It looked so pretty, so calm. As I stood on that hill, I knew that John the First would leave and that I would stay. It was impossible for it to be any other way.

Sure enough the countryside did do something magical for Edward and me and, as I think about it, I think of the wondrous small acts I have witnessed here. Edward eating his first strawberry picked from the next-door-neighbour's fruit garden. I think of his face when the local farmer's teenage lad took him for a ride on his tractor. I think of his expression of joy as he buried his face into the sweet fur of the shaggy pony that lives in the field. After John the First left, I just about managed to pay the rent and run the car. I juggled like crazy. Sometimes I would wonder why John the First wasn't there. That used to make me feel sad and lonely. But not now. That is all in the past. Everything is going to be fine.

Two hours later I'm at the local village hall with Bennie and Jamie. Once a week it doubles up as the local playgroup. I have wandered in, as I always wander in, with a vague sense of foreboding. I always feel I stand out a bit. I don't wear the right clothes. I seem to live in jeans and a tatty jumper while everyone else is always dressed in sort of middle-class trendy leisure gear. They wear makeup and have shiny hair.

I also feel fatter than everyone else. Why is everyone so slim and trim? Genevieve is slim, then again she does ashtanga yoga twice a week in the village hall. But the other mothers all seem as slim as Genevieve. Two of them, Caroline and Eleanor, had their babies when I had Jamie. Every time I see them I look at their faces and smile away, but when they are not watching I let my eyes wander down and I stare at their ever-shrinking waistlines. Why doesn't my waist shrink like theirs? Caroline is so slim, so pretty. She is younger than me and looks like an English rose – dark hair, pale skin. She couldn't be anything but English. Eleanor is slim too, but now her belly is swelling again. Her littlest is not yet one and another's due in seven months. But she'll be back in her jeans again soon after that, she tells me. She just burns off fat. That makes me wonder why I don't seem to burn off any fat.

It's eight months since I had Jamie and I still can't get

my old jeans over my hips. It's probably because I eat too much. I love to eat. I only like finishing breakfast so that I can think about what to have for lunch. Then when I finish lunch, I obsess about dinner. I'm like a human version of a Labrador dog. I hoover up the children's leftovers. I take big bites from the ice creams they have in the park. I try chunky slices of their cakes and bites of their biscuits and I nick chips 'just to make sure they're not too hot'.

I'm never really sure what I am expected to do at playgroup. We all bring our little children and then sit and chat and drink coffee. There are women here I really like. There's Genevieve with her two girls. There's Caroline with her baby boy, Harry, and three-year-old Biba. She has another daughter called Skye but we don't see her as she goes to school and school-aged children just don't exist in this little bit of our world. There's Eleanor with her two boys, baby George and three-year-old Jackson. Then there's Margot with her two daughters, Chloe, two, Camille, seven, and a son, Carlos, aged four. We never see Camille either because she is always at school with Skye. When I first met Margot I asked her why she'd given all her children names beginning with C.

'It's so much easier when it comes to sewing name tags on to clothes,' she said.

'You named your children because it makes it easier when it comes to ordering name tags?'

'Well, obviously I like their names,' said Margot, 'but it's much easier just to order a batch of tags with C Palmer printed on them than to keep ordering separate tags every year. Don't you find it a bore having to order ones for Edward and Bennie and Jamie?'

'But I don't sew name tags onto clothes,' I said, thinking

of all the miserable evenings when I have done nothing but bloody well sew.

'Well, you should. Then you won't lose things like knickers and socks and what-have-you.'

Margot is really like that – organized, efficient, knowledgeable, neat and tidy. She's the opposite of me. Her children are also terribly organized, efficient, knowledgeable, neat and tidy, apart from Carlos, who is a bit of a ruffian. I can tell Margot finds Carlos hard work. She chastises him all the time but he takes little notice. Sometimes I see her looking very angrily at him and it worries me.

Finally, there's large-bosomed Jo and her daughter, Buzzy, who has just turned four.

'I've just turned four,' she says in her sweet, proud voice every time someone asks her how old she is.

'Yes, she's really called Buzzy,' said Genevieve when I first came to playgroup and asked if I had misheard Jo's daughter's name.

'Why is she called Buzzy?'

'You'll understand when you meet Jo properly,' said Genevieve darkly.

Later on that day, I ran into Jo marching from house to house, selling what I considered to be dubious-looking natural medicines.

'Try some echinacea,' she said to me, forcing a huge bottle of pills into my hand. 'It's very good for warding off colds. That bottle retails for just under fifty pounds but you can buy it off me for half price!'

'But I don't want to buy echinacea. I am quite happy taking Night Nurse.'

'You can't take Night Nurse,' exclaimed Jo. 'It's very bad for you! Think of the children! They can't take drugs!'

'Well, what's echinacea if not a drug?'

'Oh no, no, no! It's a natural remedy.'

In the end I had to buy it to get her to go away.

Today, Jo corners me right at the start of the session. I think she is about to quiz me about her blasted echinacea when she says, apropos of nothing, 'What does your husband do?' She then looks at me expectantly, her trademark overlarge breasts heaving, very visible in her too-small cut-away top.

'He's a set designer.'

'Ooh, how wonderful!' she says over-enthusiastically. 'Does he make a lot of money?'

'He spends a lot of money,' I say, attempting a joke.

'Ooh that's a good one!'

She then gives me a card and I read:

WHERE'S THAT WACKY WHIMSICAL WAG WALLY?!
Why not hire Wonderful Wally for your child's party? Balloon tricks and party bags included in the price! Will travel anywhere in the Home Counties and the capital.

'Who's Wally?'

'My husband,' she says brightly. 'He's a children's entertainer.'

'Is he entertaining?'

'Not really,' she says, now not so brightly. 'In fact he rarely has any work. I've tried to introduce him to local mothers, you see, but there's something about him that . . .'

'What?' I am intrigued. Jo now looks a bit sad and I suddenly feel rather sorry for her.

'I don't think children like him that much.' She then grabs my hand and looks all cheery again. 'But if you have a party, you will use him, won't you? Oh please say yes. Please.'

'Well, I haven't really thought about the children's parties yet.'

'Hasn't Jamie got a birthday soon?'

'Not that soon. It's a few months away.'

'Oh please. You can have your money back if he's no good, I promise. It's just that . . . it's just that . . . oh please don't take this the wrong way . . . but Genevieve told me you sometimes have to go and interview celebrities and I thought, if you thought Wally was any good, maybe you could give them his card. Oh dear, is that too awful a thing for me to ask?'

I look at her husband's card: there is a silly clown face drawn badly – and I mean bad badly not trendy badly – in the middle of it and the type is all loopy and italicized. I start wondering what the celebrities I interview might think if I pressed a Wally card into their hands. The thought of it makes me giggle. 'Actually, I'm going to see this rock star's fridge on Friday and I think he's got a small child. I guess I could give him one of your husband's cards.'

Jo goes pink with delight. Her breasts start heaving again. 'Oh thank you.' Then she adds, 'But why are you looking in his fridge?' and I am just about to tell her when Genevieve clears her throat very loudly.

'Today, dear ladies,' she says, winking at me, 'I have brought things for the children to do! I have bought paints! I have bought paper! We are going to have fun!'

'Fun!' squeals Jackson.

'Fun!' screams Biba.

Genevieve has the ten or so children line up, except the babies Jamie, Harry and George, then troops off to find chairs and then they all sit down quietly in a circle. The rest of us watch Genevieve. None of us are sure she will achieve anything.

'This will never work,' says Eleanor, watching Jackson eyeing the blue powder paint Genevieve has produced.

Jamie sees all the children with the chairs. His eyes go round like saucers. He crawls rapidly over to me and starts climbing up my leg. Everyone loves Jamie. He has a round fat body and peaches and cream skin and blond curly hair. He has a sunny nature and virtually never cries unless Bennie has done something to him, like turn the television off.

'I don't think Jamie's going to "do" anything,' I say to Eleanor.

'Right,' says Genevieve, once we have put the kettle on for the second time. 'Today we're going to think about summer and what summer means to us.' Philippa, her elder child, who is only here because her school is closed for the day, groans. 'What does that mean?' says Genevieve brightly but looking a bit beady.

'Nothing, Mum.' Philippa mooches off and sits under the wooden toddler slide.

'Well,' says Genevieve, 'can any of you think of something you like about summer?'

'Ith hot,' says Biba.

'That's right,' says Genevieve encouragingly, 'it's hot. Now why is it hot?'

'The thun,' says Biba. 'It thines.'

'Oh you are clever, Biba! Does anyone else know anything about the summer?'

'Yes, it's boring,' mutters Philippa from under the slide. Genevieve ignores her. Jessamy starts laughing. Genevieve shoots her a look.

'You go thwimming,' says Biba.

'Yes,' says Genevieve. 'Anyone else?' She is met by silence, all those saucer eyes staring at her, mouths clamped shut. 'Right,' Genevieve sighs as she gets out the paints. 'Shall we all paint a picture of the summer?'

'Boring,' says Phillippa.

'It's boring,' says Jessamy.

'Yeth pleath,' says Biba.

The others just continue to stare.

'Erggh, blerp, ga,' says Jamie helpfully, finally joining in.

The Rules of Playgroup

Negotiating the unspoken rules and regulations of playgroup is like a complicated dance of courtship. At the base of this precarious structure is the knowledge that, by joining a playgroup, every mother is accepting an unspoken deal that she knows has to be made. There are some women you will like. Some you can't stand. But this relationship is based on the fact that you have children of a similar age, that you wish for your children to have friends and that is why you are there. You must therefore observe many rules of engagement when it comes to socializing with playgroup mothers:

Rule Number One: All children need friends therefore you must be friendly with other mothers. You must make them like you, or at least pity you, for then they will invite you and your age-appropriate offspring to their house to play. This will take the guise of, 'Oh you really must come for a coffee.' The appropriate response to this is, 'Of course, how kind,' unless you seriously hate the person doing the asking in which case you must say, 'The twenty-fourth? Why, I am busy saving the world/going to an older child's assembly/getting my mother's car serviced that day.'

Rule Number Two: The popularity of your child is a Catch-22. This is how it goes – the more popular your child is, the more other mothers will think, 'Gosh, there's a popular little boy. I wonder if (name of child) would like to be friends with that popular little boy because then, maybe, that popular little boy's popularity might rub off on up-until-now-unpopular (name of child) and make him more popular.'

Rule Number Three: This means you must practise being nice. You must learn to bake and have proper tea in your house and nice things for other mothers' children to eat. You must not be offish or patronizing. You must take a small present over to their houses when they ask you for tea. A scented candle should do the trick.

Rule Number Four: You seriously have to watch that competitive mothering thing. It's the trap I always fall into. Here is a sample conversation of what a non-competitive nice mother (who we shall call NCNM), with a popular child, says to another mother who closely resembles the rather-organized Margot but isn't her (so we shall call her OM for other mother):

OM: Is little Bennie still drinking out of a bottle?
NCNM: Oh yes. He keeps seeing the baby doing it and he so loves to.
OM: Oh how sweet. But isn't he a bit old to be drinking out of a baby bottle?
NCNM: Do you think so? I've never really thought about it.

OM: Oh yes. I've read some research that says that if babies drink from a bottle over the age of two then they do not form the correct hand–eye, eye–brain, non-sucking, non-mother-separating learning mechanisms that all two-year-olds need to develop in order to progress and not become backward and under-performing at school.

NCNM: Oh no. That would be dreadful! Thank goodness you've alerted me to this.

Rather-organized Margot, I mean Other Mother: And did you know that if you rub the teensiest bit of chilli round the tip of the nipple, which, of course, the infant is wrongly connecting psychologically to the mother's nipple, then all your problems will be solved!

NCNM: How clever! You really are so clever. I shall definitely try it. Thank you so much!

Rather-organized Margot: And if that doesn't help, you must put Bennie on the naughty step. I did that with Carlos when he wouldn't stop breastfeeding and he was going on three! You do have a naughty step, don't you?

NCNM: Oh yes! I use it twice a day and three times on Sunday. Thank you so much. Tra la la! Would you and your adorable little boy Carlos like to come for coffee on the twenty-fourth?

Here, though, is the type of thing I say:

OM: Is little Bennie still drinking out of a bottle?

Me: Oh yes. He keeps seeing the baby doing it and he so loves to.

OM: Oh how sweet. But isn't he a bit old to be drinking out of a baby bottle?

Me: Do you think so? I've never really thought about it.

OM: Oh yes. I've read some research that says that if babies

55

drink from a bottle over the age of two then they do not form the correct hand–eye, eye–brain, non-sucking, non-mother-separating learning mechanisms that all two-year-olds need to develop in order to progress and not become backward and under-performing at school.

Me: Oh really? Well, I've read that if children are allowed to develop at their own rate then they are far more likely to develop hand–eye, brain–leg, mouth–reflex, reeses–pieces, Gertheim Fflutlich technique, which, apparently, puts them in the top 5 per cent of educationally-challenging – note, not 'challenged' – children in the five-to-six-year-old bracket.

Rather-organized Margot, I mean Other Mother: Well, I've never heard that. Never. Surely you can see drinking out of a baby bottle at the age of two and a bit is, to be frank, ridiculous, childish and thoroughly out of kilter with his age group.

Me: Well, I obviously can't see that, in the same way that I, frankly, very much doubt that Bennie will still be drinking out of a baby bottle at the age of twenty-one. I very much doubt he'll be going into the pub with an outsize bottle, complete with teat, saying, 'Fill this up, bar man.' Anyway, I hear Carlos is still breastfeeding . . .

Rather-organized Margot: No Carlos is not still breastfeeding! I weaned him a month ago. I had to be tough, mind; he got so cross. Maybe you just give in to Bennie's tantrums when you try to take away his bottles.

Me: What do you mean by tantrums? I don't believe in tantrums. I believe in Bennie's right to self-expression. You know, if he wants a bottle because his little baby brother has one then I really can't see what the problem is.

Rather-organized Margot: You should take that bottle away and put him on the naughty step. He'll get buck teeth otherwise.

Me: Buck teeth? Buck teeth! As if I care. And I don't have a
naughty step. I see that as being the type of thing mad,
bored mothers use to control their children because they
don't believe in individuality and freedom and the right to
drink out of a goddamned baby bottle!

Rule Number Five: When playgroup mothers tell you that little
(name of child) goes to Tumbletots, Monkey Music, football,
baby judo, tots yoga, toddler singing lessons, tiny tots acting
classes, sea cubs, mini-hockey and rugby and cricket and
Brazilian football and they also swim, instead of saying, 'Jesus!
How on earth can any child cope with doing all that!' you should
say, 'Gosh, he sounds so talented!'

Rule Number Six: Conversely, you have to try to feel less miserable about (name of child)'s talents and the seeming lack of
talent of your own children. For have I not been moved by the
achievements of my friends' children?

When we get home from playgroup today, before Edward
comes back from school, before I start cooking broad
bean and prosciutto risotto for dinner, before I chill the
wine and call John and tell him Dougie's coming for
dinner on Friday evening, which he will probably be
happy about but may not be because he's a bit fed up
with Dougie, I decide to check my emails. I never check
my emails. I only do it when I'm trying to put off doing
something else. At the moment, I am trying to put off
thinking about Dougie and John. Dougie did ask me
once if John was worried about the nature of our relationship and I said he wasn't, which is true. What John
is worried about – or frustrated about, really – is Dougie's

seeming inability to move on from his ex-wife, Maxine.

'Why is he always at our house?' asks John whenever I tell him Dougie is coming to stay for the weekend. 'He's never going to meet a girl here!'

'But Dougie is attached to the area! He loves coming here. He is my friend.'

'Dougie should go and have sex!'

I then tell John that having sex isn't everything and why should Dougie feel he has to sort out his life by having sex?

But I once told Dougie that John thought he should go out and shag someone, and Dougie groaned and said, 'Too right.'

Dougie has always been my friend. I met him years ago, here in the local pub in the village, with Maxine. I thought he was very attractive. But then again, so was Maxine. They were drinking at the bar. They looked very together, stroking each other's hands, finishing each other's sentences. I'd popped in to buy some matches to light the fire and we just started talking and drinking and talking some more and soon a couple of hours had passed, which was not good as I had left Edward alone, asleep in his bed at home.

'Your child is home alone?' said Dougie when, after three pints of cider, I let it slip.

'I'd just gone to get matches,' I said. 'It's a tiny village. I can see the house from the pub!'

'You're a bad, bad woman,' said Dougie.

I said I had to go but then found out that the keys I had in my pocket that I thought were my door keys were nothing of the sort. Why did I think that was remotely funny? And yet I remember turning to Dougie and saying, 'They are my car keys!' I turned them over and round and round in my hands with some amazement, as if I had discovered buried treasure.

'Where are your door keys, then?' he asked me.

'In the house!'

In the end I think Maxine must have gone home for I only remember Dougie borrowing a ladder from the landlord and placing it up against my bedroom window. I was convinced I hadn't put the latch down on it properly so thought that maybe we would be able to jemmy it open and then Dougie could climb in and go downstairs and let me in through the front door. It turned out to be an excellent plan.

They were good days then. After I met John, and he'd moved in and it was a gloriously hot and blessed summer, we did things together as a foursome; pub quizzes and Sunday lunches where we ate too much. On Saturdays, when John was at work doing his set designing and Maxine was busy working on her legal cases, which seemed to be all the time, Dougie and I would take Edward swimming and then go to the pub. Dougie would push Edward on the swings and make up stories for him. Maxine didn't seem to mind the amount of time we spent together. She'd say, 'It gets him out of my hair!'

I often wondered about Dougie and Maxine's marriage. They didn't have children and, for ages, I didn't ask them why. I always think that everyone in the entire world wants children so I assumed they couldn't have them, that maybe something was wrong with Maxine. I never asked Dougie why they didn't have children. But it turned out, one day when the four of us were having a picnic, that nothing was wrong with Maxine at all. I had just found out I was pregnant with Bennie and I didn't know whether to tell Dougie and Maxine as I thought it might not be welcome news. So John and I skirted round the subject until Dougie noticed there was a bottle of champagne in the picnic basket.

'What's this for?' he said, faux-naively. 'Do you have some news to tell us?'

'I'm pregnant,' I blurted out.

Dougie leapt up and kissed me. He was laughing. 'That's wonderful!'

But Maxine just raised an eyebrow and said, 'What on earth do you want another child for? Isn't one enough?'

'*Maxine!*' said Dougie.

But Maxine just shrugged and said, 'I don't know why women want them. I really don't.'

Later on, when Maxine had gone back home to finish off some work and John and Dougie were drinking wine and I was drinking camomile tea, Dougie told us that he and Maxine had agreed to not have children.

'What *never*?' I said.

'Never,' said Dougie.

One night, I went round to see Dougie and Maxine and I found Maxine sobbing. Her head was laid on the table and tears were falling from her face onto the floor. I wanted to leave. I was an intruder. But she asked me to stay. She said she was crying because her best friend's husband had left her best friend out of the blue. They had been together for years, she told me. They had children. Now it turned out he'd been having an affair with a woman, a younger woman, in London.

'He's leaving his wife and the children,' said Maxine sniffing very hard. 'He says he wants the chance of happiness. His kids have left home and gone to college anyway. He has just upped and left.'

We all sat around the table, thinking about this. Later on, many months later, Dougie told me he thought this was the turning point. For even on that very night as Maxine said to Dougie, 'What would I do if you ever left me?' a small doubt, a little kernel, a minuscule thought, a tiny flash of realization, call it what you will, had lodged in Maxine's brain. One year later she'd gone off with the plumber and Dougie had moved out. Nothing has been the same since.

But, as my clanking old computer downloads my emails, why am I worrying about this? I have enough to worry about.

Then, finally, I open my emails.

I get a horrible shock. For there, in my Inbox, is one from John the First. I haven't heard from him in ages. I wonder what it says.

'I know this is awkward,' writes John the First, 'and I know I haven't been in touch for a long time and, Sammie, I am sure you are very angry with me, but my mother is dying. She is in Prestwood General. It's only twenty minutes up the road from you. Look, Sammie, I know this isn't ideal. I think you'll probably say no, but can I come and visit while I'm over? It would be a chance to catch up. I could meet John the Second! And Eddie – I could get to know him. I'd really like to see him . . . What do you say, Sammie? If it's OK, I'll be there in about two weeks to a month's time. I'll behave. Promise. Please, for old times' sake.'

6. Tuesday evening

It is late now and I'm thinking about this email. In fact, I think I am in shock. My natural instinct is to telephone John the Second and scream, 'JOHN THE FIRST IS COMING BACK!' somewhat in the voice my dad always used when he'd read the book about Henny Penny and the sky falling in. But I don't know what to say. So many emotions are flooding back. I am taken by surprise by them. I almost feel like crying. I am lying on my bed and the shadows of the car lights are coming and going, coming and going across the bedroom ceiling. I think about John the First. We had some years together. We travelled to sunny countries, we read books on beaches. Life seemed a good place to be. John was intelligent and funny and we liked to do things together. Somehow we became a unit. We were Samantha and John, and Christmas cards came addressed to us and party invitations had Samantha and John on them and no one ever thought we would split up for we always kissed at parties and held hands. And one night John the First turned up at our little flat in the middle of London and said, 'I've booked us a night in a hotel,' and we went to a place in the countryside and in the room there was champagne on ice and rose petals all over the bed and John the First said, 'I know how much you love the countryside, Sammie,' and I wept. Six months later we were married.

It never actually occurred to me that we were, in the

end, not the solid unit I thought we were. I felt I knew John the First so well and yet how well did I know him? Nothing had tested us. We hadn't got ill or depressed. Neither of us went bankrupt and no one close to us died or got divorced or had life-changing affairs. Nothing really came to try us until we had Edward and after Edward . . . well, I suppose we failed that test, really.

Sometimes we would drive down to Devon to visit his mother, Janet, in her holiday cottage, which was actually like a beautiful mansion with a rambling country garden. It's strange really, I always thought, for Janet actually lives near where I live now – near Tring – and has done for years and yet I have never seen her here in her home. John the First and I were always in Devon with her, for that is where she invited us to come. John the First's father had died years previously. I had never met him. Janet rarely spoke about him. But once, when we were in Devon, she said to me, 'This house used to belong to John's grandfather, as in his father's father. He gave it to me and my husband when we married and I have always been grateful to my husband's family for such a generous gift.'

I was never sure if Janet actually liked me. Then again, I don't think she had probably liked any of John the First's girlfriends. She obviously adored him. She'd talk to him all the time, faintly chastising him for his wayward behaviour and lack of obvious job whilst also adoring him as her first and only child. I think she assumed I would go away after a while and John might even go back and live with her and keep her company, and I often wondered if that was why she gave him money sometimes. When I got pregnant, she forced out a smile and said, 'That's wonderful.'

But I always liked going to Janet's holiday house because I loved the sea and I loved the house and, after John the First and I separated, Janet and I kept in touch and occasionally she would write and invite Edward and me down to Devon for a long weekend and I would go out of a sense of duty and then walk along the beach and wonder at the sea. These visits have been infrequent. The first time I went, I found it so painful to go back to a place that John the First and I loved so much that I could hardly stop crying.

I called my mother from the beach one day. I sobbed for about an hour and at the end of all the sobbing she said, 'Why go if it's so painful?' Then she said, 'But why you are crying over a man who abandoned you I really don't know.'

But I kept going, though, for Edward's sake and also for Janet because, I reasoned, she should not be tainted by the sins of her son, but after I met John the Second, then when I became pregnant with Bennie, life became more difficult. It became obvious to me that Janet did not want to accept the fact that I had got another life with another man and had more children with this man. I came to the conclusion one day that Janet just plain and simply did not want to know about my other life. Instead, she wished to phase out the bits she couldn't accept. I am sure this is why Janet never came to see Edward at my home near Tring for it would have made me and John the Second and Bennie and Jamie all too real.

But now the email has arrived from God alone knows where, saying that John the First is coming home. Janet is ill. Janet has cancer. This must be why we hadn't heard from her this year. I'd been thinking about it only the other day, wondering why she hadn't written to invite Edward and me for our long weekend in Devon. I had decided that this was the year I was going to have it out with her. I was going to say to her, 'Janet, I have three children and I cannot keep leaving two of them here without me, especially Jamie as he hates being with anyone else really, so I am only going to come if we can all come.' I wasn't relishing the thought of doing this so I suppose I was partially relieved when no letter came. Should I have done more about it? If I'd called her, would she have told me? Why hasn't she told me? And, dear Lord, why does John the First really want to visit us?

I call John. 'You're not going to believe this,' I say.

'What?'

'John the First is coming back and he wants to come and visit.'

I hear John spluttering down the other end of the phone.

'Yes, that's what I thought.'

'Sorry,' says John. 'I was just choking on my coffee in surprise. What do you mean, John the First wants to come and visit? Why does he want to come and visit? When does he want to come and visit? You haven't heard from him in ages and Edward . . . is it fair on Edward?'

'He says he wants to get to know him.'

'Well, it's a bit late now, isn't it? He calls me Dad, Samantha. Do you really think that seeing his father is a good idea? Edward's happy with things as they are, isn't he?'

'Oh yes!'

'Well, tell him he can't come over, then. Tell him you love me and we are happy and we have three children and he can stuff it up his arse. Tell him –'

'His mother is dying, John. She's in the hospital up the

65

road. That's why he is coming over. He's not coming over to mess up our life. He wants to see his mother.'

'Oh God, which hospital is she at, then?'

'Prestwood General. That's the one with the good oncology department.'

'She's got cancer? That's not good.'

'Not good at all.'

We both stay silent for a while.

John sighs. 'And where is he going to stay while he's over here?'

'I imagine he'll be based at his mother's. After all, she's not there and it's only up the road from the hospital.' There is a silence on the other end of the telephone. 'Wouldn't it be rather mean of us to say he can't come over?'

John snorts. 'Mean of us? He's hardly been overburdening us with the fruits of human kindness himself.'

'I know. I know. But isn't it better to help him, to be kind, to do as we would be done by than settle scores?'

'It's up to you. My concern is Edward. If I find Edward is upset then it will all stop. I will not have him hurt again.'

'And you think I would?' I am suddenly angry.

'Oh no, Samantha. Of course not. I'm sorry. That came out all wrong. Anyway, when is he talking about coming?'

'In a couple of weeks to a month.'

'Well, it's your call really, Samantha. I will abide by what you say.'

'I don't think I can turn him down.'

'OK.'

'He is Edward's father.'

'Yes,' says John wearily, 'I know.'

'And Janet is Edward's grandmother.'

'Yes, I know.'

'But I love you, John,' I say. 'I really don't want this to change anything.'

'I thought you wanted change, Samantha. I thought that's exactly what you did want.' And then he rings off.

I am in a panic. John the First is coming home and now I think John, my John, may be cross. And I am worried about Edward. I remember how John the First left us when I'd thought he and I were fine. What about John the Second? Is he going to leave? But John the Second is a proper person, not a scoundrel, and John the First left for many reasons. For one thing, he thought there was something possibly wrong with Edward.

All the Things That Can Possibly Be Wrong with Edward

It was Janet who first noticed how Edward had changed me. I think she saw the cracks that were about to happen before I did. John the First and I were at her house for lunch when Edward was a tiny baby. Edward was screaming. He kept arching his back. Janet tried to help me. She marched him up and down all day.

When we were about to leave, Janet took me to one side and said, 'Maybe John could help a bit more if you are finding Edward a bit of a strain.'

I nearly cried then. I couldn't see it. How could I? In the beginning there was Edward. Or maybe there was me. Who was first? Sometimes it's hard to tell. I look at him and I see me. I see something I have created – that heart was put together by me in my body. That head, those limbs, the pair of lungs and kidneys and eyes and toenails were fed by me and looked after by me and they are mine. That's how I feel about Edward. Maybe that's how everyone feels about their first-born, this terrible feeling of possession, of ownership. How I have jealously guarded him!

I have spent what seems like half my life looking out for him, protecting him, loving him, so I can't imagine what life would be like without him. Yet Edward is, without a doubt, a strange boy. What Janet Parr noticed in him all those years ago has come to pass. He doesn't say the usual things other children do. He starts sentences in the middle so that no one ever knows what he is talking about.

'Is it March or November?' he will say.

'Is what March or November?'

'It, IT,' he'll yell, getting all cross and furious.

'What's IT, Edward?'

'You just don't understand, do you?' he'll say to me and I have to tell him that no, I don't.

I can see his frustration come and go. Before I met John the Second, Edward was very difficult. He found it hard to sleep. In fact, he would find it very hard to do just about everything. Even going to the shops was a trial. I would say to little Edward, aged maybe three, 'Come on, darling, we're going to the shops!' He'd fall onto the floor, actually more like plant himself onto the floor, and refuse to move. If I tried to pick him up, he would just scream and kick and scream and bite until, bitten, scratched and punched, I would somehow drag him to the door and manhandle him into the car. There he would scream and sob and fling himself backwards and forwards. But when we reached our destination he would go into reverse.

'Right, we're here now, Edward!' I'd say brightly. 'Out we pop.'

Back on the floor he'd go. 'Me no wanna get out. Me wanna stay here!'

'You have to get out, Edward. We've got no milk or bread. Mummy needs to get milk and bread.'

'Me no like milk. Me no like bread!' And on it would go. I would drag him out and put him in the trolley and then placate him by letting him eat everything and anything his puffy little eyes set upon. 'Ooh, nana,' he'd say and I'd grab the banana and peel it for him and on this would go until, by the end of the shop, he'd have eaten two 'nanas', three Jaffa cakes, half a baguette, some chocolate buttons, a Kinder egg and half an oat cake, which he would've spat out.

I told my mother this while we were wandering round the aisles of the supermarket one day. So far everything had gone well. We walked past bananas and French sticks, chocolates and Jaffa cakes.

'I don't know what you're moaning about,' said my mother, patting Edward on the head. 'He's behaving perfectly well.'

And then we came to the oat cake aisle and quite bizarrely, as he didn't even like oat cakes, and still to this day can't stand either sight or smell of them, he started to scream.

'Me want cake-e!'

'No, Edward,' said my mother. 'You can't have cake.'

'I WANT CAKE-E!' he yelled so loudly that other shoppers started to look at him.

'Everyone's looking at us,' my mother hissed to me. 'Be quiet, Edward!'

'I WANT CAKE-E.'

My mother looked at me. 'What's wrong with this child?' she said.

If only I knew! Edward's birth changed everything. He had reflux and colic and milk allergies and he cried all night, every night in such a piteous fashion it used to break my heart. He would tense his body up and arch away from me. His little fingers would scrabble and claw away at my flesh. He would desperately search out my nipple to feed and slurp hungrily only to break off and scream. Night after night I would pace up and down the house, up and down the streets, drive round and round. Then I decided to get pro-active about it so I took him to a cranial osteopath. Baby Edward would sit on my lap and she would touch his head and press this way and that and say that yes he had birth trauma but that he was totally curable. I would heave a sigh of relief. He is curable! He will sleep! He will stop crying all the time! She would say that when we got home we might find he was a little dozy. A little dozy, I'd think. How amazingly wonderful! But Edward never was dozy.

John the First thought I was too soft on him. In fact, he thought I was probably quite mad. And so the wedge between myself and John the First grew. With every lotion and potion and cranial osteopath and Infacol colic treatment and mugs of fennel tea and teething teats and teething rings and trips to the doctor and the health visitor and the endless crying and Edward's obsession with his dummy, John the First retreated behind his guitar and then he started taking his guitar to the pub and then, one day, when I turned around to tell him that I finally thought Edward had reflux because I had heard it was very common in baby boys, I found John the First wasn't there.

After that I met many experts over the years. Edward didn't seem to be able to do much right really. He was all wrong. He was over-large, like a sausage stuffed into a too-small skin. His hearing was poor so he couldn't pick up on things easily. He became frustrated very quickly. He would bite and scratch. He found speech almost impossible. I had him referred and tested by everyone. I dogged the doctor's surgery until they agreed that

Edward should be seen by specialists. These experts tested his ears and eyes and brain. They all agreed something wasn't 'quite right', as they put it, but they couldn't agree on what the something was. Then there were friends who diagnosed him as everything under the sun. One friend thought he might have ADD, one thought he had autism. One thought he was dyspraxic, one thought he was dyslexic. The health visitor thought that he 'may well be within the spectrum of what is described as autistic' but that she couldn't be sure. I was supposed to take him for more tests but by this time I had met Dougie and Dougie told me that Edward was charming and lovely and wonderful and yes, different, but, as he said, who isn't different among us these days? So when the health visitor came round with leaflets and booklets and appointments with specialists and psychologists and forms with the words such as 'statemented' written on them, Dougie simply took them and threw them in the bin and told Edward he was just fine as he was.

A speech therapist came round once.

She told me what Edward's problem was.

'He has a big tongue,' she said.

7. Wednesday

On Wednesday afternoons, Stanley comes to play. Stanley is Edward's best friend. He is an only child. His mother, Laura, is a rather organized woman who works in 'presentational management', as she calls it, although I have never worked out quite what that means. She often turns up to our house, neat and tidy with high heels on, in her smart clean Ford Focus, at the worst possible time of day. She'll either come on a weekend just after breakfast, which means the little children always have food in their hair and milky unwashed faces, or she'll come on schooldays straight after dinner, when I've just released Bennie's nether regions to the world – Bennie hates wearing a nappy and likes to dance around naked as much as he possibly can.

'I think Bennie has no nappy on,' Laura says on these occasions, as Bennie treats her to a version of his remarkable and totally unique bottom dance. He bends over double and sticks his naked bum in the air, like a tufty duck going uptails all, and then waggles it at her. 'Does he show his bottom to everyone?' she says.

'Oh Bennie's always doing bottom dances,' I say to her. 'It means he likes you.'

Laura says she doesn't want any more children. When I ask her about it she pulls little faces and laughs a bit nervously. She says, 'Oh Stanley is enough,' and I can see that she finds our house with our three rowdy children disconcerting.

'How do you cope with all the noise?' she asked me once when she came to pick Stanley up after school and found Stanley and Edward launching Bennie and Jamie's identical Winnie-the-Pooh hot-water bottles over the banisters.

They were trying to hit Bennie, who was bouncing around at the bottom of the stairs yelling, ''it me! 'it me!' while Jamie sat just out of range clapping his hands and chirruping away to himself.

'Winnie-the-Pooh hot-water-bottle number one ATTACK!' yelled Edward, hurling a solemn-faced Pooh down the stairs.

'Pooh number two ATTACK!' yelled Stanley, following suit.

'It's all so loud,' said Laura nervously but I told her that I had become almost immune to the noise.

Then Edward spotted her and proceeded to inform her in a rather pained tone that, actually, he didn't feel that he was the noisiest one in this household. 'We had these killer whales,' he said, 'and we were going to take them to the pool up the road for a treat and Daddy blew them up with a pump, but after Mummy had put me to bed I couldn't sleep so I went to tell her but I couldn't find my mum or dad anywhere so I went to look for them in the garden and guess what I found them doing? I found them throwing the killer whales at each other and yelling and laughing really loudly, and when I asked them what they were doing they said, "This is what we always do after you've gone to bed, darling!" and I think they must've been drunk!'

'Thanks for that, Edward,' I said.

John and I call Laura 'Corporate Queen' when no one is around. Laura seems to organize people to do things, like run focus groups. She's often out meeting sets of people at ordinary hotels off motorways, such as the Milton Keynes Travelodge. She says she is trained in 'motivational speaking'. She goes on courses. The thought hit me one day, rather out of the blue, maybe she knows Nicholas? I don't know why I thought it. Why should she know Nicholas?

'Do you know Nicholas Sinclair?' I asked her the next time I saw her, when she was picking Stanley up.

'Nicholas . . . Nicholas Sinclair . . .' she said, looking thoughtful. 'Hmm. Name rings a bell but I can't place him. I'll look back in my records and see if I've ever done a course with him.'

'Oh it's all right. I just thought you might know him because . . .'

'Is he a friend of yours?'

'Well, sort of. He's married to a woman I know.'

'Well, I'll have a look and let you know,' she said. 'I have everyone's name written down in a big book at work.'

It has to be said that Stanley is a funny little boy. He has a thatch of dark hair and big thick glasses. He is a very serious child and also quite odd. He won't watch or read anything about Harry Potter as he says his mother doesn't like him to. 'My mum says *Harry Potter* is all about dark magic and she doesn't believe in dark magic,' Stanley told me once when I was about to put on a *Harry Potter* video for them all to watch. Then he told me he couldn't watch *Shrek* as his mother didn't approve of animation and that, if he was to be honest and he thought he better had be honest because his mother had told him not to lie, his mother had told him he was not to watch television at all.

Edward could hardly believe this. 'Not watch television!' he screeched at Stanley. Edward then listed all the shows he loves to watch. 'You've never watched *Scooby Doo*, then?' he said, his eyes popping out of his head.

'No,' said Stanley solemnly.

'Or *Power Rangers*?' Stanley shook his head. 'Or *Raven*? Or *Yu-gi-oh*? Or *Totally Spies*? Or *Dexter's Laboratory*?' Stanley shook his head again. 'Surely you've watched *Teletubbies*?' said Edward.

'Me watch Debbedubbies,' piped up Bennie.

'No, not even *Teletubbies*,' said Stanley. 'My mother thinks *Teletubbies* is evil!'

I asked Laura about this one time and she blushed a bit and said that she didn't like Stanley watching television as she couldn't control it. 'We had a nanny once, when Stanley was young, and all she did was leave Stanley watching television all day while she chatted to her friends on the telephone.'

I asked her how she knew that.

'I didn't know for *ages*,' she said, 'but once I came home in the middle of the day because I'd left a very important report behind and I found the nanny giggling away on the telephone and Stanley was watching a very traumatic episode of *Neighbours* where one character was shouting at another and I thought it was inappropriate.'

It also turned out that Corporate Queen checked the telephone bill – 'astronomical!' – and found out the nanny had been calling those expensive chat-line numbers.

'I asked her to leave immediately!' said Laura.

But, despite the fact that Edward and Stanley have little in common, over the years since they have been to school together they have got closer and closer. They bonded on the first day: both a bit shy, both a bit different. Then there was a period, about two years ago, when Stanley briefly went off with David Earl, the most popular boy in the class. Apparently, according to Edward, Stanley was lured by David's all-round marvellousness. Stanley later told me that he'd gone off Edward because Edward trod on all the Airfix planes Stanley had made in his room. Stanley told me that, most nights, he goes home and eats an apple and then makes Airfix models and plays quietly until dinner time. It turns out that Stanley always does the same thing when he gets home because that's what his mother always likes him to do. I once asked him if maybe he could branch out a bit and indulge in a tangerine or even a banana, but Stanley said that if he had a banana or a tangerine or something like that he thought his mother might get quite cross with him, but he was not sure why. Anyway, on that one particular afternoon, after school, Edward had insisted on having a tangerine. Stanley told him he couldn't have one as his mother wouldn't like it, but Edward would not back down and then they had an argument about it and it all ended with Edward wrecking the planes. Edward said it was an accident. When I asked Stanley why he thought Edward wrecked his planes, he thought for a bit and said, 'I suppose that's what eating a tangerine might well do to a boy.'

This afternoon, Edward and Stanley are with Bennie in the garden, discussing where would be best to look for wasps.

Laura had rung me during the day to tell me that she'd taken Stanley off E-numbers. 'It's because he's been a bit difficult recently. You wouldn't mind not giving him anything sweet, would you, because he's been barely sleeping and has been very bad-tempered.'

So I have told Edward and Bennie that Stanley cannot have sweets, chocolate, ice cream, pizza, burgers or chips.

'Poor Stanley,' said Bennie.

'Poor me!' said Edward. 'I thought we were having burger and chips for dinner.'

I told him we couldn't have burger and chips because it wouldn't be fair on Stanley. Edward then grumbled for a bit but now I am watching them and they seem pretty happy.

'I went to Mallorca once,' Stanley is telling Edward.

'Was it a nice place?'

'S'nice?' says Bennie who, as per usual, is following the older boys around.

'Did you see any churches?' says Edward.

'Why would I see churches?'

'My mum always makes me go to see churches on holiday. We were in Italy once and we went to see twenty churches in a week. I counted.'

'Me see them,' says Bennie.

'Not you,' says Edward, turning on his brother. 'You didn't see any churches. You were just a baby. Mummy wheeled you round in a pushchair.'

'No, me SAW!'

'You're such a baby.'

'No, me bad.'

'Yes, you are bad.'

'No, he's not,' says Stanley thoughtfully. 'He's just two.'

'Me two!' says Bennie.

'I think when I was two,' continues Stanley, 'I was in a car crash.'

'What?' says Edward. 'What kind of a car crash?'

'I can't really remember, but my mum told me it was

awful. She said I was thrown out of my seat onto the steering wheel. She said I had to go to hospital but I don't remember anything of it because I was only little, you see.'

'You go crash?' asks Bennie.

'I did go crash,' says Stanley.

'I was in a car crash once,' says Edward. 'I'd just met my dad. I think I was about three, and he'd just moved in with us and then Mum said he was driving too fast and we crashed.'

'Crash bang?' says Bennie.

'Yes, crash bang,' says Edward. 'I nearly lost a leg. My mum told me I had this flap of skin that was all loose and she could see my flesh and bones beneath it and that I looked all weird like an alien.'

'What colour was your flesh?' asks Stanley.

'I think a pinky yellow colour.'

'And what colour were the cars in the crash?'

'One blue and one red.'

'Hmm. And you say it was just after you met your dad.'

'Yes.'

'But how come you didn't meet your dad until then? Didn't you know him when you were born?'

'No. My mum only met him later. Before that I, well, I had a daddy, a different type of daddy but really I was only with my mummy.'

'You no daddy?' says Bennie, looking confused.

'Of course I have a daddy,' says Edward. 'Daddy is my daddy. You know D-A-D-D-Y.'

Then Edward and Stanley get into a discussion about other things they think may well have happened when they were little. Stanley says he thinks the first time he ever made an Airfix aeroplane was when he was two and a half. Edward thinks he may have once been in a taxi in London. Stanley says he definitely flew in an aeroplane because that was the only way he could possibly have got to Mallorca. Edward says he thinks he went to Africa when he was a baby because he found a photograph at his granny's house which showed him in a pushchair with a rhino behind him.

'A rhino?' says Stanley. 'Isn't that a bit dangerous?'

'My mum says that rhinos are very short-sighted so maybe he didn't see me,' says Edward. Then he tells Stanley about how, every night, he wakes up and looks out of his bedroom window.

'Why?'

'Because our cat Honey always has a fight with the barn owl. Who do you think would win, out of a cat and an owl?'

'Ooh the owl!' Stanley flaps his arms as if they are pretend wings.

'No!' says Edward. 'The cat does every night!'

Bennie, who has been listening to them, is obviously bored. 'What you do?' he asks Stanley.

'We're looking for wasps,' says Stanley. 'I found two hornets in Mallorca.'

Bennie looks around thoughtfully. Suddenly he screams, 'Bee!' and points up in the air and Edward and Stanley as one start chasing something I can't see round the garden, brandishing the fishing nets they found in the greenhouse, above their heads.

'Get it, Stanley,' shouts Edward.

'Argh,' shouts Stanley and then he makes this huge dive across the lawn.

'Have you got the wasp?' Edward is racing towards him.

Stanley looks in his net. 'No,' he says in a desultory fashion. 'There's nothing in here.'

'Hmm,' says Edward, now sitting down next to Stanley. 'I think we're going to have to whistle.'

'Why do we whistle?'

'Oh wasps hate whistling. It drives them mad. If we whistle then they'll come out of their hiding place and we can swat them with our nets.'

'Right.'

Stanley and Edward then sit there for about five minutes, whistling.

Bennie squats at their feet like a small native boy with his chin in his hands, waiting and still.

Then Edward says, 'Stanley, have you noticed something?'

'Yeah. The wasps aren't coming out of their hiding holes.'

'No, not that. Something else. Something stinky.'

'Yeah. It's disgusting. Is it Bennie?'

'Probably. Bennie, have you done a poo in your nappy?'

'Me dun poo?' says Bennie.

'Yes, have you done a poo?'

'No poo,' says Bennie solemnly.

Edward leans over and stares down Bennie's trousers into his nappy. 'Hmm,' he tells Stanley, 'it seems that Bennie is telling the truth.'

'Well, what's that disgusting smell, then?'

Edward looks around. Then he looks at Stanley's trousers. 'Oh dear,' he says, starting to giggle.

'What is it?' Stanley hasn't noticed that now Bennie and Edward are staring at his trousers.

'It's you!' says Edward.

'What do you mean, it's me?'

'You've got dog poo down your trousers.'

'Poo! Poo!' says Bennie excitedly.

'You must have skidded through one when you were chasing that wasp,' says Edward.

'Oh that's disgusting!'

'I think it's funny,' says Edward and he and Bennie start laughing even harder.

Stanley stares at them and then gets to his feet. 'I'm not playing with either of you ever again.' And he stalks back into the house.

A little later, I have sorted everything out. I have washed Stanley's trousers and sponged off his shoes and am giving them all a bath for good measure. While the three of them are in the bath, I explain to Stanley that Edward's father, John the Second, never crashed the car with him in it when he was three, and that yes Edward does have another father, called John the First, but we don't see him any more because he is travelling around so much but that, as luck would have it, Edward's father may be coming back for a visit.

'Ooh, tell me something about my father, then,' says Edward excitedly.

'Well, your father has always called you Eddie.'

'Really?' says Edward looking interested.

'Yes. I don't know why he does. It's like the way he calls me Sammie, you see. He's just that kind of man. Anyway, he may be here in a couple of weeks and it will all be very fun and you and he can go to the park and stuff.'

'Where does he live, then, my dad?'

I tell him his father doesn't really live anywhere. 'He's a citizen of the world.'

'Ooh, so Edward's father is like a pirate or a gypsy?' says Stanley.

'Yes, a bit like that.'

'That's cool!'

'Is it?' says Edward.

'Yes, super cool!' says Stanley. 'Lucky you, Edward. My dad works in a bank and that's seriously not cool at all. He says that when I grow up I'll work in a bank too but I don't want to do that.'

I ask Stanley what he'd like to do instead.

'I want to be a pilot but I bet I'm not allowed to be one. I'm not allowed anything now, you know. I can't even have a chocolate button!'

'I know,' says Edward. 'You're not allowed burgers or chips either.'

'It's bad, isn't it?'

'Dreadful.'

Once they are out of the bath, they go upstairs to play. For a while the house is quiet. Bennie is upstairs with the older boys. Jamie is happily playing with a rubber band in the sitting room. Occasionally, he pokes his finger up the dog's nose.

John rings. 'Is everything OK at home, darling?'

I tell him that Stanley is here and everything is fine, bar the fact that Stanley got covered in dog poo.

'God, that's disgusting.'

'Yes, it was rather.' I add that, as the boys are all now happily ensconced upstairs having had a long bath, everything will be fine.

'God, Corporate Queen wouldn't want Stanley coming home smelling of dog shit!'

I then tell him that I have gently introduced to Edward the idea of John the First coming to visit.

'How did he sound about it?'

'Well, he was fine. He was rather nonplussed about it all until Stanley said he thought Edward's father might be a pirate or something because I told them he travels a lot. They both got quite excited about it then.'

'Oh good, then they'll be disappointed.'

'Oh,' I say softly to him, 'are you worried Edward will think you boring in comparison, darling?'

'Dreadfully dull. Middle-aged man, father of three, never goes further than London and a walk in the woods. That's me.'

'But we love you like that.'

John laughs and says he'll be home in a couple of hours.

I decide that as everything is quiet I might well even try to do something unprecedented and actually play with Jamie. I never play with Jamie. I used to play with Edward all the time. I played Thomas the Tank Engine for years and years and years. I took Edward to see Thomas at Chinnor railway station. Every Saturday we would go to the local toyshop and buy another train for his collection. After Thomas we played Pokémon and Power Rangers. We went to the movies to watch all of the *Lord of the Rings* films and *Star Wars* and *Cats and Dogs* and anything by Roald Dahl. I spent years driving up and down the country finding things for Edward to do. But Bennie and Jamie? No one does anything with them. Bennie barely left the house and garden until he was about one. Jamie goes more places but only as an attachment. He gets to go to Edward's school to pick him up. He gets to go and watch Edward at football practice. He goes to the sports centre to get Edward after swimming class.

Today, I think I might well make baby Jamie a tower of building blocks for him to knock down. I sit on the floor. Jamie shuffles over to me on his bottom. He gurgles happily as he lays his head in my lap. He has such white blond hair, all tufty like a baby bird. I reach towards him and cuddle him and he tucks his head neatly into my shoulder and sucks his thumb.

'Oh Jamie, you are such a peaceful baby. You never get any attention and yet you are so lovely.'

'Gurgle, gurgle, gurgle,' he goes.

'And now I am going to play with you.' I sit him on the floor and build up five blocks on top of each other.

'Gurgle, gurgle, gurgle!' Jamie gets all excited. He sticks his little arm out and . . . *Wham!* The blocks go tumbling down. 'Erggh, blerp, ga!' He waves his fists in the air.

'Oh Jamie,' I laugh and build him up another tower.

Wham! Down goes the tower again. 'Erggh, blerp, ga!'

We are on our fifth tower when I hear mutterings and muted giggles behind the sitting-room door. 'Bennie?' I say. Giggle, giggle, shuffle, shuffle. 'Edward?' More giggling, more shuffling. Suddenly the door opens and standing right in front of me, stark naked, are Edward, Stanley and Bennie.

'Ta da!' they say.

'ERGGH, BLERP, GA!' says Jamie, staring at them.

I stare at them. I cannot believe my eyes. They have drawn all over each other from top to bottom in thick felt-tip pen. Edward has a crude picture of a dragon on his chest done in red and black. Bennie has what I think are

84

supposed to be blue butterflies all up his arm and back. But Stanley, oh Stanley with nothing on but his big thick glasses, has a snake whose flat green head rests just below his throat and whose body winds all the way down his chest and stomach and ends as a tiny rattle on his willy.

'Oh God,' I say.

'Don't we look great?' says Edward. 'I'm Red Dragon and Stanley is Green Snake and Bennie is Master Blue Butterfly.'

'Right.'

'We did it all ourselves,' says Stanley proudly.

'Me butfly,' says Bennie.

'Raa!' says Edward. 'I'm a dragon.'

'Ssss,' says Stanley, 'I'm a snake,' and then he wiggles his willy. 'Here's my rattle!' he says delightedly.

Just then, the doorbell rings. 'Mummy!' says Stanley, leaping for the door handle.

'Oh God,' I say.

'Raaa!' says Edward.

'Erggh, blerp, ga!' says Jamie.

'Me butfly,' says Bennie, waving his arms around like pretend wings.

And into the middle of this mess and muddle walks Laura. For a moment, maybe a mere second, she stands in mute horrified silence and then . . . and then she explodes. 'OH MY GOD!' she screams, staring wildly at my two children. She hasn't seen Stanley yet. He is behind her. She turns around maniacally to look for him and, as if in slow motion, he appears in front of her.

'Sssss,' he says archly, raising his eyebrows suggestively at her and wiggling his willy.

She gasps. And suddenly the atmosphere is broken.

She tries to grab Stanley, who is pretending to be all slithery and slippery and snakey and is proving impossible to grab, so instead of grabbing him she grabs Edward, who then 'raaas' at her so she grabs him even more tightly by his shoulders. I can see she's hurting him and suddenly Edward stops raa-ing and shouts, 'Ow, you're hurting me!'

Laura says to him, 'What's going on, Edward? I don't understand. Why are you naked? Why have you drawn a snake on Stanley?'

Then out of the blue Bennie charges at her in a very un-butterfly-like fashion and kicks her with all his two-year-old might on her shin. 'Me butfly!' he says. The shock of it makes Laura let go of Edward and look down at Bennie.

'What is going on?' she says again. Then she turns to me. 'What is going on here?' She looks panicked.

'It's nothing,' I say, feeling now rather perturbed and guilty as if it is all my fault. My God, her son has come over and Edward has drawn a snake down his willy! Why has he done that? It's because I'm a bad mother. It's so obvious. I am a terrible mother and my children are all demons and . . .

'Nothing?' says Laura desperately. 'I don't understand. Stanley didn't have a snake on his . . . on his . . . willy this morning.'

'They . . . er . . . had a bath and . . .' I say falteringly.

'Why did they have a bath?'

'Because Stanley got dog mess on his trousers.'

'How did he do that?' She stares wildly around her as if more painted children might appear out of the wood-work.

'He was chasing a wasp.'

'Chasing a wasp? Why were they chasing wasps?'

'I don't know. Something to do with Stanley seeing two hornets on holiday in Mallorca.'

'We've never been to Mallorca.' Laura looks close to tears.

'Oh.'

'Did Stanley say we'd been to Mallorca?'

'Well, not exactly.' I motion Edward to go and get Stanley's clothes.

'So, now he's lying. He's lying and he's naked and someone has drawn that, that thing on his body.'

I think she's getting a bit hysterical now. Her voice is rising up and up.

'Really, Laura,' I say in my most calming voice. 'It's just a kid thing. It's not a big deal.'

She now looks at me as if she wants to hit me. 'Not a big deal!' she says, her voice now up a full octave. 'How can you say that? How can you possibly say that?' Then she spies Stanley, who has now found his clothes. 'Come on, Stanley. We are going right NOW!'

The NOW comes out like a scream, a yelp of pain.

'Thanks, Edward's mum,' says Stanley, apparently unaware of his mother's hysterical demeanour as he is being marched out of the door. 'Bye, Bennie. Bye, Jamie. Bye, Edward.'

'Bye bye,' says Edward, waving.

Laura turns round at the car and shoots me a look of pure confusion.

'I'm so sorry,' I say.

After they have driven off, Edward turns to me and says, perfectly happily, 'Well, that was fun.'

'Oh Edward.'

★

When John comes home he finds Bennie all felt-tipped and smudged and dozing on the sofa. Edward is in the bath with some soap and a sponge. 'Look, Daddy!' he says when he hears John. 'I drew a dragon all over my body. It was a really good one! But Mummy says I have to wash it off. Do you want to come and see it before it goes?'

'Oh yes,' says John. Then I hear him saying, 'That looks amazing! It's all red and black.'

'Yes,' says Edward. 'It was the kind of dragon that went, "Raaa!"'

'Raaa! That's pretty scary.'

'And Stanley had a snake even down to his willy.'

'Right.'

'His snake went, "Ssss!"'

'Yes, I guess it would do. And what did Stanley's mother think of his snake?'

'Oh.' Edward suddenly sounds crestfallen. 'I don't think she liked it very much.'

'Never mind. It sounds like you had fun.'

'Yes, we did, Daddy, we did,' says Edward and then he goes back to soaping himself.

'Oh dear,' says John when he sees me. 'I assume Corporate Queen was none too happy about the body-drawing thing.'

'None too happy? That's an understatement. It's a disaster. A total disaster. She just drove off looking appalled and now she'll never let Stanley come over again and Edward will be totally friendless. I mean, what on earth made them do it?'

'I suppose they thought it was fun.'

'Yes, I suppose so. But really it's a disaster.'

'I'll ring her,' says John.

'Oh will you? She likes you. She likes men.'

'I'll ring her and explain. I'll tell her how lonely Edward would be without Stanley. I'll appeal to her feminine side.'

'What feminine side? She's a control freak. She won't let Stanley have E-numbers.'

'Well, I think you're just a bit upset. She was probably out of her depth. Can't you see that about her, Samantha?'

'Of course I can, but why was she so shocked?'

'Imagine coming in to find your naked son with a snake's rattle drawn on his willy! She was probably embarrassed.' He then wanders off to the study to find a telephone.

We have three portable ones and no one can ever find them because Jamie's favourite thing is to hide them in ingenious places. He's very clever at it. If he spies the telephone in a place where he thinks he can haul himself up and reach it, he'll grab the surface and rise up like a mini-diver emerging from the sea and then, with one hand flailing around, he'll find the telephone, clutch it to himself and then sink back down and shuffle off, giggling away to himself. I've found telephones all over the place: in a boot, in the dustbin, behind the sofa, in Bennie's cot, in the dog basket, absolutely everywhere. One even went in the loo. It's not worked that well since.

I can hear John swearing in the study. 'Where the bloody hell is it?' he's saying. 'For God's sake, Jamie, where have you put the bloody telephone?'

'Try the bin.'

Lots of scuffling, then, 'Found it!'

After a bit I hear lots of murmurings. I want to go and listen but feel I probably shouldn't. Eventually, I hear some laughing and then John comes back into the room smiling.

'All sorted.'

'What, really?'

'Oh yes, it's all fine. I explained to her that Edward can be a bit odd but that it's all harmless fun.'

'Yes, it is harmless fun.'

'I just think she was shocked but she's had time to calm down and she's asked Stanley about it and she now knows there was no evil intent.'

'Of course there was no evil intent. Why did she think there may be?'

'She didn't necessarily think there may be. I think she just needed reassuring.'

'And you reassured her?'

'Absolutely. Anyway, the upshot is that Stanley can still come and play on Wednesdays and some weekends.'

'Oh good. Edward will be happy.'

Just then Bennie starts stirring.

'What exactly is Bennie supposed to be?' asks John.

'Oh he was Master Blue Butterfly.'

'Right.' John then goes, very tenderly, to pick him up. 'I'll pop him in bed and he can have a bath tomorrow.' As he walks out of the room, though, he remembers something. 'Oh Corporate Queen asked me to tell you this. She says that it's all come back to her.'

'What's come back to her?'

'The thing you asked her about. She says that yes, she has met Nicholas. He came on a course once. Apparently, it was in the Lake District. She says it was like a holiday mixed with some managerial bonding and trust games. She says he was with this charming companion.'

'I don't remember Genevieve going to the Lake District with Nicholas, but maybe it was before we knew them.'

'Oh but get this. Do you know why she remembers

Nicholas?' I shake my head. 'Because he wasn't accompanied by Genevieve!' says John triumphantly.

'Oh no,' I groan, my heart plummeting downwards. 'Who was he accompanied by, then?'

'A young man! Nicholas turned up to the Lake District with a young man. And guess what? *They shared a room!*'

'WHAT!'

'Exactly!'

Then John walks out of the room with blue-painted Bennie in his arms.

8. Thursday

In the morning, John gets up early to go to work. The sun is barely up. John opens the curtains and we lie in bed together watching the dawn rise from behind the hill.

'I can see the deer,' says John. 'They're running all over the place!'

John loves to watch the deer. He will spend hours at the window, propping little Jamie up against the cold glass panes, watching the world go by. 'Look, Jamie,' he'll say, 'there's a tractor coming down the road.'

'Mmm,' Jamie will say.

'And look, there's a kestrel hovering over the field. And a man walking a dog!'

John will then jiggle Jamie up and down and Jamie will giggle and say, 'Ga! Ga! Ga!'

Today, John has opened the window. The air smells sweet and warm. I love to watch John in the morning. I like to see him come from sleep into wakefulness. I suddenly have a terrible thought. Why is everyone's life so difficult? I remember what John told me last night. Nicholas was at a bonding weekend with a young man. Is Nicholas gay? He doesn't seem gay. He is married with children. Why can't people be what they seem?

'Why do you look so worried, Samantha?'

'I'm worried about you.'

John laughs and reaches over to ruffle my hair. 'And why are you worrying about me?'

'I'm worried that maybe I don't tell you how much I appreciate you sometimes.'

'What's brought this on, Samantha?'

'And I'm worried that I don't show you that I love you enough.'

'Samantha?' He is laughing but looking puzzled.

'And I'm worried that you're going to run off with someone else of either sex.'

'What are you going on about? God, your mind works in a weird way. I thought we were happily lying in bed and you're thinking of being abandoned. I'm not going to abandon you, any of you. You don't really think that, do you?'

'No. I think I'm just worried about John the First coming and Nicholas, well, Nicholas . . .'

'Of course you're worried. Your world's gone topsy-turvy again. But stop worrying. There'll be an explanation for Nicholas's young man.'

'But what can the explanation possibly be? Nicholas is a married man!'

'Oh and no married men cheat on their wives with other men?'

'Not many.'

'But some do. Look, when it comes to Nicholas, I have no idea about it. I really don't. He may be a bit of a swinger but only time will tell on that one. And about John the First coming over to visit? Jesus, I'm worried so I'm sure you are too. But it will be fine. Trust me, Samantha.' By now, he is kissing my neck. 'Don't think about me,' he whispers. 'Just feel me instead.'

★

Some time later John is going out of the door. He is very happy. After we got up, he started whistling and his whistling made Edward laugh and then Edward started whistling and I got so cross with their endless whistling that I was very relieved when the two of them said that they were about to leave.

'Love you, Mum,' says Edward, kissing me on the lips and whirling his school bag above his head.

'Love you, darling,' says John the Second, squeezing my bottom and giving me a wink.

So they have gone and now I am chasing Bennie and Jamie round the house. They are like two hyperactive monkeys this morning. Round and round they go; up and down the stairs, behind the curtains, up the curtains, under the beds, giggling as if their lungs would burst. Even so, I still find myself mentally coming back to John's telephone conversation with Corporate Queen last night. I can't get it out of my head. Nicholas was on a management course in the Lake District with a young man. They shared a room. Who is this man that Nicholas was with? I just can't understand it. Last night I rolled over in bed and quizzed John for an age.

'What, exactly, did Laura say?'

John grunted in return.

'Did she say young man or boy, for example?'

Grunt.

'For God's sake, this is important!'

Grunt, grunt.

'This is Genevieve's marriage we're talking about! What am I supposed to say when I next see her? And I'm bound to see her at playgroup, aren't I?'

John then woke up a bit and said, 'Say nothing,

Samantha. This isn't about you, you know. This is about Genevieve and Nicholas and it's none of our business.'

And then I went off on one. 'Say nothing? Say nothing! How can I say nothing? Genevieve's husband is possibly nobbing a young man! How can I say nothing? He might be having an affair and I don't know if it's better or worse that it's with someone of the same sex! I just can't not tell her!'

Then John said I should not go to playgroup any more if that's how I felt, and then he rolled over and went back to sleep.

I call John's mobile phone. There's no reply. He's probably on the train. Damn. 'I've got to discuss this Nicholas thing with you,' I hiss into his phone. 'If you love me you'll call me back right now!'

Ten minutes later the phone rings. 'Where are you?' I say immediately.

There is a short silence and then the voice at the other end says, 'In the cow shed. Why, is that important?'

It's my sister.

'Oh it's you, Julia.'

'Of course it's me, Julia,' says Julia. 'Why wouldn't it be?'

'I was waiting for John to call back.' And then I tell her that I was just about to ring her to tell her my news.

'Your news?'

'Yes. John the First is coming back for a visit and he wants to see Edward and me, and everyone really.'

'John the First is coming back? Are you going to let him see you all? What are you going to do?'

I tell her what he said in his email and ask her what she thinks I should do.

She thinks about this for a bit and then says, 'Well, on the one hand I feel he shouldn't come and visit. He has barely been a father to Edward and he hardly deserves rights on that account. On the other hand, he is Edward's father and his mother is dying and I suppose you feel some vague sense of loyalty to him. You must, of course, think about Edward in all of this.'

I tell her I am thinking of Edward and of virtually nothing but Edward.

'It must be very confusing for him. It's all very well making a happy family with John the Second but now that his father is going to return, even temporarily, he may well get a sensation of being torn in two, of having his loyalty tested.'

'Well, there's not a tremendous amount I can do about that because I've already said John the First can come over.'

'I was reading a book the other day,' says my sister, completely ignoring what I've just said. 'It's one of the books on the course reading list, you see, and it's about how, as a parent, your job is essentially to protect the psychological stability of your children because you are an adult and they are young and inexperienced. It's really about saying no to the things you think will affect them in a negative fashion. You see, you should've said no to John the First coming over to the house.'

'Julia, it was pretty impossible to say no as his mother is dying.'

'Yes, well, that's his problem, isn't it? Edward's problem is that his father will leave him again and this will trigger feelings of abandonment in him for the rest of his life and then he won't be able to make a long-lasting commitment to any one mate and —'

I ask her where on earth she's getting all this stuff from.

'Well, there's this other book. It's about how you can map a child's future from their past. I mean, none of this is proven but I found it fascinating. You see, if we look at your past . . .'

'Oh please don't.'

'. . . we can see that it is obvious that John the First is our father and John the Second is the man you had to meet to get over our father.'

I tell her I am not in the mood for all this and that maybe she'd like to tell me why she's rung actually.

'Ah,' she says. 'I need you to come over because there's something I need to talk to you about.' She stops for a while. 'Joe's left me.'

'What!'

'He's run off with an angel therapist, and now I want to kill myself.'

I always thought that Julia and Uncle Joe had the perfect life. I have often told Julia this. Their rambling farmhouse is at the bottom of a hill. It has a little stream running through it. It has a magical willow tree and an old oak tree and looks a bit like something out of an Enid Blyton novel. Children fall out of every room and there are cats living in every drawer. In the field outside their house they keep hens and cows and sheep and an over-friendly goat.

Once when we were visiting, the goat got out and ended up trying to eat the aerial from my mother's car and she was furious. 'That's typical of Julia!' she said. 'No infra-structure!'

Perversely, even though my mother thinks I should not

have help – or 'infrastructure' as she calls it – she actually thinks my sister is mad to do it all by herself. 'Six children and no help!' she'll say.

'But you keep telling me she doesn't need help,' I said to her once.

'Ah,' my mother said, 'I didn't say she doesn't need help. I merely said that she does everything by herself. I never said I agreed with that.'

'But why should my sister have help and not me?'

'Because she has a bigger house than you.'

It is true that Julia spends half her life cleaning the house. Whenever we go round, it is always neat and tidy even though the children tramp mud in and out every day and the dogs moult and the cats moult and sometimes even the chickens come in to have a peck around. 'The house must get filthy!' my mother always says to Julia.

'It does,' Julia always replies happily. 'I was up until three in the morning cleaning!'

'Three in the morning? That's ridiculous!' Then my mother will go on to ask, 'Why don't you have help?'

And Julia will say, 'We can't afford help.'

Then my mother will say, 'Now you are being even more ridiculous. Joe earns enough money, of course you can afford help.'

Then Julia will say, smiling, 'But I like to clean the house myself.'

Uncle Joe, of course, gets away from all this. He does a job I have never really understood. He's middle management in some IT company but he seems to make quite a lot of money. He talks to me about his job sometimes, about pyramid structures and promoting brands and brand loyalty and how to make your office work more efficiently for you, but I tend to switch off and watch my sister pottering around the garden instead. Uncle Joe's work always seems to be remarkably flexible. 'I've got six kids!' he said to me once when I asked him how he managed to have a life and work at the same time. 'Your sister needs me at home to help. The office understand this.' So Uncle Joe is nice and his 'office', whoever they are, are nice and my sister is also very nice. Uncle Joe tells me that all the time. 'Your sister is so lovely,' he'll say. 'I am such a lucky man.'

But I know my sister has her insecurities. I can see that she feels nervous about things. In the past I have asked her if anything is the matter but she has just smiled and poured me some dandelion tea. When she is feeling very vulnerable she will group her children together and then gather them around her, like folds in a coat. Occasionally, she will appear from underneath them and look small and thin and drawn and then disappear back, like a nervous rabbit. At the moment, aged forty, she has become quite hyperactive, though. If she ever does engage in a conversation, her arms whirl around and she laughs like a mad thing. I feel sorry for her because I'm not utterly convinced she's that happy. Recently, I have seen some cracks. For a start, she's become obsessed with her body even though she looks very good for a woman of forty who's had six kids. But there's no telling her.

'No,' she always says when I tell her how good she looks. 'I've got a spare tyre round my middle!' But she hasn't because she's so busy all the time. When she's not cleaning, she's ironing and grocery shopping and making six packed lunches a day.

I asked her how she was going to fit her child psychology

degree in and she said, 'I've got to do something for my *brain*, Samantha!'

For a while, before she realized she had to do something for her brain – I mean, something formalized with course work and lectures and stuff – she went mad for self-help books. It all started as a bit of a joke. About a year after our father died, Uncle Joe came to see me. He told me he thought Julia had lost her mind. He said that she'd taken to cycling round the village in her nightdress in the pitch black of night. I asked him why and he said he thought it started after my father's death. He asked me to help and I thought and thought for a while and said I wasn't sure what made anyone cycle round their home village in nothing but their nightdress but that maybe he could go to the library and find a book that might help.

'You know,' I said, 'grief can make people do weird things. Maybe you need to get one of those self-help books called something like "How to Get Over Grief" and see if it works.' So he went and came back with *How to Let Go With Love*.

And so Julia read the book and one day she rang up and said, 'Oh I feel much better now,' and the week after that she rang up and said, 'Have you read any self-help psychology books yourself? They're fab!' and then she seemed to turn into a different person. She read *Chicken Soup for the Soul* and *How to Win Friends and Influence People* and *The Man Who Mistook His Wife for a Hat*. Then she read *Men Are from Mars, Women Are from Venus*. She used to rib Uncle Joe about it. 'Now, you're a hunter-gatherer and I'm a home-maker,' she'd say. 'I am in touch with my emotions and you are not. I'm a carer and you're a taker and Lord alone knows how women and men stay together at all!' Then she started reading books about child-rearing. She read *How To Say No* and the *Secret of Happy Children*. I asked her about these once and she said, 'I like them but I bet I could write a better one!'

This could well be true because Julia is a much better mother than me. Whereas my children are unruly and cheeky and uncontrollable and, sometimes, downright uncommunicative, my sister's children are lovely. They are so kind and polite and genuinely delightful. And all my children love my sister's children. They also love my sister. Last Christmas evening, as we were leaving my sister's house to come home, Edward fell over on her driveway and banged his knee on a cast-iron boot scraper. 'Arrgghh,' he wailed.

My mother was walking behind him. 'It's just a scratch, Edward!' she said in a fake bright and cheery voice.

'Arrgghh,' yelled Edward again. I went to see what the problem was, which was a bit difficult in the pitch dark.

'Stop making a fuss!' my mother hissed.

But, suddenly, out of the gloom came my sister. 'Poor you,' she said bending down with some magical injury-warning system on full alert. 'That must really hurt.'

'It does,' wailed Edward.

'And you're being so brave!'

'Am I?' sniffled Edward.

'Oh yes!' said my sister and then she picked him up – no mean feat because he is huge – and carried him into her house and then found a very fun, fluorescent, 'self-healing' whatever-that-means plaster and spoon-fed him creamy hot chocolate – one spoon for him, one for each of the kittens crowding round him.

My mother, meanwhile, sat disapprovingly in her cold car smoking a cigarette. When we eventually left again, she said, 'What a lot of fuss over nothing!' but Edward didn't care because my sister had found him a pack of Haribos and she then told him she didn't see why he couldn't throw the horrible fried egg ones out of the window as she didn't think they would pollu-whatsit anything at all. Edward was still sniffing and snuffling, though, and my mother rolled her eyes towards the heavens when she heard him.

So here I am sitting at my sister's kitchen table. Everything seems suspiciously calm and quiet and terribly homely. My sister is always baking bread and cooking delicious things. The Aga is always on. At night, the lights of the house twinkle and glisten like beacons calling in visitors. And so the visitors come. My sister never turns anyone away. Once I turned up for a coffee and a chat to find a shepherdess in the kitchen.

'Are you a shepherdess?' I asked her. I was only joking. I only asked her because she had three sheep and a collie dog in the back of her pick-up truck.

'Turns out I am,' she said in a broad Bucks accent. 'I's a shepherdess.' She then refused to budge for hours, telling us stories about how 'Patch' had released 'the big ewe' from the barbed wire. I must have drunk at least ten cups of tea. At one point I think I even nodded off. But not my sister. Oh no! Julia sat, her chin cupped in her hands, saying things like 'Really!' and 'Goodness me!' the whole way through the conversation.

As I watched the clock tick round in the kitchen and the shepherdess eating her way through yet more of my sister's home-made apple cake, I decided it was time for action. I got up, very stiffly, and said, 'Actually, I hope you don't mind but I've driven some way to see my sister and I need to talk about things with her so . . .'

'Oh right,' said the shepherdess. 'I shall take my leave, then.'

'Oh no,' said Julia, looking horrified and squeezing her arm. 'You mustn't go. I am sorry my sister is so rude. She works, you see.' But the shepherdess left and my sister turned on me. 'Oh Samantha! Why are you so mean to people? Why can't you do as you would be done by?'

Today there are cakes on the table and tea in the cups. 'Give Auntie Samantha some cake,' she says to her eldest son, Robert, as I sit down. He grunts in his teenage-like fashion and puts a slice of chocolate cake on my plate. 'Does Jamie want some?' asks my sister. 'Find a plastic plate, Robert, please.'

Robert finds a plastic plate and puts a slice of cake on it. He puts it on the floor for Jamie who slugs his way over to it, puts his little hands right in it and then smears it over his head.

'That's disgusting,' says Robert.

'Erggh, blerp, ga,' says Jamie.

'Me want some,' says Bennie, who is trying to clamber up on Robert's leg because Bennie loves Robert.

'Where's Edward?' says Robert, as he hoists Bennie up onto his lap.

'He's at school. Actually, Robert, why aren't you at school?'

Robert nods his head towards his mother. 'She said I didn't have to go today.'

'Maybe Edward should have a break from school when his father comes,' says Julia.

'Is Edward's father coming to see him?' asks Robert. 'I remember his dad. Didn't he leave?'

'Oh yes, poor Edward,' says my sister.

'Why is he poor?' says Robert now helping Bennie to some cake.

'Because his father abandoned him,' says my sister, 'just like your father has.'

'Julia!' I say.

Julia pulls an angelic face. 'She's called Suki.'

'What kind of person is called Suki?' I ask.

'I told you, she's an angel therapist.'

'Who's Suki?' says Robert.

'Oh Robert,' says my sister, 'she's the woman your father's run off with. I've told you that before!'

'Julia!' I say. 'You cannot talk like that in front of the kids. It's not fair.'

'We've never hidden anything as a family. I'm not going to start now. I've told Robert everything, so stop worrying!'

Julia says she needs some fresh air. She asks Robert if he can look after Bennie while we go for a walk and Robert, it has to be said, looks quite pleased at this idea.

'You can help me feed the chickens!' he says to Bennie.

'Oh 'es peeze,' says Bennie.

So we find Julia's dogs and dust down a perambulator from her shed and off we go. We go right into the cow field. The earth is dry and dusty. We let her dogs off. The lurcher goes like a streak of honey, skimming off the taut, desiccated land. The retriever waddles. He never does anything much more than waddle. He is too fat. He steals food off plates. Her Jack Russell is a busy, devoted dog. He runs back and forth, sniffing smells, and then comes back again to my sister to make sure she is there. He has eyes like a rat's. I don't like him that much. He bit Bennie once. We were in my mother's back garden and Bennie was throwing balls for the dogs, and as he bent down to get one to throw the Jack Russell flew out of the flower bed and bit his ear very hard.

'Oh my God!' yelled my sister as Bennie stood, white as a sheet from shock, holding his left ear. Blood was pouring out through his fingers. I scooped him up and took him into my mother's kitchen.

'What's the matter?' said my mother when she saw Bennie.

'The dog's ripped his ear off.'

'Oh let me look.' She prised poor Bennie's bloody fingers away from his ear.

Bennie howled. 'Bad doggy! Bad doggy!'

My mother looked carefully. 'It's nothing but a graze.'

'A graze?' I said. 'There's blood everywhere!'

'Oh no, there isn't. It's all fine.'

Bennie started perking up a bit until Edward came in.

'Poor Bennie. Let Dr Edward look.' This is a game Bennie and Edward like to play. Edward looks at Bennie's supposed injuries and makes him do various things like stick out his tongue and waggle his fingers before Dr Edward makes his diagnoses. 'Hmm,' said Edward. 'Yes. I can see four deep puncture wounds. Probably made by the fangs of a rabid dog. Bennie, my prescription is that you will have to go to hospital.'

"opital?'

'Yes, hospital. I think they may well have to saw your ear off and stitch it back on again. It will, without a doubt, hurt. That is Dr Edward's diagnosis.'

'Aaarggh,' said Bennie, crying again.

'Oh Edward, don't be a nitwit,' said my mother. 'Bennie, this is what happens when children play with dogs.'

Today, my sister and I walk up one side of the field as she tells me about Joe. 'Joe never wanted so many children.'

'Yes, he did! He was always so delighted when you kept getting pregnant.'

'No, he wasn't,' says Julia somewhat vaguely. 'I think he just pretended. Or maybe he thought it would make me happy and, for a while, he so wanted me to be happy.'

'But, Julia, he loved them. Don't you remember when they were babies? Don't you remember how good Joe was with them? And he was so helpful to me. You both were. I would come over with Edward and Joe would rock him and play with him and settle him down in bed. I remember that first year when I was on my own. I had dreadful flu. I fell asleep under the coats on your bed and when I woke up I saw Joe lying in Robert's bedroom and he was singing Edward to sleep in Robert's bed. It all looked so peaceful. I remember thinking that I wanted to meet a man like Uncle Joe.'

'Oh well, you don't know the half of it.' My sister sighs. She then tells me that Uncle Joe is a bully, a sex pest, a bad father, a violent drunk.

'I don't believe you! He's always seemed so peaceful and kind.'

'He's a baby. I married a baby.'

'You're just saying these things so that you can hate him. You are doing this to justify why it's OK for him to have left you.'

'No, I'm not. I don't care that he's left me. The angelic Suki is welcome to him.'

But I don't believe her. Her face is pinched and she looks angry and sad. 'How are you going to manage?'

'I don't know. I don't have any money.' She starts to cry. 'I'm trying to keep it together for the children but really I feel a little lost.'

I stop and hug her. 'Of course you feel lost. Your husband's run off with someone else and left you with six children to look after, and a child psychology course to do and, until you graduate, you have no job and a big house to maintain . . .'

'And I'll never meet anyone else,' she says, snuffling. 'Who is going to take on a woman with six children?'

'Who indeed?'

'But John took you on.'

'Ah yes, but I only had Edward.'

'True. It looks bleak, doesn't it?'

'It does a bit.'

'God, does it really?' She is getting tearful again.

'Do you want me to be honest?'

'Yes.'

'Then, yes, it does.'

After we get back to her house and have more tea, she asks me what I think she should do. I tell her I don't know really.

'I have such anger,' she says.

I tell her that of course she has anger. She is right to have anger.

'Is this how he repays me after sixteen years? All those years I've had his children and cooked and cleaned for him and now, just as I've started to branch out a bit in my life, he's gone off with an angel therapist!'

'And what exactly is an angel therapist?'

'Someone who gets visited by the angel Gabriel!'

'Is it?'

'Yes! But I'll give her angel bloody Gabriel. I'll give her bloody Raphael and Michael too!'

'I never knew you knew the names of the archangels.'

'Of course I do. The shepherdess went to an angel therapy session once.'

'The shepherdess?'

'Apparently, you meditate in a quiet room and then you call on the angels to come and visit you.'

'Have you done it?'

'No, but the shepherdess says there's a really good man who does it at the back of the crystal shop in Princes Risborough.'

'Really?'

'Yes, it's supposed to be very healing. In fact, Michael's supposed to be rather sexy. Do you think I should go and see him?'

'Who, Joe?'

'No, not Joe. I never want to see Joe again. No, that angel therapist.'

'No, I don't think you should go and see him. After all, hasn't Joe just been stolen by an angel therapist? Shouldn't you be hating all angel therapists by default?'

'You're right.' Julia is all deflated now. 'I do hate angel therapists, particularly ones called Suki. But then again . . .'

'Then again what?'

'Maybe it's not her fault. Maybe Joe was there for the stealing.'

I tell her that she is talking nonsense. 'Come on, Julia. Get angry again, it's much better for you.'

'No, it isn't. I'm too tired to be angry. I'm up till three in the morning cleaning the house.'

'Stop cleaning the house, then.'

'I can't help it. I keep thinking that if Joe comes back, I want him to see how well I'm doing, how hard I'm trying.'

'What on earth has a clean house got to do with it?'

'I want it to feel as homely as it always has,' she says. 'You know, a fire in the grate, a casserole in the oven.'

I tell her she needs to get out more.

'Or a bun in the oven!' She giggles. 'That's what Joe always used to say to me. "Let's put a bun in your oven."'

'That's not even funny.'

'It used to make me laugh. Oh Samantha, I miss him so.'

'It is totally natural to miss him but, in time . . .'

'I have to have him back. He simply must come home. I cannot cope without him. I love him. I miss him.'

'Have you told him that recently?'

'Not for a long time,' she says miserably. 'I've been so busy with the kids. You know, their homework and packed lunches and after-school activities.' Now she starts to wail. 'I've been a bad wife. A bad, bad wife.'

'No, you haven't. You've been running round after six children!'

'But I forgot about his needs. I let myself go.'

'You. Have. Six. Children,' I say. 'How many times do I have to tell you this?'

'So you think I have let myself go.'

'No, I don't think you've let yourself go. In fact, you look great.'

'For someone who has six children,' she says.

'That is not what I said.'

'You just have to understand me, Samantha. I have to have him back and you have to make him come back.'

'What?'

'He won't see me.' She is talking quickly now. 'He won't even answer the telephone if I ring.'

'Why not?'

'Oh I scratched "bastard" on his car.'

'You did what!'

'Well, actually, I didn't do it. I got Robert to do it.'

'Julia!'

'Yes,' she says happily. 'He did it in this wonderful script. It was quite beautiful really.'

'Have you lost your mind?'

'Yes. I have lost my mind. I have lost my mind because Joe has left me, and if you loved me like a sister should, you would go and find him and tell him to come back to me. Will you do it? I know where he lives. I'll give you his address.'

I tell her that I could think of, ooh, maybe eight million other things I'd rather do.

'Please, Samantha. I'm desperate.'

'Well, I can't do anything until Sunday. I've got to go to work tomorrow and my friend Genevieve is organizing some charity-lunch thing for the mothers and children at the playgroup on Saturday. The profits are going towards building an arts and crafts facility in one of the villages she used to get her Yoruba masks from.'

'That sounds fun. Is she going to cook Nigerian food?'

'I don't know, but it's five pounds a ticket and I promised I'd go.'

But then my sister starts dabbing her eyes with a

hankie. 'I think Sunday's a perfectly good day to go and see Joe. At least you know he'll be there and not at work.'

I give in. I can't bear to see her so sad. 'All right, I'll go.'

'Great! But I hope he doesn't get angry because he might well . . .'

'Well what?'

'Hit you.'

'Hit me? Uncle Joe couldn't hit anyone.'

'You don't know him,' she says darkly.

Just before I go, having taken down Joe's address and promised my sister a million times that I won't 'do anything to upset him', I remember something.

'Julia, Joe came to see me a couple of years ago. He was worried. He said you had taken to cycling round the village at night. Was that true?'

'Oh yes,' says my sister dreamily. 'I still do that when I can't sleep.'

'How often is that?'

'Oh maybe three times a week.'

'Three times a week?'

'I don't mind it. I'm used to it.'

I ask her why she cycles with her nightdress on.

'I like the way it billows out,' she says. 'I remember walking in those fields we went in today. It was just after Dad died. I saw this white swan, this beautiful white swan. It was just standing in the middle of the field and I thought to myself, "Why is this swan here? We never get swans in the field. There's no water near by." And as I was thinking this, the swan looked at me, right at me, and then it spread its wings and flew off right above my head and I felt the air from its beating wings caress my face, and then I knew everything about that swan.'

'Like what?'

'Oh don't you know, Samantha? That swan was our father. He had come to say goodbye, to tell me he was watching over me. And every time I feel sad and watchful I like to spin down the hill to the village with my white nightdress billowing out behind me because it makes me feel like that swan.'

'Oh Julia.'

When I get home I call Dougie. 'Joe's gone off with an angel therapist,' I say.

'Who's Joe?'

'My sister's husband.'

'Whoa! And what's an angel therapist?'

'I'm not really sure. I think it's someone who gets up close and personal with archangels.'

'Good grief.'

'Exactly. Anyway, she wants me to go and find him. I have his address.'

'Great. Go girl, and all that.'

'Well, it's a bit more difficult than that.'

'Why?'

'Julia says Joe is violent.'

'Oh get away.'

'Well, that's what I said, but she's insisting I don't approach him on my own. I was thinking of taking Edward but . . .'

'But he's a child.'

'Exactly. So I thought . . . what are you doing on Sunday? Could you come with me then? I know you're coming down tomorrow night for dinner, but would you mind coming back on Sunday morning?'

'Come back on Sunday to confront Joe, eh? Why isn't John going with you?'

'Oh but it will be so much more fun with you. And John will be tired. He's working flat out.'

'But how do you know Uncle Joe's going to be in?'

'I don't. We'll have to take our chances.'

'But why doesn't your sister telephone him and tell him you're coming?'

'Because Joe won't talk to Julia.'

'Why not?'

'She scratched "bastard" onto the side of his car.'

Dougie starts laughing. 'Your well-behaved sister scratched "bastard" onto his car? It's unbelievable!'

'Actually she got Robert to do it and apparently he did it in this beautiful script. My sister says it was quite a work of art!'

Dougie is laughing so much he can barely speak. 'This I have to be part of. I'll see you tomorrow and we'll get it all organized.'

As an afterthought, and just as he is about to put the phone down, I remember about Nicholas. 'Oh Dougie,' I say.

'Yes.' He is still chuckling.

'If a man goes away with another man to the Lake District and they share a room, what does that mean?'

'It means they are hard-up ramblers. Why are you asking?'

'No reason really.'

'Has John gone off rambling?' He is laughing again.

'Not John,' I say. 'So just because two men share a

room, it doesn't necessarily mean they are gay, then?'

'Oh all men are gay somewhere in their souls,' says Dougie breezily. 'Some men act on that impulse and some don't.'

'*All men are gay?*'

But Dougie has rung off.

9. Friday

Today John wakes up groaning. He is constantly ill. He groans and moans and grimaces and cries out and, quite often, if he's feeling very dramatic, he'll be sick into the loo. He says it's because he has a stomach ulcer. About a year ago he went to get it looked at and had to go through lots of tests where he had an acidometer, or whatever it was called, put into his stomach. He had to have things put down his nose and endless consultations with a stomach surgeon. Eventually, he was told that yes, his stomach was all messed up and he could have an operation, and then suddenly we had Jamie and John's never had the time to go and get healed.

When John heaves over the loo, as he is doing this morning, Bennie says, 'Daddy's sick!' and he runs off to watch him swiftly followed by Jamie – pad, pad, pad, pad – and then they sit like little dummies staring at John while he retches and heaves. Then, when Edward finally appears from one of his early morning mammoth sessions on his chair in the sitting room, during which he reads his *Simpsons* magazine, Bennie drags him by the hand and takes him to the bathroom and says, 'Daddy's sick!'

Edward stares and says, 'That's disgusting!'

When John and I first started living together I found his endless illnesses disturbing. John the First was never ill. Then again, neither was my father. I think both of them killed any potential germs they might have got with alcohol. I remember taking my father for some tests in hospital because, given that he smoked sixty a day, I was convinced he had cancer.

'I have not got cancer,' my father said crossly when I appeared at his house in London and insisted I was taking him to hospital. 'I am as fit as a flea!'

But he wasn't fit at all. He never moved out of his room. He would sit in the same armchair every day and watch *Pet Rescue*. The last thing he ever said to me, when I asked him if he really understood that he was about to die, was 'Did you know I once had badgers at the bottom of my garden?' Anyway, the tests showed that although my father had terrible cirrhosis of the liver, he had no cancer at all. My father was triumphant. 'I'm as clean as a whistle!' he said.

So I am not really used to all this illness around me because my mother would never admit to being ill in a million years and my father died before anyone had really worked out what was wrong with him. But John? Oh John will be dead before he's fifty if he carries on like this. Here is a list of what John has wrong with him: a stomach ulcer; a tendency to get flu because, as he says, he is always run down and tired; a variety of cists that move around his body; painful lumps in both earlobes; aching tendons in both shoulders complete with calcification; completely compacted lower back, which means he says 'ow' and 'ooh' and flinches every time he bends down; a formerly broken finger that 'now gives him some gyp'; a propensity to arthritis as every single member on both sides of his family has it; quite often he has aches in his buttocks; delicate shins through 'playing too much football' in his youth; dodgy ankles with aching Achilles tendons; feet that cramp all the time; and a sore little toe from the time he stubbed it quite badly once.

Here is a list of what is wrong with me: nothing.

This morning John is really bad.

'Uncle Joe's left my sister!' I tell him after half an hour of listening to him make a full range of heaving noises behind the bathroom door. 'I had to go to Julia's yesterday because she was in the cow shed threatening to kill herself!' I shout above the retching noises.

'What?'

'My sister is trying to kill herself.'

John stops retching. He opens the bathroom door. 'For God's sake why?'

I tell him all about Uncle Joe and how he's run off with an angel therapist.

'He's done what?' John looks perplexed. 'What's an angel therapist?'

'There's not enough time for me to explain. Haven't you got to get to work?'

'Oh God,' he says and rushes back to the loo.

As he starts retching again, I tell him that Julia wants me to spy on Uncle Joe.

'This is getting ridiculous,' says John, finally appearing again. 'When are you going?'

'Sunday.'

'But I'm working on Sunday.'

'I know that but it's all OK because Dougie is coming with me for protection.'

'Protection? From what?' John is now sounding mystified.

'Julia says Uncle Joe is violent.'

'No way! What on earth is going on?'

But then John notices the time and starts running round the house like a lunatic. 'I'm going to be late,' he keeps saying. 'Where are my sunglasses?'

'Glasses?' says Bennie who is remarkably good at finding things.

'Yes, glasses.'

'Ooh,' giggles Bennie and he disappears outside. A couple of minutes later he reappears with John's sunglasses. One of the lenses is missing.

'Christ! Who broke these?'

'Me!' says Bennie merrily.

'Is anyone taking me to school?' says Edward.

'Yes, I am,' says John, now hunting for his second pair of sunglasses. 'Has anyone seen my other pair of glasses?'

'Glasses?' says Bennie and he sets off out of the door again.

'You'd better hurry, Dad,' says Edward. 'I'm going to be late.'

'It doesn't matter if you're a bit late,' I say to Edward, realizing that John is never going to get out of the house in time. Bennie comes back in through the door waving John's second pair of sunglasses all covered in mud.

'Bennie!' says John.

Bennie tears off out of the sitting room and dives under my desk. 'Me bad. Bad me,' he says over and over again.

'It does matter if I'm late,' says Edward. 'You get a mark against your name and then, when you get more than ten, you have to go and see the headmaster.'

'How many have you got now?' I ask him.

'Nine,' says Edward.

John is in the bathroom cleaning his glasses. Jamie has

hauled himself up by the loo seat and is dropping stones down the loo.

'Jamie!' I say.

'Erggh, blerp, ga,' says Jamie.

'Where did he get those stones from?' I ask John.

'Me!' shouts Bennie from the study where he is still hiding.

'Bennie brought them in this morning,' says Edward.

'Why didn't you stop him?' says John.

'What's it got to do with me?' says Edward.

I am about to give him a lecture on collective responsibility when I see Edward's face. He is looking at the clock on the wall. 'Please, Dad,' he says, 'I'm going to get detention.'

John groans, pushes us aside and retches into the loo. Jamie frowns for a second. Now there is the contents of John's stomach plus the stones in there.

'You'll never be able to flush that,' says Edward.

'Christ!' says John.

This is what was supposed to have happened on this Friday morning. John was supposed to take Edward to school on time and without a fuss. I was to wait here for Santa, who was supposed to give the children breakfast. This is what happens on most Friday mornings. But this Friday morning is obviously going to be different. There is already too much to do. Once Edward and John leave and Santa is here, I have to take the dog to the vet because she is lame in her left leg. Then I must speed back home to drop the dog off before going all the way back to the vet's and beyond to get to the M4 to see this rock star's fridge. And so I booked Santa in for the day and I told everyone who needed to know – i.e. John – and it was all supposed to work like clockwork but, what a surprise, it isn't. I should be going to Bath right now and then I can come back at about 5.30 p.m., put all the children in a bath, put them in a bed, put the dinner on for John, Dougie and me and, at around 8.30, hopefully everyone will be here and we can eat it and work out what we are going to need for our Uncle Joe spying trip.

Instead, I have to take Edward to school.

'Can you take Edward to school?' asks John, his face now white.

'John, I've got to work today and take the dog to the vet and . . .'

'I AM SICK,' he says.

So I get the babies into the car all nappyless and naked and Edward goes in the front and he's in a sulk because he doesn't want detention but the traffic is not bad and we get to the school gates with two minutes to spare.

'Thanks, Mum,' says Edward and then he's off.

On the way home, the two babies giggling with each other in the back, I run through in my head what I now need to do. I feel a bit panicked. I am also a bit cross. Why can't I just get on a train and go to work and reappear eleven hours later once the house is quiet, the children fed and asleep, my dinner bubbling on the hob, like all other working people do? Why is it my responsibility to take the dog to the vet and get home in time to put everyone to bed?

I pull into the drive. John's car is not there. Santa's car has taken its place. I can hear Jamie in the back. Then I smell something horrible. I look round. Oh my God. Bennie has got poo all over his hands. He is rubbing it on

Jamie's head. Jamie is obviously finding all this very funny. He is clapping his hands and shaking his head. Bennie gives me a triumphant look. 'Me poo bum,' he says.

Two hours later I have cleaned the car, left the children with Santa and taken the dog to the vet. The dog got so nervous that she pooed all over the surgery. I told the vet I'd clean it up.

'It's been that kind of day,' I said.

Then I go home to drop the dog off.

'What ees wrong with the dog?' asks Santa, looking very glamorous in her rubber gloves. I love Santa and her rubber gloves. She wears her rubber gloves to do everything. The first time I met her she had them secreted in her bag.

She'd put an advert in the local paper – 'Brilliant au pair seeks part-time work' – so I called her up and she said, 'Hello, darling! Thees ees Santa and I wanna work for you!' And then it took two weeks to meet because she could never make it over to my house. 'Darling, I can't come today,' she'd say. 'I feel so bad, darling.' And just as I was about to give up on her, Santa suddenly appeared.

She swept in, magnificent in her short skirt with her long brown legs and a low-cut peasant top and her shiny black bob swinging this way and that, took one look at the house and said, 'Right, darling, you need some help!' Then she delved into the bag, pulled out her rubber gloves and started cleaning the kitchen floor. Whenever one of the children, whom she'd never met before, came in, she'd say, 'Out! Out! Out! and off they'd run, apart from Jamie, who crawled rapidly over to the cleaning bucket and tipped it all over the floor. 'What a beautiful baby!' said Santa, sighting hot and soapy Jamie. 'I love him!' And then she abandoned her cleaning and swept little Jamie up and covered him in kisses.

She's barely put him down since. 'Hello, beautiful baby boy,' she says when she sees him. I think she just tolerates the other two. 'Bennie is a very naughty boy,' she tells me every time she's been over to help. 'I asked him not to feed his lunch to the dog but he ignored me!' Or she'll say, 'Edward talks back all the time and I do not like it and you must do something about it!' She's immensely bossy, is Santa. She can also be completely irrational. Quite often she says to Edward, 'Edward, darling, don't play on your computer so much!' and yet, ten minutes previously, she has said, 'Edward, darling, you have been such a good boy, of course you can play on your computer!'

She drives Edward insane. 'Santa!' I hear him say. 'You just told me I could play on my computer!'

'No, I did not, darling,' she says. Edward then usually comes in and complains to me and I have to rather tactfully sort it out.

'But, Samantha,' she will say when I gently remind her that, if he has no school, Edward is allowed to play on his computer of a morning for up to one hour and that he's only been on it for, say, ten minutes, 'you are accusing me of lying!'

Santa has ambitions. She is young, twenty-seven years old, and she is not stupid. Every time I see her she has new ideas, new suggestions. She is also amazingly practical.

A couple of months back, our door fell off its hinges. All our doors have nearly fallen off their hinges and none of the handles work and our paintwork is scuffed and horrible and our sofas have got ancient encrusted breakfast cereals on them and our beautiful old wooden floors are scratched and ruined. My mother always says, 'Why do you not take care of your lovely house?' and I tell her that I do take care of my lovely house but that certain other people – i.e. my children – seriously don't. They eat wherever they please so that there are crumbs and chunks of fruit and old wrappers tucked behind tables and forced under armchairs and chucked indiscriminately somewhere towards the fireplace. They take paints and pens and draw all over the floors and the walls. They wipe their yoghurty little mouths on the curtains. They, especially Bennie, tear around the house and slam into doors which they then push open at high speed so that the doors jump up and down on their hinges and smash into the walls and take little chunks out of the plaster and then these little chunks become bigger and bigger until they look like deep ravines or scars in the paintwork. They perch on the top of the cushions on the sofa so that all the furniture is squashed and uncomfortable. In the summer, when they can't be bothered to walk the few steps it takes to get to the loo, they just urinate on the mat outside the back door.

'What's that smell?' my mother asked once.

When I told her she nearly fainted and then said, 'Far be it for me to comment but . . .' and then she borrowed Santa's rubber gloves, picked the mat up and dropped it into the wheelie bin. Now the kids just wee directly onto the patio instead.

But now we have Santa with her toolbox and she can seemingly fix anything. It's quite incredible. I don't know anyone who can fix anything. John can barely change a lightbulb, but Santa seems invincible. She found little screw things to put in the door handles so that when we turned them they actually worked. Then she helped John put the door back on its hinges after the children had banged it back and forth so much it fell off with fatigue.

'Now, Samantha,' she'd said when she saw the door lying all forlorn on the floor, 'this door needs a fix!'

'But I can't fix it, Santa,' I'd said pathetically.

'No, you can't,' she'd said, in a rather withering fashion I thought. 'But John can get me wood and then we can fix it together.'

John's eyes nearly popped out of his sockets when I told him of Santa's grand plan. 'Me? Fix a door? With wood? Oh no, I don't think I can.' But he and Santa spent a weekend banging and planeing and whatever else they did and by the Sunday night the door was back swinging on its hinges.

'It's a miracle!' I said. John looked very proud.

'My father was a very practical man,' Santa told me later. 'He told me a girl should always be able to fix things as long as it doesn't ruin her beautiful hands!'

I set off down the M4 in marvellous sunshine and turn the radio on. While I am driving I let my thoughts wander. Why has Uncle Joe run off with an angel therapist? I thought my sister was happily married. And what about Nicholas? Is he having an affair with a young man? But what will I tell Genevieve when I next see her? Surely she's found out by now.

And I suddenly see things so starkly it's as if the M4 has become the road to Damascus. I almost stop the car dead by accident.

Why on earth am I letting John the First back into my life? Look at these other people's lives! Why haven't I seriously thought about this before? I must be mad. What is it going to do to poor Edward? What is it going to do to John the Second? What about me? I haven't seen John the First for so long I haven't the faintest idea how I feel but, now I have a moment on my own in this car, I realize I am worried. It feels like a test and I don't like tests. It's a test of my marriage, a test of John the Second's and my happiness. I know John the First too well to think he'll avoid my weak spots. He always loved pressing people's weak spots. Maybe that's why he left. He pressed the biggest weak spot I had, the one that was shaped like a baby and called Edward.

But then, breaking into my thoughts, I hear the radio. 'Bad weather warning,' it says as I pass by junction 11. 'Storms, thunder and lightning, and flash-flood warnings for people driving west on the M4.' I am driving west on the M4. I look around me. It's so sunny. Surely the radio is mistaken. 'Junctions 15 to 18 are under a heavy-weather warning. If you are heading west towards that area, take great care.' I am going to junction 17 but I still can't believe it. There's not a cloud in the sky. Then I notice that the cars coming towards me have their headlights on. This does not bode well. It's an omen, I think, a bloody great big goddamned omen.

Then, at around junction 14, the blue sky gets swallowed up by big, rolling, grey-black clouds. The motorway gets darker. I put my headlights on. The warning keeps coming through on the radio. 'Bad-weather warning for people driving down the M4. There are severe storms from junctions 15 to 18.' At junction 15 the rain comes. It starts slowly, drip, drip, spit, spit, spit, spatter-spatter-spatter and then, eventually, it deluges down. The spray on the motorway is incredible. I can barely see a thing. And it is dark, so dark, and then . . . *Flash!* A streak of lightning suddenly smashes down somewhere on the left of me. I jump. The car swerves. A lorry blasts his horn at me. Christ! Then the lightning smashes to the right. I jump again. The lorry blasts away at me. I am getting very jittery. God is trying to tell me something. He's telling me I am going to die. I can't believe it. Why am I always about to die on the M4?

I start trying to take deep breaths. I try to block out the rolling thunder. I try to remember what John once told me. 'Cars are very safe in thunderstorms because of their rubber tyres,' he said. Rubber tyres. My car has rubber tyres. I must hold this thought. I drive at about 30 mph. I pass junction 16. One more junction to go. I am not the only one driving slowly. I've tucked in behind a Range Rover, which means lots of spray but at least something big and solid and bright to follow. The motorway is like a river, there is water pouring everywhere. Thoughts start crowding my mind. I think about all the things I've done that are a waste of time, like worrying about my looks. Why have I done this? Why didn't I spend all that time doing things I wanted to do, like travelling and eating and reading books and going to the pub? Why have I spent years denying myself things I really wanted to eat when, to be honest, the only person who worries about what I look like is me. I vow I shall eat chocolate if I so wish. Sod the consequences.

I eventually arrive in Bath three-quarters of an hour late. It has been a horrendous drive but, as I slowly glide down the big hill into the valley, the rock star and all of his rock-star-entourage people are standing there waiting for me with pots of tea and coffee and, as it turns out, quite a few hand-baked biscuits and I eat a whole handful of them.

When I get home late in the afternoon, having negotiated another, lesser, storm, which was sitting stagnant over Reading, Dougie is in the kitchen. He is sitting up by the breakfast bar on a high stool. He is doing sudoku. He looks remarkably cool. Dougie and I spend quite a lot of time arguing about sudoku. We don't actually argue as such, he says. He says we just 'discuss' it. He's quicker than me but not as thorough. He looks at the squares and then his eyes must do all sorts of rapid calculations because one minute later he's scribbling numbers left, right and centre. I am very boring when it comes to sudoku. I fill in every single box with every combination and then go through a process of painstaking deduction to decide which number goes where.

'You look slightly bedraggled,' he says.

'I've spent the day caught up in a storm.'

'A storm?' He raises his eyebrows. 'But it's been so hot and sunny here.'

'Yes, well, it's not sunny and hot in Bath.'

'What were you doing there?'

I then tell him about the rock-star thing.

'Good fridge?' he says.

'Yes, good, fine. Lots of yummy biscuits.'

'Good.' Dougie returns to sudoku.

Then Santa walks into the kitchen. She has her rubber gloves on. She starts doing the washing-up. The children are nowhere to be seen.

'Where is everyone?' I ask.

Santa rolls her eyes. 'Upstairs, darling.'

'Is everyone OK?'

'Yes, fine. But Bennie was very naughty. He gave Jamie all these disgusting cat biscuits to eat and now Jamie has been sick all day. He's fine now. He has thrown them all up. Oh and Edward is in a bad mood. I think your mother upset him. Oh and –' she says motioning towards Dougie, who is sitting virtually in front of her – 'Dougie's here.'

'Right.' I shoot Dougie a look. He shrugs his shoulders.

Santa sighs. She then says she has to go but that she's made Jamie some butternut squash. She hasn't had time to get the other two anything. 'I must go, darling,' she says. 'I have to pick up this new Hungarian girl from the airport. She is coming to be a cleaner. You should get another cleaner.'

'But I have a cleaner, Santa.'

'You can never have enough cleaners. And this one is a very good cleaner. I knew her in Budapest and she was always cleaning, cleaning, cleaning. I'm making her a bike so she can cycle to jobs.'

'You're making her a bike? What are you going to make it with? That's quite complicated, isn't it?'

'Don't be silly!' says Santa. 'I can't make her a bike! I will buy a cheap one and make it good for her.'

'Well, maybe we could have her one afternoon a week. It would be a help but I'll have to work out the money and . . .'

'Don't be silly, Samantha!' she says. 'I am not an idiot. It's up to you. I'm just saying, that's all!' With that, she puts her rubber gloves in her bag, kisses me goodbye on both cheeks and then, as she gets to the door, says rather darkly, 'And say goodbye to Dougie.' Then she's off.

'What's that about?' I ask Dougie.

He's frothing up the milk for our coffees. 'I don't know.' He looks away from me.

'You do know. Have you made a pass at her?'

'No! Absolutely not. I'm not saying that I don't think she's attractive. She's very attractive. It's just that I . . .'

'Just that you what?'

Dougie starts studying the sudoku puzzle again. 'I'm still pining for Maxine.'

'Fine.' I feel sorry for him now. I study him more closely and realize that he hasn't really shaved and his clothes are a bit crumpled. In fact, he looks rather thin and unhappy. 'Who's making dinner, you or me?'

Dougie perks up. 'I'll make dinner. Is John joining us?'

I tell him that yes, John is joining us and he can use any ingredients he likes from the fridge.

'You've got scallops,' he says, picking them up and sniffing them. 'Are they fresh?'

'Got them yesterday.'

'And you've got fennel. Do you like fennel?'

'Yes. That's why I bought it.'

'Ooh,' he continues, taking no notice of me, 'what's this? Monkfish. Oh la-di-da, we are going to have a feast!'

He is so busy being happy I decide I'll press him on the Santa thing again. 'Dougie, I bet you did do something to Santa, didn't you?'

'Aah. Well, she was saying that she left her last job because her boss kept making a pass at her and she found it dreadful so she told his wife and, essentially, she got sacked, and then I said something silly and facetious and I've obviously upset her.'

'What did you say?'

'Oh dear. I said, "I'd probably make a pass at you if you

insisted on wearing that wonderfully short skirt," but I didn't really mean it that way.'

'Ah.'

'Right, we must think about Sunday,' says Dougie, firmly changing the subject. 'I've been getting very excited. I've always wanted to spy on someone.'

'I'm not sure if we should do much spying. What about Uncle Joe's privacy?'

'Uncle Joe's privacy? I am afraid he forfeited that when he went off with Suzy or Suki or whatever her name is.' Dougie then tells me he has made a list of all the things we'll need. 'First we will need binoculars, that's obvious. Do you have any binoculars?'

I tell him I have two pairs.

'Good.' He ticks it off the list he has produced in front of him. 'We will need provisions.'

'Why?'

'We could be there for hours!'

I groan.

'Samantha, you've got to take this seriously. This is your sister's marriage we're talking about.' Just as I am about to say that of course I am taking it very seriously, there is an immense caterwauling from above our heads.

'Edward!' screams Bennie.

'Aargghh,' screams Edward.

They charge down the stairs, both talking at the same time.

Bennie flies into my arms. 'Mama, Edward ow my nose.'

Edward follows him all hot-headed and red-eyed. 'I-DID-NOT-hit-him-on-the-nose,' he says all at once.

'Well, why does Bennie think you've hit him?' I ask Edward, all the time keeping a fixed smile on my face.

'I didn't hit him,' says Edward. 'He's a liar. Why would I hit him?'

'Edward ow my nose,' says Bennie again, whimpering in the corner of the kitchen and giving Edward a very doleful look.

'I DID NOT!' Edward is shouting now.

'All right,' I say. 'Calm down, both of you.' I then inspect Bennie's nose and pretend that it looks awfully sore when it actually looks perfectly fine, and I slip Edward a bit of chocolate I have found in the drawer that has the plasters, and which I must have hidden in there when I was trying to give up chocolate. Then I suddenly hear the telltale sound of pad-pad-padding going on upstairs. 'Jamie!' I yell and then me and Edward run out of the kitchen, through the sitting room and stare up the stairs. There at the top, teetering on the edge, waving his little baby arms in the air, is Jamie.

'Erggh, blerp, ga,' he says. He is about to tip forwards and topple, topple, topple down when, out of the blue, Edward leaps up the stairs and grabs him.

'Phew, that was a close one,' he says. He brings Jamie downstairs, carefully holding him on his lap while bumping down on his bottom. Jamie thinks this is very funny.

I let out a sigh. 'Time for dinner, everyone.'

When we get back into the kitchen, Dougie is scribbling down numbers on the sudoku again.

'Christ!' he says, looking up and seeing Edward half-holding, half-dragging Jamie into the kitchen, 'I don't know how you survive. What a racket!' He then looks at Edward. He really likes Edward. He always has. 'Do I get a hug?' he says. Edward puts Jamie on the floor and hugs Dougie.

'Santa says you were upset when you came home. Why were you?'

'Oh yeah,' says Edward. 'Well, Granny picked me up and for some reason I started thinking about Granddad – you know, the one that's dead – and then I got really upset and then Granny told me that sometimes Granddad got so drunk on wine that he'd do a wee in the wardrobe because he couldn't find the bathroom. That's disgusting. Is that true, Mummy?'

'Sort of.' I try not to laugh because Edward looks so upset. 'It actually wasn't wine he got drunk on but vodka.'

'What's vodka?'

'Something you need never worry about. Now, tell me about school,' says Dougie, smoothly changing the subject. And off they go, chuntering on together about maths and homework and fractions and how I'm really good at spelling but no good at maths.

'Mummy's the spelling queen!' I hear Edward tell Dougie. 'But she's useless at percentages.'

I like watching Dougie and Edward together. I always think Dougie should've had children. After Maxine had revealed on the picnic that she never wanted children, I became obsessed with it. Soon after, when we were down the pub and I was still pregnant with Bennie – and even when I was pregnant with Bennie I knew I'd get pregnant again soon after because I've always wanted lots of children – I asked about it directly. 'Did you never want children, Dougie?'

'Not really,' he said. 'Maxine's never wanted them. She always thought it would ruin her career.'

'Why does she think that? I've got children and it hasn't ruined my career. You just adjust.'

'I don't think she wants to adjust. She likes her life as it is.'

But she obviously didn't or they wouldn't now be divorced.

I am thinking about this as I spoon the butternut squash into Jamie's mouth. It's going everywhere. He's smacking his lips and blowing raspberries and the golden slime is all over his face and hands and now all over my face and hands. But I don't really mind. I look at his greeny-blue eyes and his blond hair and his sweet little face. Why would anyone not want a little Jamie? Why would anyone spend their lives cold and alone? And then I look at Edward with his knowing face and I think about all the great times we have had together. Why wouldn't someone want an eight-year-old with all that history, that sense of wonderment your first child brings into your world? Then I look at Bennie. Or, more precisely, I look for Bennie. For Bennie is no longer in the kitchen. The pasta for his dinner is ready but he seems to have wandered off.

'Dinner,' I say to Edward, who is in the middle of explaining the pros and cons of being a Jedi knight to Dougie.

'They do this,' says Edward, whirling his arms around and pretending to use his light sabre, which he insists on calling a light saver.

'Tell me who Obi One is again?' says Dougie, gamefully pretending he has never seen *Star Wars* and knows nothing about it.

'He's the main Jedi knight,' says Edward – whirl, whirl, whirl. 'He fights Darth Vader. Darth Vader killed his friend Anakin Skywalker.'

'Really?' Dougie pretends to be very impressed.

'Yes!'

'But Darth Vader is Anakin,' I say.

'WHAT!' says Edward. He looks incensed. 'NO, HE IS NOT!'

'Oh dear,' says Dougie to me. 'You've offended his sense of morality.'

I am just about to explain how Anakin Skywalker goes to the dark side when I hear yet more caterwauling, this time coming from the garden. It is Bennie. He is tearing towards the kitchen door, crying almost hysterically. His face has gone red and his mouth is open and saliva is pouring down onto his chest, soaking his T-shirt. I start to panic.

'What is it, Bennie?'

'Ow, ow, ow, ow, ow, ow.' He points madly at his mouth. 'Ow, ow, ow, ow, ow, ow.'

'What? What is it?' I ask again. I bundle Bennie up into my arms. I stare down his throat. It is red and inflamed and beginning to swell. His tongue is also swelling. 'Have you been stung by a bee?'

'No, no, nooo. Ow, ow, ow, ow, ow, ow.'

'Get me some water in a cup, Edward.' But Bennie cannot swallow the water. He pushes it away and it spills down my shirt but I barely notice. 'Dougie!' I say, suddenly realizing I am not the only adult in the world. 'Do something!'

'What am I supposed to do?' he asks mildly.

'What's wrong with him?' I am too panicked to get cross with Dougie.

'I think he's swallowed something,' says Edward.

'Have you swallowed something?' I ask Bennie.

''es.' Bennie now looks almost catatonic with shock.

'Show us,' says Edward.

I put Bennie down and he takes my hand and leads me

into the garden and there, abandoned in the middle of the lawn, is a stalk bearing a cluster of red and green berries. About three are missing. Bennie points to the stalk.

'Did you eat this?' I ask him.

''es,' he says. 'Ow, ow, ow, ow, ow, ow.'

'Christ!'

'Don't be so rude,' says Edward.

I think of what to do: call my mother. No, she's on holiday. Call Maxine, she knows about plants. No, too difficult with Dougie here. I know – ask Dougie! 'Dougie, what is this plant?'

'How on earth should I know?'

I am beginning to feel really cross with him now. The phone rings. Dougie answers. It's John.

'Oh hello,' he says cheerfully. 'Bennie seems to have eaten some poisonous berries.'

I hear the verbal explosion on the end of the line. Suddenly, the phone is in my hand and I'm talking to John. I think I'm going to cry.

'Stay calm,' says John, sounding reassuring. 'Take him to hospital now. I'll meet you there.'

I tell Dougie I have to go. 'Feed Edward,' I say, 'and put Jamie to bed!'

'Right. How do I do that?'

'Oh ask Edward, for God's sake!'

Then I put Bennie, who is now choking, in the car and drive as fast as I have ever driven to hospital.

All the Times I Have Ever Been to A and E

For a whole huge pile of my life – namely from the ages of zero to about twenty-five – I had never been to A and E. I had never been particularly ill and, up until this point, neither had any of my friends and family. My first experience of A and E was with a friend of mine who had played football and got a blister. He was somewhat older than me and I told him he was too old to play football, but he'd never listen. His blister went septic and I had to cart him off to St Mary's, Paddington, where they lanced it and gave him antibiotics, and told him to stop playing football. After that, it was an age before I went to hospital again. I had to take John the First to a tiny little clinic in Camden very late on a Saturday night when he went all hot and sweaty and said his throat was closing up. They told me he had a sort of boil on his throat and they had to inject him in his backside with a big needle and I enjoyed that very much.

But then Edward got to THAT age and I felt I virtually lived in A and E for years. First of all I thought Edward had chronic asthma when he was under one year old. They inspected him and gave me a baby diffuser for him and some horrible-looking powder I was to spray down his throat. I never used it. Then, aged one, he fell down the stairs and I thought he might have concussion so I took him back to the Royal Free Hospital and they examined his eyes and X-rayed him and then sent us home. Then he fell off a swing some six months later and I thought he'd broken his arm because he said it hurt, and back we went. Then, when he was three, he careered into the metal post holding up the sides of a bouncy castle in the local park. This time he was put in one of those pods that scan your brain.

When he turned four, it got even worse: on holiday in Greece he smashed his head open twice on the rocks; cut his hand badly on a penknife he found on the beach; gave himself an electric shock when he water-pistolled some ants that were climbing up the wall of our apartment very near an electric light; went into shock having dived into the swimming pool without his armbands on, even though I'd specifically asked him not to, which meant he very nearly drowned and was only saved by the fact I'd known goddamned well he was going to jump in so I was at least prepared to rescue him. A couple of days after that he nearly drowned again even though he did have his armbands on, when taken out to sea by a freak wave. I was on the beach taking a photo of my son playing gently in the waves when he suddenly disappeared under the water. This time he was saved by an alert windsurfer who happened to be passing.

A couple of years later, we went to Italy on holiday and managed to tally up three visits to the ospedale. The first one was when Edward got stuck on an ancient carousel ride in the centre of Todi and mangled his leg pretty badly. The second was when he dived so extravagantly into the pool that he knocked his head against the side, broke his nose and concussed himself. Then, on the night before we were due to come home, John woke up screaming and pleading with God to let him die. It turned out he had gallstones and was really ill. Me and Edward and Bennie, who was only a baby then, spent hours in Todi general, with Edward pushing Bennie around in his pushchair to keep him occupied, and John sweating and swearing until, eventually, he 'passed water' and they let me take him back to the villa.

'Was everything fine?' said Julia when she met us at the airport the next day.

'Perfect,' I said.

'Daddy gave birth to some stone things through his willy,' said Edward.

'Right,' said Julia.

10. Friday evening

Bennie and I are back sitting in the waiting room of Prestwood General Accident and Emergency department, waiting for John.

After the choking fit passed he was completely silent and just sat in the back of the car, saliva drooling down his T-shirt, with his mouth open. Occasionally, he would point into his mouth like an overactive Pacman but he seemed incapable of saying anything. His eyes looked panicked, though. But once we got to the hospital he did his 'I am extremely ill' thing and screamed and screamed. This had two effects. First, he was so hysterical that when I pulled into the disabled emergency parking bay and the man in the peaked cap came up and said, 'I think you'll find that you are not supposed to park here, madam,' the force of Bennie's anguish sent him spiralling backwards.

'He's ILL,' I said. 'Can't you see that he can barely breathe?'

Peaked-cap man then sprang into action. 'Barely breathe? A little nipper like him? Park away, madam!' He then bustled us out of the car park and through into A and E and said, very loudly, 'THIS BOY CAN HARDLY BREATHE!' which meant that, secondly, a man appeared immediately, took one look at Bennie – who by now had gone catatonic again as screaming would be a sure sign that he could breathe, and our game would have been rumbled – and said, 'Nurse! Nurse!' and thus we skipped the queue. No one seemed to mind. I looked tearful and panicked. 'He's only two,' I kept saying.

We were ushered into a little room and the nurse, who seemed a bit stroppy to me, was in the process of looking at Bennie when he rolled his eyes back into his head. The nurse leapt up as if bitten by a snake.

'What is happening to him?' she said to me.

'I don't know. He ate a flower.'

'Ate a flower?' She sat down again as Bennie's little eyes rolled into focus again. 'What type of flower?'

'I don't know, but I have it here.' I showed her the green stalk with the red and green berries.

'What's that?' she said suspiciously.

'I don't know. I'm not a gardener.'

'You didn't plant it?'

'No.'

'Maybe it's a weed.'

'I'm not really sure.' I felt a trifle frustrated. 'I don't spend my time outside differentiating one from the other.'

'So you've never seen that plant before.'

'Of course I've seen it before. It grows in my garden.'

'But you don't know its name.'

'No, I don't.'

'Well, if you don't know its name then there's nothing I can do.'

'WHAT?' I said. 'What do you normally do when people come in having swallowed something poisonous, with their throat constricting and about to die? Do you normally say, "Oh I'm sorry there's nothing I can do"?'

'What do you suggest I do?'

'I don't know. I'm not a doctor! Maybe give him an

antihistamine injection. Isn't that what you do when people have allergies to something?'

Then a young and very attractive male doctor came in. Bennie looked at him and immediately started gasping and saying, 'Ow, ow, ow, ow, ow, ow, ow.'

'What's going on here?' said the attractive male doctor.

'She says,' the nurse said, nodding her head towards me, 'that her little boy has eaten a poisonous plant and that he can't breathe properly.'

'Does she know what plant it is?'

'No.'

'It's this plant here,' I said, waving the now extremely drooping and sorry-for-itself stalk in front of him.

'Hmm.' He then disappeared and came back with a huge, beautifully illustrated book. 'This should do the trick,' he said. 'If that book doesn't have it then we'll just have to pump his stomach.'

'Ow,' said Bennie.

After fifteen minutes of leafing through the book in a secondary waiting room, the corridor outside buzzing with activity, which meant it was very hard to concentrate, I found it. I turned to Bennie to tell him but then remembered that he'd seemed to get noticeably better once he'd hooked up with a ten-year-old with a suspected broken arm, and had wandered off with him.

There it was, a tall green stem with those malicious berries clustered on it. 'Lords and Ladies,' the book said. 'Can be highly irritating if eaten but not fatal. The mouth and throat may well swell up and saliva will be produced to counteract the symptoms. Treatment: irritation will decrease over time. If concerned, administer an antihistamine injection.'

'I've found it!' I yelled out up the corridor, which was now full of nobody but Bennie and his broken-armed friend.

Suddenly, the doctor appeared. 'What does it say?'

'Lords and Ladies,' I read from the book, 'is one of the most highly toxic plants known on the planet and, if not treated within half an hour, results in certain death.'

'OH MY GOD!' yelled the doctor.

'And is the common cause of lawsuits against hospitals who fail to notice that two-year-olds called Bennie are not being treated with the care they should be treated with.'

The doctor gave me a funny look. 'I can't believe you'd make a joke of this,' he said and then took the book and disappeared.

So now me and perked-up little Bennie are waiting for John and I can't decide whether to tell him the truth of our now rather unremarkable visit, or to lie and turn it into a much more exciting tale whereby Bennie nearly dies and I am the heroine who, through an amazing coincidence, happens to know that the plant is Lords and Ladies, and then saves Bennie's life by administering the Heimlich manoeuvre at the same time as recommending to the attractive male doctor that I think an antihistamine jab is the way to go and, instead of looking at me with contempt, the afore-mentioned doctor recommends me for an OBE at the end of the year and asks me out for a dinner date to Pukka Palace on the outskirts of the local town. However, one look at John's face when he rushes through the door, all white and drawn and weighed down with worry, and I realize I must tell him the truth. Unfortunately, Bennie spots him before I have a chance to tell John anything.

'Daddy!' screams Bennie. His little face then crumples with tears and he opens his mouth like a little cuckoo fledgling in a nest and says, 'Ow, ow, ow, ow, ow.'

'Oh my God!' says John, seeing how red his throat is, how swollen his tongue is. 'He can't breathe. Why can't he breathe?'

'He can breathe, it's just that he –'

John cuts me off mid-sentence. 'What does it take to see the nurse round here?' he yells, getting all Alpha-male on me. 'I DEMAND to see a nurse! My son is dying and –'

'He's not dying,' I say. 'He's fine.'

I am just about to tell him about the Lords and Ladies thing when the horrible lady nurse appears.

'Are you his father?' she asks John.

'Yes.'

'We need to administer an antihistamine injection to Bennie.'

'Fine.'

'I told you he needed an antihistamine injection,' I say to her.

'And we need your permission because your wife has behaved in an unreasonable fashion,' continues the nurse.

'An unreasonable fashion?' John says, now suddenly looking at me rather severely.

'Actually,' I say, 'I was not being unreasonable. It was that nurse who kept going on about gardens and weeds. I just wanted someone to –'

'Oh for God's sake,' says John. 'Yes, of course you can give Bennie an injection.'

'If you'll come with me, sir,' the nurse says to John, giving me a superior look.

' "If you'll come with me, sir"?' I say disbelievingly.

'Samantha,' says John, in a very serious voice. 'This is not about you. It's about Bennie.'

'Right.' I realize I'm on a losing wicket. 'Well, I'll tell you about her later. In the meantime, I'll see you back here.'

'Fine,' he says. His shoulders sag a bit as he walks off, holding Bennie in his arms.

Little Bennie looks at me over his father's shoulder. His blond curly hair is bobbing about, his cornflower-blue eyes are wide open. ''orry, Mama,' he says as he disappears down the corridor. He looks so sad I feel I am about to cry.

'I love you,' I mouth to him. For some silly reason, I have a strong feeling that I'm never going to see him again.

I sit in A and E for twenty minutes or more maybe. I watch people come in and out. A drunk man has slipped and cut his foot on something, I don't know what. His face is contorted with pain. There is a little trail of blood following him across the floor like a snail track. He smells of alcohol but doesn't seem to know where he is. It's not him who notices the way the nurse backs off from him when he speaks, or that tiny swift look of revulsion that passes across her face when he opens his mouth to speak to her. 'I've dun me – hic – foot in.'

Then there's the overtired mother with the five kids, all of whom have gone with her to hospital because the middle one's drunk a bottle of Calpol that the mother, whilst trying to get dinner, inadvertently left open on the side. There they all are, milling around her. All dirty and hungry and tired and whingeing and the mother is trying so very hard to keep her temper because what else can she do? Her bloke works nights and there's certainly no one else who'll look after the kids at short notice. The nurse sees her and tries to buck her spirits. 'We'll be with you as soon as we can, Mrs Johnson. I'm sure little Kelvin will be fine. Maybe the children would like to go to the canteen and eat?' But Mrs Johnson has no money with her so they all career around the waiting room like mini-terrorists, even Kelvin, who looks as if even a truckload of Calpol wouldn't stop him.

And then there's the old lady who can barely walk. Her body has ceased to resemble anything near that of a human being. Her back is hunched over so that her shoulders are the highest point. Her legs are short and frail and over-loaded with varicose veins. Her hair is like cotton wool. She has tripped on the stairs, 'only a little bit', she tells the nurse in a voice as thin as a reed, but she thinks she's broken her ankle. 'Can't move it, dearie,' she says. 'I'm so old, I can barely move anything.' She smells too, sort of fusty and unwashed, and her teeth are yellow. She's being supported by a woman with a hatchet face. 'This is my daughter, Melissa,' whispers the old lady to the nurse. 'She's very kind to me.' But Melissa doesn't look kind. She looks cold and angry and fed up. She is masking her face with over-bright concern but I can see that anger in her. She looks as though her mother, with her pathetic brittle bones and old person's problems, is just a burden to her. 'It's broken,' the old lady whispers to the nurse again, pointing towards her ankle.

'I'm sure it's not,' says Melissa, rather too briskly, maintaining a vice-like grip on her mother's arm.

'It is, Melissa. I can't move it.' The nurse gets an orderly to go out and find a wheelchair.

'Oh but I'm sure my mother can walk,' says Melissa.

'I can't,' says the old lady.

'I think it's best for your mother if she goes in the wheelchair,' says the nurse tactfully, 'that way it gives you a break from holding her up.' Melissa relents.

But still Bennie and John are not back. I'm getting bored now. I can't deal with everyone else's pain. I decide to go for a walk around the hospital. It is terribly quiet everywhere else. It is now maybe 9 p.m. The patients have had their dinner. Some lights are out. Some people are already sleeping. I wonder who they are? Who is at home worrying about them, missing them? I almost want to go to the maternity ward to see all those new mothers and wrinkly babies and relive, vicariously, that joyous sensation that goes with childbirth. It reminds me of something Julia told me recently. I think I was a bit low and she told me that when she's feeling a bit down she watches real-life stories on cable TV. There's a programme which apparently shows women giving birth and my sister got addicted to it. She'd turn it on, she said, to watch them give birth and to partake of every moment of worry and joy, and then cry along with them once the baby came out. 'It's powerful stuff,' she said. 'You should try it!' I couldn't, though. I thought it was too weird, but now I think maybe she was on to something.

Then for some reason I think of Janet and the fact that she gave birth to John the First, and when I think of her I realize she is here, somewhere within the walls of this hospital. I look at the list of departments on the map. Up on floor number two they are giving birth in the maternity unit. On floor number one they are dying. There she is – the oncology department, the cancer unit. It's just up the corridor. I wander along, dreading it a bit, and walk into the ward. No one is there to stop me. I feel like an intruder again. The ward is very off-putting. It's impossible to tell who is in which bed because the curtains are closed. I imagine people are trying to sleep but the lights are so bright. It all seems very uncomfortable. Imagine having to spend the last days of your life here. Oh please God, don't let this be the last place Janet sees – the lights, the curtains, the fake smiling faces, the other people she doesn't know or care about. I resolve then and there that I will not let her die like this. I've seen it in films. I shall come in the dead of night and wheel her away and out of the door and manhandle her into my car, and I shall put English roses by her bedside and a toile de Jouy lampshade on the light, and I shall make her Earl Grey tea and crumbly scones and we shall all hold her hands before she disappears from us.

Just then, a nurse finds me. She looks hassled. 'What are you doing here?'

'Er,' I say. 'I'm in the wrong department. I should be in A and E. My son is having an injection and his father –'

'It's back down the corridor,' she says. She's in a hurry. She doesn't want me to be her problem. She rushes off. I ignore her instructions and carry on wandering down the ward.

Halfway down there is a woman with her curtains open. 'Hello!' she says to me merrily. She looks about sixty-five years old.

'Hello,' I say, smiling at her.

'You're not supposed to be here, are you?'

'No.'

'But yet here you are.'

'Yes. My little boy is in A and E with his father.'

'Oh poor you. My son had to go to A and E once when he was tiny. He got his hand stuck in the mangle.'

'Ow.'

'Yes,' she says.

'Does your son come and see you?'

'No.' She is still smiling. 'He lives in Australia. My daughter lives in Canada. I look on the bright side. If I was about to die, I'm sure they'd be here, wouldn't they?'

'Yes, I'm sure they would be.'

'So I'm not near death, then, am I!'

'No,' I say, laughing.

Then the lady pauses and says, 'What's it like outside?' She looks suddenly really sad. 'I feel I've been in here so long, you see, I never really go outside.'

I tell her that actually it has been rather stormy most of the day but the ground is still a bit parched. There's a breeze and a promise of more rain later on. 'There are not many wasps this year, but lots of hornets. Apparently, it's to do with the fact that there was a warm early spring and then a cold snap, so all the wasps died off.'

'Are there any bumble bees? I love bumble bees. They always remind me of summer.'

'Yes, there are lots this year.'

Just then the nurse comes back. 'Why are you still here? You have to leave.'

'Give her a break,' says the lady. 'She's cheering me up.'

The nurse softens a bit. 'Who are you here to see?'

'Janet Parr.' I look carefully at the nurse when I say Janet's name.

'Oh Mrs Parr. Well, she's two beds down. I think she may be asleep but it wouldn't hurt much for us to check.'

'Oh thanks.'

'See you again soon,' says the lady with the distant children.

The nurse walks me down two beds. 'Here she is,' the nurse whispers. The curtains are open but the lady on the bed seems asleep.

'Is this Janet?' I ask.

'Janet?'

'I mean, Mrs Parr.'

The nurse looks at the notes on the end of the bed. She moves her hand almost imperceptibly to very briefly stroke the patient's leg. 'Yes, this is Mrs Parr.'

I look down at Janet. I wouldn't have recognized her. She is so thin. Her skin looks like a sheet of crêpe paper. And her hair? Where's her hair gone? Now she's just got a few strands of grey lying lacklustre and pasted to her head. 'What's happened to her hair?' I ask.

'Chemo, I expect,' says the nurse.

Janet's breathing is forced and laboured. She has a drip coming from one hand. Her eyes start twitching. She's going to wake up and find me standing here staring at her. I can't bear it. I don't know what to say to her. It's been too long since I've seen her and now the poor woman is dying. I start to panic.

'I have to go,' I tell the nurse.

The nurse nods in understanding. I walk as fast as I can up the ward, with the distant-children lady calling after me, 'Did you see your friend?'

When I get back to A and E it seems brimming with life compared to oncology. John and Bennie are waiting for me. I swoop on Bennie. I grab him and smell him and nestle his compact two-year-old body into mine and wrap his hair around my fingers and kiss the back of his neck.

'Mama,' he says, kissing me back.

'Steady on,' says John, laughing and then reaching forward to kiss me too. 'He's fine. He had the injection and now he's just eaten a packet of Quavers and drunk a glass of water and I should think he's starving. He won't do that again in a hurry. You should have seen his face when that nurse produced the needle!'

Now we are walking towards the car, Bennie still in my arms, snuggling up to me.

'She didn't like you!' John continues. 'What on earth did you do to her to make her feel such antagonism? She told me you were arrogant. I said to her, "That's my wife you're talking about! Don't tell me, I have to live with her!"'

And on he goes as we get into the car and I get into the back with Bennie.

'Can you take me back to the station in the morning?' John asks. 'I left the car there. I was in such a hurry and my hands were shaking and . . . I just took a cab . . .'

And all the while Bennie and I sit in the back entwined with each other, and the street lights flicker back and forth across our faces as John drives us home.

By the time we get there Bennie is asleep. John stops talking. Finally.

'I saw Janet,' I say.

'I guessed as much.' He gently takes Bennie from my arms and kisses me and somehow puts one arm around me and one arm around Bennie and we walk towards the house.

As we round the corner, there, framed by the window,

softly lit by candles, is the unmistakable face of Dougie. We watch him for a bit. Dougie is making dinner. He is stirring and chopping and tasting and licking his lips.

'What's he making?' asks John.

'I think it's griddled scallops followed by monkfish and fennel.'

'Monkfish and fennel? He's such a proper chef! But who's he talking to?'

'I don't know. He should have put Jamie and Edward to bed.'

'But someone's there.' John is watching Dougie intently. 'Look, Dougie is speaking to someone. Is Santa there?'

'No, she went home. I think they had words.'

'Dougie had words with Santa? What about?'

'Oh God, something to do with her wearing a short skirt.'

'They had an argument over Santa wearing a short skirt?'

But I am not really listening for I have seen who has just come into our kitchen.

'John,' I say slowly.

'Yes?'

I turn to look at him. 'You have to look in the kitchen.'

'What?'

'Look in the kitchen.'

John turns to look. 'Oh my God. Is that who I think it is?'

I nod.

'Well, well, well. The prodigal son returns.' For there, standing smoking in our kitchen like a ghost from my past, is tall, lean, tanned, his hair blond-tipped, John the First.

For a while I can't speak. What on earth is John the

First doing in our kitchen? He's not supposed to be in our kitchen. He's supposed to be abroad somewhere playing his guitar or, if he is here, he's supposed to be in Janet's kitchen in Tring. Maybe I'm imagining this. I turn away and then look again. No, John the First really is in my kitchen. I can't get my head around it so I just stand and stare at him and John stands and stares at him, and John the First has no idea that we are staring at him. I stare at his face. It's so familiar. I used to love that face. I slept next to it and kissed it for years, but now it seems so different. But of course he looks different; I haven't seen him for five years. Let me really look at him. Does he look different? Well, his hair is longer. He used to wear it short but now he looks a bit of a hippy. Oh so he's still smoking. But look, now he's smoking rollies. Hmm. Maybe he is a hippy. He looks older. Of course he looks older, he is older. He looks tanned, healthy, relaxed. He hasn't spent the last nine years of his life being pregnant and working and looking after children! Does he look happy? Hard to tell. He's never looked happy. Oh but see here, he has turned his head towards me. He is smiling at me. No, he can't be smiling at me. He can't see me. So who is he smiling at? Not Dougie, for Dougie is over next to the cooker on the other side of the kitchen. If I just follow his gaze . . . Christ! It's Edward! Edward has come into the kitchen. Oh God. Edward! Why is Edward still up? I can see him looking at his father.

John the Second suddenly snaps out of his reverie. 'What is John doing here now? Why is Edward still up? Why didn't John tell us he was coming over today? How are we going to explain this to Edward?' he asks all at the same time.

'I don't know,' I say in a rush, feeling panicked.

'You must have known,' John hisses at me. 'Of course you knew.'

'I did not know! Look, maybe the hospital rang him and told him Janet's got worse. Maybe they've told him she's about to die. Maybe that's why he's here now.'

'But he's not supposed to be *here*,' he says angrily. 'He's supposed to be at his mother's. Didn't he ring you and let you know?' John sounds accusatory now.

'No, he bloody didn't. Do you seriously think I'd let him arrive at our house and meet Edward for the first time in years without me being here?'

Then Bennie starts murmuring. 'Ow, ow, ow,' he says sleepily.

'I'm sorry,' says John. 'I love you, OK?'

'OK.' I kiss him very briefly and, with that, we walk in through the door.

Dougie turns when he hears the door open. He looks startled. He comes over to the back door immediately. 'Samantha. John. Bennie. Is he OK? Is he fine? Is he alive? Oh God, how awful! Oh John, erm, well, someone's here, you see. I was just cooking the dinner when . . .'

John the First walks over. He looks me up and down and then kisses me on the cheek. I am not sure if I blush. 'Sammie,' he says.

'Hi.' I give him a small hug and then I say, in a rather embarrassed fashion, 'Look, I don't wish to be rude but, John, what on earth are you doing here?'

'Oh you must be John,' says John the First, ignoring what I have said and reaching out to shake John the Second's hand. John the Second tries to extend his hand but he can't because of Bennie being slumped all over him. 'Who's this?' asks John the First.

'That's Bennie,' I say.

'Oh yes,' says John the First. 'One of your many boys, eh?'

'Well,' says Dougie brightly. 'This is a surprise! I mean, thank goodness I'm cooking a lot of food as I didn't know you were coming, John. I mean, first John.'

'Oh I'm sorry, Dougie,' I say. 'I meant to tell you about John, this John, coming back but what with work and my sister and everything else . . . there wasn't time and, in fact, John is not actually supposed to be here, are you, John?'

'I've come to see my mother,' says John the First, rather defensively. 'I got a call from the hospital saying that I ought to come right now. Apparently, my mum's got worse.'

'Which hospital is she in?' asks Dougie.

'Prestwood General,' says John the First. 'It's got a good oncology department.'

'Oh no, she's got cancer.' Dougie looks sad. Then he brightens a bit. 'Isn't that where you've just taken Bennie?'

'Yes,' I say, 'but, John, why are you –'

'Did you go and see my mother?' asks John the First.

'No,' I say. 'Listen, John –'

'Shame, she'd like to see you.'

'She may well do, but that still doesn't explain why you are here in my kitchen.'

'This is a very nice kitchen,' says John the First ruminatively. 'Didn't you make some nettle soup in here once? I am sure I called one time and you said you were making nettle soup.'

'I have never cooked nettle soup.' I am indignant. 'I've only ever made a hedgerow salad from this cookbook that told you how to survive off the fat of the land.'

'Or the thin of the land if it's a salad,' says Dougie.

John the Second then butts in. 'No offence, John, but why are you actually here in our hedgerow-salad-making kitchen?'

John the First now looks down in a contrite fashion. 'I'm so sorry. I had to fly home from the States in a hurry after the hospital called and then, when I got to my mother's house, I couldn't find the key. She said it was under the front-door mat but it wasn't and I didn't want to break a window and set off the alarm and . . . I really had nowhere else to go so I thought I'd come here and see Edward. Is that all right?' No one says anything. 'I've only got a small bag,' he adds rather desperately. 'I rang the hospital to speak to my mother but they said she was asleep and they didn't want to disturb her. It's only for one night. Is that OK, John? Or I could find a hotel . . .'

'There's no hotel near here,' says John the Second curtly. Then he softens a bit. 'You'd better stay. We've got a sofa bed in the study.'

'Oh thanks so much,' says John the First, giving him his most charming smile.

Then I remember that Edward is standing in the corner of the room. He looks half asleep. I suddenly feel angry. How could John the First just turn up without letting me know? I go over to Edward and kneel down and give him a hug. 'Are you all right?'

Edward can barely open his eyes. 'Mum,' he says to me, taking my hand, 'I think you'd better come in here.' He leads me into the sitting room and points to the floor. There is Jamie, naked and asleep on the rug in front of the fire. 'Look, Jamie's sleeping. Isn't he cute?'

I tell him that yes, Jamie is very cute but why is he not in bed and why is he, Edward, still awake?

'Dougie didn't put us to bed. I've been sitting here watching television and waiting for you to come back for hours and you just didn't come so I fell asleep and then when I woke up there was this tall man here who said he was my father.'

'Oh Edward, I'm sorry. That must have been a dreadful shock. Your father wasn't supposed to be here for another two weeks.'

'Oh so he is my dad? I thought he must have been because he called me Eddie and he brought me some chocolate.'

'He brought you some chocolate?'

'Yes. I did say thank you to him, though.'

'But where's the chocolate?'

'I ate it.'

I tell him he should clean his teeth and then I'll put him to bed.

I scoop up Jamie and tell Edward that I'll meet him in his bedroom. Then I go back into the kitchen and tell Dougie that he is very naughty for not putting Edward and Jamie to bed as I asked him to.

'I forgot, sorry,' says Dougie.

After I have put Jamie to bed, which takes no time as all I have to do is put a nappy and a clean Babygro on him and turn off his light, I go into Edward's bedroom. Edward is lying staring at the ceiling.

'I feel very tired,' he says, reaching out to me for a cuddle.

'It's been a long day.'

'I was so worried about Bennie.'

'You mustn't worry so much.'

'But Bennie could've died, couldn't he?'

'No, he wasn't going to die. He just had to have an injection in his bottom.'

'Ooh,' says Edward, giggling. 'He won't do that again in a hurry, will he?'

'No, he won't.'

I ask Edward if anything else is worrying him and he looks to the ceiling and then he says, 'Is that man downstairs really my father?'

'Yes, Edward.'

'But I don't remember him.'

'Well, you were very little when we lived with him and you haven't seen him much in years.'

'And he doesn't much look like a pirate.'

'That's because your father isn't a pirate.'

'So why did you say he was?'

I explain that, actually, it was he and Stanley who decided John the First was a pirate and that I, in fact, had never mentioned the pirate thing.

'But he's quite tall, isn't he?' says Edward.

'Yes, he's tall.'

'Why is he here?'

I tell him it's a long story.

'But I like stories,' says Edward. By now, he is virtually asleep, his head heavy on his pillow.

I tell him that we'll all talk about the long story tomorrow, for it is time for today to be over. 'Is that OK? Does that sound good?'

'Yes,' murmurs Edward.

I kiss him on the back of his neck. 'I love you, Edward.'

'Yes, Mama.' He hugs me drowsily. Just before he sinks into sleep he says, 'Mummy, do you like my daddy?'

'Yes,' I say and then he is asleep.

Now all I want to do is sleep here in this quiet dark room that smells of Edward. I want to close my eyes and never go downstairs again. It has been like a physical blow seeing John. I can remember the last time I saw him. It was when Edward was three and we took John the First to the airport after one of his fleeting visits. I remember telling Edward to say goodbye to his father. He was more interested in playing on the computer games in the arcade in Terminal Three. 'Say goodbye to your father!' I said sharply to Edward. I remember John the First bending down and kissing me on the cheek and his skin was all scratchy because he hadn't shaved. And that was it. He just kissed me and waved to Edward and I knew I wouldn't see him again for a long time. I told him that but he said, 'Oh no, you'll see me soon!' But he was wrong and I was right.

When I get downstairs John the Second has reappeared. 'Bennie's in bed. He is asleep.'

'Good,' I say.

Dougie is chatting away to John the First, who has opened a beer, and griddling some scallops at the same time. 'So, you've spent the last three years travelling across the States?' Dougie is saying to him. 'That must have been fascinating!'

'Oh it was. I just picked up my guitar and went wherever there might be work.'

'Where did you start off?'

'I went to Austin, Texas, then I kept on travelling through the southern states and then I decided to go down to Mexico for a bit.'

'Mexico! I'd love to go to Mexico.'

'Oh that was great. I was there for ages, maybe a year. I got into this mad mariachi band.'

'God, that sounds fun.'

'It was great fun. We did wedding parties and funerals and fiestas, and I learnt a lot of Spanish actually.'

'But didn't you miss everyone at home?'

'Well, not really, I –'

Suddenly, both of them notice I have come into the kitchen.

'I'm just cooking the scallops,' says Dougie nervously. 'I'm doing them on each side with a dash of lemon and some sherry vinegar.'

Dougie loves cooking. He has all sorts of recipes that he carries around in his head. He's always telling me people think he is gay because he's so flamboyant in the kitchen. Actually, recently he's started wearing odd Hawaiian shirts and I have told him that he looks rather camp in them and that looking rather camp is fine unless he wants to find a lady friend to have sexual relations with. 'No one is going to fancy you in that shirt, Dougie,' I say and Dougie pretends to look all hurt. Back during my Bennie pregnancy, he'd often fry up fish with chillies. I was mad for hot and spicy food when carrying Bennie. With Edward I wanted bloody and rare steak; with Jamie, rice pudding and biscuits. I love it when Dougie cooks. He is a fantastic, instinctual cook.

'Oh I've never been much of a cook, have I, Sammie?'

says John the First, giving me a hopeful smile.

'You probably didn't need to cook much in Mexico.'

'Oh Sammie,' says John the First, a bit reproachfully, 'don't be cross with me.'

'I'm not cross.'

'I love Mexican food,' says Dougie, a touch over-enthusiastically. 'It's all tortillas and refried beans, although I did once try to do this enchilada dish –'

'Sammie did that once, didn't you, Sammie?'

'Yes.'

'So you cooked a lot for John?' says Dougie to me brightly, obviously trying to keep the conversation going.

'Yes.'

'She does a wonderful duck dish for me,' John the Second says, finally joining in the conversation.

'I don't think duck goes with enchiladas, does it?' says Dougie. No one says anything. 'It was a joke. Oh never mind, let's have some wine. Wine is good for nerves, I think.'

'Wine is good for everything,' says John the First.

But then I remember that we haven't been able to find the corkscrew for about four weeks since Bennie spied it and hid it somewhere. Every time we are just about to open some wine, we ask Bennie where he has put it and he always shrugs his shoulders. ''S gone,' he says. Then we have to go round to the neighbours yet again to use theirs and they must think we're real drunks because some-times we go round there twice a day.

I tell Dougie we can't have wine as no one has found the corkscrew yet.

'Oh yes, they have!' he says, brandishing it. 'I found it in the fish bowl!'

We all start laughing even though John the First looks confused. 'Why do you keep your corkscrew in the fish bowl?' he says. The ice is partially broken.

But still none of us stays relaxed for very long. John the Second is quiet. I see him watching John the First but I can't read his face. I can't decide if he is feeling thoughtful or cross or angry or sad or all of these things. I can't decide how I feel either. I am, in part, furious. It's typical of bloody Dougie to think John the First is cool with his guitar and his time in a Mexican mariachi band. And I'm really cross that John the First said he hadn't missed anyone. I am also confused; I am still not sure why John the First has come back early. And Edward? Poor Edward! Why wasn't I here to support him?

To make everything better, or at least not so awkward, I open a couple of bottles of red wine and pour everyone a large glass.

After a few sips, which go to my head as I haven't eaten yet, I decide to be gracious for tonight. 'How was the mariachi band?' I ask John the First.

He gives me a look. He is not sure if I am being sarcastic or not. 'Do you really want to know about it?'

'Yes.'

'Oh I do!' says Dougie.

'It was interesting,' says John the First, 'and sort of hot most of the time.'

'Did you learn a lot?' says John the Second.

'Oh yes.'

'Like what?'

'John the First takes a long slug of wine. 'Actually, I learnt I was no good at being in a mariachi band!' Everyone starts laughing.

Then Dougie announces that the scallops are ready. 'Now,' he says to John the First, 'I can't imagine you not liking this! It was Samantha who first gave me the recipe. Samantha loves cooking. The second time I met her, she cooked me and my wife, Maxine, this fantastic coq au vin and I said to Maxine, "Isn't Samantha a good cook?" and –'

'Sammie used to cook loads. After she came back from hospital, when she'd had Edward, she went mad on making all these dishes. She did steak Diane and a fish pie, but after that she was always cooking stuff for Edward and then mashing it into some gloop.'

'That's because I wanted Edward to eat proper food.'

'Yeah, I know. But you have to admit, you did spend all your time introducing him to new tastes and pummelling avocados and lentils.'

'What's wrong with that?'

'Nothing. I was just wondering if all he eats now is chips, burgers and tomato ketchup!'

'Actually, Edward eats all sorts of things,' says John the Second. I give him a grateful look.

'You cook for the kids?' says John the First.

'All the time,' says John the Second.

'As I was saying,' says Dougie, 'maybe, John, I mean first John, you should ask Samantha to make a coq au vin while you're here because it's so delicious and –'

'I've given up meat for a month,' says John the First.

'Why?' asks Dougie, as if such a thing is inconceivable.

'I just don't like it much. The meat in Mexico is as tough as hell.'

'God, I couldn't give up meat!' says Dougie. 'Can you imagine no steak? No roast lamb? I think I'd rather die. Wouldn't you, Samantha?'

I nod, and pour more wine into our glasses.

'You eat fish, though?' says Dougie, spooning prodigious amounts of monkfish and fennel onto our plates.

'Yes,' says John the First.

'Oh thank goodness for that, or else Lord alone knows what you would've had for dinner.'

'I don't really eat much. Sammie always used to complain about that.'

'No, I didn't. It's just that you always went on about how people who ate too much offended you.'

'I love eating,' says Dougie, 'but you know, my wife – well, actually, she's my ex-wife – doesn't eat much. We once went on a trip down the Amazon and she barely ate a morsel.'

'You went down the Amazon with your ex-wife?' says John the First. 'That sounds interesting.'

'Oh she wasn't my ex-wife then. We were married for twenty years, you know. Let me tell you about my marriage break-up. I met Maxine, that's my wife –'

'Your ex-wife,' says John the First.

'I met Maxine,' continues Dougie, 'when I was at law school in Edinburgh. She was so glamorous. I loved her on the spot! I said to her, "You are the most glamorous woman in the world!" and she gave me this very haughty look and turned on her heels and walked off!'

'I met Sammie in a picture-framing shop,' says John the First. 'She was about twenty-one, just out of university, and she was wearing this kaftan thing and I thought she looked gorgeous. Actually, Sammie, you were completely different then.'

'Oh thanks,' I say.

'I didn't mean it like that. I think you still look gorgeous.

Maybe even more so. Having three children obviously suits you.'

'In what way was Samantha different?' says John the Second, cutting in.

'Oh she had long hair,' says John the First, 'and she was a socialist and she never ate meat and –'

'A vegetarian!' says Dougie.

'I never knew you were a vegetarian,' says John the Second. 'You never told me that.'

'It was years ago!' I say. 'I didn't think it was important.'

'Ah, I'm sure there're lots of things Sammie hasn't told you,' says John the First, winking at me.

'Oh really?' John the Second sounds a mixture of intrigued and put out.

'Only nice things,' says John the First hurriedly.

'*Anyway*,' says Dougie, 'I then had to track Maxine down and I can't tell you how difficult it was. I found out that she was training to be a lawyer but I didn't even know what her name was so I called every single legal practice in Edinburgh and described Maxine over the phone and asked if she worked there.'

'God,' says John the Second, 'that must've taken for ever.'

'Eight weeks and three days.'

'But why did you do it?' John the First asks.

'I was smitten,' says Dougie. 'Haven't you ever been smitten?'

'Oh yes,' says John the First, looking at me. 'I was rather smitten with you, wasn't I, Sammie?'

I don't say anything. Dougie looks embarrassed and starts clearing the plates.

'What happened next with Maxine?' says John the Second, ignoring what John the First has just said.

'Oh, same old, same old. We got married and now we are divorced.'

'Any kids?' asks John the First.

'No kids.'

'Really? God, even I've managed to have a kid and I'm hopeless.'

'That's true,' I say.

'Oh but neither of us wanted kids,' says Dougie. 'Samantha doesn't believe me. She thinks everyone wants to have kids.'

'They do!' I say, laughing. 'They're just in denial.'

'I'm not in denial!' says Dougie. 'I'm just drunk! Pour more wine!'

I pour more wine. I notice that Dougie is, indeed, drunk. I wonder if I'm drunk. I think not. I'm too nervous to be able to relax enough to get drunk.

'Well, since I'm drunk,' says Dougie, 'I thought I'd reveal that fact that I've met someone!' He gives me a big wink. John the First looks at me in a confused fashion and Dougie laughs and says, 'No, it's not Samantha. Don't be mad! She's my best friend!'

And John the First says, 'Since when did everyone start calling you Samantha?'

'After you left me, John, I just wanted to be a Samantha and not a Sammie.'

'Well, thank God you stopped calling yourself Sammie because I can't see myself as having married a Sammie!' says John the Second.

'I married a Sammie,' says John the First.

'Yes, and you left her!' says Dougie.

John the First suddenly looks a bit thoughtful. 'Actually, that's something I've come to regret.' John the Second

164

gives me a meaningful look and raises his eyebrows. 'I've sort of come back to apologize, Sammie.' John the Second gives out a low whistle. 'If that's all right with you,' John the First says to John the Second.

'Yes, well, that's fine,' says John the Second.

'I do feel really bad about leaving. I just . . . I just . . .'

'It's OK.' I am now feeling really embarrassed. 'I don't think now is the time and the place . . .'

'But I want to tell you,' he says. 'I had to go and see if I could be a musician.'

'Right. Fine,' I say.

'Yes, now what's for pudding?' says Dougie.

'But I found out that I couldn't, Sammie,' continues John the First. 'That's what I'm trying to say. I've failed at being a musician really and so now I've come home not just to see my mother but also to make amends with you and Edward.'

'Oh.' I pour out more wine.

'Is that OK?' asks John the First.

'You're drunk,' I say to him.

'No, I'm not. I've just been worrying about you.'

'Why have you been worrying about Samantha?' says Dougie, who has just downed another glass of wine. 'She's done all right for herself, haven't you, Samantha? You've got a nice bloke, nice kids, nice house.'

'Yes.' I reach out to hold John the Second's hand. 'I've done very well, thank you.'

'I've got to hand it to you, Sammie,' says John the First. 'You've got the life you wanted really. In fact, you're turning into your sister! By the way, how is your sister?'

But just before I can tell him about Uncle Joe and the angel therapist, Dougie bangs his fist onto the table. 'Sod

Samantha's sister! Doesn't anyone want to know who it is I've fallen in love with?'

'Me!' I say. 'I want to know!'

'Oh wait until you meet this girl,' says Dougie. 'She's got a sleek black bob and endless hair and her name is . . . Santa!'

'I knew it was! And you always deny it!'

'Ah but who says I am telling the truth now? I may be lying. I may be lying to protect the identity of a lady.'

'Oh what are you talking about?' John the Second sounds exasperated.

'Maybe it's another who has taken my eye,' says Dougie. 'You have to guess. It could be more than one.'

'Then give us a clue,' I say.

'No clues.'

'Oh for God's sake, Dougie,' says John the Second. 'Give it a break.'

Dougie looks a bit crestfallen.

'But why did you and Maxine break up?' asks John the First.

'Over a window!' says Dougie, swaying on his chair. 'I've never really told anyone this, but I love a cold house. I really do.'

'God, you're like my sister,' I say. 'She has all the windows open all the time. Her house is like a refrigerator.'

'But Maxine loves a warm house,' continues Dougie, 'and we used to argue about it all the time and then, one day, I just flipped. The house was baking. Maxine had shut the windows, even though it was the summer, and she'd turned the heating up and I felt so claustrophobic, and I just told her everything bad about her and . . . she never forgave me really.'

'You split up over whether or not to have the window open?' says John the First incredulously.

'Essentially, yes.' Dougie now looks very remorseful. 'If only I'd . . . if only I'd . . .'

I think he is going to cry. He reaches for the wine bottle. I take it off him.

'Come on, Dougie,' I say softly. 'It's time for us all to go to bed.'

John the Second goes off to make the beds – one in the upstairs spare room that is always known as 'Dougie's room' and one sofa bed in the study downstairs for John. On his way out of the door I hear him say to John the First, 'Here's your bed. Stay as long as you like.'

Just as I am about to go upstairs to bed, John the First catches me by the hand. 'There's a lot I want to say. We have a lot of talking to do.'

'Yes, I'm sure there is a lot to say. And since my husband has kindly said you can stay, I'm sure we'll have a lot of time to say it in.'

'I want to talk about you, Sammie. I am sorry. Truly I am and I want you to know that I've changed and –'

'John, you've already told me this. I would have thought that you'd like to know about the last five years of Edward's life.'

'But, Sammie, I want to talk about you and me.'

'You and me? There is no you and me, John. You are here. We are letting you stay and that's enough. I would have thought the only conversation we need to have, or the only conversation you should really be interested in, would be one about the welfare of your son.'

'So you're still cross with me, are you, Sammie?'

'Not really.' I am now so weary. 'Look, John, it's been a

long day. My two-year-old nearly died. I'm tired. I want to go to bed.'

'But when can we talk?'

'Tomorrow. But, please, don't delve into the past. It's just not worth it. Let's just stick to Edward.'

'OK.' He blows me a slightly flirtatious kiss. 'See you in the morning, Sammie.'

When I get to bed, John is dozing in a semi-drunken fashion. 'He's not that bad,' he says to me as I inch towards him.

'Who isn't?'

'Oh you know. Your ex. I mean he's a crap dad. It's a bit odd that he turned up unannounced saying he couldn't find the key. He obviously wants to stay here. I suppose it's because he's one of those men who can't stand their own company. That's probably why, and he's prone to talking about himself, but he's all right really, isn't he?'

'Is he?'

'Yes.' John props his head up on his elbow and looks at me in a quizzical fashion. 'Come on, *Sammie*. He apologized to you. That's what he was trying to say, wasn't it? That he regretted leaving you and that he is sorry. Isn't that what everyone wants to hear from their ex? I mean, as far as I'm concerned, he can stay for a week or so if he's so desperate for love and affection.'

I suddenly have a sense, an overwhelming sense, of being utterly and swirlingly alone. I look long and hard at John. 'What on earth are you talking about? Why should he stay? Why should I care about his need for love and affection? And he hasn't apologized to anyone. Has he apologized to Edward? No. Is he going to apologize to him? Probably not. He is a selfish man.'

'I think you're being a bit harsh.'

'Do you? Then why did he turn up unannounced? Why did it not occur to him that I would need time to prepare Edward for seeing his father again? It's because he didn't bloody think about it. All he's thinking about is what to do with his life now he's finally realized he's a failure. It's all about what he needs but when has he ever thought about what Edward needed? Edward hasn't seen him in years. I can't imagine what Edward's thinking now!' And then I start to cry.

'Oh Samantha.' John now reaches out for me and holds me. 'Edward's fine.'

'How can he possibly be fine?' I sob. 'Why don't you understand this?'

'But Edward is fine,' he says, stroking my hair. 'He is happy with us. He has a support system around him, Samantha. He'll be fine.'

'But we don't know that!' I am getting increasingly anguished. 'Why was I not here for him? I've always been there for him, John. Always!'

'You had to be with Bennie. You can't be with everyone all at the same time!'

'I let him down. If only John had let me know he was coming early then I could've prepared him. I could've –'

'Shh, Samantha.'

'I'm going in to see him.'

'Who?'

'Edward.'

'Why?' John groans slightly.

'I want to make sure he's asleep.'

'He is asleep.'

'How do you know? How do you know he's not wide awake worrying?'

'Because, if he was, he would be in here telling you all about it. Come on, Samantha. Edward hides nothing from you, you know that.'

He's right of course. Just John saying this makes me calm down.

'Can I change the subject?' he asks.

'No,' I say in a thick voice.

'I just thought you might like to know that John still fancies you.'

'No, he doesn't. It's not funny, John. I can't concentrate on this.'

'I'm not trying to be funny. Your ex fancies you and you know that.'

'Don't be silly. No one fancies me.'

'I fancy you. I think you look amazing.' He makes a playful lunge for me. I push him away.

'But no one else does. John the First probably thinks, "God, that ex of mine has put on weight."'

'Do you want him to fancy you?'

'Not really. I just want someone to say, "You know, even though you are married you look amazing." No one ever does that. No one ever looks at me. I've become an invisible woman.'

'No, you haven't. People do look at you. The other day in the shop a man really gave you the up and down look.'

'The up and down look?' I begin to relax a little.

'You know.' John suddenly leaps out of bed and struts around like a cockerel, giving me one of those lascivious long looks going from head to toe.

'Who did that?' I start to giggle.

'A really good-looking man.'

'How old was he?'

'Oh maybe about seventy.' I throw a pillow at him. 'Ah,' says John, coming back to bed and holding me again, 'have I cheered you up now?'

I tell him that he has.

'Good.' Then he rolls over and goes to sleep.

But later, when he is gently snoring, I look down at my body. Childbirth has changed it. My breasts have never really gone back to what they were. They have always been big and full but they didn't used to be this big. The last time I was pregnant, with bluey-green-eyed Jamie – how do all my children have blue eyes when mine are brown? – I produced so much milk I expressed it, bagged it up and gave it on a weekly basis to a man who came from the local hospital to collect it. It was incredible really. My milk fed all these other babies whose mothers had little non-milky breasts. I felt like the community wet nurse. But now, having been pumped dry, my breasts sag. My bottom's all right but I've got a fleshy stomach. Bennie loves to wobble my stomach. He gets into bed in the morning and goes, 'Ooo, ooo, ooo,' and pummels me with his little fists. One time, not too long after I had Jamie, Edward said, 'Mum, look at your stomach! Have you eaten Jamie?' I burst into tears then. My arms are chunkier too and my hips are broader.

I look at John. He looks the same. He hasn't given birth.

Recently, a taxi driver in London asked me when the baby was due and I felt like crying. 'I've just had a baby,' I said, but it's a lie. Jamie is no longer a newborn. And a lady at the local shop congratulated me a couple of weeks back. I've lost confidence. I used to swing down London streets in short skirts and high heels. Now I keep to the shadows, a bag clasped over my stomach. Santa is as slender as a reed. She wears tight tops and short skirts and Dougie does fancy her. And John the First doesn't fancy me any more. I can just tell.

11. Saturday

The next morning Edward gets up early, as usual. For once Bennie, probably exhausted by the exertions of the night before and all that antihistamine in his little rump, doesn't wake up. Edward creeps past Dougie's bedroom and quietly lets himself into our room.

'Mummy,' he says, 'who's that man asleep in Dougie's room?'

'Dougie.'

'Dougie?'

'Yes, Dougie, as in my friend Dougie.' I look carefully at Edward. He seems chirpy enough.

'Oh Dougie!' says Edward. 'Was he here last night?'

'Yes, Edward. He was here and he was supposed to put you and Jamie to bed because I had to take Bennie to the hospital up the road.'

'The hospital where I went when I banged my head on the bouncy castle?'

'Yup.'

'The hospital I went to when I mangled my leg?'

'No. That was in Todi.'

'Where's Todi?'

'It's in Italy.'

'What was I doing in Italy?'

'We were on holiday.'

'When?'

'Two bloody years ago!' says John the Second emerging

from under the bedclothes, now obviously awake.

'You shouldn't swear, Dad,' says Edward.

'I'm sorry. It's just that I was half asleep and then I heard you and your mother having one of those conversations again.'

'What conversations?'

'Those ones that go round and round and never get anywhere.'

'Do we have conversations like that, Mum?'

'Hmm,' I say, joshing with him, 'what do you think?'

'Maybe.'

John groans and hides his head under the pillows.

Edward starts giggling. 'There's a strange man in the study,' he says.

'He's your father, Edward.'

'My *father*?'

'Yes, your father,' says John in a rather muffled voice as he emerges from the pillows again.

'What did Daddy just say?'

'He said, he's your father.'

'Of course he's my father,' says Edward. 'Of course you're my father,' he says to John.

'Not him, Edward,' I say gently. 'He means the man in the study is your father, your genetic father.'

'My genete-whatsit father? When did my genete-whatsit father come here?'

I explain to Edward that his father came last night. 'You saw him, remember? He gave you chocolate.'

'Oh that tall man? Oh yes, I remember him.'

'Look, Edward,' I say, 'the thing is . . .'

'Samantha,' says John warningly as he levers himself out of bed.

'The thing is,' I continue, 'that your father – your genetic father – has come over to see your grannie – do you remember her, the one that's called Janet? – because she's not very well and she's in the hospital near us, you see. And the hospital phoned and –'

'Which hospital?'

'The hospital Bennie went to.'

'Oh you mean the hospital where I went when I banged my head on the bouncy castle?'

'Yes,' says John, a bit impatiently. 'That hospital, Edward.'

'But why is my grannie that's called Janet in hospital?'

'She's not very well, and your father has come over to see her and he's also come to see us but he had to arrive suddenly –'

'Has she mangled her leg?'

'No. She's got a long-term illness so your daddy – your genetic daddy – is going to see her and he's going to spend some time with her and I just really want to let you know that everything is OK and that me and Daddy – this daddy here – are here for you, Edward.'

'But why wouldn't you be?' Edward looks puzzled.

'Exactly,' says John, pulling on his jeans. 'Why wouldn't we be?'

I shoot him a cross look. 'It's not that, Edward. It's just that you haven't seen your real father in years and, some-times, these types of things can be difficult for everyone involved . . .'

'Especially when people *go on about it*,' says John.

'. . . and I just wanted to let you know that Daddy and I love you,' I continue, 'and you can tell us anything and –'

'But how does my genete-whatsit daddy know my grannie that's called Janet?'

John groans.

'Your father is your grannie Janet's son,' I say to Edward.

Edward looks astounded. 'I never knew that!'

'Well, who on earth did you think your grannie Janet was?' says John. 'I mean, you've known her since you were a baby, Edward! I know you haven't seen her for a couple of years but didn't you ever realize who she was?'

'I didn't recognize my cousin Robert once,' says Edward happily, 'and that was because he'd put on a pair of glasses!'

John shakes his head. 'Oh Edward.'

Just as John and I are about to start on one of our 'what are we going to do about Edward' conversations, we get interrupted. Dougie comes into the bedroom. He looks sleepy and tired. 'Good morning,' he says. He rubs his eyes like a child. I tell him that he is obviously hung over and must go back to bed immediately.

'I'm fine. I want to get up really.'

'Hello,' says Edward.

'Oh hello, Edward. Have you done the board yet today?'

'The board!' says Edward, suddenly looking delighted. 'Oh no, I haven't!'

'Shall we go and do it, then?' says Dougie. They go off down the stairs.

'What do you think Edward will write?' says John.

'I don't know,' I say.

The board is a whiteboard on the fridge. Everyone in our household writes down on the board things that they need or appointments they've made. For a while it worked very well. I'd write down nappies, milk, bread, cucumber, wipes, Marmite, Santa would add rubber gloves and John would add AA batteries, and then whoever was going to the shops – usually me – would know what to buy. I would also use the board to remind John of everything that needs doing, like Walk the Dog and Book Jamie Injections and Edward Haircut and Bennie Playgroup Tuesday 10 a.m. This meant that John wouldn't annoy me every day by asking things like 'What does Bennie do today?' when Bennie does the same thing at the same time every week. In fact, the board has become quite a useful means of communication. It holds all the secrets of the minutiae of our family life without anyone having to say anything at all: Edward £3.50 jujitsu Wednesday; Tumble Tots 10 a.m. Friday £2; baby milk, dog food, cat food (not biscuits), bread, milk, apples, school pens for Edward.

All this was fine until Edward began subverting it. He started to write things like Chocolate for Edward and then I'd write No Chocolate for Edward and then underneath that he'd write No Chocolate for Mummy and on it would go until we'd filled the board. Then one day, when Edward and John had an argument, he wrote, John is Bad, Edward is Good, and then he made up boxes with Good, Funny and Bad on them and we all started filling in people's names, depending on how well we thought they had behaved. In the good box there is always me and Beady the dog. In the bad box there is always Bennie and Honey the cat. In the funny box there is often Jamie, especially when he does his weird head-waggling thing when he wants something. As for the Daleks, it depends on who is writing: they are in the bad box if it's me or in the good box if it's Edward. Edward often puts Daddy in the bad box unless he's bought him sweets in which case Edward rubs out the Daddy in the bad box and transfers him to the good box.

This morning, once we have all got up and come downstairs, we peer at the board. I'm in the good box and so is the dog. Bennie is in the bad box, 'for eating that plant,' says Edward. Jamie is also in the bad box.

'Why is Jamie in the bad box?' I ask him.

'Because he fell asleep on the floor.'

I tell him that that was hardly Jamie's fault but Edward is implacable.

'It's about time Jamie went into the bad box.'

'Why is Santa in the funny box?' asks John.

'Because she says "blaady hell" and she's a girl and she knows how to fix doors and that's funny because not many girls can do that, you know,' he giggles.

Edward is in the good box along with Daddy x 2, Gameboy, chocolate and light savers.

'Where are you going to put me?' asks Dougie.

'I don't know.' Edward looks at him very carefully.

'Put him in the bad box,' says John.

'Why?'

'More bloody fun!' says John now making the coffee.

Edward rubs the 'x 2' off the 'Daddy x 2' in the good box and puts a Daddy in the bad one. 'That's for swearing, Daddy. I think I'll put you –' he points towards Dougie – 'in the funny box with Santa until I work out where to put you because you are very good for talking to me about *Star Wars* but very bad for not giving me any dinner last night.'

'That's fine,' says Dougie. 'Being funny is better than bad, isn't it?'

'Not always,' says Edward darkly. John the First then walks into the kitchen. 'You're in the good box!' Edward tells him.

178

'What are you talking about?' says John the First, who also looks half asleep.

'You know, along with light savers.'

'Oh right.' John the First blearily inspects the whiteboard.

'At first I thought I'd put you in the bad box,' continues Edward, 'for not seeing me for years.'

'Oh sorry.' John the First looks rather embarrassed.

'But I swapped you back just now because you bought me some chocolate. See? And here's my other daddy and he's in the bad box because he swears. Do you swear, Dad?' he asks John the First.

'No,' says John the First. I choke on my coffee.

'I don't swear either,' says Edward. 'My little brother Bennie once said "uddy bell" and I think he was trying to say –'

'Well, good morning, John,' says Dougie, overriding Edward's monologue.

'What do you mean, no dinner?' I ask Edward, finally realizing what he said to Dougie.

'He didn't give me any dinner,' says Edward, rubbing Dougie's name out from the funny box.

'I'll get you bacon and eggs,' I say.

'Bacon and eggs?' says Dougie. 'I'll have some of those. In fact, I'll make them! Anyone else for bacon and eggs?'

'I've put you in the bad box,' Edward says to Dougie.

'Now where's the bacon, where're the eggs?' says Dougie. He opens the fridge door. 'My, oh my, Samantha,' he says, 'you've always got so much food! You must spend a fortune on it!'

'We do,' I say.

*

All the Food We Get Through in a Week

The reason we spend so much money on food is because we get through acres and acres of it. I only have to see a loaf of bread for it to disappear. An entire pack of yoghurts can vanish in a day. Mini chocolate croissants last only half a day. But what we buy – what we actually buy in terms of a shopping list – is tricky, as John the Second tends to do most of the elaborate cooking and yet constantly fails to tell me what he needs for his recipes. I will find him, night after night, poring over cook books and humming and ha-ing and then saying things like, 'I think I'll make a tasty lamb stew tomorrow.'

But when I ask him what he might need for the aforementioned lamb stew, he'll say, 'Lamb!'

I'll say, 'What type of lamb?' for I know that there are many different cuts of lamb and maybe he wants neck, leg or shin.

And he will look ever so slightly annoyed and say, 'Just lamb!' all over again.

So, if I am doing the food shop, I will never come back with all of the right ingredients and he will have to drive the half an hour back to the supermarket and the butcher's and the grocer's and start all over again.

Conversely, if it is him doing the shopping, it will be even more disastrous for, as the week goes on, I write down on the whiteboard what we need but then, once it starts to fill up, I sort of get bored of writing it all down and just keep a vague idea of what we've run out of in my head. Therefore, when John the Second goes to shop, he copies down what is on the whiteboard and then says those magical words: 'Is there anything else we need?'

And I want to reply, 'Yes, you blind numbskull, there is tons of stuff we need but as it is the same stuff we need every single week, how come you don't know what it is!' Instead I say, 'Just get the usual.'

This means that he'll spend about an hour staring at a blank sheet of paper which he calls the Shopping List. When I ask him why his sheet of paper is blank, he'll say, 'I am going to write down what we need in an aisle-by-aisle format.'

'An aisle-by-aisle format? Why?'

He will then go on to explain that it makes more sense to do the shopping list that way as it means that when he is in the supermarket, he doesn't waste time going backwards and forwards from, say, the fruit and veg bit to the milk bit at the diametrically opposite side of the shop, just to find himself going back to fruit and veg again for something else.

'But don't you scan the list and then work it all out once you're in the shop?' I'll say. 'Surely you don't just read the first item and see carrots, for example, and go to get the carrots and then move your eyes one millimetre or so downwards and read milk and then go and get the milk and then think, "Oh darn it!" because right under the word milk is bananas? Surely that's not what you do? Only an idiot would do that.'

'I am not an idiot,' says John, but generally he comes back with about three bags of shopping, compared to my ten, and I have to go back to the shops a day later as we've run out of food again.

So this would be our general shopping list on a Monday:

Milk (6 pints). Bread. Bagels (plain and cinnamon). Small choco-latinis. Cheddar cheese. Babybels. Dairylea cheese triangles. Petits Filous. Frubes. Choc ices. Frozen peas, frozen beans and oven chips. Captain Birdseye fish fingers. Cod in breadcrumbs. Ham (pack of organic). Organic chicken. Organic chicken thighs.

Organic chicken drumsticks. Beefburgers (fresh). Aberdeen Angus meatballs. Lamb chops. Lamb for Irish stew (any). Frankfurters. Fresh pasta (tagliatelle). Margherita pizza (3). Garlic bread (3). Fresh pomodoro pasta sauce. Baked beans, cannellini beans, chickpeas, spaghetti hoops, tinned tomatoes, Heinz tomato soup. Shreddies, Rice Pops, Cornflakes and Branflakes. Dog food. Cat food (in jelly NOT gravy). Dog biscuits. Cat biscuits. Eggs. Sugar. Coffee. Tea. Teabags. Self-raising flour for baking. Plain flour. Basmati rice and wok noodles. Biscuits. Small packs of raisins. Nutrigrains. Marmite. Orange juice. Apple juice (6 small cartons for Edward's packed lunch). Crisps. Filled crepes (for Bennie's lunch). Apples. Bananas. Grapes. Melon. Carrots (organic for us, non-organic for the horses up the road). Potatoes. Broccoli. Green beans. Salad vegetables. Fresh tomatoes. Cucumber. Butternut squash (5). Tomato ketchup.

Then, by a Thursday, lots of this will have disappeared or John the Second may have finally decided what he is going to cook later on in the week and added it to the list, so this is what I may well get on a Thursday:

Loo roll (forgot on Monday, ditto washing powder, fabric softener, washing-up liquid, bin bags, floor cleaner and bathroom cleaner, sponges, washing-up cloths and J-cloths and bayonet lightbulbs). Bread. Bagels (plain, the kids prefer them to the cinnamon ones). Chocolatinis (gone in one day). Frubes (gone in two days). Crisps (also gone in two days). Bananas. Grapes. Nappies size 3 and 5 and baby wipes. Fresh orange juice. Dairylea triangles (gone in three days). Organic chicken for stir-fry (fancy that for my dinner). Fish for fish pie – cod, smoked haddock and salmon. Potatoes for fish pie. Sea bass (for me). Ginger and spring onions for sea bass. Cumin. Paprika. Cinnamon. Turmeric. Bay leaves.

Bouquet garnis. Star anise (for John the Second's spice cupboard). Turnip. Swede. Parsnip. More butternut squash. Leeks. Celery and mushrooms (for John the Second's soup). Streaky bacon (smoked). Back bacon (unsmoked). Prawns. Monkfish. Clams. Coriander and parsley (for fish stew).

These are the things I might go back and buy on a Friday as, having just thought about my 'Celebrity Fridge' copy, I will be obsessed with superfoods and having a balanced diet and omega 3 fatty acids obtained from oily fish:

Peppered mackerel. Smoked salmon. Tuna fish in a jar. Blueberries. Danone superbifidous yoghurt or whatever it is called. Oatcakes. Cottage cheese. Spinach. Spring greens. Couscous. Pine nuts. Bulgar wheat for tabbouleh. Mint. Red onions. Oranges. Avocado. Fillet steak. Reduced-fat hummus.

I think that's it. On Fridays, I love to look at the fridge heaving full of delicious food with such wonderful potential.

By Monday it has all gone and the whole ritual starts all over again.

Dougie starts heating oil in a frying pan, then John the Second says he is not staying at home.

'I've got to go to London,' he says apologetically.

'Why?' I ask him.

'To look at a space.'

'What kind of a space?'

'A place to build sets.'

'I don't understand. You've never needed a place to build sets before.' He usually just does them on site.

'I have to go. I need somewhere quiet to work. There are too many people in this house at the moment. It is too noisy with all the kids and I just can't concentrate. Didn't we discuss this before?'

'I would have remembered it if we'd discussed it before.'

'We discussed it last week. I said that if you want me to earn more money then I need to get more work and that means working all the weekends.'

'I don't remember telling you that you have to earn more money.' I add that, today, I don't care about his earning any money. I only care about the fact that he is intending to go to London without having previously informed me of this, and to leave me alone with three children and – and I motion my head towards John the First, who is busily discussing the politics of the white-board with Edward.

'I don't think I want to be good,' John the First is saying. 'I think I'd actually like to be bad.'

'Oh for goodness sake, Dad,' replies Edward. 'You don't get the point of it, do you? You don't get to choose which category you go in. I get to tell you, you see?'

'I'm going to the bathroom,' says John the First in response.

'Me wanna go dondon,' says the unmistakable voice of Bennie who has suddenly appeared downstairs perched on Dougie's back.

'I heard him crying upstairs,' Dougie says apologetically. 'I thought I ought to get him up and make sure he's OK.'

I ask Bennie if he's OK.

'No,' says Bennie, looking at his father. 'Me not OK. Me wanna go dondon.'

'Well, you can't,' says John.

Bennie bursts into tears. 'Me wanna go. Me wanna go!' he yells. I now hear the telltale sound of Jamie shuffling into the room.

'Oh yes, Jamie was awake too,' says Dougie. 'I think Jamie's got a smelly nappy.'

'Melly nappy?' says Bennie.

'Where's his changing stuff?' says John the Second.

I tell him all the changing stuff is in the bathroom but I think he'll find John the First is in there.

'Oh John,' says Dougie, 'I'll give you a lift to the station to pick up your car. I'll go back to London as well. I've got lots of work to do.'

'Thanks,' says John, now cuddling Jamie.

'Oh great,' I say. 'Now you're abandoning me too.'

'I'll be back tomorrow morning,' says Dougie, sounding hurt. 'It's just that I've got to pick up some stuff in London.'

Bennie suddenly perks up. 'ME GO DONDON!' he yells.

'GA!' yells Jamie, getting very excited.

'No, neither of you is going to London!' says John firmly to both of them.

Bennie bursts into tears. 'Nooo, Dada Dada Dada.'

'Oooo, ma-ma-ma-ma-ma,' says Jamie.

'Mummy!' says Edward, still fiddling around writing on the whiteboard but now paying attention as his father is no longer there. 'Jamie just spoke! He said "mama". Say it again, Jamie.'

'Erggh, blerp, ga,' says Jamie.

'I didn't hear him,' says John.

'But he did say it,' says Edward.

'You're all mad.' John puts Jamie down and walks out

of the room. He tries the handle on the door of the bathroom. It is locked. John sighs and goes upstairs back to our bedroom. I follow.

'That was a bit off,' I say, looking at him. He seems unperturbed. 'What's the matter with you this morning?'

'Nothing.' John is hunting for a pair of socks. 'What could possibly be the matter?'

'You seem to be in a bit of a bad mood.'

'Samantha, the baby stinks, Bennie's crying and you're having a go at me about the fact that I have to spend today in London. I mean, do I want to go to London? No. Do I want to go to the loo? Yes. Can I change either of those situations? No, I can't! I mean, what has a man got to do to go to the loo in his own house!'

I tell him that maybe we should forget the loo thing and that, actually, what I really wanted to say was that he deliberately negated what Edward was saying. 'John, first of all you tried to stop me from talking to Edward this morning about the fact that his father has materialized from nowhere –'

'No, I didn't. I was just suggesting that it may be better for Edward if we don't make a big deal out of it.'

'But it *is* a big deal! And now you've pretended that you didn't hear Jamie say "mama".'

'But I didn't hear Jamie say "mama".'

'Are you calling Edward a liar?'

'Oh God, Samantha, you're just being paranoid and over-sensitive. Did you hear Jamie say "mama"?'

'I heard it most clearly.'

John turns away from me. 'Well, maybe when your ex-husband finally makes it out of the bathroom, he can spend all day listening to Jamie and then he'll be able to tell me all about it when I get home today. After all, he has nothing else to do.'

'Ah, so this is what it's all about. You're cross about John.'

'I'm not cross about John. I've just woken up and realized that I'm not sure why he is in our house. I mean, don't you think it's a bit odd? When I'm at work and people say, "What are you doing tonight?" and I say, "Oh well, I'm going home to have dinner with my wife – oh sorry, the former vegetarian that I didn't know about – and her ex," don't you think they might just think it's odd?'

'I don't care what they think because it is our life and not theirs and, in case you've forgotten, last night it was you who invited John the First to stay, not me.'

'That's not the point!' John is now getting a little angry. 'It's the fact that it's pretty weird and disconcerting. Last night was sort of fine. It's not that I even have anything personal against the man, it's just that now, in the light of day, I think it isn't fine at all. I don't like having this man, this man who has known you since you were a kaftan-wearing hippy-girl, in our house. Surely even you can understand that?'

'Yes, that's all well and good, but how many times do I have to say this? I DIDN'T ASK HIM TO STAY! Anyway,' I say, playing devil's advocate, 'John does have some right to be here. He is Edward's father.'

'Yes, I know. And you're making a bloody song and dance about it.'

'No, I am not!'

'Oh yes, you are. You're doing all this "Oh poor Edward, having to re-meet his real father," but do you know something? He's not Edward's father. Where are the photos, then? You know, "John and Edward aged two". They're not bloody here because he wasn't bloody here! I'm the one who's been bloody here!'

'We discussed this, didn't we?' I say. 'Or was it just me having a one-sided conversation that went something along the lines of "Do you mind if John the First, father of my eldest son, wastrel, hopeless musician with mother dying up the road, comes to visit?" And did I then reply to myself, "Oh no. Of course you must not only ask him to visit but we must also let him stay because he's a sad self-obsessed bloke who needs a bit of love and affection." Who was it who said that or something like it?' I ask.

'I said it,' John admits.

'And now you are back-tracking, aren't you?'

John turns round and does something completely unexpected. He takes my face in his hands. 'I love you, Samantha,' he says as he goes to kiss me, 'but sometimes you can be very stupid.'

I am about to kiss him in reply, when I hear a yell from downstairs. It's Edward.

'Mum, come quick!' he yells. 'Jamie's fallen behind the sofa and can't get out.'

All I can see when I get downstairs is a pair of little legs. Jamie has somehow fallen backwards over the sofa and has got his head wedged between that and the heavy dresser next to it.

'Waaaa!' says Jamie.

'Jesus Christ!' I say.

'"e's stuck,' says Bennie.

'John!' I yell.

'Yes,' says a voice. It's John the First, now finally out of the bathroom.

'Where's John?' I yell at him.

'I'm here,' he says.

'Dad!' yells Edward.

'Yes,' says John the First.

'Not you!' I say. 'His other dad.'

'Why is Jamie down the back of the sofa?' says John the First.

'I pushed him,' says Bennie.

'You pushed him?' says John the First. 'That's not much fun for Jamie, is it?'

Edward starts giggling.

'Waaaa!' says Jamie as I start trying to heave the sofa to one side.

'Why did you push him?' asks John the First.

'Cos 'e's norty,' says Bennie.

'Because he's naughty!' says John the First. 'Well, your mother used to be naughty, very naughty but I never pushed her behind the sofa.'

Edward starts giggling even more.

'Shall I tell you about it?' asks John the First.

'Ooh yes,' says Edward. Bennie's eyes are round like soup plates.

'Oh hello, everybody,' I say, easing poor Jamie out of his hole. 'Look, here's poor injured Jamie that no one's interested in.' Jamie clings to me like a little marsupial.

'Erggh, blerp, ga,' he says sorrowfully. I go to get Jamie some hot milk while John the First settles down to tell his story.

'Well, one day . . .' I hear him say, and then he goes on to tell the story of how once, when we were on holiday, we were on a train and I had my headphones on and I was so carried away by the music that I forgot everyone else couldn't hear it and I let out an enormous . . .

'I broke wind!' I yell out from the kitchen.

'Mummy farted?' says Edward, utterly amazed. 'But Mummy says she never farts.'

'Well, she did then,' says John the First.

'Mummy dun a pump?' says Bennie.

'Oh yes,' says John the First.

'Thanks for that,' I say. Then I remember about John the Second. 'Where's John?'

'I'm here,' says John the First.

'Oh please don't start that up again,' I say. I go to the hall and look for Dougie's car. It's not there. 'John's gone!'

'For ever?' says John the First.

'Oh for God's sake,' I say. 'Did he say goodbye to anyone?'

'No,' says Edward. 'Daddy, can you tell me more stories about when Mummy was naughty?'

'Oh yes,' says John the First. 'Oh I've known your mother for a long time and the stories I could tell!'

I leave him and Edward and Bennie sitting on the sofa and go into the study with Jamie who is now quietly sucking on his bottle of milk. I call John the Second on his mobile. It rings and goes to answerphone. 'Hi, it's me,' I say. 'You and Dougie left without saying goodbye. Why did you do that? Why didn't you help me? Jamie was stuck behind the sofa! Didn't you know that? Ring me, please. I don't understand what's going on and I need to understand and I'm sorry I said John could stay and –' *Bleep!* The message cuts out.

Just then the telephone rings. It's my sister.

'What are you doing today?' she says. 'I thought I'd come round for coffee and . . . Oh hang on a minute, it's your playgroup charity morning today, isn't it?'

'Oh my God, the charity morning!' I say, suddenly remembering about Genevieve and her possibly gay husband.

'Didn't you tell me on Thursday that you were busy this weekend because that friend of yours – Genevieve, is it? – had arranged some Saturday-morning activity for the parents and children and that's why you can't go round and spy on Joe till tomorrow?'

'Oh God. I'd totally forgotten. There's too much going on here and John the First has arrived and –'

'John the First has arrived already?'

'Yes.'

'How do you know? Did he ring you?'

'No, *he's here!*'

'What, here as in the country?'

'No, *here as in my kitchen.*'

'But why?' My sister sounds astounded. 'Hasn't he come a bit early?'

'Yes. Apparently, the hospital rang him and told him to come as soon as possible.'

'Oh that's not good.'

'No. Then he went to Janet's house and he says he couldn't find the key so he said the only place he could think of to go was here and so, when we got back from hospital, he was cooking dinner with Dougie.'

'Your friend Dougie whose wife left him? I didn't know he could cook.'

'He's a marvellous cook. He always says that people think he's gay because he's a good cook.'

'Is he gay? Maybe that's why his marriage broke up.'

'No, he's not gay. He fancies our au pair.'

'Oh.'

Then Julia asks why I was at the hospital and I tell her

all about Bennie eating his poisonous plant and she makes lots of sympathetic noises. Then she asks when John the First is leaving to go and find Janet's door key. I tell her that, in a fit of generosity, John the Second has said he can stay with us temporarily, and my sister makes a tutting noise.

'Think about Edward,' she says. Then she sighs. 'Well, then you'd best get out of the house with Bennie and Jamie and let John and Edward do some bonding.'

'Yes,' I say miserably.

'Oh what's wrong with you? Why are you in such a bad mood? My husband's left me and I'm more cheerful than you!'

I tell her I'm just finding everything a bit tricky.

'You think your life is tricky? You should try mine. Now get out of the door and you'll feel better. I'm going to take Robert out to look for a car! Toodle loo!'

Just as she puts the phone down I realize that she is sounding suspiciously cheerful. Why is this? And why is she buying Robert a car? He's only fifteen. I call her back. The line is constantly engaged.

An hour later, I am in the car park outside the village hall. I have, rather reluctantly, left Edward with John the First. Edward was very affronted that I was taking Bennie and Jamie to playgroup and not him.

'Why can't I come?' he wailed.

'Because your father is here,' I said.

'I don't mind,' said John the First, picking up a newspaper. 'Why don't you all go to playgroup?'

'Why do you think? You haven't seen Edward in years. Why don't you take him to the park?'

'Me go park,' said Bennie.

'Bennie wants to go to the park,' said Edward. 'Why doesn't Bennie go with my daddy and I'll come with you?'

'Because Bennie is not your daddy's son, you are, so you are going to the park, Edward. And, anyway, why on earth do you want to go to playgroup? It's full of women and small children!'

'But you're taking Jamie and Bennie.'

'I am taking Jamie because he is a baby and Bennie is two, and there's no way I'm leaving your father to look after two small children.'

'I can look after small children perfectly well!' said John the First.

'John, stop being irritating and get off your bottom and take your son out and have some fun.'

'Fine. But, er, Sammie, I don't have any money.'

I gave him a twenty-pound note. 'Now look,' I said to him while Edward was off finding clothes, 'be nice to Edward.'

'Sammie, I told you, I've changed!'

'Well, prove it. Be nice to him and spoil him.'

'Right.' John the First then pulled me to him and kissed me on the top of my head.

'John! Watch it.' Then I remembered about Janet. 'Aren't you going to see your mother today?'

'Might do.' He turned away. 'But what about me, Sammie? I haven't seen you in years either and you're abandoning me.'

'I have to go to this playgroup thing because I promised my friend Genevieve I would and she's organized it.'

'It sounds dull.'

'It might sound dull, but it's raising money for an arts

193

and crafts facility in a small village in Nigeria. We're all paying five pounds and having a light lunch and it's a good thing to do.'

'It sounds even more dull. What kind of a man marries a woman who has a playgroup charity morning on a Saturday?'

'Her husband's name is Nicholas. He works for an oil company and he's off playing cricket this morning.'

'Oh God, he sounds far too conventional for me. The whole lot of them do.'

'Well, count your lucky stars you're not going. And tomorrow I have to go and spy on Uncle Joe because I promised my sister I would, and as for not seeing me, you promised you'd love me and cherish me and keep me safe and warm for ever and you didn't, so, really, that was the way you played it, John, not me.'

'Oh, Sammie, I'm really sorry, I – But why are you going to spy on Uncle Joe? That sounds much more like fun!'

So I told him all about Uncle Joe running off with an angel therapist and my sister wanting to know what he's up to.

'An angel therapist?'

'I'll tell you about it when I get home. I'm busy and I have to go right now, this minute.' Then I felt a bit bad. 'Look, I'll cook you dinner and we'll have a night in, the two of us.'

'Oh is John not coming home tonight?' asked John the First in a really irritatingly bright manner.

'Of course he's coming home. He lives here with me and his three children and you're very fortunate he's said you can stay here.' And I picked up Jamie and Bennie and left and then, halfway to playgroup, I had a blind panic.

What if John the First didn't take Edward anywhere, or forgot to feed him, or let him play in the street, or gave him alcohol? I remember once going out (oh once! Hooray!) when Edward was a baby and when I came home he had on an hours-old shitty nappy, he was stuck in his cot, which was where I had left him some hours previously, and John the First hadn't thought to give him lunch. The thought of this panicked me so much I had to pull over and call Santa.

'Santa, please go to my house and rescue Edward.'

Then I explained the problem in detail and she said, 'Blaady hell!' a lot and said she'd be over immediately.

On my way into this special lunchtime playgroup I notice that poor Jamie has a cold. He always seems to have a cold. He has constant slugs of snot trailing down from his nose towards his mouth. It's very unappealing. I asked my sister once why all babies have snotty noses and she said, 'It's because they drink too much milk, you know.'

'But all babies drink milk. What kind of baby doesn't drink milk? So there's nothing anyone can do about it?'

'There's lots you can do about it,' she said sternly. 'For example, all my children were raised on soya milk, apart from Robert because he only liked nanny-goat milk.'

'That sounds disgusting.'

'It may well do, but they've never had colds. I said that to Joe the other day. I said to him, "Have you noticed that our children never have colds?" and he said he had noticed and he thought it was amazing!'

I then told my sister she was a marvellous mother. In fact, a much better mother than me and that I bowed down to her soya/nanny-goat milk routine.

'You're making fun of me, aren't you?' she said suspiciously and rang off.

So I haven't taken Jamie off his milky diet. He spends his life pouring milk down his neck and I am sure it's not that good for him, for I have started to believe that if Jamie stopped drinking so much milk and, instead, ate a better range of food other than butternut squash, he might not have those slugs running down his face. I wouldn't mind the slugs, as such, but it makes him so unkissable. I see people rear back when they see him. 'Ooh look at your sweet baby,' they say, reaching out to tickle this adorable little bundle of blond hair, and then this little poppet pumpkin will turn his head to give them a kiss and – *yuk!* This horrible snotty face lurches towards them. Today I have lots of tissues with me. John always laughs at my tissues. He says I leave them everywhere as if they are little reminders of where I have been, as if I am worried that I may lose my way at some point. I tell him all parents carry tissues with them. I stuff them down the side pockets of the car, in the nappy bag, in my coat pockets, my jeans pockets, down the sides of sofas, on my bedside table, on his bedside table, in my handbag, and in some obscure place in each of the children's rooms.

But now I can wipe poor Jamie's nose. He hates having his nose wiped.

'Erggh, blerp, ga,' he says, looking very sorry for himself.

'Poor Jamie,' says a voice behind me. It is Eleanor. She has George and Jackson strapped into a double buggy, one on top and one below, like a New York garage stacking system.

'How are you?' I ask her, almost forgetting she is pregnant for George is still so young and the same age as Jamie and I couldn't imagine having another one so soon without dying of exhaustion and stress.

'I'm fine. I was wondering, do you know what we are doing today? I called Genevieve to see if this five pounds covered lunch for us or just for the kids but she sounded upset about something.'

'Oh,' I say nervously. God, I hope Eleanor doesn't register my nervousness. 'I wonder why Genevieve was upset?'

'Probably something to do with Nicholas,' says Eleanor airily. 'They're always arguing about something!'

'Oh dear.'

'Don't worry. It will blow over. It always does.'

Just then the front door of the village hall opens. It's Genevieve.

'Hey,' she yells. 'Come in. We've been waiting for you!'

When we get into the hall I find Margot there as well as Jo and Caroline.

'The usual crowd!' says Genevieve happily. She follows my glance as I look at what's on the table. 'It's wine! I've decided that, for my charity lunch, we should stop organizing things for the kids to do and have a wine-tasting instead! Here, I've got some wine and some snacks and some cake and juice for the kids and –' She suddenly stops speaking and notices that everyone is staring at the wine in shocked silence.

'I'm sorry,' says Margot. 'Did you just say that we should not organize the children but sit here and get drunk instead?'

'Oh no!' Genevieve laughs in a rather high-spirited fashion. 'I thought we could just chat and eat some of these crudités and dips; it's just that I've also brought some of the wines that Nicholas likes. He's very into wine, you see – well, we both are. He trained as a sommelier in a previous life and he suggested that we try them. He's told me all about them and I thought it might be fun to have like a wine-tasting really. You know, you don't have to swallow. You can spit if you like, if you, um, know what I mean.'

'Yes, I know what you mean!' says Jo a bit too over-enthusiastically. We all stare at her. Then we stare back at Genevieve.

'But isn't it a bit irresponsible to get drunk on a Saturday lunchtime in front of our children?' continues Margot, ignoring Jo's comment entirely.

'I'm not suggesting we should get drunk,' says Genevieve a bit more snappily. 'I just think it's a fun thing to do to brighten up a weekend. I mean, my husband's off playing cricket and we never do anything in this playgroup. We discuss the kids and that's it. We never talk about anything real and important.'

'I consider my children to be very real and very important,' says Margot somewhat primly.

'Oh I know that, Margot,' says Genevieve, 'but what about us? It's the weekend. Why don't we live a little?' There is a long pause. No one looks at anyone else. Genevieve tries again. 'I mean, why don't we do something for ourselves for once?' She looks beseechingly at everyone in the group. 'It's only meant to be a bit of fun. There's nothing criminal in that, is there? What do you think? Shall we give it a go?'

I catch Eleanor's eye and she gives me a funny look. I follow her into the kitchen as Genevieve sets about finding the corkscrew she has somewhere in the bottom of her bag.

'Do you think this is madness?' I say to Eleanor.

'No, but I am not sure why you are going along with it.'

'Because I think Genevieve needs to do this.'

'Why?' Eleanor is making herself some tea.

'Because she seems a little depressed to me. Does she seem depressed to you?'

'No. It's more like that she's gone temporarily insane.'

Back at the table, I set about cutting the rich, dark, home-made chocolate cake Margot has brought in. Margot notices that Eleanor is drinking tea. 'If you hadn't got pregnant again so quickly,' she motions towards Eleanor's steaming mug, 'then you could've had wine with the rest of us.'

'Oh you're having wine, are you, Margot?' I ask her, pretending to be surprised.

'Yes, I am. I don't really approve but . . .' then she whispers loudly, 'if that's what Genevieve wants then I think we should indulge her.'

Just then Bennie comes up to me. 'Me want cake.'

'That's for the grown-ups,' says Margot.

'No, me want cake!' says Bennie a bit more loudly.

'Well, you can't have it. It's for the grown-ups and little children can't have that. It's not good for you. Why don't you have an apple or something?' She asks me if I've brought Bennie an apple. I tell her I haven't.

'ME WANT CAKE!' yells Bennie. I cut him a slice and give it to him. 'Tanks,' he says and wanders off.

'Really, Samantha,' says Margot. 'You cannot expect Bennie to be a disciplined boy if you don't back up rules and regulations.'

'I don't expect Bennie to be a disciplined boy. He's two, and he wants cake.'

'But he shouldn't have cake. It's not good for him.'

'It's not good for us either but that doesn't seem to stop us from eating it.'

'Well, would you give him wine, then?' Margot's eyes are glinting. 'I mean, we all drink that so why not let your children have it? That's what you're saying really, Samantha, isn't it?'

'No, I am not saying that, but yes, I would let Bennie drink wine.'

Margot then gives me a disparaging look and walks off to reposition herself next to Caroline.

As I sit there, watching Genevieve, I start wondering what today is all about. I think there's a lot about Genevieve I don't understand. I don't understand why she spends her life organizing things. When she and Nicholas have a dinner party, they don't just invite a few friends over for a relaxed meal, they invite only *certain* people and then Genevieve will work out a placement so that everyone has someone who shares their interests to talk to. It must take for ever! Then, after dinner, everyone will play parlour games which Nicholas will like to win. Genevieve gets pretty tense when someone else wins. Maybe Nicholas gets cross with her later. Sometimes I think Genevieve wants to cry when this happens because she understands the fragility of life. All this competitive socializing and stuff means nothing. She and Nicholas go camping and skiing and they are the *best* campers and the *best* skiers and, during their weekends, they are constantly walking everywhere super-fast with their girls dragging along. But maybe Genevieve knows that this apparently happy family she has made could all dissolve with one small word. Maybe Nicholas really is having an affair. He's never at home. He's always off on business. Maybe one day, as Genevieve is pummelling the dough for her muffins into nice round, neat, uniformed shapes or polishing those beautiful masks, he will lean over to her, casually almost, and tell her he is leaving. Then Genevieve will finish her muffins and pick Philippa up from school, and lord alone knows when she'd find the time to let herself cry.

Then again, sometimes I think I have Nicholas all wrong. Occasionally, I feel sorry for him because I think he is nervous of his children. I see him with them. He is like any parent who works too hard and spends too little time around his children. He doesn't really understand them. He doesn't see that they are that incredible combination of absolute innocence and utter manipulation. He horses around with them and pushes them in a faux-matey way but when it gets all too much and they fall over and cry, I see his face drop. Then, on hearing her children's combined wailing and crying, Genevieve will come running out of the house and say, 'Oh Nicholas!' and the little girls will run and sit on their mother's lap and shoot small looks of triumph at their father.

One day I found Nicholas in the cellar of their house. I had gone to look for some wine. I could hear Nicholas humming in the dark, which I thought was a bit strange, so I called out, 'Nicholas?' I turned on the light and there he was in the corner, fiddling with something. He jumped back and said, 'Dim the lights! Dim the lights!' and then he called me over to show me what he was doing. In his hand he had a mouse. It was small and brown and shiny.

'Why do you have a mouse, Nicholas?'

'The house is infested with mice!'

I asked him what he'd done to get rid of them.

'Well, I bought these humane traps. The mouse goes into the trap and gets stuck in there and then you take your trap and open it and release the mouse back into the wild rather than killing it.'

'Does that work?'

'No. I released the mice at the bottom of the garden but they kept coming back. I knew they were the same mice because I dabbed them with Genevieve's Chanel nail varnish.'

'Oh.'

'Then I had to think of something else, so I came up with Plan B.' He then showed me a small cage he had perched on a table next to him. He told me that he now puts the mouse into the cage and takes it on the train with him when he goes to work. 'I release it at the next station.'

'What? Don't any of the other passengers mind you carrying a squeaking mouse around and then releasing it under their feet?'

Nicholas looked thunderstruck. 'It never occurred to me to ask them!'

The wine is surprisingly good. The first one is a South African white.

'Right,' says Genevieve to everyone, 'Nicholas chose this one because he felt it's got this slight dryness, it's got a hint of oak and –' she puts the wine glass to her nose, swooshes it around and takes a deep breath – 'am I right in saying zestiness? Everyone try their wine.' We all try our wine as instructed. 'Does anyone else get a zesty sense from this wine?' Margot puts her hand up.

'It's not school, Margot,' I say.

Genevieve looks at me reproachfully. 'She's just joining in, Samantha.'

'I think it's got a bit of a lemon taste,' says Margot.

Genevieve nods. 'You see, something with this type of citrus acidity goes very well with dark chocolate. It offsets the sweetness of the chocolate but complements the darkness, the slight bitter quality that the chocolate also possesses.' We all take a bite of chocolate cake and a slurp of wine.

'Mmm,' says Jo, her mouth half full. 'This is yummy, Genevieve.'

Genevieve looks delighted. 'Now this one,' she says, 'is a Chardonnay.' I pull a face. I hate Chardonnay. 'Now don't be like that, Samantha. You're just being a snob.'

'No, I'm not. I just don't think they drink Chardonnay in Yoruba villages, do they?'

'No.' She gives me a look. 'But the point of today is to raise money, not stay within the traditions of the Yoruba tribes.'

Then she turns towards the group who are now all gathered round the small play table, sitting on little children's chairs. 'Now, Samantha is actually right to turn her nose up at Chardonnay because there are so many poor ones on the market but this one –' and she looks at the bottle and caresses it lovingly – 'is a pure Chardonnay made with grapes that grow in the Brescia region of northern Italy. Now try it and tell me what you think.' We all take another bite of cake and a slurp of the Chardonnay.

'What do you think of this one?' says Genevieve.

'I love it,' says Caroline, who has taken a massive gulp. 'It's not at all buttery. Goodness. I think it's even fruity!'

'That's exactly it!' says Genevieve happily. 'Everyone

thinks Chardonnay is buttery but this one is a light, fruity number. It's smooth, yes, but not insipid.'

And on it goes. We try a Sauvignon Blanc and a Riesling and we all get merrier and merrier and the noise level rises and I start feeling a bit light-headed. I go slurp, gulp, bite, gulp, slurp, bite and I keep trying to look for the children but I start seeing a bit wonkily. At one point I see two little Bennies come up and eat my cake, bite, and I think I gave him a slurp, gulp, of my wine because I remember hearing Margot say, 'Samantha!' but I probably just giggled in return. But then, into my slurping, gulping reverie, I hear Genevieve say, 'Now does anyone have anything they want to share with the group?'

For some reason I find this very funny and I start giggling. So does Caroline. Then Genevieve says, softly and bizarrely intuitively, 'Is there something you wanted to say, Samantha?'

'Yes,' I say. Everyone turns to look at me. I take a huge gulp of Chardonnay or Riesling or whatever it is. 'It's not a big deal. In fact, it's all very silly and I don't know why I didn't tell you before, it's just that it seemed so much easier not to because once I start going into the whole thing it makes life sort of more complicated yet simpler and . . . does anyone understand what I am saying?' They all shake their heads.

'You haven't told us what "it" actually is,' says Eleanor, who is now drinking herbal tea.

'Oh right.' I try to concentrate. 'Well, the thing is . . . John the Second is not Edward's father, which really doesn't matter because, in this day and age, who is anyone's father really? But what I am trying to say is that John the First has come to stay with us and it's freaking me out a bit, that's all.' Everyone stares at me.

'Let's unravel this a bit,' says Eleanor. 'Who is John the First?'

'Edward's real father,' I say.

'And were you married?'

'Yes.'

'And who left whom?'

'He sort of left me.'

'And how old was Edward when you split up?'

'Two.'

'And does he know John the First is his real father?'

'Yes.'

'Ah-ha!' says Genevieve, still sipping her wine. 'So what's the problem? Edward has a different dad that you never told us about. We don't care! We love you and we love Edward and Edward loves John and –'

'Which John?' says Eleanor.

'John the whatever,' says Genevieve, 'the one she lives with. We don't care who Edward's daddy is, do we?'

'Of course not,' says Margot, now drinking water. 'But, Genevieve, you've forgotten the main problem. Samantha said that this first John has come to stay.'

'Oh.' Genevieve looks glum. 'That's not good, is it?'

'No,' I say.

'Why has he come to stay?' asks Margot.

'His mother is very sick with cancer. She's at Prestwood General and he wants to see her and he wants to see Edward and me, I suppose. He says he's changed.'

'No one ever changes,' says Margot, 'and you shouldn't really let him stay. It was very childish of him to ask.'

'But they were married,' says Caroline.

'He is Edward's father,' says Eleanor.

'His mother's got cancer!' says Genevieve.

'Has she tried any naturopathic remedies?' says Jo. 'There's a book about it called *How to Beat Cancer the Natural Way* and my friend got cancer and she swears by this book.'

'Jo!' says Caroline. 'We're trying to help Samantha.'

'I was trying to help!' protests Jo.

'What does John – I mean, the John we know – feel about it?' asks Caroline.

'I don't think he's happy about it,' I say, 'but we're just going to have to cope with it.'

'Is he good-looking?' asks Jo.

'Who?' I say.

'Your ex-husband.'

'Yes.'

'Ooh, bring him along here!' says Jo. 'We could do with a bit of excitement!'

'Jo!' says Margot.

Then Genevieve says, 'Nicholas wrote me a two-page letter.'

'What was the letter about?' asks Margot.

'Sex,' says Genevieve. Suddenly, everyone else stops talking about my predicament and we all look at Genevieve. I look at Genevieve the most. She blushes. 'I mean, more about the lack of sex.' Oh no, I think. Of course they're not having any sex. He's gay! He has a young male lover!

Margot leans forward and takes Genevieve's hands in hers. 'You don't have to talk about this now,' she says gently.

'Yes, I do,' says Genevieve. 'I'm a bit drunk and, anyway, I want to talk about this now. You're all my friends, right?'

We all nod. I nod a lot. 'Well, then you won't mind me talking about it and maybe you can help me.' We all nod solemnly again.

'What I mean to say,' says Margot, now almost whispering, 'is I don't think we should be discussing this in front of the children!'

'Oh for God's sake!' says Genevieve. 'Look at them!' We all look at them. They are happily playing. 'You see? They are fine. I'm not going to go on about this but I just feel a bit low and I want to share this because it's about me and I don't seem to be sure about me any more. I am so busy with the children that no one asks me about myself or how I feel.' She stops to take a breath. We are all captivated now but I have a terrible sense of foreboding. I am almost willing her to stop. Our wine glasses stand untouched on the play table. 'We've all given Samantha advice, hopefully good advice, and now I need some,' she says, 'and I don't know who else to ask. OK? Is that OK?' We all nod, including Margot, but now I am feeling desperate.

'Right. The thing is –' Genevieve takes a deep breath – 'Nicholas and I don't really have much sex.' We all now look down nervously, bar Jo, who is staring at Genevieve intently. 'We used to, when we first met, but we've had the girls and Nicholas is always working and I'm always tired and we just, we just rarely do it or anything like it really.'

'Right,' says Margot, now putting a brave face on and trying not to seem embarrassed when she so obviously is, 'but when you say you never do it, how often do you mean?'

'Maybe once a month.'

Eleanor gets up to make some more tea. 'I'm going to think about this one in the kitchen.'

'Once a month,' says Margot, mulling it over. 'That's not really enough, is it?'

'Obviously not.' Genevieve is a bit tearful. 'I mean, it's worse really. Nicholas says all sorts of awful things in this letter. He says I'm a control freak who can never let go of my emotions! He says I'm more devoted to the children and my ashtanga yoga than I am to him.'

'Well, I think that's a bit rich,' says Margot.

'He says if the situation doesn't improve he'll . . . he'll leave me!'

'Oh that's ridiculous!' says Caroline. 'How can he give you such an ultimatum? That's cruel!'

We all nod enthusiastically in agreement – well, bar me. Poor Genevieve, there's nothing she can do, apart from have a sex change, I think. Then I wonder if I'm still a bit tipsy.

'Very cruel,' sobs Genevieve.

'Well, how often would he, in an ideal world, like to have sex?' asks Margot.

'He says every day.'

'Is Nicholas a sex maniac?' I ask.

'Yes,' says Caroline. 'He must be. No woman who has kids and a home to run and mouths to feed and schools to organize and pets to look after has any energy left for sex. To have sex you have to feel sexy. You have to feel desirable, not exhausted and covered in stretch marks.'

'Well, that's how I feel!' says Genevieve. 'I've never got my figure back!'

'But you're so slim,' says Margot.

'Like a boy,' I say.

'I don't feel slim like a boy. I feel fat and tired and now I'm so worried that Nicholas will leave me, I'm getting paranoid about everything.'

'Of course you are,' says Margot soothingly. 'But you are going to have to try. I mean I wasn't having much sex with my husband but I realized that, in order to show him I loved him, I had to get on with it. You know what men are like. If you don't give them sex, they'll find it elsewhere.'

'That's what I'm worried about.' Genevieve now begins to cry again. 'I'll hate him if he does that. I'll leave him!'

'He's not going to leave you,' says Caroline. 'It's not at all helpful to say that if you don't have sex with him, he'll find someone else who will. No, you must point out to him that he is not around enough. You can't have sex with him if he's not there!'

'That's true,' says Genevieve, sniffing a bit.

'In the meantime,' says Caroline, 'you have to try to make yourself feel sexy again.'

'But how am I going to do that?' wails Genevieve.

Suddenly, Jo leaps up and says, 'Viagra!'

We all look at her.

'That's for men,' I say.

'Oh no, it's not.' She looks triumphant. 'I wasn't having any sex with Wally because I just couldn't be bothered really and, to be honest, when he comes home after work looking like a clown it's hardly a turn-on, but then I saw an episode of *Sex and the City* and that older one in it – what's her name?'

'Samantha,' I say drily.

'Ooh yes, Samantha!' Jo giggles. 'Just like you! Anyway, she took a Viagra pill and was at it all night.'

'Yes, but that's a television programme. It's not real, you know.'

'Ah but I got some from the doctor,' says Jo. 'I pretended

it was for my husband and we took them and . . .' Her face colours.

'Good God!' Margot is shocked.

'It was amazing! We were at it all night. Honestly, we did things I hadn't even read about in books! And now we're so much better at it. My husband rushes home from work at night with his make-up already removed, just to see me. Before we discovered Viagra he was trying to tout for business all the time and if he wasn't doing that he was in the pub all night and lying to me about it, saying he was working!'

There is a crushing silence. Then Caroline says, 'Do you still take them now?'

'Oh yes! I've got tons of packets of them. I'd recommend it to anyone, really I would.'

'Would you give me some?' says Genevieve desperately.

'Of course! I'll give you a whole stash!'

Later on, as we leave, I can tell Genevieve feels embarrassed. She won't really look at me, or at anyone. She has the empty wine bottles in her bag and they are clanking together like a reminder of what she has just revealed. 'Was I horrible about Nicholas?' she says.

'No. You were nice about him but he's done something not very nice to you.'

'What do you mean?'

'You know, writing you that letter. That whole sex thing. It's not a very nice thing to do.'

'But he does do nice things.'

'I know.'

'He saves mice!' she says, smiling. 'He lets them out at Beaconsfield station.'

I tell her I know that as I saw him catch one once when I went to get wine from her cellar.

Genevieve looks at me a bit suspiciously. 'You know more about Nicholas than you let on, don't you, Samantha?' Then she walks off with Jessamy in tow.

I finally get Jamie's coat on – always nearly impossible as he clamps his arms down to his sides like a wooden soldier and it takes me an age to prise them away.

Eleanor is waiting for me in the car park. 'Wow! You've got a mysterious ex-husband and Genevieve's not having any sex. Fascinating!'

'I am sure it is.' I thank her for the coffee that has sobered me up or else I probably would have left playgroup without either of my children or, more likely, ended up going off with someone else's without meaning to.

'I mean, God, Jo takes Viagra! That's so scary!' continues Eleanor.

I tell Eleanor that I agree that Jo can be very scary. I tell her about the time I drove past a whole deer, dead on the road. It must have been hit by a car but I couldn't see any damage, only a little bit of blood trickling from its fine nose. I was with Edward. He couldn't stop looking at the deer. 'It's a male,' he said, as we slowed to pass it without running it over as there was no way I wanted my tyres to spoil its sleek coat and shining eyes. Edward then got very upset and spent the whole journey moaning about people who take the lives of one of God's creatures.

'It's in that song, Mummy,' he said.

'Which one?'

'You know, that one about the animals.'

'"All Things Bright and Beautiful"?'

'That's the one.' He then proceeded to sing it the whole way into town and back along the valley road until he saw Jo standing next to the deer with a huge hunting knife in her hand. I stopped the car and wound down the windows.

'What are you doing?' asked Edward.

'I'm skinning this deer and then I'm going to eviscerate it and take it to the gamekeeper,' she said.

'What does eviscer-whatsit mean?' Edward asked Jo as she cut into the deer, a neat, sharp incision just above its knee on its foreleg.

'It means to take its insides out,' said Jo. 'You can make this wonderfully potent healing skin cream from the fat of a deer's belly. Do you want to help, Edward?'

'Oh no,' he said, recoiling back into the car and looking queasy. As we drove off, Edward turned to me and said, 'Who is that lady? How does she know me?'

I told him she was Jo, as in natural-remedy-selling Jo, and that he'd met her when she came round to sell us echinacea.

'She's mad and scary,' said Edward.

'Too true,' says Eleanor now. 'Jo with a hunting knife and Viagra? That's very worrying.' Then, just as I am about to get into the car and leave, she adds, 'I don't want to sound scary myself but I was watching you, only because I'm a mad, pregnant, stressed-out mother of two. I saw your face. You looked so upset.'

'Oh well, I am upset. I'm upset for Genevieve.' I get into the car and turn the engine on.

'Look, I hate to ask this, but do you think Nicholas is having an affair?'

'I don't know.' I avoid looking at her directly. All I can

see in my rear-view mirror as I drive off down the road is her thoughtful face.

Half an hour later, I have manhandled a sleeping Bennie out of the car and laid him on the sofa and now, as I am spooning globs of butternut squash into waiting Jamie's little mouth, I hear a car pull up into the drive.

'Erggh, blerp, ga,' says Jamie as I leave off feeding him to run to the back door.

Then I hear laughing. Who's laughing? I see John the First come in through the back gate. He is grinning from ear to ear. This is odd. John the First never grins from ear to ear. Well, at least he never grinned from ear to ear when he was with me. Behind him comes Santa. She seems to be laughing about something. Behind her comes Edward, holding a large pack of pick-and-mix sweets. He is concentrating very hard on sucking something.

'Hi, everyone,' I say.

John the First doesn't respond. He just ruffles the top of my head and walks in through the door.

'Blaady hell!' says Santa happily, picking Bennie up for a cuddle. 'Bennie's got so heavy.' She puts him back down on the sofa in the sitting room. 'You should put him to bed, Samantha. He is so tired.'

'Yes, well, he had a late night last night. John arrived when we got back from hospital so . . .'

'You went to hospital! Why?'

I tell her what happened to Bennie.

'That is blaady awful.'

I then notice that Edward has come into the house and not yet spoken a word. 'Edward, are you OK?'

'Mmm,' he murmurs.

'He's got a bag of toffees,' says Santa. 'John gave them to him.'

'Have you all had a nice time?'

'We had a great time!' says Santa. 'We played crazy golf and John was so funny and Edward loved it and then we had an ice cream at the café and John told us all about his life and it was so fascinating.'

'Was it really?'

'Oh yes. He was telling us how he trekked across the States from one place to another because he'd been promised a gig and then, when he got there, the man who had booked him had died and the new manager didn't want him so he had to turn around and trek back again. Isn't that funny?'

'Hilarious.'

'Then he told us about how he once went to Colombia to learn to play merengue but the man who was supposed to be teaching him stole all his money and he had to work playing love songs in a bar to get home. Isn't that amazing? He is a real character. Is that how you call it, Samantha?'

I tell her that yes, 'character' probably is the best word for it.

Then she suddenly pulls in a breath. 'Not that I don't think your John is a good man. He is a wonderful man. I love him! It's just that . . . I think you should give this other John a chance.'

'A chance to do what, Santa?'

'To know Edward, to get involved with him, to be part of your family.'

'Well, in case you haven't noticed, that's exactly what I am doing.'

'Of course you are, Samantha!' she says happily, 'and

John is very grateful. He told me that. He is so sad about his mother and he so wants to make everything right with Edward.'

'Don't worry. I am sure everything will be fine.'

'Wonderful! Now, I have to go. Tell John goodbye and tell Bennie he is a monkey and I'll see you next week!' With that, she spins around and is gone.

I turn round to find that Jamie, now obviously bored of not being fed, has tipped the plate of butternut squash all over the floor. The dog is happily licking it up. 'Erggh, blerp, ga,' says Jamie, giggling and rubbing the remainder of the butternut squash into his hair.

'Oh goodness, Jamie. Now there's nothing left for your dinner.' Jamie starts crying. 'I'll find something for you.'

'He can have some of my pick and mix,' yells Edward from the sitting room. 'I think I've had too much. I feel sick.'

I tell him that if he's going to be sick, he has to be sick in the loo. I hear him get up and rush off. Then I hear shouting. 'The loo's locked!' he says. 'Dad's in it.'

Oh God. I grab a bowl and give it to Edward. 'Be sick into this,' I say and then I knock on the bathroom door. 'John! What are you doing?'

'What do you mean, what am I doing?'

'What are you doing?' I say impatiently. 'You've been in the loo for ages.'

'No, I haven't. I've been in here for about ten minutes. Can't a man go to the loo in peace and quiet?'

I tell him that no, a man can't go to the loo in peace and quiet when he's fed his child too many sweets and consequently that child is feeling sick.

'Get Eddie a bowl.'

'I have got him a bowl, but he needs to come into the loo.'

'For Christ's sake!' says John.

Then I hear just about everything happen all at once. I hear the lock slide back in the door. I hear Edward making heaving noises. I hear Bennie stirring and starting to cry. I hear a God-almighty crash from the kitchen followed by the biggest cry I have ever heard.

'WAAAAAA!'

I shoot into the kitchen to find Jamie and his high chair all crumpled and broken on the floor. 'Oh my God!' I whip Jamie up and hold him very tight and very close. 'This is not your day, Jamie, is it?' He is whimpering now, almost worse than the crying.

Edward, who has obviously finished retching, is standing at the door surveying the carnage. 'That chair's collapsed!' he says.

Even Bennie has been stunned into submission. He pokes his little white face round the door. 'Ow, ow, ow,' he says.

Then John appears. 'What on earth is wrong with this household? First Bennie eats a poisonous plant, then your baby gets stuck down the back of your sofa, then I find out your sister's husband has left and you are going to spy on him, and now your baby has destroyed his high chair and dislocated all his limbs in the process. Do I detect foul play? Black magic? Or are you just an overworked, in-attentive, clumsy mother who has taken on too much and can't cope?'

I tell John that he's not helping matters.

'I mean, I'm surprised men actually stay with women like you who have children. I've had Edward all day and we've had a great time. He's come back safe and sound whereas both your other children seem to have some latent death wish. And what's the difference between these children? Edward has spent all day with me while the other two have been with you.'

'Well, that is all wonderful and marvellous,' I say, 'and I'm glad you've had such a great day with your son but has it occurred to you that looking after your son for one day, along with the au pair, does not make you a child expert?'

'Ah but when children are with women,' he continues, 'they whinge and whine and hold on to their skirts. They say they're not going to do this and they're not going to do that yet you women all have to think you are right all the time!'

I tell him he hasn't the faintest idea what he is talking about and that I have better things to do than hang around here being lectured by an up-until-now-absent father about how badly women look after their children.

'You think I know nothing about children, don't you?'

'Yes.'

I am now trying to run Jamie a bath with one hand while, at the same time, not drop him in it. 'How can you possibly know about children, John? You've never been involved with any.'

'You wouldn't let me! You're just like your sister.'

'No, I am not.'

'Yes, you are. You're all "Oh let's have freedom of information, let's all be equal!" but the truth is, you rule this family. You decide who knows what about whom and who does this and who does that. You won't even let Jamie eat anything apart from butternut squash!'

I tell him that he's being ridiculous. 'I'd love for Jamie to eat something other than butternut squash. I've tried everything but . . . Why on earth am I explaining this to you? It's got nothing to do with you. Anyway, what's wrong with you? You're in a bad mood for someone who's just had a good day with your son.'

'I am not in a bad mood.'

'I know what it is. You're up to something! You always used to get in a bad mood when you were up to something.'

'I am not up to anything.' He is getting angry. 'You're just really annoying me now.'

'Oh sorry,' I say sarcastically, now balancing Jamie in the bath.

'Oh I'm not surprised I left you, and I'm not surprised Joe left Julia. You're both horrible.' And then he walks out of the bathroom and before I can send Edward to get him back, I hear the front door slam and he's gone.

Two hours later, everyone bar Edward is in bed. Edward has thrown up three times. 'Sweets!' said Bennie, staring into the loo.

Jamie has thrown up twice. 'Baked beans,' Edward said after inspecting Jamie's sick-spattered Babygro. 'Why did you give Jamie baked beans, Mum? You know he only likes butternut squash.'

I tried to explain that all the butternut squash was now in the dog but Edward wasn't listening. He is now curled up on the sofa watching *Star Wars*. His long, long legs are tucked underneath him. He looks pale and serious.

'Are you all right, Edward?'

'Mmm,' he says, not looking at me.

'I've just had to read Bennie seven books to get him to go to sleep!'

'Mmm.'

'And then he wanted milk and water and an apple. Honestly, his teeth are going to fall out, Edward, just like yours!'

'Yes.'

'Edward, are you listening to me?'

'Mmm.'

I get up and turn off the television. Edward rears up like a cobra about to bite.

'What have you done that for?' he says crossly. 'You are so mean, so so so mean. I was watching that!' He then buries his head under a cushion.

The Politics of Television

This is a tricky one. There are, as all mothers know, great benefits to the television and, in particular, a television-watching child. I will never forget when Edward first saw Teletubbies. *As soon as he spotted those strange round multicoloured creatures with televisions in their stomachs, he was hooked. 'Eh-oh,' they'd say. 'Eh-oh,' said Edward, bouncing up and down on his little bottom. It was quite a revelation to me to see him so entranced, so involved, so happy. I went out and bought every Teletubby video known to mankind. I bought him Tinky-Winky, Dipsy, La-La and Po cuddly toys. John the First disapproved greatly of all the* Teletubbies *watching but I pointed out it wasn't he who got up every morning at 5.30. So there Edward would sit, eh-ohing away while everything else fell apart around him. Eh-oh. Eh-oh. Teletubbies say, 'Bye bye.' In fact, when I think about the ending of my relationship with John the First, I think of many things: the empty wine bottles, the alcohol-fuelled arguments, the copious amounts of cigarettes we smoked, the screaming rows, the silences . . . but all these memories are punctuated by that one overwhelming sound. Maybe we eh-ohed ourselves into non-existence.*

But now it's all different. Now I am a proper grown-up with John the Second and two other children who don't wake up at 5.30 a.m. and therefore do not have to be force-fed television to get them to shut up. Edward still gets up stupidly early and is, without a doubt, a committed television addict. John the Second and myself have talked about this often. Some time after John the Second moved in, we all had THAT conversation.

> *Me: I think Edward watches too much television. What do you think, John the Second?*
>
> *John the Second: Oh I think it's fine. I did nothing but watch television at Edward's age.*
>
> *Edward: Yippee! Told you so, Mummy.*
>
> *Me, now looking very significantly at John the Second: What, at Edward's age?*
>
> *John the Second shifts around a bit from one foot to the other: Erm, no. Maybe I was older or, er, younger.*
>
> *Edward disappears outside and kicks a ball around.*

Since then, of course, we have circled round the issue with Edward like wary vultures, occasionally swooping in, picking at a bit of rotting flesh. Sometimes the discussions about the television-watching seem dead in the water, other times they feel never-ending. Some mornings, when it's 5.30 and we hear Edward creep down the stairs, we just can't be bothered to argue with him. Edward doesn't seem to mind watching Open University, which is the only thing on. When he's not watching that, he's gawping at Scooby Doo videos even though he knows he is not supposed to watch videos before 7 a.m. Once we went to Lyme Regis and, on the way there, I was trying to tell Edward how fossils are formed and he kept yawning and looking out of the window, and eventually I exploded at him and said, 'You don't listen to a word I say! I'm trying to tell you something interesting!'

Edward looked at me very patiently and then said, 'But I know how fossils are formed.' He then went on to explain, in great detail, about the earth's formation and peat and all those things that I've never really understood.

When I asked him how he knew this stuff, assuming he'd been taught it at school, he said, 'I saw it on early morning TV.' After that he told us about how and why volcanos erupt, how the Romans built straight roads and how zombies come into being. 'That last one,' he said sagely, 'is from Scooby Doo Goes to Zombie Island.'

'Right,' I said.

So here are my television-watching rules: Edward can watch it in the mornings because a) no one wants to get up with him, and b) it seems to be relatively educational. In the evenings, he should not watch any other television apart from The Simpsons or something an adult wants to watch. Be warned: Edward will watch television night and day if left to his own devices. It has corroded his heart. He will lie to babysitters, to Santa, to my mother, to anyone if it means he can watch one second's more television. It is all very weird.

Bennie, however, couldn't be less interested in television, which, again, has its plus points but also its definite downside. For example, when you need to make lunch for the two babies, which generally involves boiling and mushing and whirring things, there is no point in trying to distract Bennie from what you are doing by turning on the television. Bennie might pretend he wants to watch the television. He might yell 'Pat!' and 'Nornee', which is his word for Fireman Sam, and 'Beebies' for the CBeebies channel but, in reality, once he realizes you are busy and in the kitchen and thinking he is safely ensconced in the sitting room, he will get up to all sorts of mischief. These are the types of things he gets up to: drawing on the walls with Edward's felt-tip pens that he has found hidden under the chest of drawers; finding the stick that the dog has left under the sofa and proceeding to torment the dog with her own stick by poking her in the eyes; sneaking a yoghurt out of the fridge and smearing it over the sofa; weeing on the window sill; taking all the videos out of their boxes and trying to ram them into the DVD player; and, if Jamie is with him – for Jamie, strangely for one so young, loves the television, especially Harry Potter movies – deliberately switching it off so that Jamie cries inconsolably.

The only time Bennie actually likes to watch the television is when he is supposed to go to bed. He will then sit as if superglued to the sofa. He only budges if Edward makes the fundamental mistake of moving out of his seat, for Bennie covets Edward's seat. I see him watching Edward out of the corner of his eye. Edward always sits in the armchair next to the light, the window sill, the remote controls. Everyone loves that seat. Few get near it. In the mornings, when Edward has carted Bennie out of his cot, I hear them both running for that chair. Thud thud thud. Pad pad pad pad pad. Edward always wins. Bennie always cries. During the rest of the day, while Edward is at school, Bennie has first dibs on the chair but, of course, never goes near it. But as soon as Edward's home there's a lot of caterwauling to be done. But Bennie's no fool. He bides his time. As soon as Edward gets up, Wham! Bennie is in there like a shot.

He then refuses to move until I come and prise him off, kicking and screaming, and make him go to bed.

Some nights, usually Fridays when John works late, I can't be bothered to put anyone but the baby to bed. Jamie has no will power. At 6 p.m. on the dot, he starts yawning and conks out by 6.30. But Bennie, Edward and me stay up and have Friday Night Film Club. It used to be just Edward and me but now Bennie's joined. I cook salty and sweet mixed popcorn and make big bowls of cut-up fruit and we watch Lord of the Rings *and* The Incredibles *and* Harry Potter *until Bennie's little eyes glass over and he falls asleep like a fat milky puppy curled up half on my lap, half off.*

'Edward, we need to talk.'

'About what? I don't want to talk to you. You've just turned off *Star Wars* and it was the best bit!'

'Was it the bit when Luke Skywalker finds out that Darth Vader is his father?' I ask gently.

'No, it is not! It's the bit when Han Solo gets frozen. See? You don't know everything, do you?'

'I never said I did.'

'Yes, you did. When I asked you once if Burger King was open you said, "No, it's not open on a Sunday," and then I said, "How do you know that?" and you said, "Because I know everything," and then when we drove past it, Burger King was open!'

'Well, Edward, I don't know everything. For example, I don't know how you are feeling now.'

'Why are you always asking me how I feel?'

I sigh.

'When is Daddy coming home?' he asks.

'Which daddy?'

'The one who lives with us.'

I tell him I think John the Second is coming home in an hour.

'Can I stay up and see him?'

I tell him probably not but that John will come into his room and kiss him when he gets back. Then Edward looks at me terribly sadly. I go and sit next to him and put my arms around him. 'What's the matter, Edward? Is this all too much for you?'

'My brain hurts,' he says.

'Of course your brain hurts. This is all very difficult to take in. Your father shouldn't have just arrived without telling me. It was unfair of him to do that.'

'But I like him, Mummy. I like him calling me Eddie. We had real fun in the park. He made me laugh and he didn't shout at me like Daddy does.'

'That's because your daddy has to work and help with the little ones. Your real father doesn't have the same responsibilities.'

'Well, I like him not having those things that begin with r.'

'Responsibilities.'

'Yes, them. Does my genete-whatsit daddy make you laugh?'

'He used to.'

'Did you love him?'

'Yes, I did. But we just wanted different things.'

'You wanted me, didn't you, Mummy?' Edward snuggles into me.

'Always you,' I say, stroking his hair back from his face.

'But what if my genete-whatsit daddy wants me too?'

'Well, he's having a bit of you now and, if he comes

back to live in this country, you can see each other as much as you like.'

'But will Daddy mind?'

'No. He will understand.'

Then Edward thinks for a bit and says, 'I don't suppose you and my real father will ever live together again, will you?' and suddenly he looks so hopeful it makes me want to cry.

Oh Edward, I think, how can I explain this to you? How can I tell you that one afternoon of being a father is nothing compared to a lifetime? How can I show you what John the Second has done for you? How can I help you understand that his shouting and his occasional flare of temper is because he is a kind and loving family man who has too much on his plate sometimes?

But, before I can try to reply, Edward says, 'But why did my genete-whatsit daddy leave?'

'Because he wanted to go travelling and I wanted to stay at home because I thought it was better for you.'

'Oh no, not when I was little. I mean why did my genete-whatsit daddy leave just now?'

'I don't know.'

'Was it because you asked him to get off the loo?'

'I don't think it possibly can be.'

'Maybe he was late.'

'Late for what?'

'Late for dinner.'

I tell him that John the First couldn't be late for dinner because we'd arranged that I would cook him dinner.

'But he's having dinner with Santa, Mummy.'

'No, he's not, Edward. He barely knows Santa.'

'But he is! I heard them arrange it. He said to her, "What

are you doing tonight?" and she said, "Not blaady much," and he said, "Let's go out for dinner and then you can show me around." He said he didn't know the area very well and she said, "OK, then." I remember that, Mummy. You know how good I am at remembering what people say.'

This, it has to be said, is very true. Edward can't remember his homework or what his address is or even what his home telephone number is, but he is brilliant at remembering dialogue. He can recite, word for word and including actions, great long scenes from movies. He could probably act out the entire first *Star Wars* movie. It's quite remarkable.

'Does it matter that my genete-whatsit daddy's gone for dinner with Santa?'

'No. I'll cook the food for Daddy instead.'

And then I put him to bed with a strange heavy heart and wait for John, my John, to get home.

While I wait for John the Second I get out my old photo albums and look through them. Look, I say to myself, here's John the First and me at a party. John has his arms around me. I am smiling. And here's the first flat we lived in when we had just moved in with each other. I must have been about twenty-four, him maybe twenty-six. We both look so thin and young and tanned. Where had we been? Oh yes, I remember. Spain! We had a row in Ronda and I ran off and got lost in a crowd of flamenco dancers and I started to panic and then, out of the blue, John was in front of me and I felt such relief. I remember him laughing and everything seemed rather funny.

I turn the page. Oh and look, here we are again in

France. I do remember that holiday. That was the one when I got some terrible illness and had to go to the doctor who gave me every pill known to mankind and they knocked me out and that meant I couldn't take part in the great oyster challenge. We each had to eat twenty a day and see who chickened out first, and we were only on day two.

Here's a photo of Janet and me sitting on the lawn in the sun. That was the day John said he'd cook us lunch and then he produced nothing but potatoes. I thought it was so funny but Janet was cross. But now I'm feeling a bit weepy about Janet for Janet is going to die. Why hasn't John been to see her yet? He should have gone today. Oh but this is too depressing.

I look at another album. Oh! It's Edward's birth album. Here I am in labour. God, I look huge! Was I that huge? And here's Edward all scrunched up with that red Z on his forehead and his little white hands clasped together. Here's me holding him for the first time. I look so proud! And here I am breastfeeding him, and standing behind me is John the First and he's holding two packs of chicken and chips that I'd made him go and get late at night because I was so hungry! Oh look at John's face! He loved us then. He looks so happy, so proud, gazing so lovingly at the two of us. And I want to turn to him and show him this picture and say, 'Look. See.'

And then I think about how carefully John the Second trod when he came into our little unit and how the photos changed from just me and Edward to me and John the Second and Edward and suddenly I think it's all so unfair. I remember those first few months, after John the Second had moved in, and Edward would try to come into our bed. He had always slept with me, on and off, but now he was obsessed with it.

'I want to sleep with you,' he'd say. 'Please let me sleep with you!' John the Second would roll over to let him in and Edward would say, 'No, not with *you*!' and then try to kick John out.

It went on for what seemed like an age. Sometimes, John would get up and go and sleep in Edward's bed. Sometimes, he would just try to cope by teetering on the edge as Edward snuggled into my back. But everything changed when I got pregnant with Bennie. Edward was amazed, thrilled. In a way, anticipating Bennie's birth made him grow up. He'd say, 'Ooh, I can't sleep with you when the baby comes. I might wake him up!'

'But why do you think it's a boy?' I asked him.

'Oh of course it's a boy, Mummy. I've asked God for a little brother!' And, once we had Bennie and Edward had gazed for a long time at him, he said, 'Now we are a proper family, Mummy,' and he went and hugged John the Second and then the midwife took a photo of the four of us together. We are together, I think. We should be together, we should all be with our children. Then I think, 'Where the hell is John the First?'

As I am thinking about all of this and getting really rather tearful, John the Second finally comes home.

'Hello, darling,' he says, coming over to kiss me.

'He's not here.'

'Who isn't here?'

'John the First.' Then I ask him what the time is because I have no idea myself. 'I haven't put the dinner on yet. I could've been sat here for an hour or a day.'

228

'Ten thirty.'

'Why are you home so late?'

'I've had a horrible day.'

'Me too. Edward threw up three times, Jamie threw up twice and it all went everywhere and I had to clean it up.'

'Oh God.' John looks alarmed. 'Are the kids all right?'

'The kids are fine but I can confirm our suspicion that Jamie doesn't like baked beans.'

'But you know Jamie doesn't like baked beans. He only likes butternut squash. Why were you trying to feed him beans?'

I tell him all about the high chair collapsing and the piggy dog who ate up all the butternut squash from the floor leaving poor little Jamie with nothing to eat.

'The high chair collapsed? With Jamie in it?'

'Yes. But he's fine. He threw up only because of the beans.'

'But why didn't you call me? He could've been injured!'

'Well, he wasn't injured and if I hadn't made that mistake with the beans he would've been as right as rain.'

'Why didn't you make him more squash?'

'Because John the First said I was being too controlling.'

'What on earth has it got to do with John the First?'

I then ask John the Second if he thinks that I am, in fact, too controlling.

John takes me into his arms. 'No, darling. You are wonderful. Now what's brought this on?'

'I've been looking at photo albums.'

John sees them on the floor. He opens up Edward's birth one. 'Oh dear. Have you been getting a bit remorseful?'

'Not remorseful.'

'Sad?'

'A little bit.'

'Of course you're sad, Samantha. John was a big part of your life. He is Edward's father. Janet is his mother and she is dying. It's all very emotional. Didn't you expect this to be difficult, Samantha?'

I tell him that of course I knew it was going to be difficult but that I didn't expect to have to deal with it on my own and why did he walk out this morning in a bad mood?

'I called you and left a message and you didn't ring back,' I say.

'I'm sorry. I behaved like an idiot.'

'You're not the only one. I had to go to playgroup today so I left Edward with John the First.'

'Did it go OK?'

'Yes, it was all fine because I got Santa to come and help.'

'Oh thank God.'

'But John the First and I had a row and now he's gone off with Santa for dinner. He said me and my sister drive men away. He says we are control freaks who don't let men into the family. He says I wouldn't let Edward love him!'

'This is not true, Samantha.' John the Second is holding me close and smoothing my hair down and comforting me like he comforts Bennie when it's all too much for him.

I tell him that I think Edward is finding it difficult. I don't tell him exactly what Edward said but I give him the gist of the conversation.

'Oh dear,' he sighs. 'I thought this might happen.'

'I don't want our family ruined.' I start to cry. 'Maybe I shouldn't have let John come and visit!'

'You did what you thought was best, darling. John chose to let you go. He chose to have virtually no contact with Edward. It is not your fault and it's very kind of you to let him see Edward, so please stop worrying. But I do think it's a bit odd that John's gone off for dinner with Santa. What on earth is he playing at? Oh Samantha,' he says, stroking my hair, 'what a merry web we weave.'

12. Sunday

Sunday morning finds me, Dougie, Edward, Stanley, Bennie and Jamie all sitting in the car on a small nondescript road outside a nondescript house that may or may not be Uncle Joe's house in the small town of Flackwell Heath.

'Why are we here so early?' asks Dougie, yawning.

I tell him that the early bird catches the worm. 'Also Stanley's mother had to go to Stratford to oversee a training course so she had to drop Stanley off early.'

'Yes,' says Stanley, cleaning his glasses with a cloth. 'My glasses keep misting up. Why is that?'

'It's because it's cold at this time in the morning,' says Dougie, wrapping his coat tightly around him. 'And what are we supposed to find out?'

'My sister wants to know if this angel therapy woman is living with Joe.'

'Right. So we just sit and wait. Which house are we supposed to be looking at anyway?'

'She's not sure of the number,' I say, 'so we'll have to keep our eyes peeled.'

'I've brought my binoculars,' says Edward.

'So have I,' says Stanley.

'You got noclars?' says Bennie.

'Yes,' says Stanley, rubbing Bennie's head affectionately. 'I told my mum we were going aeroplane-watching because if I told her we were going spying I don't think she would have let me come.'

232

I tell Stanley he's getting surprisingly good at lying.

'Why wouldn't she like spying?' says Edward.

'I don't know. I told her your dad was a spy or a pirate or a gypsy and she didn't look very happy at all. She said, "I thought Edward's father was a set designer," but I told her that he's not really your dad. He isn't, is he?'

'Well,' says Edward, 'there's a daddy who lives with me and my genete-whatsit daddy who doesn't so I suppose they are both my daddies really and they're both called John, which is pretty handy actually.'

'Is Edward's genete-whatsit father a spy?' says Stanley.

'No. He's a musician.'

'A musician!' says Stanley. 'That's super cool.'

'And where is John the First this morning?' Dougie asks me.

'I don't know and I don't care. He picked a stupid fight with me last night and walked out, and I haven't seen him since. He's probably still in bed.'

'Where was he yesterday, then?'

'He and Santa took Edward to the park and then I said I would cook dinner for him because he had been complaining he'd hardly seen me, but he went out for dinner with Santa instead.'

'He went out for dinner with Santa?'

'Yes. John stormed out and then Edward told me he was meeting up with her.'

'Meeting up with Santa? Why?'

'I don't know. Anyway, they must have had a good time as I didn't hear John come in.'

'Maybe he didn't come in.' Dougie looks perturbed. 'Maybe he stayed out.'

I tell him that I am sure he didn't stay out and that the

reason I didn't hear him come in, which I am sure he did, was that I had finally found my earplugs so my sleep was blissfully undisturbed.

'Oh dear,' says Dougie.

Just then Edward, who has been scanning the street and all the houses and the driveways and the cars in the driveways, says, 'Look, there's a car just in front of us that is just like Uncle Joe's. It's got something written on the side. What is it?'

'Me see,' says Bennie, trying to grab Edward's binoculars.

'No!' shouts Edward, grabbing them out of Bennie's grasping hands and inadvertently bashing Jamie on the head.

'Waaaaa!' cries Jamie.

'Shh,' says Stanley.

The curtains in the house we think is Uncle Joe's start twitching. 'You've blown it now!' says Edward to Jamie.

'Waaa!' says Jamie.

'Quickly,' I say to Dougie, 'undo Jamie's straps and give him to me.' Dougie bundles Jamie over to me and I cuddle him until he calms down.

'Me see.' Bennie is trying to grab the binoculars again.

'No!' says Edward.

''es,' says Bennie, making a second lunge. Edward parries the move and Bennie falls to the floor. 'Arrggh!'

'Shut up!' says Edward.

'You have to share,' I say, now trying to reach Bennie's head to comfort him while balancing Jamie on my lap.

'Me want noclars,' says Bennie sorrowfully from virtually under my seat.

'Let him have a go, Edward,' I say.

'No!' Edward swings away from me so that I can't reach the binoculars.

234

'Christ almighty!' says Dougie. 'I'm just going to get them off you, Edward.' And then, as he shifts position to lean towards the back of the car to grab Edward's binoculars, there is an almighty sound.

Beeeeeep!

'Dougie, you're leaning on the horn!'

'Arrggh,' says Bennie.

'Waaaa!' says Jamie.

'For God's sake!' says Edward.

The curtains twitch again.

'Shh,' says Stanley.

Suddenly, everyone is quiet and we sit, terrified of our discovery, in the car. The curtains stop twitching. We breathe a collective sigh of relief.

'Edward's mum,' says Stanley.

'Yes.'

'I've been looking at your sister's husband's car through my binoculars and I have worked out what's written on the side of it.'

'Ah well, Stanley, I'm not sure if –'

'It says "bastard". That's a rude word, isn't it? My mother told me I must never say that word so I must apologize for having said it.'

I tell Stanley that he's not to worry about saying the rude word because I certainly will not tell his mother he said it.

'I will,' says Edward, giggling. 'Is Uncle Joe a bastard?'

'No,' I say, 'he's just being a bit antagonistic to Auntie Julia.'

'What does antago-whatsit mean?'

'Well, it means he's sort of left her.'

'Hmm. That's not a nice thing to do, is it? Now she'll be lonely.'

I say that she will, no doubt, be lonely.

'Do her children mind? Does Robert mind?' Edward is very fond of Robert because, as he says, 'Robert plays cool computer games.'

'I am sure all her children do mind. But we're not going to talk to them about it, are we, Edward? Because that would be tactless.'

'Oh right. So when I see them I shouldn't say, "Oh I hear Uncle Joe has left you?"'

'No, Edward. We won't say that because that might upset them.'

'Why are we spying on him, then?'

I tell him that Auntie Julia wants me to talk to Uncle Joe and find out what's going on in his life.

'Right.' Then he thinks for a bit. 'I don't like Uncle Joe any more. I'm going to call him Evil Uncle Joe!'

Stanley starts giggling. 'Evil Uncle Joe. My mum won't like that. I'm not allowed to say words like evil.'

'You've just said it!' says Edward.

Forty minutes later, during which everyone has played endless games and Edward and Stanley have discussed the pros and cons of the word 'evil' in all its many contexts, we are all stuck on playing I-spy.

'I spy with my little eye, something beginning with p!' says Edward.

'Erm, policeman,' says Dougie.

'Where?' says Edward.

'There isn't one,' says Dougie.

'I know, pavement,' says Stanley.

'No,' says Edward.

'Noclars,' says Bennie.

'No, Bennie, binoculars don't start with a p,' says Stanley.

'Why does he say "noclars" to everything?' Edward asks me.

'Because he doesn't really know any words. He doesn't know his alphabet.'

'Talking of binoculars,' says Dougie, 'has anyone seen what's going on at Uncle Joe's house?'

There is a flurry of activity in the back of the car as Edward and Stanley grab their binoculars and focus them.

'Wow wee,' says Stanley. 'It's a lady!'

'Give me the binoculars, Edward!' I grab them and focus them and, sure enough, walking down the driveway and past Uncle Joe's car is a blonde lady.

'Give them here.' Dougie nicks them off me. He stares through them. 'Hmm, tall, blonde, thin, in her thirties maybe, pretty good-looking actually.'

'Is that her, do you think?'

'Yup. I'd say that was our angel therapist.'

I ask Dougie how on earth he knows that. After all, we still don't know for sure it is Uncle Joe's house.

'Does she have wings?' says Edward, bouncing up and down on the back seat.

'Me got noclars now?' says Bennie to Stanley as he hands his binoculars to him.

'Yes, Bennie,' says Stanley. 'Now it's your turn.'

'Ooo,' says Bennie, looking through them the wrong way.

'She's walking towards us,' says Dougie. 'Quick, act normally.'

'What's normal?' says Edward.

'Erm, pretend you're playing with Stanley, and I'll talk to your mother. Quick, Samantha, put Jamie up your jumper and act as if you're breastfeeding him so it looks as if that's why we have stopped.'

I grab Jamie and tuck him under my jumper and at first he seems very surprised but then starts protesting and beating his little fists against my tummy. 'Erggh, blerp, ga,' he says.

The blonde lady walks past the car. She looks in at us a bit and we all smile back at her and on she goes.

'I think she's pretty,' says Stanley.

'She doesn't have wings, though,' says Edward.

'Now what are we going to do?' says Dougie.

We debate this for a while and decide these are our options: a) we could wait in the car some more and see if Uncle Joe comes out, and, if he does, we could pretend we were just parked on his street, all six of us, in happenstance, because we were on our way to the supermarket but had to stop for me to feed Jamie.

'But I stopped feeding Jamie months ago!'

'Yes, but Uncle Joe doesn't know that,' says Dougie.

Option b is that we all get out of the car, knock on his door and, if Uncle Joe is there, go in for a coffee.

'He might not have coffee,' I say.

'Hmm,' says Dougie, 'maybe there are too many of us.'

'Maybe we should knock on his door and run away!' says Edward. 'That's a game, you know. Someone told me about it. It's called Knock On Charlie.'

'But what's the point of the game?' says Stanley.

'I think it's just to irritate someone,' says Edward. 'You know, they have to answer the door and there's no one there!'

'My mother says it's bad to irritate people.'

'Well, we're not going to irritate anyone,' I say.

'Can't we just go home?' says Edward.

'Well, that's option c,' I tell him. 'The give-up-and-go-home option.'

'I'm bored now,' says Edward. 'I really want to go home.'

'We still haven't caught a wasp,' says Stanley.

'That's true. Mummy, please can we go and catch a wasp?'

I tell him that there's a slight problem. 'I promised Julia I'd talk to Joe for her. I just don't feel I can leave before I've done that.'

'Why don't you go and talk to him and we'll wait here?' says Dougie.

'But I'm so bored!' says Edward.

'Why don't we all go to a café in town and come back for Mummy in half an hour?'

'Nooo,' groans Edward.

'There's hot chocolate and croissants at the café.' Dougie winks at me.

'Why are you winking?' asks Stanley.

'There's no hot chocolate, is there?' says Edward. 'You're lying, Dougie!'

'No, I'm not. I just can't guarantee it because I don't know which café is open. But all cafés have hot chocolate.'

'That's true.' Edward is now placated.

'So that's what we are doing, then,' says Dougie to me.

'Fine, but get everyone something to eat. Jamie must be starving and Bennie didn't have any breakfast.'

'Me take noclars?' says Bennie hopefully.

'Yes, Bennie,' I say. 'Of course you can take the noclars.'

I watch them all set off before I pluck up the courage to knock on Uncle Joe's door. I keep remembering what my sister said about him. 'You don't know what he's like,' she'd said on the telephone yesterday morning. 'He can be violent. Take someone with you.' Yes, well, I did take someone with me. I took Dougie and now he's taken my children off for hot chocolate because I forgot about Uncle Joe's terrible temper. This is ridiculous, I say to myself. That man has always been a pussy cat. He may be big. In fact, he's always been big – big and strong and strapping. I think he used to row at university. I remember Julia saying he was rather good at it. I bet that's why she liked him. He's sporty and blond and quite good-looking.

I stride up to the door and knock. Rat-a-tat-tat. Nothing happens. I knock again. Still nothing happens. I peer through the letter box. I see no signs of life. Maybe Uncle Joe doesn't live here. Maybe the blonde lady is not Suki the angel therapist at all but someone who innocently lives here. But the car! The bastard car! That's certainly Uncle Joe's, no mistaking that. So he must be here! Just as I am about to give up and run, in blessed relief, down the street and try to catch up Dougie and the kids, I hear a voice saying, 'Coming, coming.' It is the voice of Uncle Joe. Damn. I peer back through the letter box. God, he's wearing a bath robe. He's obviously been up all night having sex with bloody Suki and now he's having a bath.

Uncle Joe opens the door. 'Samantha!' he exclaims. He is obviously surprised. He looks at me. I look at him. He looks well – tall, blond, slimmer than usual, trendier haircut, no bags under his eyes, healthy-looking skin. This is not good. 'Samantha!' he says again. 'Where are your children?'

'My children?'

'Yes, the boys, where are they?'

'Oh they're with Dougie at the café in town.'

'Oh. Who's Dougie?'

I tell him that Dougie is Dougie, as in my best friend Dougie, as in Maxine's ex-husband.

'What's happened to Maxine?'

'She ran off with a twenty-six-year-old apprentice plumber.'

'Good on her. I always thought Dougie was a bit too serious and at least Maxine's found a man who's good with his hands!'

I'm beginning to not like Uncle Joe now. I thought he was a nice, kind man, not an oversexed idiot who walks out on his wife and children. I tell him that Dougie is, in fact, very upset but that I have obviously not come round to discuss Dougie.

'Oh yes, well, I'm sure you haven't.' Joe sounds contrite now. 'Sorry, come in. I'll get you a coffee.' The kitchen is a bit of a mess. There are empty champagne bottles everywhere and two open condom wrappers. 'Ah right, well,' says Joe when he sees I have seen them. He scoops them up, along with the wrapping of some expensive smoked salmon and some mackerel terrine, and puts it all in the bin.

'Well, at least you're being responsible,' I say.

'Yes, a bit of a night last night, I'm afraid.'

'I really didn't need to know that.'

While the coffee is being made, I snoop around the house. I establish from all the evidence that Uncle Joe is leading a bit of a bachelor lifestyle – no food in the fridge, only champagne, unmade bed with covers everywhere, denoting much activity in the night, bedside light toppled over, clothes scrumpled in a heap on the floor, dirty bathroom with unwashed towels, shoes kicked down the stairs, nothing unpacked from the removal boxes. I deduce that Suki is probably not living with Joe yet but there are tiny pieces of evidence to show she exists. There's some girly shampoo in the shower, the type women buy directly from the hairdresser for vast amounts of money. There's a female's thong tossed over the back of a chair. A thong! Best not tell my sister that. And there's a *Marie Claire* lying open on the table in the sitting room.

Over coffee I ask Joe if he knows why I am here.

'Yes. Julia sent you.'

'I have come to plead, on Julia's behalf, for you to go home. She wants you home, Joe.'

'I'm not going home, Samantha. You must tell her that.'

I tell him that he has to think very long and hard about what he wants to do. 'You have responsibilities, Joe. You have six children. You can't expect my sister to look after them single-handedly with no money and no job prospects until she finishes her degree.'

Joe says that he doesn't expect her to live off no money and with no job prospects and that he is quite happy to give her money and pay for an au pair.

'That's not the point! She needs you and she loves you and you can't possibly throw away sixteen years of marriage without giving it a chance.'

But he tells me he has given it a chance. He says they haven't really got on for years. He says Julia never really liked the things he likes. She doesn't drink champagne and he loves it. She likes animals and he doesn't. He only wanted three children and she refused to stop. 'And I've met Suki. Suki is . . .' and he gives a secret little smile.

'Well, I can see what Suki is!'

'No, you don't understand. Samantha, I want you to hear me out. I want you to promise me that you won't butt in or say anything until I've finished. There is something you have to understand.'

I tell him I shall try very hard.

'People get married for many reasons. There are couples who marry when they are not in love. They think they are in love but they are not. It usually happens when a woman wants children. She picks a man who she thinks will be a good father, who will earn money, who will look after her and be a good provider. But what she doesn't do is work out whether or not she genuinely loves the man she has married. Do you know how that makes that man feel?'

'Dreadful?'

'No. He doesn't notice it until someone else comes along whom he falls in love with and she falls in love with him. And then he feels . . . well, he feels amazing. He promises himself that he will do anything to be with this woman. He looks back at his past life and sees the compromises he has made and he thinks, "No! I shall not do that any more for I have only one life and to have lived that life as a moral man but a man who has never known the passion of love, that is no life at all."'

For a while we both sit in silence, staring into our coffee cups. I tell Joe that that's the most I've heard him speak in years.

'Is it shocking to you that I feel this way?'

'I'm not sure. I don't know if I agree with you. I bet my sister was just as exciting as Suki when you first met her and you didn't have children and a mortgage and all those other things.'

'No.' He is smiling now. 'Your sister was never like Suki.'

I point out to him that he is just in the throes of early passion, that everyone feels like that when they've met someone they click with. 'That's why they have affairs. Think about what will happen when the passion dies and then you'll have to face the fact that in pursuit of your own sexual satisfaction you ruined six children's lives and walked out on your wife. How are you going to feel about that, Joe?'

'I'm not giving Suki up.' Joe looks a bit threatening.

I'm getting a little tired of Joe now. I tell him I have to leave. I give it one final shot. 'Joe, listen to me. All that sex with Suki will fade. Everything fades. But your children won't fade. Julia's love for you won't fade. Think about it from their point of view. You've abandoned them and her.'

'No, I haven't. Your sister never loved me. Ask her about that.'

I tell him that she says she loves him and she wants him back and can't he just consider it for a while before doing anything drastic.

Joe suddenly swoops round the table and grabs my elbow very hard. 'You tell your bloody sister to leave me alone. Do you hear me? She's a nutcase. She scratched my car. Tell you that, did she? Did she?'

'Yes, she did tell me that. Now, Joe, please let go of my elbow. My children need me and they are waiting for me in the car.'

Joe softens his grip. 'I'm sorry.' He looks ashen. 'It's just . . . this is all very hard for me.'

'Yes,' I say drily. 'I can see.'

'No. I mean not seeing the children. Please ask Julia for

me! I'm begging you. Ask her to let me see the kids. Please, Samantha. You know I love them.'

I say I'll ask her but that I really must go now.

Uncle Joe walks me to the car. Edward sees him and pops his head out of the window. 'Hello, Uncle Joe,' he says brightly.

'Hello, Edward,' says Joe.

'We've been to a café and had two glasses of hot chocolate each.'

'Two!' I say.

'Bennie and Jamie knocked them over so Dougie bought us some more.'

'Me got noclars,' says Bennie, squeezing his head out from underneath Edward.

'Oh hello, Bennie,' says Uncle Joe. 'Why have you got binoculars?'

'Because,' says Edward, 'we've been spying on . . .'

'. . . people in the town for a project we are doing at school,' says Stanley, whose head has appeared out of the other rear window.

Joe's eyes narrow. 'Have you been spying on me, Edward?'

'No.' Edward looks hurt. 'How could you say such a thing, Uncle Joe?' Then he puts his head back into the interior of the car, swiftly followed by Bennie and Stanley.

'Sorry,' says Joe.

I just shrug my shoulders. 'Well, see you, then.'

Joe goes to kiss me but I turn away.

'Think about it,' I say.

'I will.'

In the car everyone is quiet. Dougie looks at me for a bit and says, eventually, 'How did it go?'

'Not great. I don't know. He's in denial.'

'Is he evil?' pipes up Edward in the background.

'Maybe a little,' I say.

'Oh that's cool,' says Stanley.

When we get home the house is quiet and cold. Dougie disappears. I make the children some lunch.

'John's bed's not been slept in,' says Dougie, coming back into the kitchen.

I sigh. I tell him that, right now, I have ceased to care. 'I have to call my sister and tell her what has happened. She'll be waiting, Dougie.'

'Are you going to phone Santa? You need to find out where John is.'

'Why do I? He's a grown man. I hope he's at the hospital seeing Janet. Maybe he came in last night and got up late and made the bed. Maybe he did sleep here after all.'

'Did he used to make the bed?' asks Dougie suspiciously. 'He doesn't look like the type of man who would ever make his bed.'

I tell him that actually John the First was surprisingly neat and tidy when it came to making his bed but that if he, Dougie, is really concerned then I could give him Santa's number and he could just ring and ask her. 'Wouldn't that be simpler?'

'I'm not going to do that!' says Dougie. 'Anyway, she's too young for me.'

'She's twenty-seven! You're jealous, aren't you?'

'No, I am not. You know I am still in love with Maxine!'

'Oh I give up on your love life. I don't know who is in love with whom any more.'

I go into the study to call my sister. I can see Edward and Stanley and Bennie back outside looking for wasps. Jamie has fallen asleep on the sofa. Julia picks up on the first ring.

'Did you see him?'

'How on earth did you know it was me on the phone?'

'I've got caller ID,' she says impatiently.

'How did you get that?'

'You just call up your telephone service and ask them for it.'

I ask her how she knew about caller ID considering that she is usually about eight million years behind everyone else when it comes to the technological revolution, bar our mother who still calls record players gramophones when no one even buys records any more.

'I'm not that bad,' says Julia. 'Robert showed me how to start the computer yesterday. It was fascinating.'

'But how did you get caller ID?' I ask again.

'Tessa the shepherdess showed me how to use it.'

'The shepherdess is called Tessa?'

'What's wrong with Tessa?'

'I thought a shepherdess would be called something far less middle class and more country-ish, such as Dorcas or Demelza. And how come she knows about telephones?'

'Her boyfriend works for BT.'

'The shepherdess has a boyfriend? You're joking!'

'No, I am not joking.' My sister then tells me that I am straying from the subject, which is that of her errant husband. 'Come on, Samantha, did you see him? Put me out of my misery please.'

So I tell her. I don't tell her everything. I don't tell her about the mystery slim, attractive, blonde lady who came out of Uncle Joe's house. I also don't tell her about the thong. I don't tell her about the love-speech thing. But I do tell her that he's drinking champagne and that he seems to be eating nothing other than smoked salmon and mackerel pâté.

'Has he lost weight?'

'Yes.'

'I knew it! He's not feeding himself properly. It's because he has no nourishment for his soul. That's what my book says.'

'What book are you reading now?'

'*Soul Food*. It's about how you have to nourish not only your body but your mind as well.'

'How on earth do you do that?'

'You have to eat raw food and beans and pulses and seeds, and you have to be happy and live a righteous life, and Joe is not doing that.'

'No, Joe is certainly not doing that!'

'What do you mean by "Joe is certainly not doing that"?'

'I just mean it's not very righteous to walk out on your wife and kids and set up as a champagne-swilling single man in a nearby town.'

'What do you mean by "champagne-swilling"? He's never even liked champagne.'

I tell her that he must like champagne now, judging from the number of empty bottles he has on the sideboard.

'What did he say about me?' Julia asks, now sounding really worried. 'Did you talk about me? Did you talk about Suki?'

'Yes.'

'Oh God, so there is a Suki!' she wails.

'Probably. But you knew that, didn't you?'

'I hoped it wasn't true. Oh God, he's having sex with her, isn't he?'

'I think he may well be.'

'Arrgghh!' Then there is a small silence.

'Julia, don't do anything crazy, will you? Don't just go round and scratch his car again or have a row. Just . . . just try to stay calm.'

'Samantha,' says Julia quietly, 'is Joe coming back?'

'No. He says he is not.'

There is an even longer silence.

Then she shouts, 'BASTARD!' and puts the phone down.

13. Sunday night

For most of the evening, I can't stop thinking about my lie-in tomorrow. All night, after Corporate Queen came to pick up Stanley and while Dougie and I talked and John the Second listened and we waited for John the First to come home, I have been thinking about it. I had to barter hard to get it.

'You were supposed to have a lie-in today!' said John the Second when I told him of my intentions.

'How could I have had a lie-in today? I had to go and spy on Uncle Joe!'

John the Second thought for a while and then he said, 'But that was your choice!'

'But what else was I to do? She's my sister!'

John the Second nodded some more and thought some more and, eventually, he said that he'd given the lie-in situation all due consideration and that he had decided, in fact, to give up his Monday lie-in for me. 'You deserve it. After all, what a week you've had.'

But soon after that, we had words. It started quite innocently when I asked him to put Bennie to bed and he gave me one of those 'God, can't you?' looks.

'What's the matter?'

'Nothing.' He pretended to flick through a newspaper.

'Don't you want to put Bennie to bed?'

'Quite happy to put Bennie to bed. It's just that I've been at work all day and I just want a bit of time to relax, have a glass of wine and take a look at the papers. Then I'll put Bennie to bed.'

'But Bennie's tired. We've been out all day spying on Uncle Joe and I think he really kind of needs to go to bed now.'

'Well,' said John evenly, 'if he needs to go to bed now, why don't you take him?'

I wanted to say, 'I don't want to bloody well take him because it's so difficult putting him to bed,' but I didn't. Instead I said, 'I thought you loved being with the kids.'

'I do love being with the kids.' John was sounding rather exasperated. 'I just want five minutes or so. Does five minutes matter really or have you decided that Bennie must go to bed right at this minute for reasons you cannot explain to me?'

'No, not that,' I said meekly. 'It's just that it's your turn, that's all.'

How to Put the Kids to Bed

Edward

Edward should not be that difficult to put to bed. He is eight. He should, of course, put himself to bed but he doesn't. This is because Edward has learnt the art of procrastination. This is what happens.

> Edward, who is sitting on the sofa glued to The Simpsons:
>   I'm hungry.
> Me: Why didn't you eat all of your dinner, then?
> Him: I didn't really like it.
> Me: It was lamb chops. You like lamb chops. You asked me
>   to cook you lamb chops and I did!

Him: There was too much meat on them.

Me: Of course there was meat on them. They're lamb chops!

Him: Well, I never want to eat them again.

Me: Don't be ridiculous. If you won't eat chops, what else am I supposed to cook you?

Him: Pasta and pesto.

Me: You can't live off pasta and pesto.

Him: Why not?

Me: Because it's full of carbohydrates and you should try to eat something from every food group each day.

Him: What do you mean, food group?

Me: You know – proteins, carbohydrates, dairy, that type of thing.

Him: OK, well, I'll have a glass of milk with it.

Me: And vitamins and minerals and fresh vegetables!

Him: Well, I'll have a raw carrot and some cucumber with it. Is that OK? (Edward then gets up, wanders into the kitchen and finds an apple.) Here I am, you see? I am eating an apple. An apple! Is that OK? Does that fit into a food group?

Me: Edward, you are now being simply ridiculous. And I know what you are doing.

Him: What am I doing?

Me: You are deliberately asking me stupid questions to avoid the fact that The Simpsons has finished and you don't want to go to bed.

Edward will continue to insist he is hungry and he'll go on and on about it until I say, 'Oh for God's sake, get yourself something to eat, then!' He will decide he wants an 'alien' bagel, as he calls it – he puts the entire bagel into the toaster and incinerates it and then eats it whole and unbuttered – and a fruit plate. Then he will sit like an immovable Buddha on the sofa, staring at the blank screen of the television and eating very, very slowly. If he wants to be really annoying, which is quite a lot of the time, he will take all the toy cars and fire engines Bennie has carefully left all queued up and ready to play with the next morning, and scatter them round the room. And on it goes.

When I finally get Edward up the stairs he will start worrying about whether he has any water, which means he has to go and check and, if he doesn't have any, he will have to go back down the stairs, rather laboriously and complaining a lot. Then he will insist I read him a chapter of his book and when I say that no I can't possibly because he is eight years old and is perfectly capable of reading to himself, and that Bennie is also waiting for me to read him a book and he is two and cannot read to himself, Edward will writhe around as if being bitten by a thousand snakes saying, 'It's not fair, it's not fair. You read to Bennie and you won't read to me!'

'Stop procrastinating,' I'll say to Edward.

'What does procrasto-whatsit mean?'

I'll then have to promise that I will read to Edward but only after I've put Bennie in his cot.

This means the whole bedtime process takes two hours. Two whole wasted hours.

Bennie

Bennie is the worst to put to bed. He never wants to go into the bath or clean his teeth or put his night nappy on or go up the stairs or have his pyjamas on or let Edward read him a story or let me read him a story or get into his cot or anything. To get round this problem, I have had to learn the art of cajoling. Let's say I have caught Bennie – not an easy feat but you can only try. Let's say I have lured little Bennie into taking the flower pot off his head by offering him pops. Let's say little Bennie is now happily sitting on the kitchen floor eating a ramekin of pine nuts and raisins, which he actually prefers to pops. What do I do now? I think of a way to entice him up the stairs. I say, 'Ooh look, Bennie. I've found another ramekin full of pops. Do you want these pops as well?'

Hopefully, Bennie will say, ''es!'

I will then say, 'But these pops are the pops that can only be eaten upstairs in your bed!'

Little Bennie will look very suspiciously at me now. 'In me bed?'

'Oh yes. Only in your bed. These pops are special bed-eating pops but if you don't go to your bedroom, they will disappear back to pop land known as the cupboard.'

'Pops be bye-bye pop land?'

'Absolutely!'

Bennie will then, hopefully, run lickety-split up the stairs and into his bed.

There are, however, problems with this plan. Problem number one is Edward. Here are the variations on what Edward may do to totally ruin my getting-Bennie-to-bed plan: a) Edward may well appear out of the bathroom incandescent with rage that Bennie has been allowed food before bedtime.

'Why aren't I allowed pops before bed?' Edward will say. 'You don't let me have anything! You are lovely to Bennie and horrible to me!'

Bennie, who will now be convinced that Edward means to steal his pops, will grab the bowl and then run under the desk in my study and refuse to come out, and the whole cajoling thing will have to start all over again.

Or b) Edward may appear from the bathroom in the middle of brushing his teeth and then fly into a moral outrage about

Bennie having pops because he hasn't brushed his teeth and he, Edward, has had to.

'You can't have pops before bedtime!' he will rage at Bennie. 'You haven't cleaned your teeth!'

He will then accuse me of favouritism and Bennie, who will now be convinced once again that Edward is going to try to steal his pops, will zoom back into the study.

Here are the other things that might startle Bennie into not going to bed: the telephone may ring, the doorbell may go, his father may come home just in the very nanosecond I am getting Bennie up the stairs, Santa may come to babysit, the cat might be on the stairs (Bennie is afraid of the cat because the cat is an evil misanthrope who scratches anyone who comes near him. 'Bad cat. Cat bad,' Bennie will say if he sees him), the dog may bark, Bennie may decide he wants no more pops.

But, generally, Bennie will now not go to bed unless Edward is going to bed. So I have to coax Bennie up the stairs while, at the same time, persuading Edward to come out of the bathroom and go upstairs too. But when Edward wants water, Bennie wants water. When Edward wants a story, Bennie wants three stories. When Edward wants me to go downstairs to read him a story, Bennie wants me to stay upstairs and lie with him until he goes to sleep. It's no good really. I got into the habit of nodding off on Edward's bed when he was tiny and it took me seven years to get him out of the habit. Seven years! I am not spending seven years lying with Bennie.

And then, when you have eventually got Bennie into his cot, he wants this tape on and that tape on, but not that one. Yesterday he liked a Postman Pat tape. Today you'll put it on for him and he'll say, 'No, not Pat! Pat's 'orrible. I hate Pat!' and then you have to go through the long and boring process of selecting a tape for him.

'Fireman Sam, *Bennie?*' *you say hopefully.*

'No, *'orrible,*' *says this little muffled voice from beneath the bedclothes.*

'Animals of Farthing Wood?'

'No, hate animals.'

'Noddy, *maybe?*'

''orrible.'

It can take an age. But if you lose your temper it's a disaster, as Bennie will start screaming and crying and then bang on the walls of his cot so hard he'll wake Jamie and then the whole house is awake and you are back where you started. No, you must take care when you bed down a little Bennie. You must find a tape that is acceptable. You must tuck him in surrounded by a bottle of water and a bottle of milk and his ramekin full of pops. You must put his night light on and kiss his little creamy forehead and then creep quietly down the stairs and read Edward a chapter of his book using your most quiet mouse-like of voices and then creep, creep, creep down the last set of stairs and pray to God that you don't hear Bennie's little voice piping up, 'Muummyy?' For if you do, all is lost. You have to start all over again.

Three hours lost, then, you see.

Jamie

Jamie, though, is easy to put to bed. You just pop him in the bath and then wrap him up in one of his baby towels that has little ears on it. You carry him upstairs and lay him down and massage his baby body with some oil and he wriggles and stretches out and coos, and then you put his nappy and his Babygro on and pop him into his cot. When you put him down, he sighs and rubs his eyes and gives you a smile, pops his thumb into his mouth and goes to sleep. You then don't see him for the next twelve hours. It's miraculous!

Mind you, Bennie used to be like that and now look. He spends half his life careering around with a plastic flower pot on his head.

Anyway, early last night it all blew up slightly over the Bennie issue and, in the end, Dougie offered to put Bennie in his bed and – surprise, surprise – it worked! Dougie carried Bennie up the stairs like a prince, all replete and happy with his big, fat, white belly. This left me and John downstairs with all things to discuss. I asked John why he thought Uncle Joe had left my sister.

'I don't know. It's all very strange.'

'Do you think it's because he's having a mid-life crisis?'

'I think everyone's having a mid-life crisis.'

Then, before we could get any further, Dougie re-appeared downstairs. 'Is there any chance of having something to eat?'

'Actually, are we having dinner?' said John the Second. 'I don't want to complain, Samantha, but I haven't had dinner for two nights in a row.'

'I have given up cooking. I've had a lot on my plate, in case everyone hasn't noticed.'

'Everyone's got a lot on their plates,' said Dougie, uncorking a bottle of wine. 'It's just that it's not food! Oh well, we shall have to drink instead.'

'Dougie,' I said, 'don't you think you're drinking a bit too much?'

'No.'

I then asked him and John why one of them couldn't make dinner.

'I've been at work!' said John the Second.

'I only want to get drunk,' said Dougie.

'Do you think we should make up his bed again?' John asked me, watching Dougie downing the wine.

I said I thought that yes, we better had.

'This house is like *Groundhog Day*,' said John. 'Right, Samantha's going to make some dinner and I'll make you up a bed, Dougie.'

'You sound as if you are up to something,' said Dougie, peering at John out of one eye.

'No, nothing, Dougie. I just think you should get a good night's sleep.'

'Everyone should get a good night's sleep.'

'I am sure we all will. Now what would you like to eat?'

'You're treating me like a child,' said Dougie.

'Yes, you are a bit, John,' I said. 'Dougie may be getting drunk but he's not stupid.'

'No, I'm not stupid,' said Dougie, drinking his swift third glass of wine. He then got off his chair and tried to hug John. 'Don't be cross with me. I've been spying through noclars all day and I'm a bit of a wreck.'

'Why are you a wreck?' asked John.

'Santa,' I mouthed at him.

'Maxine,' said Dougie. 'I still love her. Everyone still loves her and she's left me.'

'Well, I don't love her,' said John, motioning me to start heating up the baked beans, which were about the only quick-cook thing I could see in our entire kitchen.

'You don't love her?' said Dougie, now plonking himself back into his chair. 'Yes you do! Everyone does. Everyone keeps telling me so. They keep telling me what an idiot I was for letting her go over that window thing and now she won't come back because she's screwing that, that young person!' Dougie sank down onto the table, his head on his arms. 'Oh why, oh why, oh why!' he wailed. 'What can that, that, that plumber do for her? What? He's like a pixie, a fairy, a sprite. It's almost illegal! Almost paedophilia!'

'You're better off without her,' said John.

'I'm miserable without her!' Dougie reached for another glass of wine.

'Only because you want to be miserable.'

'Not true. I spent twenty years with her. Twenty. How long have you two been together?'

'About five.'

'Exactly! Five years is nothing. I knew everything about Maxine. I knew her weak spots. That's why she loved me, because I understood her.'

'She wouldn't give you children, Dougie!'

'I never wanted children. I said that the other night, John. It was a joint decision.'

'Well, I always thought it was a great pity. You know how much you love children. It was cruel and mean of her not to let you have any. You may have loved her, but if she'd really loved you she would've given you what you wanted.'

'Oh it's all right for you,' said Dougie, now sounding a bit fed up. 'You're the most fertile couple in the land. Oh we all know how much you two love children. How simply brilliant you are as parents!'

'Dougie!' I said, stirring some pesto into his beans.

'Oh it's true.' He downed more wine. 'Couldn't you see how you made Maxine feel? She'd come round here for a cup of tea and come back almost in tears. "She's the bloody perfect woman!" she'd say about you, Samantha. You and your permanently pregnant belly and your wonderful children and your bloody potato-print pictures on the walls and your playgroup friends. You made her feel sad and lonely and inferior.'

'That's bullshit, Dougie.' I stirred some parmesan into his beans for extra taste. 'I never spoke to Maxine about why she didn't have any children. It was she who kept going on about it and how they were like little aliens! It was she who banged on about how successful her career was and how stupid I must be for being at home with the kids more than working. And it wasn't me who bloody left you, Dougie. I'm still bloody here!' And I got so cross and upset that I tipped some dried chillies out from the jar I suddenly saw in front of me and added them to Dougie's beans.

'I'm just drunk,' said Dougie apologetically. He put his head in his hands. 'And I did want children, you know. I just never made a fuss. Why didn't I make a fuss? I was pussy-whipped. I'm so pathetic.'

I put Dougie's beans down in front of him. 'What are these?' He looked at them suspiciously.

'Baked beans, Dougie. I have added pesto to them to make them taste nice, even though you don't deserve them.'

'Sorry.' Dougie took one mouthful then he leapt up as if bitten by an adder. He covered his mouth with his hands. He was panting and sort of jogging on the spot. 'Fuck! Fuck!' He spat a mouthful of beans out into the sink and grabbed a glass of water. 'What did you put in them!' he demanded, staring at me with wild eyes.

'Chilli. You deserved it.'

'You can be a real bitch, you know, Samantha.' He then walked out with John following after.

*

So now, here we are, waiting for John the First to come home and, when he does, it is like having a stranger in our midst. He says, 'Sorry I haven't been around much,' and 'Is Edward still up?'

'Of course not,' I say. 'It's after midnight!' Then I tell him it doesn't matter he hasn't been around much although his absence has, of course, surprised me as I thought he wanted to have dinner with me the night before, but oh well, never mind.

'Oh well, never mind,' repeats John the First. 'I promised I'd take Santa out.'

'Yes, what is this thing with Santa?' asks John the Second.

'I like her. She's refreshing. I'm lonely. My mother is dying. And, in case no one else has noticed, she's also very sexy.'

Also very sexy. Suddenly, these words permeate through the fog of my brain. 'Sorry, what did you say? Did you say that Santa was very sexy?'

'Yes.'

John the Second can see where this is going. He reaches out to hold my arm. But there is no stopping me.

'I'm sorry, John, but I thought you said you'd changed.'

'I have changed. I have come back to make a commitment to you and Edward.'

'And what kind of commitment might that be?'

'Oh you know,' he says, nonchalantly helping himself to a glass of wine. 'See Edward, take him out, earn some money, give you some of it.'

'So it's commitment that has made you disappear all day with Santa, is it?'

'I'm sorry, but I don't understand what you are getting at.'

'Don't you see how inappropriate this is?'

'What do you mean?' He carelessly reaches for the wine again.

'This isn't a bloody bar.'

'What?'

'Anyway,' I say, 'what do you mean by "what do you mean"? This is not a difficult thing to understand. You have come over here to see your mother because she is in hospital. You've asked to stay with us because you are my ex-husband and Edward's father, whom he hasn't seen in years. And then, instead of coming in and eating humble pie and begging Edward's forgiveness for all the years you haven't seen him, sent him money or birthday presents or cards, let alone go and visit your poor mother, you go and get off with my au pair! It's sick! It's so bloody juvenile, the bloke who gets off with his wife's au pair. Can't you see that?'

'Ah but you're not my wife any more, so I can do exactly what I want to do. So, no, I don't think it's sick or juvenile. I think it's fun. And anyway, you're assuming I've "got off" with Santa, as you so eloquently put it. I may have but then again I may well not have, but whatever has happened, it's got nothing to do with you.'

'Nothing to do with me! In case you haven't remembered, I'm Edward's mother and anything that affects him has got something to do with me!'

'So, when are you going to let him off your apron strings, Sammie?'

'Oh you're just a selfish bastard. You're just trying to get at me because you feel guilty about nobbing Santa. I don't know why I expected any better from you. Everything's always been about you and what you want to do and where you want to go. You've never done anything to suit Edward. You've spent your life letting him down and now you're doing it again. Since when did you care about him more than yourself, John?'

'Listen, Sammie. Can't you see what's obvious? I don't love Eddie like you do. I never did and I never will.'

'That's very sad,' says John the Second, finally getting an opening in the conversation.

'Oh well, don't cry over your bloody precious wine,' says John the First, now turning to glare at John the Second. 'You've got Eddie now. Enjoy him. Be happy and let me get on with my life.'

Just then the telephone rings. None of us moves.

'Your phone has a habit of ringing at crisis points,' says John the First.

My sister! Oh God!

I pick up the receiver. All I can hear is silence and then something rather muffled. 'Who is this?' I now hear sniffing. 'Who is this?' I ask again. 'Julia, is that you? It's one in the morning. Julia? Please talk to me.'

And then I hear a small, Julia-like voice say, 'Joe's in hospital.'

'What? What do you mean, Joe's in hospital?' I can see that the Johns have stopped their conversation. 'What happened to him? Is he OK? What's going on?'

'He got stabbed in the arm and severed some artery and he's lost lots of blood and . . . it's pretty touch and go.'

'Oh God, Julia. Please don't tell me you had a row with him and stabbed him and now you're going to go to jail for manslaughter. Please don't tell me this. Please, Julia, please.'

'Oh no, it wasn't me! I didn't throw a plate at him and attack him.'

'How do you know someone threw a plate at him and attacked him?'

'I was there. I saw it!' She is very overexcited.

'You saw it? How can you have seen it?'

'Well, you have to promise not to be cross with me because I know you told me not to go round but I did because I was very upset after I spoke to you and I decided to go round to talk to him, or scratch "bastard" on the other side of his car or something like that if he wouldn't talk to me. Anyway, I was outside Joe's front door when I saw him come home and he looked so sad that I went to speak to him and, Samantha, do you know what he did? He just held me and told me he'd made a great mistake and, honestly, Samantha, I think he was crying! Yes, crying! I knew he'd miss me. I was about to tell him how much I'd missed him too but then I noticed he kept looking nervously around and then, suddenly, he broke away from me and said he had to go but he told me he loved me and would see me soon.'

'And then what happened?'

'Well, the next thing I knew, this blonde woman came running up the drive like a Fury. I mean, I was hiding behind a bush so she didn't see me, thank God, because I was so scared. Actually, Samantha, you never told me she was blonde.'

'You never asked.'

'Yes, but you didn't tell me deliberately, did you, because you know how nervous blondes make me feel?'

'Yes, that is precisely why I didn't tell you.'

'Anyway, this blonde woman was hammering on the door and then, when Joe opened it, she sort of flew at him and she was screaming at him really loudly and yelling, "I saw you! I saw you!" And poor Joe, my Joe, was trying to push her away and I could see he was looking for me because you know how kind and thoughtful he is. He really is a marvellous man and he was obviously very worried that Suki might see me and attack me! Then I crept away and got in the car and drove like a maniac back home and I was trembling, I can tell you, but as I got in the door the phone was ringing and it was the police and they asked me to go to the hospital because Joe wanted me there and then they told me what had happened. Suki attacked him! She must have seen him kiss me.'

'Kiss you?'

'Oh yes. Didn't I mention that? Anyway, I've just got back from hospital and I don't know if he's going to pull through and . . .' Julia is now crying and babbling at the same time. 'And I don't know what to do or who to turn to and then I thought of you. I thought, I know who'll know what to do – it's you! Oh Samantha, you must help me. You always know what to do. What should I do?'

I tell Julia that I am very confused. It's late and everything's all messed up and both the Johns are here.

'Hello, the Johns!' yells my sister loudly down the telephone.

'Hello, Julia!' they yell back in unison.

'How are you, the Johns?'

'Fine!'

'JULIA! Have you been drinking?'

'A little bit.'

Oh God, she'll be pissed on one glass. This is not good. 'You have to listen to me,' I say. 'You need to talk to the police and tell them what you know.'

'But I have. Oh it's such fun. I told them that I was there with Joe, you know, my husband Joe, and I told it to them just like that. I said, "Well, there I was with my husband having a chat and a kiss and then he asked me to leave and this mad, slim, blonde, attractive woman came and attacked him!" That's what I told them!'

'But you didn't exactly see her attack him, did you?'

'No, not exactly.'

'And isn't it a bit weird that you left and drove home, which would have taken you – what? Twenty minutes?'

'Actually, it took me ten. It's very fast at night because the roads were so clear and I was so messed up about what was going on and about all the kissing that I think I drove much faster than usual.'

' "The kissing"? I thought you said you had one kiss?'

'Is that important? How many kisses we had?'

'No. But really you are telling me that in those ten minutes Suki stabbed Joe with a broken plate after they'd had a row and then called an ambulance and the ambulance came and took him to the hospital and the police then called you to tell you he wanted to see you? All in ten minutes?'

'Yes. Weird, isn't it, how fast things move? Anyway, what should I do?'

'First, you must calm down. You are going to have to tell the children what's happened, so you must stay calm.'

'Right. I'll have another glass of wine. Maybe that will help.'

'Wine will not help.'

'But you drink wine.'

'Yes, but I'm used to it.' I then tell her that she must go to the hospital in the morning. 'This is your chance to win him back. You must visit him and feed him grapes and get it all back together again.'

'But I don't want to go to the hospital on my own. You

know I don't like hospitals. Everyone knows you end up getting more sick in hospital than you are when you go in so I don't trust them really and I think, actually, that Joe should discharge himself and come home and let me look after him instead.'

'Yes, but realistically speaking, a severed artery can't be treated at home, can it?'

'Hmm. I've got a herbal remedy book here somewhere. I know you think it's nonsense but that remedy you got from the health food shop worked for Edward's chicken-pox, didn't it?'

'Yes, it did.'

'Ah here it is. I've got the book in front of me and it says that the thing that helps blood clot is called natto. Have you heard of natto?'

'No.'

'Neither have I. Apparently, it's made of steamed soya beans. Oh yuck! Do you think steamed soya beans can help clot blood?'

'I have no idea. Look, Julia, I'll come to the hospital tomorrow to give you moral support, OK? Where is he?'

'Prestwood General.'

'Prestwood General? That's where Bennie went when he swallowed those berries.'

'Swallowed some berries? Now I bet the book has a remedy for that. Oh here it is! The book says you need to get some –'

'JULIA! I shall come to the hospital tomorrow morning. All right?'

'Right,' says Julia.

When I get off the telephone, I find that the two Johns are discussing the whole Julia/Uncle Joe scenario.

'Do you know Uncle Joe?' says John the Second to John the First.

'Of course I know Uncle Joe! I remember when Sammie's sister married him! I always thought it wouldn't work out. I said that, didn't I, Sammie? At the reception, I said, "She'll leave him, mark my words. He's too boring for her." And look what's happened!'

'Yes, but he left her,' says John the Second.

'Too true, too true. Banged to rights, guv'nor. I was wrong!' He starts laughing until I tell him that we are both going to the hospital the next morning.

'Oh right.'

'We can all go together – you, me and Edward – and I can visit Uncle Joe and your mother in one visit. That makes sense, doesn't it?'

'Right.'

'And you –' I look towards John the Second – 'can look after the children.'

'Right.'

I notice John the First seems uneasy. 'You do want to see your mother, don't you?'

'Oh yes.'

'Then why are you being so hesitant about it?'

'It's not about my mum, Sammie. I'm worried about your sister.'

'Of course you're worried about my sister. Her husband has been stabbed and she's taken to the bottle. We should all be worried about my sister.'

'No, it's not that. Look, have you thought about what your sister just told you?'

'No, obviously I haven't bloody well thought about it because she's only just bloody told me.'

'Hey, cool your boots. I was just thinking . . .' and then he hesitates.

'Yes?' I say impatiently.

'What if, erm . . . What if your sister is lying?'

'What do you mean? Why should my sister lie?'

'Well . . .' He now looks desperately at John the Second.

'I think what John is trying to say,' says John the Second smoothly, 'is that the timing is so strange, you know. Your sister apparently drives home in ten minutes and in those ten minutes somehow Suki does the stabbing and calls the ambulance and so on . . . Something somewhere doesn't add up.'

'Hang on a minute. Are you trying to tell me that it was Julia who stabbed Joe?'

'Well,' says John the Second, 'who else's word do we have? What if Julia came round and she and Joe didn't make up but had a row instead?'

'Yeah,' says John the First, 'your sister could have gone round to scratch "bastard" on the car and then Joe could've seen her and they could've had a row and she could've stabbed him!'

'What? My sister stabs her husband in the street? I don't think so!'

'Of course not,' says John the Second, 'but maybe your sister went round to chat and it got out of hand and she lost her temper and broke a plate and inadvertently cut Joe's arm with it and then, when she heard Suki at the door, ran out of the back and left.'

'Or what if Suki never came round at all!' says John the First. 'Your sister could have left and then telephoned for the ambulance from a phone box.'

'Oh right. So that's why the police are charging Suki with assault, then?'

'But are they charging Suki?' says John the Second. 'Is that what Julia said?'

'Not exactly, but I assume that the police will catch up with Suki and charge her eventually.'

'Yes, but you don't actually know that Suki stabbed Joe, do you?' says John the Second.

'No. I don't.'

'Exactly,' says John the First. 'Your sister has stabbed Joe!'

'We don't know that, John.'

'Oh yes, we do.'

'How?'

'Because it's obvious. Your sister is madly jealous and now she's going to prison for attempted murder!'

'John! That's enough! My sister has not stabbed anyone. She is a kind and thoughtful person and no one is putting her in prison!'

'Oh Samantha,' says John the Second kindly, coming towards me to hug me. 'She may just be a bit mad at the moment, darling. That's what love does to you when you get jealous.' He then looks at John the First in a meaningful way.

'Hey,' says John the First, throwing his hands in the air. 'I don't even know who's jealous of whom right here and now. I really don't.'

When we are in bed, I ask John, my John, what he meant by that comment. 'Who do you think is jealous of whom?'

He is tired and sleepy. His head is lolling a bit to one side. He has started to make a vague snoring noise. He does it all the time. It is half a grunt mixed in with a snore and a snort at the end. Tonight I try the gentle pushing method of waking him up.

'Oh Samantha,' he says, rolling towards me, 'I can't talk about this now.' His eyes are shut and he won't open them.

'Please tell me, John. I really want to know. What did you mean when you said about that jealousy thing?'

'Oh I can't even remember what I said. I am so tired, Samantha. Please can we talk about it in the morning?'

'No.' I push against his chest a bit more. 'I won't sleep. Really, I won't.'

John sighs. He hoiks himself up on one elbow and opens his eyes and looks at me. 'I think I mean that everyone is jealous of everyone else. It's human nature.'

'Well, who's jealous of whom in this household?'

'Well, maybe Dougie is jealous of our family life. Not in a horrible way but maybe a bit of a sad way. He's also jealous of John being with Santa.'

'Is John with Santa?'

'Yes, he is. Of course he is. And you don't like that because you are, in part, jealous of Santa.'

'Am I?'

'Yes, you are jealous of how she looks and you are very jealous of her and John.'

'No, I am not!'

'Oh but you are. You are cross because you wanted to have dinner with John last night and Santa has moved onto your patch.'

'And who are you jealous of?'

'Oh I'm jealous of your ex.'

'No, you're not! Please don't tell me that you'd rather have his life than your own. John, would you?'

'Oh Samantha, of course I wouldn't. Not in reality. Just bits of it, the fantasy freedom bits. Come on, Samantha, it's a game we all play. If I were free, would I . . .'

'Would you what? Have no children? Have no me?'

'No, darling, because I can see John's jealousy so clearly.'

'Oh what's that about?'

'It's about you.'

'Me?'

'Oh yes.' John is now stroking my hair and kissing my eyes. 'It is you, my sweet. He loved you then and he still does now and how could I blame him for you are a jewel, Samantha, a bright sparkling jewel, and once someone possesses you, they should never let you go and he did and the thought of that, the knowledge of that, is killing him. That's why he is here, to claim you back.'

'No, he's not. He's here because his mother is dying and now he wants to have sex with Santa. He may even have already had sex with Santa.'

'Well, I just think you should be aware of his intentions, that's all.'

'Oh he doesn't have intentions like that! And I have no interest in him, anyway. He's so tiresome and selfish.'

But now John is drifting off to sleep. He looks very handsome to me all of a sudden. I roll towards him and cuddle him. 'I do love you,' I say.

'I know,' he murmurs and then, almost into the night's air as sleep comes up and steals him away, he says in one breath, 'but your sister has gone quite mad, you know!' And then he's gone.

14. Monday

So today I want my lie-in very much but I am obviously not going to get it. Edward is in the bedroom doing a rain dance or something like it. He keeps hopping from foot to foot and clapping his hands above his head. It's all very weird.

'What are you doing, Edward?'

'Trying to wake you up!' he says, grinning at me.

'But why are you trying to wake me up?'

'We're going out with Daddy today!' says Edward happily. 'I'm not going to school. We're going to the hospital!'

'How do you know that?'

'Because Daddy told me! Daddy said, "We are going to the hospital today to see your grannie," and I said, "Hooray!"'

And then off Edward goes down the stairs. Thump. Thump. Thump. Thump.

'Hmm, I notice he calls my nemesis "Daddy",' says John the Second from under the sheets. I roll over and find him, naked as a baby, under the bedclothes.

'Don't worry about it,' I say, kissing him. 'John will be gone soon and you'll have Edward back again.'

'Don't know if I want him back again.' John untangles himself and presses up against me. He's all hot and slightly sweaty.

'Are you ill? You're very hot.'

'Hot for you,' he says, kissing my ear. 'Shall we make another Edward?'

'Oh God, not an Edward,' I giggle.

'How about another Bennie or Jamie, then?'

'John, I am going to hospital today to see a dying woman and a man who may or may not have been attacked by my sister.'

'Oh but you're not going now, are you?' He is running his hands up and down my thighs in a rather appealing fashion.

'Well, not exactly now,' I say, turning towards him and kissing him. I love kissing him. Sometimes it makes me want to swoon. But today his mouth is slightly stale. He smells of alcohol. 'You smell like a wino.'

'Oh that's not very sexy, is it?' He gently rolls on top of me.

'It'll do for now.' I caress his back and close my eyes. John has his hands under my bottom, pulling me up towards him. I open my eyes to look into his but all I can see, just over the top of his left shoulder, is the door opening and there, with blue eyes like saucers and watching us intently, is Bennie.

'Daddy, what you do?' he says, leaping onto our bed and smacking his father on the bottom. 'You all naked! Me naked too!'

It's true. Bennie has not a stitch on.

'Why have you got no clothes on, Bennie?'

'Me dun wee wee,' he says sorrowfully. 'Me all wet.'

'Well,' says John evenly, with his hand on my breast, 'why don't you go downstairs and ask Edward to run you a nice hot bath so you can get clean?'

'No. Me want Daddy come bath.'

'Bennie, Edward is perfectly capable of running you a bath.'

'Nooo!' wails Bennie. 'Daddy come!'

'We're going to have to give up on this, aren't we?' says John, kissing me lightly on my forehead.

I nod.

'Maybe later?'

I nod again. 'Tonight.'

Then I lie in bed and watch the sunlight throw patterns on the walls. I hear the familiar sounds of the house beneath me and around me. I can hear Dougie, who has now contrived to stay virtually the entire weekend, stirring in the spare room. He is moaning and groaning a bit. I bet his head hurts. I can hear Edward downstairs, chattering on to his father about everything and anything.

'I've put Dougie on the bad list today,' he's saying, 'because he made such a racket when he came to bed!'

'Right,' says John the First.

'But you're on the good list, Daddy, because you've got up to make me breakfast!'

'And what would you like for breakfast, my son?'

'An alien bagel!'

'Right!'

Goodness how things have changed. A few days ago, John the First would have no idea what an alien bagel was, but here he is making one for his son. I realize I like to hear them together. It's what I have always wanted, for Edward to be loved by his father.

Then I hear Bennie splashing in the bath.

'Five little ducks went out one day,' John the Second is

singing to him, 'over the hills and far away.' Bennie is squealing with delight. 'Mother duck went . . .'

'Quack, quack, quack, quack,' says Bennie.

'But only four little ducks came back.'

'Yaaay!' shrieks Bennie.

For some reason I feel content. This is my life. I have my three boys and my three men all loving me under this one roof. What woman wouldn't love this? I can hear Jamie playing in his cot. 'Ma-ma-ma,' he is saying to himself. I suddenly feel suffused with love.

But then I remember what John the Second said to me last night. Is he jealous of John the First? He shouldn't be. John the First always told me he could never find happiness, and that made me so sad. 'But Edward and I make you happy, don't we?' I'd say to him, but he would never reply.

That's the difference between the Johns. John the Second is happy with his family. He is happy with me. Nothing makes John the First happy. I then list all their differences in my head: John the First is good with money (oddly so for such a hopeless man); John the Second is atrocious with money. John the First is musical; John the Second can't even play the spoons. John the First is thin; John the Second is not thin. John the First is well travelled; John the Second has barely been abroad. But, and this is a big but, John the Second likes sex. John the First did not seem to like sex, or maybe it's that he didn't like sex with me. John the Second is not very argumentative and when we do have an argument it is over and done with very quickly. John the First is very argumentative and hangs on to moods for hours and days and yet even more hours and days. John the Second loves children, his children, all children. John the First hates all children. John the Second takes care of me. John the First left me. There. That says it all really.

Then I hear John the First trying to talk about *Star Wars* with Edward.

'I really think Darth Vader is an interesting character,' he is saying. 'You know, brought up by a good, well-meaning man who takes on the role of father but really his father is a much deeper, darker character who just needs time to learn to love his son.'

'I don't know what you mean,' says Edward.

I realize that the singing in the bathroom has stopped.

'Well,' continues John the First. 'Sometimes people have more than one father.'

'Oh I have two fathers,' says Edward happily. 'You – you're my genete-whatsit daddy – and Daddy, the daddy who lives with me.'

'But only one of us is really your father, Eddie, isn't that right?'

'Is it?' Edward now sounds puzzled.

I leap out of bed, grab a robe and tear downstairs. At the same time John the Second appears from the bathroom with Bennie wrapped up in a towel. I can see John's face. He is furious.

'John –'

He turns to me and says, almost under his breath, 'This has to stop. What do you think this is doing to Edward's head?'

'I don't know,' I hiss at him.

'Well, you should think about it.' Then he picks Bennie up and disappears into Bennie's bedroom.

I go into the kitchen.

'Time to get dressed, Edward,' I say.

'Oh why?'

'Because we are about to leave for the hospital.'

'Now?' says John the First.

'Yes, now!'

Once Edward is out of the room, I tell John we need to have a talk. I tell him he is being not just tactless but deliberately provocative and that I won't have it.

He holds his hands up. 'No, no, no.'

But I tell him he is to stop going on about who is Edward's real father. I tell him that John the Second has brought him up and that he, John the First, owes my John, John the Second, a huge debt and that he should actually thank him for being such a good father to Edward.

I am about to go on when Dougie walks into the kitchen. He looks terrible. His hair is sticking up, his skin is sallow and he smells.

'God, Dougie!' I say. 'You look terrible.'

'I feel terrible! I feel as if someone put chillies in my baked beans!'

John the First looks at me. 'Sammie, did you put chillies in Dougie's baked beans?'

'Yes, I did, but only because he was being drunk and annoying.'

'You can be such a cow sometimes,' he says.

'That's what I said,' says Dougie, 'but I used a different word!'

'What word did you use?' says Edward, who has now come back downstairs wearing a pair of ripped trousers that could not be more tatty if he rolled around in the mud and then hoisted them up on a flag pole.

'Oh, Edward,' I say. 'Why are you wearing those dreadful trousers? Grannie will think I don't dress you properly.'

'They're my lucky trousers,' wails Edward. 'My friend Stanley says they make me feel happy!'

'A pair of trousers makes you feel happy?' says John the First.

'You should try them on,' I say to him.

'Oh *touché*,' he says in return.

'Right, children,' says Dougie. 'Enough bickering. What time are you leaving for the hospital?'

I then realize that Dougie doesn't know about the stabbing of Uncle Joe.

'No!' he says when I tell him.

'That's not all,' butts in John the First. 'I think Julia did it herself!'

'Good God!' says Dougie.

'What?' says Edward, who was busying himself with the whiteboard but has now stopped. 'Auntie Julia has stabbed Uncle Joe?'

'No, of course not,' I say.

'Yes, she has!' says John the First.

'I'd better put her on the bad list, then,' says Edward.

So now we are all in the car, me, John the First and Edward, and on our way to the hospital. I have called Julia, who sounded even more upset than she did last night, to tell her we'll meet her in the reception.

'Reception? It's not a hotel, Samantha, you know. It's a hospital! I don't even know if they have such things as receptions!' She rang off.

I then managed to call my mother to tell her what was going on.

'I can barely hear you,' she said. 'This is a ship-to-shore phone.'

'I know that. Where are you, anyway?'

'I'm near Aswan. I'm having the most marvellous time!' She said that she knew what had gone on because she talked to Julia this morning. 'I told your sister I wasn't at all surprised it had come to this. I told her I knew it would be a disaster before she married him,' she said in the tone of voice that people use when they are talking to deaf people.

'Why didn't you tell her that then?'

'She didn't ask. I have to go now, we're coming into dock!' she said and rang off.

In the car Edward sits in the back playing some imaginary game which involves him pulling moronic faces and throwing a pretend hat up into the air. Jamie and Bennie are at home with John the Second and Dougie. They are all going to the pub for lunch.

'I wish I was going to the pub for lunch,' said John the First.

'Well, you're not,' I said. 'You are going to see your mother.'

He then pulled a face at me and put his hands over his eyes, which is the thing he always used to do when he was being particularly annoying.

As I pull into the car park, Edward sees Julia hanging around outside the entrance of the hospital. Robert is with her.

'There's Auntie Julia!' he says excitedly. 'There's Robert! Can I go and see them?' He then leans out of the window. 'Robert!' he yells. 'It's me, Edward. I've got the day off school!' Robert waves back in a rather embarrassed fashion. 'Hey!' continues Edward. 'I hear your dad's left you!' Robert looks away.

'Edward!' I say.

'What? Can I get out, Mummy, please?' I let him out and he runs off to join his aunt.

'God, he's tactless!' I say to John.

'A bit like you, then.'

I turn to look at him and am about to make some biting retort when I see he looks incredibly unhappy. 'John, what on earth is the matter?'

'I can't go in. I can't see her. I don't want to see her.'

'Why ever not? She's your mother. She needs you.'

'I can't explain, Sammie. I'm scared of her. We haven't been that close for years really and now . . . I fear what she is going to say to me.'

I can understand that. It takes me back to the time I had gone down to Devon to tell his mother that John the First and I had separated. Janet had invited the three of us to join her there for a week's holiday but John had left a month previously and I knew I had to go and tell her. She just looked out to sea as I recounted how John had packed his bags and left.

'He'll come back,' she said.

I told her I didn't think he would.

'But why didn't you make him stay?'

'I couldn't be his keeper. He wanted to go. What would have been the point in making him stay?'

'He probably wanted to stay, but you forced him out, didn't you?'

I could see that she was angry. I tried to stay calm. I told her that I had come to see her because she was Edward's grandmother. I told her that she could see Edward as much as she liked. She didn't respond and so we sat there, in the late summer, in her orchard full of heavy fruits. I remember the drone of the wasps.

And then Janet suddenly got so angry that she started shouting at me. 'John is your husband! Your place is by his side.'

I kept telling her that he didn't want me by his side, that he didn't want Edward by his side either, but she wouldn't hear of it.

'You should have made him stay with you,' she said again. 'You should have put him first.' Then she grabbed me by the arm and, with Edward trotting along behind me, walked me round to the front courtyard, showed me to my car and asked me to leave. 'I will write to you,' she said. And so she did and, over the years, Edward and I made those trips down to Devon every year, but it never felt the same after that really.

So I say to John now that yes, I think his mother probably can be very scary.

John takes my hand and squeezes it affectionately. 'But you'll look after me, won't you, Sammie?'

I tell him he's behaving like a little boy and that he should stop being so pathetic. He pretends to bat his eyelids at me. I ask him if he's told his mother that Edward and I are coming to visit her today. 'I don't want it to come as a shock.'

'No, I've told her, and she's so looking forward to seeing you and Edward.'

'And have you discussed John the Second with her, and the fact that I've got two other children?'

'Of course I have.'

'And what did she say? I mean, Edward and I have stayed with her in Devon when I've been pregnant and she's never said a word about it!'

John looks away. 'I don't think I'd better repeat it.'

'Oh great.'

John then looks at me and starts clasping my hand even harder. 'She believes in marriage for life. That's why she was so upset when we split up.'

'You mean, when you walked out?'

'You didn't give me a chance! And by the time I realized I had been a total idiot, you'd gone off with John.'

I remind him that I didn't actually go off with John. 'I didn't go off with anyone! I was on my own with Edward for ages. Not that you helped in any way whatsoever!'

'Can you not mention that to my mother?' says John rather nervously.

Just then there is a tap on the window. It's Julia.

'Are you two ever going to get out of the car?'

We get out and John the First goes rather awkwardly to shake Julia's hand but she reaches out and hugs him. He looks very embarrassed.

'Ah hello, Julia. Long time no see.'

She pulls back from him and looks him up and down. 'You look good, John. How are you? We haven't seen each other in years!'

'Oh I'm fine.'

'What are you doing here? Have you come to see Joe?'

'No.' John now looks a bit alarmed. 'I've come to see my mother.'

'Oh she's ill, is she?' says Julia brightly.

'JULIA!' I say. 'I told you this. John's mother is in the oncology department.'

'Oh right,' says Julia with one of her looks of concern on her face. 'Oh dear. That's very difficult, isn't it? Poor you.' Then she looks at John intently. 'May I ask what kind of, what kind of, you know, that thing beginning with c, your mother has?'

'Julia!' I say again.

'No, it's all right,' says John the First. 'It started in her ovaries and now it's spread throughout her body.'

'Started in her ovaries?' murmurs Julia. 'Spread throughout her body . . . Oh dear, that's not good. That sounds like an aggressive form of the . . . erm . . . of the c-thing.'

'His mother's got cancer, Mum,' says Robert. 'Why won't you just say cancer?'

'I'm a tad superstitious,' giggles Julia. 'I've always thought that superstitions are more than just folklore. I think they are things we learnt as children that lodge somewhere in our brains. For example, "don't walk under ladders" is an obvious one. Throwing salt over your left shoulder when you've spilt some is to do with the devil sitting on that shoulder, so that sort of makes sense. But that one about a black cat crossing your path? I've never really understood what that –'

'MUM!'

'Right, sorry. We must go our separate ways. Robert is desperate to see his father as, of course, am I.'

I agree to meet John the First in the oncology department after Edward and I have visited Uncle Joe.

So the four of us – me, Edward, Robert and my sister – head off to Ward G where Joe is staying.

'It is like staying somewhere, isn't it?' says Julia. 'It is sort of like a hotel! You're so clever, Samantha, calling it a hotel.'

'I didn't call it a hotel. I only said that we should meet in the reception.'

'Oh but that's what you meant! Anyway, if I think of it being like a hotel then I don't feel so nervous about it.'

I let her chat on as we walk down corridor after corridor. The two boys are playing I-spy.

'I spy with my little eye, something beginning with g,' says Robert.

'Glue?' says Edward.

Robert shakes his head.

'Gunge?' says Edward hopefully.

'Where's the gunge?'

'Oh everywhere. You know, like the gunge that comes out of people's legs when they have to be chopped off.'

'No, it's not gunge.'

'Is it, erm, is it great big hospital?'

'No,' Robert laughs. 'It's not great big hospital. Do you give up?'

'Yes.'

'It's a gurney!'

'What's a gurney?'

'Can you find Ward G?' I ask Edward.

Off Edward goes, like a bloodhound in full pursuit. 'To Ward G and beyond!' he yells.

'Is he like this every day?' says Robert.

'Now, Robert,' says my sister reproachfully. 'Edward is a lovely boy.'

And then Edward is back with his news. 'Ward G is just ahead on the right. And I've seen Uncle Joe. What on earth did you do to him, Auntie Julia? He looks terrible!'

In all truth, Uncle Joe doesn't look that terrible.

'He looks fine,' I whisper to Julia as she goes towards Joe with her arms out.

'Oh Joey, oh Joey,' she says. 'What has that woman done to you?'

Joe looks up and, seeing Julia, smiles weakly. 'Hello, my

pet,' he says to her, trying to hold his own arms out but failing dismally because he has a great big intravenous tube running into his arm. 'They're having to run the blood back into me,' he says.

'Hello, Uncle Joe – I mean, Joe,' I say somewhat warily.

'Hello, Samantha.'

Robert goes and gives his father a hug. Joe ruffles his hair.

'Robert does love it when his father ruffles his hair,' says Julia, beaming proudly at them.

'I hate it when my dad ruffles my hair,' says Edward.

'Which dad?' asks Julia.

'Either of them.'

And while Joe is hugging Robert and asking him all sorts of questions about school and homework and moped lessons and how all his sisters and brothers are, Julia has decided to quiz Edward about the two Johns. 'Now, Edward, a little birdy has told me your genetic father is staying with you for a while . . .'

'That's right. My genete-whatsit dad is staying with us.'

'And is that all fine?'

'Oh yes. But, Auntie Julia, what does that word, that genete-whatsit word mean?'

'It means the man who helped make you.'

'Wasn't that God?'

'No, it was John the First.'

'Oh right. But which little birdy told you he was staying with us? I didn't know birdies could talk. Mind you, when I was little I used to think there was a birdy tweeting in my wall because, at night, you could hear it and I told Mum but she said, "Don't be so ridiculous, Edward," but I wasn't being ridiculous because –'

'I told Auntie Julia your father was here,' I butt in.

'Now, Edward,' my sister continues, 'I was wondering how you feel about having your father to stay.'

'Oh I quite like it. He seems quite nice.'

'Right. So you don't feel any conflict?'

'What does conflict mean?' Edward looks confused.

'Well, it means, it means . . . well, it's quite complicated. What I meant was, it must be hard for you to know your daddy and so hard for your daddy to know you.'

'Julia,' I say warningly.

'I am just saying that daddies need to know their children.'

'Yes, but Edward's daddy chose to live several thousand miles away, in case you've forgotten.'

'I haven't forgotten. I just thought Edward might want to discuss it.'

'Discuss what?' says a voice. It is Uncle Joe. He and Robert are now listening to our conversation.

'We were just chatting about how important it is for boys to know their fathers,' says Julia, looking meaningfully at Joe.

'Were we?' I say.

'Yes, we were. I was asking Edward how he feels about the fact his father is staying with him. I mean, you haven't seen your father for years, have you, Edward?'

'I don't think so,' he says.

'And that's hard for a little boy,' says Julia. 'Children need to be with their parents. Both their parents.'

I point out to Julia that Edward has always had me and has also, in the last few years, had John the Second, so it is pretty rich to imply he hasn't been properly parented.

'Oh no, I wasn't saying that. I was just saying –' and

now she looks in the most exaggerated fashion from me to Joe and back again – 'that a caring father would never leave his family. Don't you agree, Samantha?'

I tell her that of course I agree. Julia seems satisfied. She kisses Joe on his cheek and announces she's desperate for a cup of tea and would the boys like to come with her and get a hot chocolate.

'I always get a hot chocolate when I go to visit Uncle Joe,' says Edward.

So here I am on my own with Uncle Joe and I'm really not sure what to say. He sits quietly looking at me with his head cocked. I look anywhere but at him. I shuffle my feet a bit and read the health notices on the wall all about how nurses should sterilize everything before they use it and where chemical waste must go and who is on which round.

'Oh it's Nurse Khan today,' I say in a pretend-jolly voice.

'Her name is Gita. The nurses like to be called by their first names, apart from Sister who likes to be called Sister.'

'Oh right.' Then we are silent again. I keep looking at the door, hoping that my sister and Robert and Edward are going to appear soon, with some chocolate for me to eat. The doors stay closed. 'But do you think Sister has a Christian name?' I ask Joe.

'I'm sure she has a first name. But I don't know what it is. She's a West Indian lady and pretty fearsome on the surface. The nurses are all scared of her but she's a honey underneath.'

'Right.' I am now willing the doors to open. Where is my bloody sister?

'You're wondering where Julia is, aren't you?' I nod. 'Oh she'll have met some poor, lonely, hopeless case in the

288

canteen and will be listening to their boring story and the boys will probably be going up and down in the lift. That's what usually happens around Julia, isn't it?'

'Gosh, Joe. You sound so weary of everything! I am quite taken aback.'

'I do feel weary, Samantha. I've nearly bled to death. Your sister has brought me more grapes than an army of men could consume and now she's giving me a hard time over Robert. You've just heard her do it.'

'But I thought you and Julia were sorting things out?'

'It'll take a lot more than an accident with a plate to sort this one out.'

'An accident? But Julia told me Suki stabbed you.'

'No,' he says, even more wearily. 'That's just something your sister has made up. Suki wasn't there. I was making dinner and I'd had too much champagne and I went to put the plate in the dishwasher but I slipped over and somehow the plate shattered and, as I fell onto the floor, a shard of it went into my arm. If you'd continued your day of spying, Samantha, you would've known that.'

'Well,' I say hotly, 'I can't spend all day spying on you! I've got three children and two husbands to think of. Let alone Dougie . . .'

'Yes, I can see you are busy. Well, thanks for coming.'

'I didn't mean it like that.' I now feel a bit dreadful. Poor Joe. 'It must hurt, your arm.' I motion towards the large bandage wrapped around his forearm. I can just see a dark patch of blood oozing out beneath the gauze.

'It does hurt a bit,' he admits, sinking back down on the pillows.

I shift up so that I can look at his face properly. 'Joe, why don't you go home? Julia will look after you. She'll find something in that alternative medicine book she has – essence of pussy willow or something – and rub it on your arm to make it better. She loves you, Joe, so do the kids.' Joe closes his eyes. I think he is going to cry. 'Oh Joe.' I suddenly remember that I've known this man for nearly half my life. He is Joe, the man my sister married sixteen years ago. He is not evil. He is not a wife batterer. He's just a poor, tired, sad man.

'I can't go back to her.' He is almost whispering, his eyes still closed. I can barely hear him so I bend forward and lean right over him. My hair falls from my face and brushes against his mouth.

'Why not?' I whisper to him, as low as a caress.

Joe suddenly snaps his eyes open. I rear back in fright but his uninjured hand is up out of his bedclothes and he is gripping my forearm, and he is surprisingly strong and I just cannot move. 'Because your sister is bloody mad, that's why!' he says in a low, threatening voice.

I pull my arm away and walk as fast as I can out through the door of Ward G.

After ten minutes of searching along endless corridors and wards full of ill people and their visitors, I find Julia. She is still in the canteen, which is ostensibly closed. The sign on the door says CLOSED. The canteen is empty. There is no one around to serve tea or biscuits or sandwiches and I am so desperate for something to eat and drink. My sister has an empty cup of tea on the table in front of her. She is sitting next to an old man who is blubbering into a handkerchief.

'Julia!' I hiss at her. 'You have to come now.'

'Oh hello, Samantha! I was just talking about you. I

WAS JUST TALKING ABOUT MY SISTER, WASN'T I, MR LUDMAN?' she shouts at the old man. 'He's a bit deaf,' she says to me, 'and very upset because his wife, Vera – VERA, WAS IT?' she shouts at him again and the old man nods, 'has just died. Just today in this very hospital! Isn't that sad?'

'Yes,' I say, motioning at her with my hand to come to the door, 'but Joe has gone mad and I think you'd better go and see him.'

'Oh no,' says my sister dreamily. 'Joe's not mad. MY HUSBAND'S NOT MAD,' she shouts at the old man and the old man shakes his head.

I suddenly wonder what on earth I am doing here. Why am I visiting my sister's husband who has nearly killed himself by accidentally cutting his artery open with a broken plate, if he did accidentally cut open his own artery? Why am I trying to have a conversation with my sister who is hell-bent on saving everyone else but herself? Why am I standing here in a state of extreme hunger and thirst while an old man I have never met before grieves the death of his wife?

'That's it,' I say to Julia. 'I'm going.'

'You can't go! I need you here.' The old man tugs at my sister's sleeve. 'I'M JUST TELLING MY SISTER I NEED HER HERE!' The old man looks at me and nods his head.

'Look, Julia, I have to go and see Janet. She is dying somewhere in this hospital and John is waiting for me there and Edward and I must go now.' But I can't see Edward. He is not here. 'Where is Edward?'

'I don't know. DO YOU KNOW WHERE THE BOYS WENT?' she asks the old man. He shakes his head.

'For God's sake, Julia. Why aren't you looking after them?'

'They're not small boys any more. They're nearly grown up.' The old man is tugging at her sleeve. 'I SAID THEY'RE NEARLY GROWN UP.'

The old man tugs again, more urgently. He is pointing behind me. I turn around to find Edward flying past me on a gurney.

'G is for gurney, Mummy!' he yells before crashing into a table and chairs. 'Oh hello,' he says, on spying the old man.

'THIS IS MR LUDMAN. HE'S JUST LOST HIS . . .'

'Get up, Edward,' I say. 'We've got to go and find your father.'

Robert then saunters into the room. 'Went a bit wrong, did it, Edward?'

'We're going,' I say to him.

'I'll call you later,' says my sister, waving at us. 'I SAID I'LL CALL HER LATER.'

'Poor Mr Ludman,' I say to Edward. Edward doesn't say anything.

'What are we looking for?' asks Edward, who has found a map of the hospital.

I tell him we need to go to the oncology department.

'Now, I remember I was in A and E and then I went up and left and . . . there it is!' I show Edward where we need to get to because Edward is good at directions, and as we go along – left here and right here, he says – I tell him about his grandmother. I tell him that when he was a little baby, his grandmother came to stay and she held him on her lap and rocked him to sleep and that, somewhere in all the boxes we have in our house, I have a photograph of him with his grandmother. I tell him how we used to go to her house in Devon on holiday sometimes and that we would sleep in a huge room called the pink room.

'Why was it called the pink room?' asks Edward.

'Because everything in it was pink: the bed, the carpet, the bedspread, the curtains, the en-suite bath and sink and loo and loo roll and soap and the very pretty, porcelain, pink soap holder that you broke, when you were one, by swooshing it off the side of the bath while I wasn't looking.'

'Oh dear,' giggles Edward. 'That was a bit clumsy of me.'

'Yes it was most clumsy and I had to give Janet twenty pounds to replace it.'

Then I tell him that his grandmother had made a cot up for him in the pink bedroom and that she'd dressed the antique heirloom cot in pink blankets, which I thought was a bit odd because Edward was obviously a boy. John the First told me it was because Janet never liked things not to match but I was so nervous of hefty baby Edward breaking the antique cot, as Janet had told me again and again how priceless it was and how emotionally attached she felt to it, that I put Edward in the bed with us and, in the morning, ruffled up all the pink blankets to pretend Edward had slept in the heirloom cot.

'And do you know what I found in that pink cot?'

'No,' he says, his eyes like saucers.

'The biggest spider I have ever seen!'

'No!'

'Oh yes. It was sleeping in your blankets!'

'Was it a girl spider?'

'I didn't check.'

But then I get more serious. 'Your grandmother may have only seen you once a year, Edward, but she's always sent cards and money for you on your birthday and at Christmas.'

Edward says he knows all that. 'I've always liked going on holiday to the grannie that's called Janet's house. I love that house near the sea. She has lots of pictures on her walls and lots of shells, doesn't she?'

'You're absolutely right. Lots of pictures and shells.'

'Didn't she have a picture of me as a baby on her mantelpiece?'

'Yes, she did. She put it up the last time we went to see her, which must be . . . nearly two years ago, Edward.'

'Where was Daddy?'

'Lord alone knows,' I sigh. 'Probably practising with the mariachi band in Mexico, for all I know.'

'No, not genete-whatsit daddy. Other daddy.'

'Oh he stayed at home to look after Bennie. Bennie was just a tiny baby then. In fact, I think I was pregnant with Jamie.'

'Why didn't Daddy come with Bennie?'

'Well, the grannie that's called Janet is not grandma to Bennie, only to you, so I don't suppose she'd have wanted Daddy and Bennie to come.'

'Doesn't she like Daddy?'

'She's never met Daddy.' I go on to tell him that his grandmother is very sick.

'Is she sick like Granddad was?'

I tell him that yes, it is pretty similar. 'This may be the last time you see her, Edward.'

Edward looks very sad. He takes my hand in his and I stop and crouch down and take him in my arms and hold him. 'Why do people die?' he says.

'I don't really know why, just that everybody dies in the end.'

'Are you going to die?'

'Yes, one day, I too will die.'

Edward starts crying. 'But I don't want you to die,' he sobs. 'I never want you to die.'

'Well, I don't want to die either, and guess what? I'm not dying for a long time and, by the time I do die, you will be reconciled to it.'

'What does recon-whatsit mean?' he sniffs. Then he says, 'Stanley had a goldfish that died. He flushed him down the loo.'

'Yes, I think that is what people do to goldfish when they die.'

'But that means that goldfish can't go to heaven, doesn't it?'

'I'm not sure if animals do go to heaven.'

'Of course they do! Auntie Julia gave me a book about it.'

'What kind of a book?'

'She told me not to tell you but it was after one of her cats died and I told her we had a cat and she gave me this book to read in case our cat died too.'

'And what did the book say?'

'I don't know!' Edward sounds exasperated. 'Honey hasn't died yet, has he?'

'Sometimes, you are very literal, Edward.'

We get to the swing doors of the oncology department. 'I found the way!' says Edward, now all happy again and seemingly forgetting about the death conversation. I look around for John but I can't see him. I can see so many other people. They all look dreadful, like phantoms.

'Where's Grannie?' says Edward loudly.

No one moves, though. They all lie still in their beds, those thin-framed beds.

I gave birth to Edward on one like that and then had to spend the night trying to get to sleep on it. God, that was a night! John the First had gone home and I was left with Edward in some plastic cot thing while I was supposed to 'rest' in the maternity ward. How on earth do you rest in a maternity ward? The babies cry all the time. The women groan. I groaned a lot. I had no idea how painful childbirth was. I assumed you popped the baby out and then had friends round for dinner. I had no idea that my private parts would end up looking like a battleground. The midwife insisted I looked at myself with a mirror. I couldn't believe what I saw. It was unrecognizable. It was swollen and painful and bloodied and scarred. It made me feel profoundly depressed. I refused to urinate for a week, it hurt so much. Consequently, I got ill. And that first night with Edward, I sat bolt upright staring at him because I couldn't get the bed to go horizontal and no one came to help me. It's all coming back to me, the birth of Edward, while I am surrounded by all these dying people.

Then I wonder where the lady I spoke to is. The one with the far-flung children. I stop a nurse. 'I know you're probably busy . . .'

'Yes, I am very busy,' she says curtly.

'But I wondered if you could tell me where the lady is who was in that bed over there?' I point to the bed six down on the left.

'Isn't that her?' says the nurse, squinting down the ward.

'No, I think that's a man.'

'Oh. Are you related to the woman who was in the bed?'

'No.'

'OK. So what was her name?'

'I don't know.'

'Do you have anything for me to go on?'

'She is old and her children live in Canada and Australia and she probably likes to talk about them a lot.'

'Hmm,' says the nurse.

'Is she dead?' I feel almost as if I am intruding now; after all, I barely knew the woman, but suddenly it seems very important.

'Not necessarily. We move people around a lot so she might be in another ward.' The nurse tells me she'll try to find out. I don't hold out much hope.

Just then I notice Edward peeking his face out from behind a screen further down the ward, on the right. 'She's here,' he mouths at me. Then John sticks his head out and gives me a nod. He looks pale and stressed. From birth to death, from death to birth . . .

Suddenly, I remember going to see my father when he was having one of his lengthy stays in a private hospital in London. It was like a hotel. He had a button he pressed and people came running out of doors and went hither and thither trying to find out what it was sir wanted today.

'Langoustine, I think,' he'd say, and off they'd go running down Marylebone Road and then – *Beep!* He'd press that buzzer again and they'd all come back.

'What, sir, what?'

'From Harrods,' he'd say. 'I only like langoustine from Harrods,' and then off they'd go again.

The only things they wouldn't get him were cigarettes

and booze. He'd ring me and plead. Couldn't I hide some vodka in my handbag? A whole bottle would barely stick out. OK, then, a half bottle. OK, then, a miniature. 'If you love me, my Samantha, you'll bring me vodka.'

'I'll bring you oranges,' I'd say.

'Why don't you inject the oranges with vodka?' he'd say, and then how sad and how angry he would be when he peeled back the skin on those ruby-red oranges and taste nothing but orange in their zest.

And this one time, the time I am thinking about now, he was eating his oranges but his hands shook so that I had to feed them to him like a baby, and Edward lay in his pram in the corner of the room and looked up at the water-sprinkling system. When it got very bad, just before my father died at home, he had to wear a sort of adult nappy and when he had fouled himself I would have to change him and he would become as distressed as Edward.

Janet is about to die. I can tell by her skin tone but I cannot say this as I am not sure if she knows. She is sitting up in her bed. She has obviously made an effort as she has combed her desperately thin hair forwards and has put on some bright red lipstick, and I really want to take the napkin she has tucked into her nightdress to stop the water she is trying to sip from running down her chest and making her wet, and dab the lipstick off her. It makes her look like a stick-thin, ancient geisha. I feel so sorry for her. She tries to smile when she sees me.

'Samantha,' she says. 'Samantha, you look –' She breaks off to cough. Spittle comes from her mouth. John leans forward and brushes it away with the napkin. 'You look so . . . so –'

'Different?' I am suddenly aware of how much bigger I am now than when I first met her.

'No,' she tries to laugh. 'So beautiful.'

'Oh thanks.' I feel immensely self-conscious.

'And Edward,' she says almost in a whisper as Edward perches on the side of the bed and puts his head in her lap, just like a puppy. 'He's grown into such a big lovely boy.'

'Oh thanks again,' I say.

'You're a polite boy, aren't you?' she asks Edward, who nods away happily. 'I remember you as a baby. You looked so like your father but now . . .' She looks at me. 'Oh now you're your mother's son. I can see that.' Then she starts coughing again and has to stop speaking.

'You've got a photograph of me as a baby on your mantelpiece,' says Edward in a dreamy fashion. 'I went to your house once near the sea and saw it.'

Janet is still coughing too hard to reply.

'I remember that photograph,' says John the First. 'You were wearing some dreadful green Babygro your mother bought you from Gap.'

'Yes, you were, Edward,' says Janet, now recovered and weakly laughing.

'Was I a nice baby?'

'No,' I say at the same time as John says, 'Yes.'

'You were a character,' says Janet. 'That's how I'd put it. I used to rock you to sleep at night when your mummy and daddy came to stay with me on holiday.'

'Then why haven't I seen you for ages?'

'Oh you will, Edward. I've been a bit ill so it's been difficult, but I promise that when I come out of hospital I will see you every month. Is that OK?'

'Oh yes. That would be good.'

But Janet is getting tired now. She asks John to go and get her more water. Then she chats on in her hoarse small voice, asking Edward what he's been up to and what he likes to do and what his bedroom is like. Then she tells him all about what John liked to do as a boy.

'Your father used to play golf,' she says. 'Golf! Can you imagine a little boy playing golf? But he used to go out with his mini-clubs and practise. He was very serious about it, you know.'

Edward laughs. 'Tell me more about my father.'

'Well, he loved music and he loved the sea. When you were a little baby, and we'd go to the house in Devon, you would come down to stay in the pink room and you'd sleep in my old antique cot and, in the morning, your father would put you on his back and take you walking for miles.'

'What else did Daddy do with me?'

But Janet is coughing very badly now.

'Edward,' I say, 'I think we'd better go.'

Janet motions with her hand that she'd like us to stay. I wait uncomfortably for the coughing to stop. 'No, please stay,' she says hoarsely.

'When are you going back to the house in Devon?' asks Edward.

'I am not sure,' says Janet.

'Will you go there when you're better? Can I come and stay with you there? But it's far away, isn't it?'

'Well, I don't live in that house all the time. I also live in a house quite near here.'

'But we live quite near here! We're only down the road!' Then he stops and thinks for a bit. 'But, Grannie, if you live so near, how come you never come to our house?'

Janet closes her eyes. 'I don't know why,' she says weakly.

'We live in a lovely house! And my daddy, not my genete-whatsit daddy but my other daddy, can make you some food. He makes really good food! Mind you, I don't like it when he makes stews because it has gravy in it and I hate gravy! My brother loves gravy, though! You can meet my brothers when you come to my house! They are very naughty, you know. They –'

At this point, John walks back into the screened-off area carrying a bottle of sterilized water. 'Here you are, Mum. I think we'd better go now, Sammie. Mum's getting tired.'

Janet looks sad.

'I really think we must go,' I say.

'Oh but I've barely talked to you,' protests Janet, trying to take my hand.

I tell her she looks tired and that I am worrying that this is all too much for her.

'No, I'm fine.'

'Mum, Sammie's right. You look like you've had enough. You need to get some rest.' John leans forward and gives her a kiss.

She opens her arms to give Edward a hug. Then she looks at me. 'He's a credit to you.'

'Thanks,' I say, as if that is the only word in the world I know. 'I'll bring him back soon. I promise.' I give her a small, embarrassed wave goodbye.

'Please do,' she says as she sinks back onto her pillows. I think she has tears in her eyes.

We are all very quiet when we get into the car to go home. Edward looks out of the window and then, pretty soon, his head begins to loll forward and he dozes off. I turn the heating up.

'Why is the heating on?' asks John the First irritably after about ten minutes. 'It's like being in an oven in here.'

I nod towards Edward in the back. I explain that the heating helps Edward get to sleep.

'Well, he's asleep now, so just turn it off, would you?'

I do as he asks. I am in no mood for a fight. But I can tell he is spoiling for one. He always wants a fight when he feels guilty about something. He always wants to accuse someone, anyone, of anything and everything, to shift blame away from himself. He is the past master of shifting blame. He leans back in his seat. I know he's looking at me. God, this takes me back. I remember one time when we were driving down to see Janet in Devon on a summer's morning. I had the CD player on. 'Gonna find my baby. Gonna hold her tight. Gonna grab some afternoon delight.' I turned round to watch Edward, who was burbling away in the back, happily putting his feet into his mouth. 'Hey, baby Edward,' I said. 'Sky rockets in flight. Afternoon delight,' and Edward was chuckling away and, suddenly, John the First turned the stereo off.

'I hate that song.'

'Well, I like it. It makes me feel happy. It makes Edward laugh.'

'I don't care. We're not listening to it.' He refused to let me put it back on. I never found out why.

I wonder what he wants to fight about now. Probably his mother, knowing John.

'Why did you want to leave the hospital so quickly?' he says.

'I didn't want to leave the hospital quickly. I thought we both agreed that your mother looked tired and needed to get some rest.'

'But you virtually ran out of the ward. Is it because Edward started talking about his brothers?'

'No. Anyway, Janet looked perfectly happy when Edward was about to tell her his stories about the family.'

'She thinks you should've stayed with me.'

'I don't believe you, John. I don't think your mother cares who I am with as long as Edward is happy.'

'But she does care. She told me before you came in how our marriage break-up probably started her cancer. She said she found the whole thing so stressful that she thinks that's when she got sick.'

'But that was years ago, John. Your mother didn't have cancer until recently.'

'Apparently, she's had cancer for ages and not told anyone. That's what she told me today.'

'Oh poor Janet. She must have been lonely with no husband or son to take care of her. Why on earth didn't she ring me?'

'You know, Sammie, we could help her. Today she asked me if there was any chance we would get back together. She said, "You were so happy with Samantha, darling. Can't you sort it out?" But I told her you had your new John and your other children and I think it really hurts her to think about it, and that's your fault, Sammie, not mine.'

That does it. I pull over to the side of the road, inadvertently almost knocking a cyclist off his bike. I turn round to say sorry but the cyclist sticks two fingers up at me. I smile at John. I lean over and open his car door.

'Out,' I say pleasantly.

'What?' He looks astonished.

'Out.'

'Why?'

'I won't have it, John. I will not have you come back into my life after all these years and mess it up and I will not have you mess Edward up either, or my John or my marriage or my other children. I am a happily married woman with three children. It is what I have chosen. So if you don't like it because you missed out, that's your problem.'

'Missed out? Do you think that's the kind of life I wanted? All that noise and mess and early mornings?'

'No. I imagine that's precisely what you didn't want, so good luck to you. But I won't have you sit in my car and insult me, so now you can get out and find your own way home.'

'I don't believe you, Sammie.'

'Well, I'm not going anywhere until you get out. Or you can apologize to me.'

John gets out and slams the door. I wave at him as I drive off.

When I get back home, I feel so exhausted I fail to see Santa's car parked opposite the house. Before I have even reached into the back to gently wake Edward up, Santa has run out of the house and into the driveway, looking very distressed.

'Where is John?' she says desperately.

'Which John?'

'You know! Your first John! He rang me. He was in a phone box. He said you'd made him get out of the car! Did you?'

'Yes, I did.'

'How could you? How could you? He was so upset. He was crying about you and crying about his mother.'

'Crocodile tears.'

'Samantha,' says Dougie, who has now also come out into the driveway. 'What's happened? Where have you left the poor man?'

'On Wycombe Hill.'

'But why, oh why?' wails Santa. 'You are too mean to him. He is suffering. He is sad. Why have you left him?'

'He was rude to me.'

'In my country, when someone is grieving, they are allowed to be whatever they want to be! You should be looking after him. Not leaving him alone and in the dark.'

I tell Santa that, in case she hasn't noticed, it's not dark and that she should stop being so melodramatic. 'Anyway, it's not far for him to walk home.'

'Walk home! From Wycombe? No! That is too cruel. I go find him now.'

Dougie looks at her in desperation. 'Santa, you can't just go off and drive around Wycombe. He could be anywhere by now.'

'No, Dougie, I have to go.'

'Yes, Dougie,' I say, 'if she feels she has to go and find him then she has to go and find him.'

'Santa!' says Dougie as she sets off towards her car brandishing her keys.

'Oh what, Dougie?' She sounds annoyed.

'Nothing,' he says miserably.

We go back into the house. Bennie and Jamie are in the bath. I can hear John the Second singing with them. 'Five little ducks went out one day, over the hill and far away.'

'Wasn't John singing Bennie the same song in the bath when I went out?' I ask Dougie. He nods his head. I don't think he is speaking to me. 'Dougie, are you speaking to me?' He shakes his head. 'Why not?' Dougie won't answer. Instead, he just looks at me.

John appears from the bathroom. He has nothing on but his jeans. He is carrying a double bundle of a soaking wet Bennie and an equally soaking wet Jamie, each wrapped up in a white towel. They look like two naughty angels. Jamie crows when he sees me and sticks out his little hands. 'Ma-ma-ma-ma,' he says.

'Oh he's said "mama" again,' I say.

'Yes, he has, hasn't he?' says John.

I take Jamie and he nestles into my shoulder. 'You sweet baby,' I say to him, kissing his naked back. 'You lovely beautiful baby.'

Bennie struggles out of John's arms. 'Me a lovely boy too,' he says, tugging at my jeans.

John, all wet with a few bubbles on his chest, comes over and kisses me. 'Are you OK?' He is trying to sound cheerful.

'No. Dougie's not speaking to me.'

'Oh,' says John. Then, 'Where's Santa?'

So I tell him what happened.

'Oh,' he says again. 'Well, it all sounds dreadful. Personally, I think you were absolutely right to sling John out of the car, but I imagine Dougie's sulking about Santa. You see, we went to the pub today for lunch. We had a lovely time, didn't we, Dougie?'

Dougie, who has now come into the sitting room, nods.

'And Dougie finally told me something momentous. Quite momentous.'

'What?'

'Dougie is now no longer in love with Maxine!'

'Thank God for that!'

'There's a downside, though. He is, in fact, now totally convinced that he is in love with Santa.'

'Oh.'

'Exactly,' says John.

'Who is in love with Santa?' says a voice. It's Edward. 'I woke up and you weren't there,' he says in an accusatory voice. 'I had to unstrap my doo-da and get out of the car and that's quite difficult for a boy of only eight, you know.'

'Edward, I am very sorry for forgetting to get you out of the car.'

'I was fast asleep, and then I woke up and no one was around and I didn't know where I was so I thought, "Hmm, I wonder where I am?" and then I thought I had better find out so I looked around me and thought, "Oh look. I'm in my driveway." I thought I'd sit and wait for someone to come and get me but then no one came for ages and ages and . . . Where's my dad? I thought he was in the car with us, wasn't he?'

'Yes, he was.'

'Where is he now, then?'

'I made him get out of the car.'

'Made him get out of the car?' says Edward, as if this is a thoroughly new concept. 'Why did you do that?'

'He was being contentious.'

'What does contente-whatsit mean?'

'It means he was being insulting, and I didn't see why I should put up with it.'

Edward then asks where I left him.

'Wycombe Hill.'

'Wycombe Hill?' says John. 'You didn't tell me you'd left him on Wycombe Hill. Are you out of your mind? That's miles away!'

I tell him that's why Dougie is cross with me. If I hadn't turfed John out of my car, then Santa wouldn't have gone to pick him up and if Santa hadn't gone to pick him up, she'd probably be here now chatting away to Dougie.

'So you've ruined his day,' says John.

'That would seem to sum it up, really.'

'Is Dougie in love with Santa?' says Edward.

'Um, no,' I say.

'Who is, then?' he asks again.

'Everyone.'

'But that means I must be in love with Santa when I don't really know if I am.'

'Me love Tanta,' Bennie pipes up suddenly.

'Ma-ma-ma-ma,' says Jamie.

'Oh Jamie just loves you, Mummy,' says Edward.

'Me love Mummy,' says Bennie.

'And I love you,' I say to Bennie.

'I can't stand this,' says Dougie. 'I am going. Please ask Santa to call me.'

On his way out, I try to give Dougie a hug but he won't respond.

'Dougie . . .'

He turns around to look at me. 'I don't know how you stand this yourself. How can you watch your ex-husband, this man you once loved so much, go off with your au pair and react as if it was no more than some scientific dating experiment? Where are your feelings? I feel so angry, so hurt, so . . . so . . . disappointed that I could bloody kill your ex-husband.'

'Hang on a minute, Dougie.' I then point out that of course I care but that I have a husband, three children, a sort-of job, a cat, a dog, a suicidal sister and a friend whose husband is having an affair to deal with. 'I do not have the time or the energy to get all het up about Santa and John the First. I care about the effect it may or may not have on Edward but that's it really.'

'I don't believe you,' says Dougie. 'I've seen you look at him. You like him!'

I tell Dougie that I never said I didn't like him but that, when it came to John the First's love life, I am prepared to accept the fact that he is a grown-up and should, therefore, take responsibility for himself, and as much as I actually seriously do not like at all the idea of my ex-husband and my au pair getting it on together, there is not much I can do about it. I also point out that, actually, as Dougie had been, until a couple of days ago, in constant denial over his love for Santa, refusing to admit his feelings about her every single time I have asked him, I could hardly be blamed for assuming that he did, after all, still love Maxine. In the same way, I could not be blamed for finally accepting his protestations that he and Maxine were in accord over not having children, despite my better instincts, until his angry outburst last night telling me and John we were smug bastards and how unhappy he felt about being childless. 'The truth is,' I say to Dougie, 'you are not honest with yourself or with others and it has to stop, Dougie, really it does. You have to stop drinking so much and you have to stop lying to yourself and everyone else around you. You know what? If you want Santa, go and tell her. Go and have pistols at dawn with John the First on Wycombe Hill for all I care but, for once in your life, do something, Dougie!'

Dougie looks astounded. He stands on the doorstep and just stares at me and then he reaches forward, gives me a huge hug and says, 'You are right! You really are right!' and then he drives off.

'What a day!' I say to John.

'Yes, what a day.'

Later on, when the children have gone to bed and it is all quiet and peaceful and the dog is laid out on the sofa and the cat is asleep, probably dreaming of the owl-infested night ahead, John the Second makes a fire as the light fades from the sky and we lie, naked and half-baked, in front of it. We drink red wine and talk and kiss and become engulfed in each other and, this time, no one interrupts us for a very long time and when we are all finished and done we say we love each other and that we must promise to make more time for each other. Then I tell my John that soon everything will be over. I murmur to him that Janet is dying and John will leave and our family, our happy little family, will all return to where it was before.

'What could go wrong now?' I ask.

What indeed.

15. Tuesday

Today is the day my sister is coming to playgroup. I have warned everybody she is coming. I have telephoned them all and explained that my sister is a teeny bit depressed and that her husband has left her and that, although she doesn't have a small child as such, she has six bigger children so maybe she can come without a child and just sort of give us tips.

'Is she a good mother?' asked Margot.

'She's a great mother.'

'Then why isn't she bringing one of her many children?'

'Because they are all at school. Her youngest is five.'

'Oh right. Well, I shall try to be nice.'

'Margot will *try* to be nice!' I said to John the Second when I saw him later.

'Don't worry about it,' said John. 'It'll all be fine!'

But I am worried.

Julia rang yesterday evening and said, 'I've been thinking. I need a life. I have no friends. I must make friends. I've been reading a book about making friends and how supportive they can be in your life and I just must find some.'

'You can't just find friends,' I said. 'You have to meet them. You have to go out and chat and invite them round and bake cakes and be nice about their children and then they are nice about your children and . . . It's a whole social minefield and I'm not sure why you'd want to start doing all that friend stuff with everything you're going through right now.'

'Hmm,' said my sister. 'So where have you met your friends?'

'I sort of meet them during my day-to-day life.'

'Well, I have a life and yet I seem to have no friends. Why is that, Samantha?'

'Probably because you got married and had children when you were young. You haven't had time to meet friends.'

Then she asked me if I had local friends and I told her that yes, of course I had.

'Well, where did you meet them?'

'Playgroup.'

'Right, I shall join a playgroup.'

I pointed out to her that to go to playgroup you had to have a child aged under five and she certainly didn't have one of those, but if she ever wished to borrow Bennie . . .

'Oh that's kind but wouldn't everyone think it rather weird to turn up to playgroup with a child that isn't your own?'

'Well, people might think it was a little weird but maybe you could say I'd died and you'd adopted him or something.'

'No, Samantha, I am seriously not that desperate.' But she must have been because she rang me back an hour later to say that she'd had a brainwave. 'I can come to your playgroup!'

'But what's the point? My playgroup is nowhere near where you live.'

'I just want to see how it works. I'm out of touch. Maybe it'll help me learn how to meet people.'

'But, Julia, your kitchen is always full of people popping in for a tea. You actually have loads of friends.'

'They are not my friends. They are just people I know and they are all boring.'

I gave in. I told her to come to the next session, and the next session is today.

I have worried about it ever since. 'I don't think Julia should come to playgroup tomorrow,' I said to John last night once we'd finally given up trying to contact Santa, who wasn't answering her mobile phone, and Dougie, who wasn't answering his, either.

'Why shouldn't your sister come to playgroup?'

I explained to him I was worried that she wouldn't like it.

'Of course she'll like it. She'll love it!'

I then told him I was worried that she'd like it too much and then try to come all the time. Or that maybe no one would like her or that everyone will like her or . . .

'You're worrying too much.' He laughed. 'I am sure it won't affect your life too much, Samantha. Julia's lonely. Let her come just once.'

So here I am waiting for her. I've told her I'll meet her in the car park next to the village hall.

'I'm hopeless at finding things,' she said.

I said, 'Don't be ridiculous. There's nothing else here.'

I am standing here looking down the hill into the valley. Bennie is playing in the car park, running in and out between the parked cars. Jamie is in the car, waiting patiently. It's a beautiful sunny day. 'Look, Bennie,' I say, grabbing him as he careers past me. 'Can you see the cows?'

'Moo!' says Bennie excitedly, craning his neck to look into the field sloping away from us.

'Can you see the sun?' He points at the sun. 'What colour is the sky, Bennie?'

'Boo!' says Bennie.

'No, it's b-l-ue, Bennie. B-l-ue. What colour is the sky again?'

'Boo. Boo. Boo!'

'Boo to you too,' I hear a voice saying. It's Genevieve. She's got Jessamy with her.

'Hello, Jessamy,' I say.

Jessamy ignores me. She looks at Bennie and then, for no discernible reason, suddenly lunges forward with both arms outstretched and pushes him over.

'Arrggh,' yells Bennie, who is now lying on his front on the car park tarmac holding his head in his hands. 'Ow, ow, ow.'

'Jessamy!' shouts Genevieve. 'You are a very naughty girl!' Jessamy stands with her back to her mother. 'You say sorry to Bennie!' Jessamy doesn't budge.

'Ow, ow, ow,' whimpers Bennie sorrowfully to himself.

'I said, say sorry to Bennie!' says Genevieve. 'I'm so, so sorry,' she says to me. 'I don't know why she's being like this. I really don't. She's been in a bad mood all day. I think it may be because Nicholas left for Brussels this morning. She gets so upset. She said, "Is Daddy going away again?" and it nearly broke my heart. I don't know what to do about her aggression. I really –'

Genevieve stops dead. Her face goes white. Then she emits a bone-chilling screech the like of which I have never heard before. 'JESSAMY, NO!'

I turn around almost in slow motion to see what is going on. This is what I see: Jessamy crouching over Bennie with the fingers of her right hand entwined in Bennie's hair. She is pulling with all her might, pulling his head backwards and upwards and she looks as if she is about to smash his head into the tarmac. Bennie's little face is contorted with pain. His mouth forms a wordless O. Then, before I can move, before Genevieve can get to Jessamy, before poor little Bennie has vocalized his pain, before Jessamy does, in fact, smash little Bennie's head onto the ground, my sister appears. I suddenly see her, out of the corner of my eye, marching across the car park.

'LITTLE GIRL!' she says loudly to Jessamy when she gets close to her. 'LET GO OF BENNIE'S HEAD NOW.'

Jessamy, now looking utterly stunned at the intervention of this woman she's never met before, lets Bennie's head go. *Clonk!* Bennie's head sinks onto the tarmac. Within half a second, Bennie is up and attached to my leg, looking white and petrified. I crouch down to cuddle him.

'Jes'my hurt Bennie! Me got ows!'

'Oh my poor Bennie.' I kiss his poor hurt head and his grazed hands and grazed knees and his tearful eyes.

But I also keep watching my sister. She has Jessamy in her grasp. She has one hand clamped on Jessamy's arm so that she cannot escape and she too is crouched down. She is on the same level as Jessamy and she is looking at her long and hard in the eyes. She is talking to her, her mouth is moving constantly, but I cannot hear what she is saying. Then she lets go of Jessamy's arm and stands up. Jessamy looks nervously over to me and Bennie. She looks at her mother. Genevieve is standing like a statue – mute and immovable – but she looks terribly close to tears. Jessamy comes over to me and Bennie.

'Sorry, Bennie,' she says. I look at her. She actually seems genuinely contrite. Then she goes over to Genevieve. 'Sorry, Mummy,' she says. Genevieve looks even closer to tears.

'Oh Jessamy! Do you know, that's the first time you have ever apologized to me.'

Jessamy smiles at her mother. 'Sorry, Mummy,' she says again.

Genevieve then looks at my sister. 'Who are you? Jessamy has never apologized to anyone about anything, ever. You must be a miracle-worker or something. Are you Super Nanny in disguise?'

'No,' says my sister, smiling back at Genevieve. 'I'm Julia. I'm Samantha's sister.'

Ten minutes later and the usual group of us are all sitting round the table. My sister is sitting next to Genevieve, who has made her a coffee and has found a packet of biscuits.

'Do you know that Julia –' and she points to my sister – 'got Jessamy to apologize to me.'

'No!' says everyone at the table.

'Oh yes. This woman here is Samantha's sister and I think she deserves a round of applause.'

'Oh dear me no,' says my sister, going pink with pleasure. 'No applause. I just did what any parent would do to avoid conflict.'

'I avoid conflict by doing colour therapy,' says Jo. 'I went to one of those classes. What are they called, again?'

'Colour Strings?' says Julia.

'That's it! They told me that I was a summer person, which means that I should wear pale blues and peaches and pastels.'

'Oh that explains it,' says Eleanor.

'Explains what?' says Jo, looking hurt.

'All your beautiful, peachy, little summer tops,' says Eleanor somehow managing to keep a straight face.

'What kind of conflict?' says Margot to my sister, leaning forward to hear her reply.

'Well,' says my sister, 'Jessamy and Bennie obviously have a history together. Am I right in saying that?'

'Yes!' says Genevieve.

'Oh yes!' says everyone else.

Oh no, I say to myself. Bennie has absolutely no history of conflict with Jessamy. It's Jessamy who always beats him up while he generally chooses just to ignore Jessamy most of the time.

'So what we have here,' says my sister, warming to her theme, 'is a classic situation of a child – Jessamy – with low self-esteem who feels threatened by a younger but physically bigger child: Bennie.'

'Do we?' Genevieve looks like a stunned rabbit.

'Oh absolutely! You see, if we notice, Bennie is bigger than Jessamy even though she is older than him. So, Bennie is a threat on a physical level. But he is also a threat in other ways. If Jessamy is a dominant force at playgroup . . . Is she a dominant force at playgroup?' she asks Genevieve.

'Yes, she is,' says Genevieve. Only because she's a bully, thinks me.

'Well, then Bennie threatens Jessamy's dominance.'

'He's not a bloody chimpanzee,' I mutter.

'What's that, Samantha?' Julia looks at me as if I am a naughty little girl.

'Oh nothing, Julia.'

'Now,' she says, 'when Jessamy's position in the herd is threatened – and I use the word "herd" deliberately, for what Jessamy does is entirely animalistic – she reacts by protecting herself. And how does she protect herself?' she asks the group. They all look at her, their mouths agape.

'By hurting the person who threatens her?' says Genevieve.

'Exactly!'

'So that's it?'

'Well, sort of.'

'But how do I stop her from doing it?'

'Lock her in a darkened room and throw away the key?' I suggest.

'Samantha!' says my sister.

'It's only a joke,' I say to Genevieve.

'You have to find a way of making her feel unthreatened,' says my sister. 'If you watched what I did with her, I went down to her level, I stayed calm, I took her hand – that's a bit of reassuring physical contact, you see, so she knows you're not being all cold and aloof – and then I looked her in the eye and spoke to her. I was firm but fair.'

'I see.'

'I said to her, "Now, little girl" – I called her little girl because I didn't know her name. Obviously, if I had known her name I would not have called her "little girl" because it sounds a bit derogatory. I said, "Now, little girl, you have hurt that little boy and although you see him as being a big boy, he's not and now he is hurt and crying and your mummy is hurt and crying and you must say sorry to him and sorry to your mummy." Then I said to her, "Do you think you can do that, because that really would make everyone feel very special and if you make everyone feel special then you will be the most special little girl in the world!" And she thought a bit and nodded her head, and that's how it happened.'

'But it's a miracle! Jessamy has never ever done anything nice like that before.' Genevieve hangs her head a bit. 'And you, you have helped her and I cannot tell you how grateful I am.'

'Oh it's no problem. I've got six children.'

'Six!' says everyone in unison.

'Oh yes. I know everything there is to know about children.'

'Did you have a naughty step?' asks Margot.

'No. All that naughty-step stuff and standing in the corner and going up to your room, I don't believe in any of that.'

'Don't you?' says Margot in obvious astonishment.

'Oh no. Punishing children in that way, excluding them, constantly highlighting their bad behaviour, it doesn't work.'

'Doesn't it?'

'No. It just ruins their self-esteem.'

There is a pause while everyone thinks about this. I go into the kitchen to make coffee. Eleanor is in there making tea.

'Your sister is incredible! How on earth has she managed with six? She must have help. A cleaner? An au pair?'

'No. She's done it all herself. She's never even had a babysitter.'

'My God, she must have endless patience. She ought to write a book, you know. Or do talks or be on television. She was marvellous about Jessamy and so right. All of us could see it but it's impossible to tell your friends about their own children. I remember Jessamy once beating up Jackson and I was furious and I wanted to tell her off but Genevieve said, "Oh it's six of one and half a dozen of the other," but it wasn't and I really wanted to say that to her. I wanted to say, "No, it's Jessamy who kicks and bites and it's Jessamy who has problems and you need to accept this and do something about it!" But I couldn't say anything.'

I tell Eleanor I know what she means. It happens all the time. You want everyone to love your children. You want your children to fit in and be popular but, occasionally, you get lumbered with a disturbed child who just can't quite handle life.

'But Bennie's a dream!' says Eleanor.

'Oh not Bennie. Edward. He used to bite and kick and he couldn't speak properly for ages. I could see the mothers at nursery never wanted him round to play and it broke my heart.'

'That's terrible! What's he like now?'

'I think he's learnt how to manage it now. He's happy but he only has one friend really and he's completely weird so they rather suit each other. They spend their life whistling for wasps.'

'Whistling for wasps?' Eleanor starts to giggle. 'That's really cheered me up!'

When we get back into the main hall, carrying our coffees and teas and some home-made chocolate brownies that Eleanor has baked – 'Nesting, you see,' she says apologetically – we find Julia still surrounded by all the mothers. They are clustered around her, looking at her intently, straining to hear everything she is saying. I cannot believe it. I don't think Julia can either. She is still talking to them at length about bringing up children without naughty steps.

'Children don't inherently mean to do wrong,' my sister is saying.

'What do you mean?' says Margot. 'I always think children know *exactly* what they are doing.'

'But your children are so well behaved!' Caroline says to Margot. 'They never do anything wrong.'

My sister pricks her ears up. 'Really?'

'I have two girls and a boy,' says Margot rather primly, 'and they behave like little angels.'

'Yes, but you are pretty strict with them,' says Genevieve.

'Am I?' Margot sounds a bit prickly now.

'Yes, Margot, you are.'

'How do you mean, strict?'

'Well, they're not allowed to do anything much, are they?' says Genevieve, warming to her theme and seemingly incapable of realizing the effect she is having on Margot. 'Remember when you came to our swimming party last year?'

'Yes,' says Margot.

'They came in matching swimsuits! Then they were only allowed to swim in the shallow end even though they can all swim because you take them to swimming lessons religiously every week because you can't bear the thought they might not achieve anything and everything. Then they weren't allowed cake or juice or fizzy drinks or peanut butter sandwiches . . . I mean, come on, most children would've strangled you by then but your children, well possibly apart from Carlos, just say "yes, Mother" and "no, Mother" and it's weird! It is weird, Julia, isn't it?' Genevieve, suddenly toppling to the fact that Margot is looking thunderously at her, stares beseechingly at my sister.

'I don't think I can go into individual cases,' says Julia, ignoring the disappointed looks on Eleanor's face and mine and deliberately not looking at Margot who, I can see, is about to explode. 'What I will say on this is that children do, of course, need to learn how to accept the parent's word. There is a very good book called *How to Say No* and I urge you all to read it. Children do have to have boundaries, of course. I couldn't have had six children doing exactly what they wanted to do and going exactly anywhere they wanted to go, because the whole structure of our family would have broken down. But I also feel we have a system of loving respect in our family. We try not to hurt each other or wreck each other's things. We try to be accommodating. It is based on love, you see. I surround my children with love. I am always there for them. When I ask them not to do something, I explain why I don't want them to do it. I don't shout or swear at them. If you dominate your children, if you rule them with an iron fist, they will turn on you. Mark my words. Very well-behaved children tend to turn into dreadful rebellious teenagers.'

'Well,' says Margot, looking at my sister in a rather concerned fashion, 'I can't see my children will be like that. They are lovely, well-behaved children because that is just the way they were brought up.'

'I am sure they are lovely,' says my sister.

'It's not my fault that I can't cope with all the noise.'

'No, absolutely not.'

'I do try, you know.' Margot now looks as if she is going to cry. 'I just found it hard at first, you see. I was so good at my job. I used to be a deputy headmistress.'

'Oh that's wonderful.' My sister nods her head in encouragement.

'I was a very good teacher.'

'I am sure you were.'

'I won an award and my school did so well and I was

so happy. Then I had Camille and, and, I couldn't cope. She just cried and wailed and I was up all night and then, when she was six months old, I went back to work but I couldn't concentrate and my teaching standards slipped and no one paid attention to me. The school was going downhill and, try as I might, I couldn't seem to do anything to stop it because I was so tired and Camille still wouldn't sleep and . . . to cut a long story short, I gave up work, stayed at home and decided to make my children behave so that I would never feel so out of control ever again.' Margot then sits, bravely, looking at all of us.

'Crikey,' says Eleanor.

'Oh I'm so sorry.' Genevieve gets up and wraps her arms around Margot.

'And you see,' Margot says, now sounding tearful again, 'when you talk about how well behaved my children are, I do know it's because I dominate them all the time and now I feel really bad about it.'

'Oh you musn't feel bad!' says Genevieve.

'But you don't dominate your children,' sniffs Margot.

'Yes, but look at them! Philippa's a supercilious know-all and Jessamy's a thug.'

'Oh no, she's not!' says Margot.

Eleanor and Caroline and I shoot each other a look.

'Oh yes, she is!' says Genevieve. 'She's a horrible little bully and I don't know how to handle her.'

'I think,' says Julia, 'that Jessamy has low self-esteem. I could tell that as soon as I talked to her. She doesn't think she is worth anything and so she wishes to make others worth nothing, just like her.'

'Oh no! That's terrible!' says Genevieve. 'Why would Jessamy have low self-esteem?'

'Do you praise her?'

'Yes.'

'Do you tell her all the time how talented and clever she is?'

'I tell Buzzy that all the time,' says Jo. Genevieve shoots her a look. Jo shakes a large pill box she has in her handbag at Genevieve and mouths 'Viagra!' rather gleefully at her. Genevieve blushes.

'Do you tell Jessamy how clever and talented she is?' my sister asks Genevieve again.

'Yes, of course!'

'And who is mostly at home with her?'

'Me.'

'What about her father?'

'He's never at home. He works very hard, you see.'

'Aah,' says Julia. 'And here we have the source, the root of all Jessamy's problems.'

'What do you mean?' Genevieve sounds a little defensive.

'She is trying to get attention from her father.'

'Is she?' Genevieve is astounded.

'I am afraid so. Where does your husband work?'

'He works for an oil company and, and . . . he is away a lot and he works very hard.'

'But why is he away a lot? Why does he work so hard?'

'He, he –' Genevieve starts to cry and then she says, in a strange, high-pitched voice, 'He has another family to support!'

'WHAT?' say Margot, Eleanor, Caroline, Jo and me all at the same time.

'Oh God,' says Genevieve. 'I shouldn't have said anything.'

'Oh yes, you should,' says my sister. 'We are all here to

support you. You can be honest here! We should all be honest with each other.'

'Yes, you're right. Why shouldn't I tell you all? Why should I deny what has been happening? Why should I say I am fine when I am not?'

'Yes, why should you?' says Julia. 'I mean, my husband has just left me for an angel therapist! He won't even speak to me. He told my sister I was mad. How do you think that makes me feel?'

'Dreadful,' says Margot.

'No! Angry!' says my sister. 'God, I have sat on my family secrets for so long and now I say, "No more!" No more sitting on secrets! No more feeling guilty for things that are out of our control!'

'You're right,' says Genevieve. 'No more lies!' Then she tells us that, as a twenty-one-year-old man, Nicholas had a relationship with an American lady he met when he was working as a trainee sommelier in the French Laundry restaurant in California.

'There's nothing wrong with that,' says Eleanor.

'No, absolutely not. It was years before I met him.'

'And the French Laundry's a great restaurant!' I say.

Genevieve goes on to explain that Nicholas came home a year later, saying goodbye to the lady, and he thought that was that. Then, five years after that, the lady turned up on his doorstep in London with a little boy, claiming that he was Nicholas's.

'Nothing wrong with that either!' says Eleanor.

'Nothing wrong at all,' says Genevieve. Having established that this was his son, Nicholas then got very attached to him and married the mother so that she could stay in the UK. They never lived together. Nicholas, now successful, bought the American lady a house down the road from where he lived and the boy lived at both his parents' houses.

'That sounds ideal!' I say, thinking of how I have judged Nicholas as a parent in the past, only to find out he has been this committed father. It makes me think of Edward. It makes me think of John the First and how useless he is. Why didn't he come and live near his son? Why hasn't he been a committed father?

Everything was fine until Nicholas met Genevieve on that aeroplane back from Lagos. They fell in love and the upshot is that Nicholas divorced the American lady and married Genevieve.

'But this is all fine,' says Margot. 'Who on earth would have a problem with that?'

'Well, it was all fine, until we married. Nicholas's ex was furious, even though, when it came to the divorce settlement, he was very generous with her because he wanted her to be happy and he wanted his son to be happy.'

'He is devoted to his son, isn't he?' I say.

'Absolutely.'

'So what's the problem?' Jo asks.

'Since the divorce, the ex-wife has got very greedy. She keeps telling Nicholas that if he doesn't pay her more money then she won't let him see his son! She says she'll take him back to the States and he'll never see Nicholas again.'

'That's blackmail!' says Margot.

'I know. I've told Nicholas that he should tell her she's getting nothing more, but he won't do it.'

'That's terrible!' I say. 'God, I've given John, Edward's dad, all rights to see his son and he's never even bothered to take me up on the offer or pay me any money!'

'That's even worse!' says Genevieve. 'What a selfish man! Poor Nicholas is desperate about the thought of losing contact with his son.'

'But his son must be in his early twenties now, isn't he?' I say, remembering what Corporate Queen told John about Nicholas and the young boy he took on the management training weekend. Of course! He took his son! God, what was I thinking? I must have been mad. I can see it all now.

'Yes, he's just turned twenty now.'

'But he's a grown-up!' I say. 'Surely it's up to Nicholas's son whether he sees his father or not.'

'But Nicholas's ex-wife keeps telling him horrible stories about Nicholas and trying to poison him against his father and, of course, he feels protective of his mother who claims, wrongly, that Nicholas abandoned her. It's all very difficult and it means that Nicholas works all the time to pay this woman this money and he can be very distracted sometimes.'

'And that makes you feel cross,' says my sister.

'Yes,' says Genevieve miserably.

'I'm going to think about this one,' says my sister. 'But you must speak to your husband and tell him this situation is intolerable. You must tell him to stop paying this woman. He has you, his wife, and two small children to think of. This older child is now a young man. Nicholas must trust his relationship with him. He must understand that he has behaved well. He has helped his mother out financially and he has been more than a good and loving father to his eldest child, but now he needs to concentrate on you.'

'Right. But what if he refuses to do so?'

'Then you tell him you will leave him,' says Julia. As

she gets up and gives Genevieve a hug she whispers quietly, but loudly enough for me to hear, 'You need something to do, Genevieve. I can see it in you. You are bored and frustrated. Use that wonderful brain of yours.' Then she kisses her on the cheek.

Now everyone is silent. We have all forgotten about our children. They are playing away happily around us. Out of the corner of my eye I see Jamie slugging across the floor towards me. He has seen the chocolate brownies. 'Ga!' he says, trying to climb up my leg.

'I thought Jamie only liked butternut squash,' says my sister.

'Yes, but since you gave him chocolate cake at your house, he's developed an obsession with it.' I give him a brownie and pull him onto my lap where he sits squishing it in his hand.

'You see,' says my sister to no one in particular, 'your children are happy at the moment. You are not hovering over them, you are not fighting their battles for them. They are playing together and sorting out their own way of being together as a group. You should all feel very happy about that. In fact, you should all give yourselves a big clap.' At first we all sit there but then, encouraged by my sister, everyone starts to clap. 'And you, Samantha,' says my sister to me, noticing that I am reluctant to join in. So I clap too.

'Well,' says my sister as we go towards the car park. 'I think that went well!'

'Very well.'

'Do you really mean that?' says my sister. 'Oh bye, Margot,' she calls, waving at Margot, who is waving enthusiastically back.

'You certainly put the cat among the pigeons,' I say.

'Oh no, I didn't,' she says, now waving goodbye to Genevieve whose telephone number she has taken down. 'Remember, Genevieve,' she yells out, 'you are a strong woman! Give those children all that love you have inside and be firm but loving with that man!'

'OK,' shouts Genevieve as she gets into her car.

'I think I'm quite good at this,' says my sister.

'Good at what?'

'You know, women's things.'

'Eleanor thinks you should become a counsellor or write a book or something like that.'

'Oh maybe I should become a counsellor!'

'Good idea.'

'Well, I think I'll come next week and see how they are all doing.'

'Great, that's just great.'

'Is everything OK with the Johns?' she asks as she gets into her car.

'I seem to have misplaced John the First.'

'Good thing too!' She blows me a kiss and drives off.

I don't even have time to ask her about Joe.

When I get home, having struggled to get the kids in the car because Jamie is covered in chocolate brownie and keeps trying to smear it over Bennie, who is having none of it, the telephone is ringing. I pick it up.

'Hi!' says Genevieve.

'Oh hi, Genevieve,' I say, holding Jamie away from Bennie with one arm.

'Jamie, no!' Bennie keeps saying while trying to push Jamie away.

'Is now a good moment?' says Genevieve.

'No, not really,' I say as Jamie wriggles from my grasp.

'I just wanted to say that I thought your sister was amazing, and that we raised thirty pounds on Saturday, which will buy five full art sets for the new centre in Nigeria!'

'Great! Jamie, stop doing that!' I say sternly as he finds another bit of chocolate brownie on his shoe that he is trying to feed to the dog. Bennie is now slumped like a crash-test dummy on the sofa. He looks exhausted.

'Oh sorry,' says Genevieve. 'Is Jamie being a bit difficult?'

'No, it's fine. I'll just pick him up.' I then launch myself at Jamie and grab him.

'Erggh, blerp, ga,' he says happily, wriggling his feet around like small, independent-minded caterpillars that just happen to be attached to his legs.

'I just really wanted to say that I'm sorry about how useless Edward's father has been. It must have been difficult hearing about Nicholas and his own son.'

'Oh no, don't worry. I suppose I resigned myself to John the First's behaviour some time ago, although I do think it is marvellous of Nicholas to feel so strongly. It's very admirable.'

'Thanks for that, Samantha. Anyway, I've also rung up to see what your sister's situation is because I think she could be a good motivational speaker.'

'Right. Well, I'm not sure what she's up to. Her husband, or estranged husband or whatever he is, is in hospital.'

'Oh why?'

'It's a long story, but someone stabbed him with a broken plate.'

'Well, she may need some financial help, then. Nicholas

knows this woman – I can't remember her name – but she runs these courses for big companies and she gets experts to come and talk to them about how to sort out their company problems.'

'Right.' I am now trying to pinion Jamie to the sofa by his arms as he has decided the best thing to do in life is to smear chocolate all over my hair.

'Ma-ma-ma-ma,' he's saying.

Suddenly, Bennie perks up from his slack-mouthed reverie on the sofa. 'Ooh, Ma-ma-ma-ma!' he says, dancing around.

'Blerp ga!' says Jamie, now off the sofa and crawling rapidly to the open back door.

'Ooh blerp ga!' mimics Bennie and off he goes.

I rush, telephone cradled between my chin and my left shoulder, to shut the door.

'Ma-ma-ma!' yells Jamie, getting faster.

'So,' carries on Genevieve, seemingly oblivious to the fact that a mini-revolution has broken out in my house, 'if I can get the name of the woman, do you think your sister would be interested? She'd be great at talking to people about their children and how to manage them. She could then relate that to big business, if you know what I mean. It's a boom industry, really it is. They pay really well, you know.'

'I'm sure she would be really grateful.' I am now careering towards the door.

'And you get to travel, you see. Nicholas once went to the Lake District and had a great time.'

I have now wrenched Jamie away from the door and am in the process of grabbing Bennie before he tastes too much freedom in the garden. 'No, Mummy!' he says.

'The Lake District? Oh I know the woman you mean.

It's Edward's friend's mother. Her name is Laura. Is that the one you were thinking of?'

'That's her. Laura! Funny woman with an odd son?'

'Oh yes, that's her.'

'Well, Nicholas thought she was very good. He really enjoyed that course she did.'

Now all I have to do is put Bennie back in the sitting room and . . . 'Is that because he had his son there?'

Genevieve suddenly goes very quiet. Jamie is now setting off towards the bathroom.

'That woman Laura told you Nicholas had his son there?' Genevieve says quietly.

'Ma-ma-ma,' says Jamie, sticking his hand down the loo.

'Well,' I say, trying to wrench Jamie's hand back out again, 'she didn't exactly say son. I think she said he was accompanied by a young man.'

'So you already knew Nicholas has a son?'

'I didn't know he was Nicholas's son.' I try to out-stare Bennie, who is blocking the door and staring at me truculently.

'Well, who did you think he was?'

'I didn't know who he was.' I am flailing around now, trying to pull Bennie back into the sitting room. 'I just didn't think about it.'

Genevieve knows I am lying. There is a long silence then she says, 'Oh my God. You thought he was Nicholas's lover, didn't you?'

'No,' I say, rather desperately.

'Yes, you did! Samantha, how could you? He's a married man with children!'

'Well,' I say, yanking Bennie back from the door again and now feeling rather defensive, 'it's hardly unknown for men who are married with children to be having affairs with men, is it? MPs are always at it. My God, people even think my friend Dougie is gay because he can cook!'

'You're pathetic, Samantha,' she says, ice cold. 'I thought we were friends but obviously we are not!' Genevieve slams the phone down.

I turn around to find Jamie joyfully scooping the water from the loo into his mouth.

'Mmmmm!' he says happily.

When I finally have the two of them secure – Jamie in his spare plastic high chair that attaches in a rather rickety fashion to our kitchen chairs and Bennie on his bigger chair – I call my sister.

'Listen, Genevieve has called and she thinks you should do some speaking.'

'About what?' My sister then tells me that she can't chat for long as she's going up to the hospital to give Joe some naturopathic pills that playgroup Jo recommended. 'I got them in the local health food store. They're a mixture of charcoal and something else and they boost your immune system and I think Joe's immune system needs boosting, don't you?'

'I have no idea, but I think you should listen to what I have to say because it could work to your advantage. Genevieve knows someone, who happens to be Edward's friend's mother, who could probably get you some work as a motivational speaker.'

'A motivational speaker? What's that?'

'I don't actually know exactly, but I think it may be to do with talking to high-ranking businessmen about their businesses and somehow relating how they run, say,

Microsoft, to the way you bring up children.' I suggest that maybe she should talk to Corporate Queen about it.

'Oh no, I don't want to do that. I don't like the idea of talking to businessmen about how to run their companies in the same way as people should rear their children. That doesn't sound very holistic, does it?'

'Maybe you should think about not doing the big business side of the job and just do the child-care bit. Genevieve has suggested that perhaps you should think about doing talks to mothers about children and how to bring them up. You know what she means, don't you? Everyone wants to know how to help their children to be happy, and think about what you did this morning. You sorted out the entire problems of the playgroup!'

'Oh no, I'm sure I didn't!' says Julia, but she sounds thoughtful.

'Anyway, give Genevieve a ring, will you? She'd love to speak to you and, you never know, something may come out of it. Genevieve says it pays very well.'

'I could do with the money.' Julia sounds even more thoughtful.

I then tell Julia about what has just happened between Genevieve and me and why.

'Oh dear,' says Julia. 'I can see why she's upset.'

'I meant no harm. I was confused. I didn't know what to do and John said I shouldn't get involved.'

'Yes, but John was wrong. Essentially, you thought Nicholas was having an affair and it is actually immaterial whether it was with a woman or with a man. An infidelity is an infidelity.'

I tell Julia rather crossly that I didn't think Genevieve was cross because I failed to inform her of her husband's supposed infidelity, but because I assumed he was having an affair with his own son, as it turned out.

Julia says that she will talk to Genevieve about it for me. 'I am sure this can be resolved easily. I've always found that the only resolution to disruption in female relationships is for everyone to be honest, so now everything is out in the open I am sure there is hope. You see, when female friendships break down, one of the parties takes a line. It's almost as if they draw a line in the sand over which they will not cross, and what the other person has to do is –'

'Is that the time? Sorry, Julia, but I've got a million and one things to do, and don't visiting hours finish soon?'

'I have to go and see my Joe now,' Julia squeals and off she goes.

Bennie and Jamie have finished their lunch now so I pop Jamie up in his cot and snuggle Bennie down on the sofa to watch a *Postman Pat* video – 'Pat 'orrible,' he says but then happily cuddles up next to the dog and starts sucking his thumb – and then I look at the whiteboard. LAUNDRY it says. I go into the laundry room. It is a disgrace. There are knickers and socks and pants and trousers and John the Second's crumpled-up shirts everywhere. I sigh. I hate doing the laundry for it must be one of the most boring chores in the world. Food and laundry. Laundry and food. Is this what my life has become?

In order to put off the moment when I have to brave the laundry, I telephone Dougie. His mobile rings and rings and then it says, 'This is the T-Mobile messaging service. Please leave your message after the tone. *Bleeeeep.*'

'Dougie! Why are you not answering your phone? I

want to know what is going on! I want to not have to do the washing. Call me now to prevent an outbreak of tedious domesticity.'

I then call Santa. I get her messaging service as well. I leave a bit of a frosty message for her. 'Santa, I am not sure when you are coming to look after my children again. Neither do I know where my ex-husband is. If you have any information for me on either of these matters, please ring. Bye.'

Hmm. So, it's the laundry, then.

How Much Laundry I Do in a Week

This is what I know to be true about my laundry: WE DO FAR TOO MUCH OF IT! How do I know this?

1) *I know this because I put the washing machine on at least every day and, even though I changed my washing machine to be one of those eco-friendly ones, I am sure I am swamping Oxfordshire with the ridiculous amount of dirty, sud-filled water that must pour out of the back of my machine on a daily basis. Whenever my mother comes round and she hears the familiar whirr of the blasted washing machine she says, 'Not washing again, are you?' and then she tells me that although she had two children, she only ever did a wash once a week, which is exactly the number of baths we had a week. When I tell her that we put the machine on at least once a day and that the children bath every day, bar Edward who hates having a bath, my mother looks very disapproving and says, 'No wonder there's a water shortage in this area.' I tell her that the water shortage is nothing*

to do with my consumption of it and everything to do with the fact that the water companies have not renewed their pipes since cavemen roamed the earth and that, therefore, these pipes leak out far more water than they pump through into my household, and my mother says, 'Nonsense. You're just wasteful, Samantha.'

2) In fact, I have tried to cut down on washing in this household but it seems to be in vain. It starts from the top. Every day, John changes his shirt, underpants and socks so there is always his little mini-pile scrunched-up and strewn around our room. Because John is always in a desperate rush in the mornings, and also because he is too lazy to just bend down a little bit and pick up his dirty clothes and then gingerly hold them and take them down the stairs and put them in the laundry basket, it means that muggins-me has to do it. Every day I think, 'Right, well, I'm not going to do John's washing for him today. I am going to leave all his socks and pants and shirts to have a cosy little conversation on the floor with each other and see how long it will take him to actually bother to wash his own clothes.' Sometimes I wonder how long it would take for John to realize this is what I am doing. Would he start putting his stuff in the laundry or would it get to the point when, having finally run out of shirts and pants and socks, John would look around and see a mountain of his dirty washing piled up on the floor and be astounded by this as if seeing reality for the first time? And would I then say, 'Oh look! The washing fairy has been on strike and you've only just noticed!' Or would I graciously pick it all up and take it downstairs, safe in the knowledge that I had made my point? But I'll never find out because I get so irritated by

the messiness of it all that I always give in and take his stuff down to the wash.

3) It is also almost impossible to cut down on the washing because of the children. In the morning, Edward gets up and, ignoring the school uniform he wore the day before which I have lovingly cleaned, scrubbed and then straightened out and placed oh-so-carefully at the end of his bed, lunges straight for his cupboard and grabs a whole new uniform. Even if I say to him the night before, 'Oh look, Edward. See this uniform I have rescued from your floor and made all nice and clean-looking. See how I am placing it at the end of your bed so that when you get up you can wear it again!' he has totally forgotten about it by the next morning. He wakes up, finds his new uniform and takes it downstairs, which means he gets changed in the sitting room and abandons his pyjamas on the armchair in front of the television and someone – John usually – then puts Edward's pyjamas plus yesterday's uniform in the wash. When I say to John that he should not put Edward's clothes in the wash for, surely, Edward doesn't need to wear a new school uniform and new pyjamas every day, he says, 'Samantha! You cannot possibly think it is a good idea for Edward to go to school in the same uniform all the time?' But I tell John that I am not suggesting that. I tell him that a) I have made Edward's uniform all nice and clean for him, and b) why, if John feels so exercised about Edward's washing, does he not feel so excited about his own? John then just stares at me as if I have walked out of the lunatic asylum.

So, with the uniform and pyjamas, that's half a load. With Bennie and Jamie there's even more washing than with Edward. Bennie gets through at least two pairs of trousers a day because he either urinates or defecates in them inadvertently, or takes them off and puts them carefully in the dog's water bowl – 'Look! A boat!' – or he'll sit down in the middle of a mud patch on the way back from playgroup and do a bottom dance in it. I think that Bennie doesn't really like wearing trousers at all and, therefore, has just devised ways of making me take them off. With Jamie, it's T-shirts and tops that get dirty because he hates anyone feeding him so he spends a vast proportion of the day trying to spoon butternut squash into his mouth and failing. 'Erggh!' he'll say as he grabs his plastic spoon off you. 'Blerp!' he'll say as he sticks it into his butternut squash, and then he'll give out a long 'Gaaa!' and fling the squash all down his T-shirt.

'Why don't you put a bib on him?' Santa asked when she first saw Jamie decorate himself, the kitchen table and the wall with his pale yellow gloop.

'Be my guest!' I showed her where we kept all the bibs we had been given and which nobody has ever used apart from guests who come round with their own much cleaner, much better-behaved babies.

'Right, lovely baby,' said Santa, choosing a soft blue one with a picture of an elephant on it. 'Here is a bib, my darling. It will keep you clean and beautiful!'

'A bib?' said Bennie, eyeing what Santa had in her hand. 'For me?'

'No, darling,' said Santa. 'It's for your baby brother.'

'Ooh noo,' said Bennie, putting his hands across his eyes in pretend horror.

Santa advanced towards Jamie.

'Erggh, blerp, ga,' he said sweetly to her. Then he saw

the bib. 'Erggh, blerp, ga!' he said, now looking suspiciously at her, and as she went to tie it round his neck he whipped his head round as quick as a shot and sank his teeth into her hand.

'Arrgghh,' said Santa as she recoiled backwards clutching the bib. 'That really hurt me, Jamie!'

'ERGGH, BLERP, GA!' said Jamie triumphantly.

'Blaady hell, Samantha,' said Santa, looking upset. 'Why didn't you tell me Jamie hated bibs?'

'I tried to, and, anyway, I thought it might work.'

So, once we have John's things and Edward's uniform and underwear and pyjamas and Bennie's endless pairs of trousers and Jamie's endless butternut squash spattered T-shirts we are up to one load a day.

4) Then there's the bed linen. I change Bennie's cot sheet and duvet cover once a week and Jamie's almost every day because he's constantly sicking up milk and his sheet always smells of sour milk, which is disgusting. I change Edward's sheet and duvet cover once a week and mine and John's mattress protector and sheet and duvet cover – all superking size – once a week, and all that probably takes about three to four loads a week so our weekly tally so far is eleven washes. Eleven washes and we haven't even talked about the weekend yet!

5) The weekend wash is the worst. There is always at least one dirty school uniform to go in, plus a tie, a blazer, Edward's weekly sports kit (shorts, T-shirt, two pairs of football socks, one pair of gym socks, a tracksuit top and bottom and a fleece), Edward's swimming trunks and towel, Bennie's swimming trunks and towel, all of Bennie's

340

discarded trousers that I have found stuffed in the dog basket where he likes to hide them, endless odd socks that are hanging around the house, and all of the clothes used over the weekend which have got muddy. This usually comprises two pairs of trousers, three T-shirts, two sets of underwear, a pair of tracksuit bottoms, a sweat top and two jumpers, plus the usual endless pyjamas for Edward; five pairs of trousers, eight pairs of underpants, five pairs of un-matching socks, three T-shirts, three jumpers, four vests and two pairs of pyjamas for Bennie; six T-shirts, six jumpers, three pairs of trousers, five pairs of socks, three bedtime Babygros and two vests for Jamie. And then there is my washing and what do I wash? My knickers and socks, maybe a T-shirt, and one pair of jeans all week!

Total laundry, including separate white washes, which I always forget to do and then get into trouble about with John the Second and Edward because all their lovely white shirts and T-shirts are now a sort of off-greyish whiteish colour: 20–24 loads, which is two a day. And then I have to unload the washer and put it all in the dryer and then, when it has all dried and we have ratcheted our electricity bill up by another million pounds, I have to sort it all and fold it all and try to match up the socks that never match and try to work out which are Jamie's vests and socks and T-shirts and trousers versus Bennie's vests and socks and T-shirts and trousers, and then find the labels and look at them because it is hard to separate whose stuff is whose because Bennie and Jamie are so close together in age and therefore size and then I have to put all the laundry away carefully in their drawers and then start all over again the next day when it all reappears. I have it down to a fine art now, though. I am like an octopus with my sorting and folding, and then I run upstairs *and . . . Whoosh! It's all in the drawers – maybe not so neat and tidy but it will do.*

Sometimes, though, my system fails. I once went into Edward's room to kiss him goodnight and found him struggling with a pyjama top.

'I. Can't. Get. It. On,' he said as he tried to squeeze himself into a blue stripy flannel top.

'I think you'll find that's Bennie's.'

And the other day John went to work wearing a pair of Simpsons socks. None of us said anything, though. We all just smirked at him.

But, just before I am about to venture into the mayhem that is the laundry, I hear footsteps at the back of the house.

Then I hear, 'Daaarling! We are back!' It's Santa. 'Hello, darling,' I hear her say to Bennie. She comes through into the hall and sees me. 'Samantha!' she says, bending forward to give me a kiss. 'Oh Samantha, I got your messages and here I am, darling, and you mustn't be cross with me and I mustn't be cross with you and . . .'

'Why are you here?' I ask her a bit coldly.

'Oh but you are cross! Why, Samantha, why?'

I tell Santa that actually I am not cross with her but that, as I had no other way of finding out what had happened to John the First, I had hoped she'd ring last night.

'Oh but I couldn't ring last night!' She flicks her shiny black bob back behind her ears. 'I had to find John and then he was so upset and he needed me to comfort him so we went for this dinner at a beautiful place in the middle of nowhere and it was lit with candles, and John – oh

342

Samantha, he told me everything! He told me about how he loved you and how you went off with Edward and –'

'Santa! That is just not true! You cannot trust him and you must believe me when I tell you that!'

'Well, that is what he said,' says Santa defensively, 'and I do not believe you at all. Honestly, Samantha, was it the right thing for Edward to force John to leave? Was it?'

'Actually, Santa, I have no intention of discussing any of this with you.'

'Is it because you only think of me as being an au pair?' She looks all indignant.

'No, it is nothing to do with you being an au pair and everything to do with the fact that everything you are talking about happened a long time ago and that John the First is a habitual liar.'

'He is not! He truly loves you and Edward, you know. I mean, he doesn't love you like . . .'

'Like what, Santa?' She goes pink and her eyes shine.

'Like he says he loves me, but he wants to make everything up to you! He told me he was going to take you and Edward for dinner last night and that he was going to tell you about me and him but then you chucked him out on that horrible hill and –'

I then tell Santa that I chucked him out because he was being utterly annoying and that I still feel utterly justified in leaving him on Wycombe Hill. 'All I actually want to know now is whether John has any intention of coming back to see his son?'

'Of course he does! John already has come back!'

'What?'

'He is here now. He is waiting in the car!'

'Why?'

'Oh,' she says sadly, 'I almost forgot to tell you. You have to leave now.'

'I have no intention of going anywhere, thank you very much.'

'No, Samantha, you must go now. Janet has rung John. She wants to see you.'

'Oh.'

'Yes, she says it is very important and she wants to see you and John together and he is waiting to drive you there and I will stay here and look after the children. You must go, darling. Really you must.'

As I leave, I ask Santa if she has heard from Dougie. 'No, darling. My phone was off.'

'But didn't he leave you a message?'

'Dougie?' She looks surprised. 'Why would Dougie leave me a message?'

'Never mind.'

16. Tuesday evening

Everything in the hospital is quiet now and John and I are sitting round Janet's bed in virtual silence. There is not much to say to each other. All I can hear is Janet's heavily laboured breathing. Hurhh, she breathes in. Urhh, she breathes out. Hurhh, she breathes in. Urhh, she breathes out. Hurhh. Urhh. Hurhh. Urhh. A machine next to her head blinks red and occasionally bleeps, which makes me jump out of my skin. Hurhh. Urrh. Hurhh. Urhh. *Bleep!* The next time it does it I get a fit of the giggles.

'Sammie!' says John the First sharply. 'Now is not the time to laugh.'

He is sitting a bit apart from me on Janet's bed. I am on a chair in the corner, shrouded by the canvas of the portable screens that stand like guardians looking over each and every patient.

John the First is in an odd mood. I knew it as soon as I got in the car. He just said, 'Hi, Sammie,' and then left it at that. He didn't bang on about me leaving him on Wycombe Hill. Neither did he tell me about his new-found love affair with Santa.

We just sat in silence for the journey and I looked out of the window at people's faces and I thought, 'I wonder what's happening in their lives today?' For right after my father died and I walked out of his house and down the street, I imagined every single person who saw me could see that my father had just died. I could not understand how they could not have seen it. Wasn't that grief written on my face? Did I not look wild-eyed and stricken? But when I went into the newsagent's to buy a paper, the lady at the till went wittering on – 'Ooh you'll never believe what happened in that house opposite here last night!' – for so long that eventually I turned to her and said, 'My father's just died.' She then looked all nervous and shocked and didn't even charge me for the paper. Now, when I myself look at all these strangers, I understand that our faces reveal nothing. No one can spot a serial killer or an adulterer or the person who is living in pain or dying of cancer, or those whose hearts are pumping away right now trying to keep them alive, to stop those arteries from furring up. We all walk around in blissful ignorance of each other, of even ourselves. I think it's almost a miracle.

So I could not tell what was behind the odd mood John the First was in and, after watching him for a bit, his face set in an immovable mask as he negotiated roundabouts and traffic lights, I gave up trying. I wanted to tell him about Nicholas and Genevieve and Nicholas's twenty-year-old son. I wanted to say to him, 'Why aren't you more like Nicholas? Why is it that Nicholas was not an absent father and you are? Since when did you think you get to make that choice?' But I decided to bide my time.

When we got to the hospital John the First turned to me and said, 'I called my mother this morning, Sammie, and she didn't sound good.'

'Right.'

'She told me she didn't think she has much time left.'

I sighed then. 'I'm sorry, John.'

'She wants to see us together.'

I told him I knew that because that's what Santa had said.

'I didn't think you would agree, Sammie.'

'But here I am.'

And so here we are with nothing much left to say to each other about this. I am here, hanging slightly back from Janet's bed, with my ex-husband, and feeling awkward all because a dying woman wants it this way. Why does she? Does she wish to die having maintained some illusion? The thought of all this makes me feel quite angry. Why have I let this go on? Why did I not puncture these pretences some years ago? Why did I not turn up in Devon with beautiful Bennie and a wailing Jamie? Why did I not say, 'These are Edward's brothers and he loves them so you must love them too'? And where is Edward? Surely, if we are to play happy families for this one last time, Edward should be part of this. And the thought of Edward, now probably safe at home playing with his brothers and arguing with Santa about how long he's supposed to be on the computer, makes me calm down. Of course Janet would not want to put Edward through this for she is a good woman. That I know.

Just as I am thinking about all of this, Janet wakes up.

Bleeep!

'What's that?' she says weakly.

'It's the machine,' says John.

'Is that you, John?' she says, reaching out her hand. She is obviously having trouble focusing.

'Yes, it's me, Mum.'

'I can't see much.' Her voice sounds panicked.

John reaches forward and takes her hand. 'It's probably because you've just woken up, Mum.'

'No, no.' Her voice is as thin as paper. 'I'm losing my

sight, John. I can tell. It's going so quickly. Yesterday I could see a bit from the window and today the nurse took me over and I couldn't see anything!' She is crying now.

John takes both her hands in his. 'No, Mum, you're not losing your sight. It was raining today. It makes the sky dark. You are not losing your sight!'

Tears roll down her face. 'I am losing everything, John,' she says hoarsely. 'I've lost my taste completely. I barely eat. There seems no point in it. I derive no pleasure from it.'

'But, Mum,' says John, and I can tell he is close to tears, 'you've always loved to eat!'

'I don't think I shall ever eat again. I don't think I shall do anything ever again.'

'You will, Mum, you will!' he says desperately.

'No, John.' And he leans forward to hear her for her voice is so faint now. 'I shall never do anything again. I am losing my life, John. I can feel this darkness entering into my heart. I am so tired, John. I just feel I must give up and let go.'

'No, Mum, no! You can't go. Please, Mum.'

But now Janet talks as if her mind is wandering. 'All I have now are my memories,' she is saying. John has sunk down onto the bed. He has his head on her breast and she is absent-mindedly stroking his hair. 'I remember that summer I first planted the buddleia in Devon. Do you remember that, John? You were tiny then and just crawling. You were covered in earth and you smelled all peaty. And you kept trying to eat the earth and your mouth was all dark.'

'I remember that, Mum,' John says softly, almost as if in a trance.

'And do you remember the smell of that bush as it grew up at the back of the house? You grew with that bush, John. You grew strong and healthy just like that buddleia. I will never smell that buddleia again, John.' She seems quite calm now. She has stopped crying. Then she says, 'Everything must grow and change, John.'

'I know,' he says, but his words are muffled.

Suddenly, Janet sort of shakes him. She gathers up her strength and pushes his shoulder. 'You must think of Edward. He is your son and . . .'

'Sammie's here,' says John to his mother.

'Sammie?' Janet now looks up wildly and peers around dementedly. 'Where are you, Samantha? Are you here? I can't see you.'

'I'm here, Janet.' I move out of the shadows.

'Oh you've come, Samantha.' She sounds relieved. 'I wasn't sure you would.'

'Yes, I'm here,' I say again.

Janet motions for me to come nearer. 'I want you to sit near me and take my hand, Samantha.' I do as she asks. John also sits near her and takes her other hand. 'Here you two are.' She sounds contented. 'You are together again, as you always should have been.'

'Janet –' I say.

'Here you are,' she says, cutting in and now sounding surprisingly strong. 'Edward's parents. What a wonderful child he is. He is your son, Samantha, and you should be very proud of him.'

'I am very proud of him.'

'You are a good mother, Samantha. Your children will flourish.'

'Her *children*?' says John the First.

'Yes, John. Edward will flourish and so will the other two. They will be happy because Samantha is happy, aren't you, Samantha?'

'Yes, I am.'

Then Janet turns to John. 'Will you please go and ask the sister for some painkillers? I have run out and now I am getting tired and I am in pain. Would you do that for me, darling?'

'Yes,' says John, but he looks confused.

'Go now, please.' She sounds weak again. John goes off and Janet grasps my hand even tighter. Her eyes are closed. 'Samantha,' she says, almost like a sigh. I don't know what to do. Suddenly, Janet seems so intense and yet so weakened by it.

'Janet, you must rest.'

'No! I need to tell you something. I want to tell you that I am sorry. I have done this all wrong.' She starts coughing and sinks back a bit onto her pillow.

'No, there is nothing to apologize for.'

'Yes, there is,' she says so quietly that I can barely hear what she is saying. 'There is so much I want to say, Samantha, but I haven't the energy.' I lean forward towards her. I can see she has tears edging out from her closed eyes. It makes me start to cry.

'Janet, please.'

'No, Samantha. I should have come to see you. I should have met your children and your husband and I am so sorry that I was so blind, so very blind. I just couldn't let go.'

'It's fine, Janet.'

'No, it's not fine. I've been such a fool! I never invited you to my house, Samantha. I never went to see you and it must have been hard for you.'

'It was.'

'And I was no help to you!' She is getting distressed. 'I just couldn't accept that my son, my only son would . . .'

'Please don't get agitated. It's all in the past. There's nothing we can do about it now.'

'But there is,' Janet whispers softly. 'I want you to listen to me when I tell you this.'

'I am listening.'

Janet leans towards me and opens her eyes. 'Look in the bedside cabinet,' she whispers. 'There is an envelope in there. It has Edward written on the front.' I look and find the envelope on the bottom shelf. 'I have written Edward a letter. I have told him in this letter that I love him and that I am so very proud of him, for I fear I will never see him again.' There are tears running down her face.

'Oh Janet.' I am now weeping as if I will never stop.

'In this letter,' she continues, 'I tell Edward many important things but I don't want anyone to open it until after my death. You must promise me this, Samantha.'

'I promise,' I say desperately.

'It is my goodbye to him, to you all, you see. It is my last goodbye, Samantha.'

'No,' I say and I sink down onto my knees at her bedside, sobbing into her nightclothes. Then I hear John the First's footsteps coming back down the ward.

'Samantha,' whispers Janet, so hoarsely now, 'you will survive all this, you know. You have a good family. Keep it that way.' And then she closes her eyes.

17. Tuesday's end

John the First and I come back from the hospital. We don't speak in the car. I want to ask him what Janet said to him, for I left them alone together for a good quarter of an hour, but when John came out he had hard eyes so I don't say anything. I just sit and stare out into the black of the night. And then when we come home and Santa runs to the door looking beautiful and concerned, he just pushes past her and goes to the kitchen.

'Samantha! What is it? What is the matter with him?'

I tell Santa that I don't know. 'His mother talked to him, but I don't know what she said.'

Santa looks very hurt. 'He just pushed me out of the way.'

'I think he's very upset,' I say, by way of explanation. Then I remember. The kids! It seems like days since I saw them, not hours. 'The children!' I say to Santa. 'Where are they? How are they?'

Santa tells me not to worry. 'They are in bed. Jamie ate some baked beans and threw up but only a little bit.'

'He only likes butternut squash,' I say distractedly, suddenly feeling the clean edges of the envelope Janet gave to me in my coat pocket.

'And it took two little pots of pops to get Bennie up the stairs, and Edward . . .'

'Yes, Edward,' I say, realizing I haven't seen Edward all

day and suddenly missing him very badly, 'how is my darling Edward?'

'He is fine, but I told him you had gone to the hospital with his father and he was a bit upset because he said he wanted to go with you.'

'Oh no.'

'But I told him you would be back tonight and that if he was worried he should come downstairs and talk to you.'

'Great.'

Then Santa tells me I have three telephone messages. 'Your mother rang to say that she is back from holiday and she had a great time and that she might drop in tomorrow but that she can't pick Edward up next Tuesday because she has met a friend on the cruise and she is going over to her house for tea. And John rang to see how everything was and he spoke to Edward and he told me to tell you he'll be back late tonight because of some work thing he has to change. Oh and your sister rang and she talked to me for ages! Does she always talk a lot?'

I tell Santa that my sister talks all the time non-stop.

'She left a strange message. She said that Genevieve is fine with everything . . .'

'That's a relief.'

'. . . and that – what is it? Is it Joey or something? Joey has gone a bit mad! Does that make sense?'

'It does to me.'

Santa then says she has to go now. 'I am babysitting tonight.' She looks nervously towards the kitchen door. 'Do you think I should . . . ?'

'No, Santa. I think he wants to be alone.'

'But you are here!' she says accusingly.

'I'm his ex-wife. I've known him for years, Santa.'

She then asks me to tell John that she is on her mobile if he needs her. 'I will come any time of day or night for him. You must tell him that, Samantha.'

I tell her that I will tell him.

On the way out she tells me that there was another call. 'Dougie rang!' she says.

'Oh. Did he say anything?'

'Yes.' Santa looks rather puzzled. 'He said to tell you that he thinks he may have got the last thing he told you all wrong but that everything is OK and that he is all right.'

'And did he talk to you much?'

'No. It was very odd. Normally, he likes to talk to me on the telephone but he just asked me to give you that message and then he rang off. It was quite surprising.'

'Very surprising.'

When I get back into the house, John is sitting in the kitchen with his head in his hands. He seems broken, shattered. I open a bottle of wine. For a while we don't speak. We barely move. I just sip wine while John does . . . I'm not sure what. I think he is crying as his shoulders are moving very slightly up and down, up and down.

I want to tell him it is too late. Janet is dying. She is just holding on to this tiny thread of breath, this little faint murmur of a heartbeat, this minuscule globule of blood, of red oxygenated blood that is weakly managing to meander round her system.

I want to tell him that soon, maybe even tonight, Janet will do what so many other people do, what my father did not so long ago. She will simply cease to exist. All these little things that are valiantly keeping her alive will gradually stop working. Her lungs will stop inflating. Her breath will go. Her fading eyesight will finally leave. Her heart will stop. Her pulse will fail. Everything that is and was Janet Parr will, in that tiny, inevitable second that no one will ever know about, bar possibly Janet Parr herself and maybe even she won't recognize it for what it is, finish and end for ever. She will deflate, as my father deflated.

I remember going to see him as he lay dying. I drove up the M4 and I cannot remember a single other car being on the motorway. I remember being flashed by a speed camera but I didn't care. Edward was next to me, curled up and asleep, tucked in with colourful blankets. I watched him sleep. I watched my speedometer rise and fall. I remember thinking, 'I shall never drive up the M4 again like this.' Everything seemed almost like a celebration or as if I was on some hallucinogenic drug that suddenly lets you see the truth. I saw trees and lamp posts in London that I had never seen before. I entered the square in which he lived. I parked the car and sat in the square, watching and waiting. I could hear Edward's breath gently inflating his lungs. I watched him breathe in and out. What a miracle that he could breathe! I sat and knew I would never see my father alive again. I waited for the nightmare to begin.

All this I want to tell John the First. I want to tell him how shocking it is to see a dead body. I want to tell him how death brings some people together but causes fissures between others. I think Julia and Joe were never the same after my father died.

When Joe told me once that Julia changed after she saw our father's body I started giggling because I remembered what happened the next day. We had the heating on full blast. My sister insisted on it.

She said, 'I don't want Dad to be cold.'

'He can't get cold. He's dead!'

'He may not be dead.'

'He hasn't breathed for hours! His eyes haven't blinked.'

'I'm still not sure. Maybe he's just slipped into a coma.'

'If that's the case then we must take him to hospital!'

'What's the point of that? He's dead!'

So we left him on his bed in his bedroom and notched up the heating and sat with a bottle of whisky and watched him lie so still and deflated until the morning when the doctor came.

The doctor wasn't our father's usual GP, who had gone skiing, but he knew about him. This doctor said he had been told he might have to examine our father. He explained to us that he had brought the death certificate with him but that he really had to agree with the regular doctor, and that he would have to examine our father to establish the cause of death. I remember that it was about this time I got the giggles. I had had far too much whisky during the night, much to the disapproval of Julia, and I was still a little tipsy.

'Well, here we are, then, Mr Smythe,' said the doctor, talking to my father as if he was alive and a simpleton. 'I'm just going to examine you.' My father lay still and unblinking. 'I'll just warm up my stethoscope,' said the doctor. He looked like something out of a Hardy novel with his fine clothes, fob watch and pale, slightly moist skin. 'Is there anywhere I can warm my stethoscope, Miss Smythe?'

I was about to suggest he asked my father when Julia cut in. 'Of course,' she said. 'I shall heat it in the kettle.' So then we all had to wait as the kettle boiled away.

The doctor kept looking at my father. My father kept looking at the ceiling. The doctor kept up a one-sided conversation. 'It's quite warm for this time of year, isn't it, Mr Smythe?' and 'Aren't the leaves on the trees a wonderful hue?' and eventually my sister reappeared with the warmed instrument. The doctor felt my father's head with his hand. 'You're surprisingly warm, Mr Smythe,' he said. 'Miss Smythe,' he said, addressing me again, which was beginning to get irritating, 'what makes you think your father is dead?'

'Oh,' I said, suppressing a rising giggle. 'I think it's because he hasn't blinked or breathed for hours.'

'Ah-ha,' said the doctor and then, as if to himself, 'no rigor mortis. Warm body. Hmm. Hot room. Hmm.'

'My God!' My sister had now gone ashen. 'Do you mean he isn't dead? Do you mean we've had our father in this boiling room for all this time and he isn't dead?'

'Oh no, no, no,' said the doctor. 'What I mean is he is surprisingly warm for a . . . ahem –' and then he turned his face away from my father as if fearful of hurting his feelings – 'dead person.'

'Do you mean that we could've saved him?' said my sister, now almost shouting. 'Maybe he wasn't dead,' she said wildly. 'Maybe if we'd taken him to hospital they could've saved him. Maybe we've killed him!'

'Calm down,' the doctor pleaded with my sister. 'I am sure Mr Smythe is dead and that nothing you could have done would have saved him.'

'But you don't know that!' My sister was now in a state of near-hysteria and fled from the room, which was probably quite a good thing for when the doctor bent down to press the stethoscope to my father's chest, my father let out a long, endless fart. 'Never mind, Mr Smythe,' said the doctor. 'Corpses often have wind.'

I am afraid that was it for me.

'Maybe it did hit her hard,' I said to Joe when he came to talk to me about it.

'She thinks she killed him,' said Joe. 'She thinks she could have saved him.'

'Nothing could have saved him. You must tell her that. He died of over-living. That's what the doctor put on the certificate: "Mr Smythe died of exhaustion."'

'How could anyone die of exhaustion?'

'Oh I don't know.' I suddenly felt exhausted myself. 'Anyway, if my sister's unhappy, why don't you try to help her?'

But of course I now know that he didn't help her at all.

And now here I am sitting opposite this man who is about to lose his mother and suddenly I start feeling angry with him too. Where was he when my father died? For all he knew, I could've been cycling round the village in my night-dress. I remember trying to telephone him but I couldn't find him. I was crying and didn't know who to turn to and Edward was in bed and I almost passed out with grief, and when I woke Edward was pouring bleach all over the carpet.

'Where were you when my father died?' I ask John the First.

John raises his head. His eyes are red. He looks pathetic, wrung out. 'What?'

I know he feels exhausted. I can see it but I am not in the mood to be careful or gentle now. I am in dangerous territory and I don't care. 'I said, where were you when my father died?'

'Where was I?'

'Yes, where were you?'

'I don't know. When was it again?'

'Five years ago.'

'Let me think.' He pours himself a glass of wine. He pretends to think. 'Had I joined that bluegrass band then?'

'I don't know. I didn't know you were ever in a blue-grass band.'

'Didn't I tell you about it?' He is suddenly enthusiastic.

'No.'

'Oh it was great. We toured round the southern states. God, we had fun. But then . . . I suppose we just went our separate ways. Bits of flotsam and jetsam on the wind, like a tumbling . . . Did Eddie ever get that tape I sent him?'

'No. Did you actually send him a tape?'

John the First looks tired again. 'No, probably not.' Then he looks at me with all the sadness of the world in his eyes. 'I don't know where I was when your father died, Sammie. I really don't. I'm sorry.'

'I don't know if sorry is good enough. I'm here for you but you were never there for me, were you?'

'No, I wasn't. Don't worry. My mother's told me all about it.'

'What do you mean, your mother's told you all about it?'

'She said, "Samantha's a better person than you," and I think that's probably the last thing she'll ever say to me.' Then he starts to cry.

Four bottles of wine later and he is still crying and now I'm crying too but I think I'm just drunk. I can't really concentrate on what he is saying. I keep catching vague words and sentences, and then I think I catch a sentence which says, 'I love you more than I have ever loved anyone in my life.' This sentence seems to hang in the air as if suspended on strings.

'I'm sorry?' I slur.

John the First looks at me very intently but I can see two of him and it's very disconcerting. 'I said I love you. I have always loved you.'

'What?'

'I love you, Sammie. I have come here to tell you this. This is why I have come. Not to see my mother, but to see you.'

'Are you mad? You haven't come to see me because, if you have, how little time we have spent together! You've spent more time with Santa than you have with me.'

'Santa means nothing to me. She is merely a diversion.'

'Merely a diversion! That's probably how you describe Edward!'

'I have never described Eddie as a diversion.'

'Well, you've never truly loved him.'

'I did love Eddie! I do love Eddie, but he's so much your child now. What did you expect me to do?'

'What did I expect you to do? I expected you to love him like I did. I expected you to be happy with him and care for him and feel some parental warmth towards him.'

'I did, I did!'

'No, you didn't!' Now I am crying for all those years of love and pain and sadness. 'You turned your back on me, on him! You went off on some dream of becoming a guitar player in a band. You didn't even send a postcard to tell us where you were. We loved you! I loved you, John! Me,

360

myself, I loved you and you left me! How come a man like Nicholas, a man you dismissed as being "too conventional", has managed to have a relationship with his son by his ex-partner and you haven't? Tell me that, John!'

'I have no answer to that,' John says quietly. 'I only wanted you to know that I love you. And hey, Sammie, no one could love Eddie the way you do. You just don't let it happen.'

'It's my job to love him.' Suddenly, I feel really upset and sorry for Edward only being loved by me, and sorry for myself for reasons I'm not sure about, and then, before I know it, John the First has grabbed me and is kissing me and I'm crying and kissing him back as if I have never kissed anyone but him in my entire life, and then, through my drunken, teary haze, I look up and standing right there watching us is Edward, my Edward, and he's not looking at all happy.

'What are you doing, Mummy?'

'Oh Edward.'

'What are you doing, Daddy?'

'I'm kissing your mother,' says John the First.

Edward looks confused. Edward looks in pain. Edward looks desperate. I reach out to comfort him but he backs away from me. 'Were you kissing Mummy?' he asks his father.

'Yes.'

'But she's wearing a marry ring,' says Edward, his eyes filling with tears. 'She's married to Daddy, my other daddy.'

John the First tries to grab Edward and hug him but Edward moves away from his grasp. 'Well, she used to be married to me.'

'But Mummy's not married to you now. She's married to my daddy.'

'But I got there first. And, Eddie, I am your daddy.'

And Edward turns to me like he did when he was a baby and I can see his eyes are bottomless and filled with tears. I can see his confusion, his fear. 'I don't understand, Mummy. Why are you kissing my genete-whatsit daddy? I thought you loved my other daddy.'

'I do love your other daddy.'

'Do you?' says John the First.

'Yes, I do!'

'You loved me, remember?' says John the First. 'Can't you remember that?'

'But I don't love you now.'

'I don't believe you, Sammie. Why were you kissing me if you don't still love me? I know you, Sammie. I know you better than anyone else. We can make a life together, you, me and Eddie.'

And now Edward is crying. 'My name's not Eddie!' And he comes to me finally and he buries his head in my lap and I can smell that smell of his. I know it so well, slightly acrid yet with a certain sweetness.

I am crying and crying and I say to him, 'It's all right, my darling. It's all right, my darling. I am so sorry. I am so sorry.'

John the First is saying, 'Eddie, listen to me. I held you up in my arms and I felt like a king. I saw you born and I felt like a prince. I've written songs about you, Eddie, hundreds of them, and I'll sing them to you and I'll take you to places you couldn't imagine in your wildest dreams where we can surf all day and eat fresh fruit from the trees and I'll treat your mother like a princess, Eddie. I promise I will because I love you so and I am so full of this love because this is how you and your mother make me feel now.'

But Edward isn't listening because there, standing at the door, is John the Second.

'Daddy!' yells Edward, flying into John's arms. 'Daddy, Daddy, Daddy!' John lifts him up and kisses him.

'What is going on?' says John the Second looking from me to John the First. Neither of us says anything. I am looking down at the table. I cannot look up. 'Why is Edward up?' he asks me. I do not reply. 'Why are you up, Edward?'

'I couldn't sleep!' says Edward. 'Mummy wasn't here when I got home from school and Santa told me she was at the hospital and that my grannie is really ill now and I've been crying about it in my bed and then when I came downstairs to tell Mummy, she was . . .'

'What was she doing, Edward?' says John the Second carefully.

'Nothing.' Edward looks down towards the ground.

John the Second turns and looks at me. I can feel him looking at me. Then I look up to face his gaze but his eyes are scanning the room: four empty wine bottles. He then looks at John the First. John the First winks at him.

I wince. This is not good. This is, in fact, dreadful. This is the terrible thing I've dreamt about. Everything I have worked for is about to collapse and it's my fault, my own stupid fault. And I realize, as I did absolutely in the very moment when John the Second walked in through the door, that I could not bear to lose him.

'I think you need to go to bed now, Edward,' says John the Second very calmly. 'You go upstairs and I'll bring up some hot milk and tuck you in.' But Edward still clings to him. 'What's the matter, Edward?'

'Nothing's the matter,' says Edward rather desperately. 'I just don't want to go to bed, Daddy.'

'Oh I'll put you to bed.' John the First walks towards him. 'All right, Eddie?'

'No,' says Edward, burying his face in John the Second's shoulder. 'I don't want you to.'

'He doesn't want you to,' says John the Second. 'Now back off and leave it to me.'

'Back off? Well, I don't think I'm going to be doing that now, John. Eddie is my son.'

'You know something, John?' says John the Second, looking John the First square in the face. 'Edward may be your son but I have brought him up and so I think I really can tell you to back off if I want to.'

'Really? You really think you can convince me so easily that you are the protector of this supposedly loving and happy family?'

'Yes. Because that is what we are, John. We are kind. We are loving. We are happy.'

'Really?' John the First is smirking a bit. 'If you are that happy, then why has your wife spent the last half an hour snogging my face off?'

John the Second puts Edward down. He advances towards me. I daren't look at his face. He must be so angry for he knows it is true.

'John,' I say.

'Don't say anything, Samantha.' He then turns to face John the First. 'Do you think I care that she's kissed you?' he says to him very quietly while putting an arm round my shoulders and holding me close. 'Do you think that I am going to get cross and angry about something so petty? Do you think I am going to shout and scream at my wife, at the woman I love, and walk out of the door because of a few pathetic kisses? For what are you to me,

John? You are nothing, and I am going nowhere.'

'I don't think you understand.' John the First is now a bit perplexed. 'She kissed me! Doesn't that mean anything to you?'

'Of course it means something to me. It means that she was probably drunk and hurt and upset and confused. It means that for a small while, for an infinitesimal moment in time, my Samantha lost her way, as she does sometimes. Do you think I don't know this about her? Do you not realize that part of the reason I married her was to protect her and look after her, not leave her like you did?'

'Well, what about Eddie?' says John the First desperately.

Edward runs to my side and I hold him as tightly as John the Second is holding me.

'He is my son. I could ask for custody.'

My head flies up. Custody? John the Second holds me even tighter. 'Of course you could,' he says, 'but I'd like to see you try. No court in the land is giving you Edward, as well you know. Stop trying to hurt everyone. God, you'd even use your son to try to destroy our happiness. Well, you will not succeed. Me and Samantha and Edward and Bennie and Jamie are a family and nothing you can do, none of these silly little victories you try to score over us, will change anything. Other marriages may fail. Everything Samantha has trusted – you, her sister's marriage, her friend's marriage – might crumble and fall, but not me and not us. We are strong and safe and warm and, with that in mind, John, you may pack your bags and leave our house right now.'

We all stand there absolutely stunned. I cannot move. I cannot speak. I want to weep. I want to hold John the

Second and Edward as tightly as they are holding me but my arms, my legs, my feet, my vocal cords are like lead. I look at John the First. I think he is about to say something. Suddenly, the telephone rings.

Ring ring! Ring ring!

It makes us all jump. The silence is broken. John the Second reaches for the telephone. John the First turns on his heel and walks out of the kitchen. Edward runs into the sitting room and throws himself onto the sofa, sobbing.

'It's the hospital,' I hear John the Second say. 'They want to speak to John.'

I cannot reply. John the Second leaves the room, clutching the telephone in his hand.

Finally, I make it to the sitting room. I sit down next to Edward and take him in my arms. I rock him back and forth, back and forth. 'I used to do this to you when you were a baby,' I tell him. 'I used to sing to you and rock you to sleep and you always loved it.'

'Would you sing to me now, Mummy, please?' Edward says in a muffled, small, tired voice and so I sing to him those songs I sang way back then.

I sing 'Lulaylula My Little Tiny Child'. I sing 'Away in a Manger'. I sing 'Iko Iko': 'My grandma and your grandma, sittin' by the fire. My grandma said to your grandma, "I'm gonna set your flag on fire . . .".'

'Is my grannie dead?'

'I don't know, but I think she probably is.' I stroke Edward's hair, his thick thatch of hair, back from his brow. The skin on his forehead is as pale as the moon.

'Oh dear,' says Edward and he begins to cry.

'I am so sorry, Edward. I should not have put you through all this.'

He cuddles into me. John the Second comes back in with some hot milk for Edward. He sits down next to me and puts his capacious arms around us both. 'I am the glue,' he says. 'I am the Airfix glue that holds you both together!'

Edward giggles a little. 'Mummy,' he says, 'has my daddy, my genete-whatsit daddy, gone now?'

'I don't know but I think he probably will go quite soon.'

'Will I ever see him again?'

'I am sure you will.'

Then Edward says, 'But I don't want to see him again. What if he steals me?'

I tell Edward that if his father had wanted to steal him, he probably would have tried to do so by now. 'He won't steal you. He wouldn't dare.'

'Steal you?' says John the Second. 'No way, Edward. You have made your choice and your father, your real father, knows that.'

Then Edward looks at John the Second and he says to him, 'You are my real father, Daddy,' and, for the first time in a long while, I see tears in my John's eyes. Then Edward thinks a bit more. 'I don't think I like my genete-whatsit daddy very much.'

'Sometimes it's fine to feel you don't like some people very much, Edward, especially when they have hurt you.'

'Mummy,' says Edward, 'I'm going to put him on the bad list!' and I say that I should think that putting him on the bad list is a very good idea indeed, and as I take Edward upstairs to bed I hear the sound of a car pulling away from outside our house and it sounds very much like Santa's.

★

When I get back downstairs, John the Second has made a fire. He is sitting in front of it and he is smiling at me and the room is so warm and he is so warm and I sink into his embrace and I curl my head into his chest and I cry for a while and he strokes my hair and says, 'It's all right, Samantha. It's all all right,' and when I have composed myself I sit back and look at him. I see his blue eyes and his handsome kind face and the wrinkles that have grown there over time and his greying hair and then I look at his broad shoulders and flat hands with his long fingers, and I lean forward and kiss him and I tell him I love him over and over again, and just as I am about to unbutton his shirt and his belt and see him naked in the firelight, the telephone rings.

'Oh God,' says John, getting up rather wearily.

'Don't answer it.'

'I must, it could be John.'

'That's why you shouldn't answer it!'

'I have to.'

He goes out but is immediately back, a look of confusion on his face.

'It's your sister. She's . . . well, she's . . . I think she'd better tell you herself.'

I take the phone. 'Julia, what on earth is the matter?'

'Oh, Samantha.' She sounds oddly excited. 'You'll never guess where I am!'

'No, I won't. Where are you?'

'I'm at Oxford police station! I've been arrested for . . . oh hang on a minute.' My sister now turns away from the telephone. I hear her say, 'Excuse me, officer, what have I been arrested for? Oh thank you so much!' Julia turns back to the telephone. 'I've been arrested for Attempted Bodily Harm. They call it ABH, you know.'

'WHAT?'

'Apparently Joe said I stabbed him with that blasted plate, but of course I didn't!'

'Of course you didn't!'

'Well, it's Joe's word against mine, apparently, and this very nice police officer told me that I was only allowed one telephone call so I've called you!'

'And what am I supposed to do?'

'Oh I don't know. I think I need a solicitor. Do you know any solicitors?'

'No,' I say desperately. 'Oh God, Julia, we've had the most awful night here. I don't even know if I'm in a fit state to drive over.'

'Oh.' Julia sounds dreadfully sad.

Suddenly, I see John the Second waving at me. 'Dougie,' he mouths at me.

'Oh my God! Yes. Dougie!'

'What about Dougie?' says my sister.

'He's a solicitor! I'm going to ring him. I'm going to get him over there as soon as possible. Don't you worry, Julia! Dougie will save the day!'

'Hooray!'

Dougie answers the telephone on the tenth ring. 'Mmm, who is it?' he says sleepily.

'It's me.'

'Samantha? It's two in the morning. Why are you ringing me?'

'I need your help. My sister is at Oxford police station. She's been arrested for stabbing Uncle Joe.'

'Oh dear, poor her. Call me in the morning and tell me how you both got on. Bye bye.'

'NO, Dougie! You don't understand. Julia has been arrested for ABH and I can't go over to the police station right now to help.'

'Why not?'

'Because I've drunk too much.' I then go on to explain the events of the evening to him. 'Janet is dying, in fact Janet is probably actually dead, and I kissed John the First –'

'You what?' Dougie now sounds wide awake. 'What on earth made you do that?'

So I tell him I was drunk and emotional and not trusting anything. 'But it's fine because John, my John, has forgiven me and so has Edward . . .'

'Edward! What on earth was Edward doing there?'

'He couldn't sleep. Anyway, it's all worked out because John the First has gone off with Santa . . .'

'Oh there's a surprise.'

'. . . and John and I are here and . . . well, we're just here being loving to each other.'

'But your sister?'

'Yes, right. Now the thing is, Dougie, you have to go to Oxford police station right now.'

'Oxford police station? I'm in London!'

'Well, it won't take you long. There'll be no traffic at this time of night.'

'And what am I supposed to do when I get to Oxford police station?'

'You find my sister and you get her released.'

'What? I can't do that!'

'Why not? You're a lawyer. Go and do whatever it is you lawyers do.'

'I'm a commercial lawyer, not a criminal one.'

'What's the difference?'

'"What's the difference?" It's entirely different.'

'But you must've studied criminal law at some point in your career, didn't you?'

'Of course I did! You have to study all the areas of law to be able to practise it.'

'Well, just put on a suit and pretend you're a criminal lawyer.'

'Samantha, I can't just put on a suit and –'

'Yes, you can! You have to. I told my sister you would. Please, Dougie. Please!'

There is a silence at the other end of the telephone. I can hear Dougie sighing. John the Second looks at me and raises his eyebrows. I shake my head and give him a little frown.

Then Dougie comes back on the line. 'OK, Samantha, have it your way. I'll go now, but God help me if they find out I'm a fraud.'

'You're not a fraud, Dougie! No one could ever think you were a fraud! You're a very good man. You're the best friend a girl could have!'

'Hmm,' grunts Dougie and then he hangs up.

'He's going!' I say to John the Second. 'Dougie is going to save my sister!'

John the Second gives me a big hug and I hug him back. 'It's the beginning of something, Samantha! I can just feel it. Something has changed. I just don't know what it is.'

'No, neither do I!' I say happily. 'But it feels pretty good, doesn't it?'

'Oh yes.'

Then we sit back down on the warm rug beside the fire. Neither of us can stop smiling.

'You didn't really think of going off with John, did you?'

John the Second asks me, gently taking my T-shirt over my head.

'No, John! Not even for one small second.'

And then I start unbuttoning his shirt and undoing the belt on his trousers, and tonight, almost as if it is the first night we have ever been together, we lie in the firelight and eventually we go to sleep replete, peaceful, contented.

Epilogue
Sunday

It is early autumn now and yet it is still warm. I can see the trees from my bedroom window. The leaves are changing colour. I love to watch the leaves. In the spring they are green and soft and furled and shy and they are so clean that I always want to taste them, to put them in my mouth and feel the soft new furriness on my tongue. And then in the summer, as the heat rises off the fields, the leaves start to crackle and dry and become parched and brittle and they sort of sigh when the odd drop of rain comes and they get all excited and reinvigorated, only for the sun to suck them dry again a day later. But now, in this early October sunlight, there is a chill in the air and the new spring greenness and the parched summer yellowness have given way to the deep russets and reds and oranges and pinkish hues that make the leaves look as if they are all dressed up for their final flourish.

I am standing at my open window looking at everyone outside. It is Jamie's first birthday. We hadn't intended to celebrate it but, some days after John the First had left, Edward said, 'I think we should give Jamie a birthday party,' and I knew what he meant.

Later that night, after everyone had gone to bed, John the Second said to me, 'We have much to celebrate, Samantha,' and I sank back into his arms and felt whole and secure.

The next day I got up and rifled through my purse and found what I was looking for.

Jo sounded ecstatic when I rang. 'You want to book Wally?' she said excitedly. 'You want to book Wally for Jamie's first birthday party?'

I told her that yes, I certainly did want to book Wally.

'Oh he will be so pleased. I mean, he's wonderful with little children. He's really, really wonderful with them. He could do some balloon tricks and bring a rabbit and maybe have a little disco.'

'Jamie's only going to be one.'

'But one-year-olds love to dance!'

'Jamie can't walk yet, Jo,' I said, but she wasn't really listening.

'Oh yes, and then he could do some magic tricks and some card games and . . . oh but, Samantha, I will give you your money back if you don't think he's any good. Honest, I will! But you'll love him. I know you will. This is his big break. I can just feel it.'

'Jo,' I said patiently, 'I have to go. And please bring Buzzy to the party.'

'Bring Buzzy? Oh how kind! Buzzy will love it! She's always talking about Bennie you know and . . .' and off she went for half an hour until I persuaded Edward, who was loafing around my study trying to secretly eat a packet of Maltesers he'd found in a drawer, to pretend to be a crying baby.

'Oooeeeewaaa!' he went, trying not to giggle.

'Oh Jo, there's Jamie crying. I must go!'

'Jamie? That doesn't sound like Jamie.'

'Waa, waa, waa!' went Edward.

'I never knew Jamie had such a deep voice!' said Jo.

'Oh yes, Jamie is renowned for his deep voice,' and then, finally, I hung up.

'Phew,' said Edward. 'I thought you were never going to get off the phone.'

'Neither did I.'

'Who were you talking to?'

'Jo.'

'What? That Jo who cut open the deer?'

'Yes. Her husband's a children's entertainer and I've booked him for Jamie's party.'

'Is he funny?' asked Edward suspiciously.

'Er, Jo says he's not funny at all.'

'Oh that's quite funny,' said Edward, giggling.

But I am watching Wally in the garden now and he's really not that bad. He's hopeless at entertaining babies but, then again, how do you entertain a baby? Jamie is sitting in the flower bed eating the crumbs of chocolate birthday cake that he has found deposited in his hair. Harry has tipped himself up on his bottom to drink the water from the dog's bowl and George is smearing the poster paints that he brought as a present for Jamie, all over his face. Wally is doing balloon tricks for the older children – Bennie, Buzzy, Jackson, Biba, Philippa, Chloe, Carlos and Jessamy. Skye and Camille are not here. They have gone ice skating with Margot's husband. Stanley is here, it being a weekend, and he and Edward are standing a bit apart, watching the balloon tricks.

'Now, what do you think this is?' says Wally, bending a long, thin, blue balloon into a slightly different long thin shape.

'Is it a sausage?' says Philippa.

'Nooo,' says Wally, 'but that's a good guess.'

'Is it a gun?' says Carlos.

'Nooo, try again.'

'Is noclars?' says Bennie.

'Nooo, it's not whatever it is you said you thought it was, little boy. Doesn't anybody know?' Wally puts the balloon up to his mouth.

Buzzy puts her hand up.

'Yes, my Buzzy?'

'Is it a cigar, Daddy?'

'Yes! It's a cigar!'

'What's a cigar?' asks Jessamy.

'Time for the disco!' says Wally.

'Yippee,' say the kids.

Wally then puts on 'Hit Me Baby One More Time' and gets his bow tie to spray water at the children and they all run round the garden giggling.

'Erggh, blerp, ga!' says Jamie as Bennie runs past him.

Then Wally turns the music up and the children all start dancing in the strange little way that they do – all wiggling hips and waggly bottoms – and the next thing I know, Jamie has crawled out of the flower bed and is in the middle of the garden, bouncing away rather rhythmically on his capacious baby bottom. His hands are in the air. He is clenching and unclenching his fists and smiling.

'Ma-ma-ma-ma!' he says.

'Come on, Jamie,' says Edward to his brother. 'You look funky!'

Just then, my sister walks into the garden.

'Auntie Julia!' Edward runs over to her and gives her a kiss.

'This looks like a great party!' Julia says to Edward.

'Is Robert here?'

'He's just parking the car.'

'Robert can drive?'

'Well, he's not supposed to but I let him sometimes.'

'You let Robert drive?'

'Yes, Edward. I am trying to encourage him to be independent, as learning to be independent is a very big deal for a child. Actually, I think I might write a book called *How to Encourage the Independent Child* and . . .'

'Driving's awesome,' says Stanley.

'What does awesome mean?' says Edward.

Robert comes into the garden. Bennie sees him and runs into his arms. 'Bennie,' says Robert affectionately, rubbing Bennie on the top of his head and reaching down to pick him up.

'Me got gar,' says Bennie, showing Robert the long thin balloon that he has somehow stolen from Wally's bag.

'What's gar?' says Robert.

'He means a cigar,' says Stanley.

'Look at Jamie!' Edward says to Robert. 'He's dancing on his bottom.'

Julia and Robert turn to look at Jamie. 'Oh I very much approve of this!' says Julia. 'Babies like nothing more than music. Lots of people think babies can't dance but they love to move to a rhythmic beat. It helps them get a spatial sense of their own bodies.'

Jo sees Julia and comes over to give her a hug. 'How are you?'

'I am very well, thank you, Jo,' says my sister. 'And how are you?'

'I'm great!' says Jo. 'Have you met my husband, Wally? He's the children's entertainer.'

'Well, he's doing a very good job. I was just telling Edward how much babies like music –'

'That's what I said to Samantha!' says Jo. 'But she pooh-poohed me!'

'Oh don't worry about Samantha! She never listens to a word I say.'

Then Julia says she must have a quick chat with Genevieve. 'I'm so sorry,' she says to Jo, 'I don't want to spoil the fun but I need to run through some things with Genevieve.'

'Oh have you heard about Nicholas?' continues Jo. 'I think my Viagra is doing them the world of good! And it's all worked out with his son. Apparently, once his mother found out Nicholas was not going to give her any more money, she went back to the States.'

'Oh that's wonderful!' says Julia.

'And how is your husband?'

'He's out of hospital.'

'Has he moved back in?'

'No,' says Julia. 'I think too much has gone on for that.' I hear her go on to tell Jo what happened on the night of her arrest. 'I don't know why he did it! I mean, why on earth would I have stabbed him? I know I was angry with him and I know I got Robert to scratch that word on his car, but to stab my husband? I'd never do that!'

'Well, why do you think he accused you of it?'

'I think he went a bit mad in hospital. I think he had nothing else to think about but our marriage. He became quite convinced that I had never loved him, you know, so I suppose, once he'd discovered that's how he felt, he realized he was very angry with me. I imagine that the hospital must have seemed very claustrophobic and I think Joe also felt guilty about running off with Suki and so, to get rid of his guilt and anger, he decided to get me arrested. But, of course, once he'd done it he felt terrible and had to tell the police not only had he made the whole story up but that actually the whole plate-stabbing thing was an accident as he'd fallen on it himself!'

'Was it scary at the police station?'

'Not really. But, you know, Joe and I had both gone mad. I was no better really. I accused Suki of something she didn't do because of my own anger and guilt.'

'But how did you get Joe to admit he'd lied?'

'Oh Samantha dispatched her friend Dougie to help me. Do you know Dougie? He's a lawyer.'

'Oh yes. I've heard Samantha talk about him. Didn't his wife leave him about a year ago?'

'Yes, that's him. Well, he realized quite quickly what had gone on and he suggested the police confront Joe with all the evidence, and that was it really.'

Julia is now beckoning to Genevieve, who gets up from the grass. 'Look at Jessamy, Julia,' she says as she comes over. I watch them as they watch Jessamy, who is laughing and dancing with her sister. 'She's a different girl.'

They then go on to discuss my sister's new venture, a book and a speaking tour entitled *How to Bring Children Up the Natural Way* (also known as *Ban the Naughty Step!*) by Julia Smythe, Mother of Six. My sister came up with the idea after she'd talked to Genevieve that afternoon a few months back and then, about two weeks later, my sister called me up and said, 'If I am going to become a motivational speaker then I need someone to organize me.'

Just as she said it the same idea came into both of our minds at the same time. 'Genevieve!' we both said.

'She used to organize people to buy African artefacts,' I said. 'She was terribly good at it. And she organizes charity lunches and painting sessions at playgroup. And she's bored!'

'Part of the profits could go to her arts and crafts project,' said my sister dreamily. 'I like that. It's good karma.'

'That's if there *are* any profits.'

'Oh yes,' says Julia hurriedly, 'that's if there are any, of course. No one may come! It may be a disaster!'

It turns out, of course, that Genevieve has been amazing. She and my sister speak every day. Today, Julia says to Genevieve that she needs to finalize some dates for her speaking commitments. 'I've spoken to the mothers' group in Amersham,' says Julia, 'and they want me to do the fourteenth, which is next week, and that's a bit soon for me so I think it needs rearranging.'

'Oh don't worry,' says Genevieve, 'I'll call them and shift it because, actually, you're booked into that hall in Aylesbury at the end of next week and the tickets are sold out, so you can't possibly do two talks in one week. Then there's been a lot of interest in you doing a mini-tour in the West Country, a bit in Devon and Cornwall and coming back via Bristol and Bath.'

'Oh that would be exciting! But remember, I've promised Dougie a ticket to come to the Aylesbury talk. He rang and said he really wanted to come.'

Genevieve raises her eyebrows. 'Dougie, eh?'

'I like Dougie,' says Robert who has now put Bennie and his balloon down.

'Seen a lot of him, then?' says Genevieve.

'Oh he just pops round,' says Julia airily.

'Doesn't he live in London, though?' Genevieve smiles at Julia.

'He taught me how to drive around the farm,' says Robert, 'and he helps us with our homework.'

'He loves children,' says Julia, as if by way of explanation.

'Well, I guess that's a plus if he's going to go out with you, Mum,' says Robert.

'I am not going out with Dougie,' says Julia. 'We are merely good friends.'

'Yeah, right.'

But now I am no longer concentrating on them for John, my John, has come into the bedroom and is standing behind me, his arms round my waist. 'And what are you listening to, you naughty ear-wigger?'

'Oh I'm listening to everybody and everything.'

'Is that Jamie dancing on his bottom?' John asks when he sees Jamie's little hands waggling up and down.

'Mmm.'

'And is that our little Bennie playing with Jessamy over in the corner of the garden?'

I look and see Bennie and Jessamy playing on a plastic tractor. Bennie is sitting on the tractor and Jessamy is pushing him along.

'Wonders will never cease,' I say.

'But where's Edward?'

'I don't know where he is. He's gone off somewhere with Stanley.' Then we both listen and we hear them coming up the stairs.

I am about to call out to Edward when John says, 'Shh!' and puts his finger over his lips. 'They're talking,' he whispers. We creep to the bedroom door and listen to them.

'Edward,' says Stanley, 'did your dad, that one we thought was a pirate, ever come and see you?'

'Oh yes. He came in the summer but it turns out he wasn't a pirate but he was very tall.'

'Did I meet him?'

'I don't think you did. He didn't stay very long.'

'Why not?'

'Well, my grannie died and then he left.'

'My grannie died a few years ago,' says Stanley, 'and I was quite sad but I didn't cry because my mum told me it's bad for my sinuses to cry. Did you cry when your grannie died?'

'No, I didn't cry because she told me that if I ever needed to talk to her or if I ever thought of her and missed her then I should know that she's in heaven and she's watching over me. She wrote me a letter to tell me that and I could show it to you, if you like.'

'Oh yes, please.'

After some rustling we hear Edward say, 'Ah-ha! Here it is. Right, Stanley, this is how it starts: "My darling Edward" – she always called me darling – "My darling Edward, by the time you read this I will be dead but I want you to know that I am very proud of you and I love you very much."'

'That's nice, isn't it?'

'What is?'

'The "I love you very much" bit,' says Stanley. 'What else does she say?'

'Oh she says . . . erm, let me see . . . she says that I must be nice to my mother and I must be nice to my new daddy and my brothers, and then she says, oh this is the best part, she says, "In my will I have left you a house in Devon."'

'A house in Devon? Awesome.'

' "It is the house near the sea where you and your mother came to stay. I think you will love it as I always loved it and I want you, and your family, to enjoy it as much as I have." '

'Gosh,' says Stanley, 'that's a big present to give someone, isn't it?'

'Well, I don't get my present now and I have to share it with my brothers, but when I'm older I can go and live there with them. Actually, Stanley, we could both go and live there because there are lots of wasps there. I remember I went there with my mum and there were wasps everywhere.'

'I think I'd like that. I like wasps.'

'Shall we go and draw a picture of a wasp?'

'Ooh yes, and we could draw on our bodies again, couldn't we?'

'That's a good idea.'

'Bagsy I'm a snake.'

'Oh no,' I groan, as John leads me from the door and back to the bed.

'Oh it'll be all right. Forget about Corporate Queen right now. When Stanley is with us, he is part of our family and if our family decide the one thing they want to do is to paint snakes on their willies, then so be it.'

'Are you going to tell her that?' I say, lying down on my back and watching the sunlight drifting across the ceiling.

'Absolutely!' Then John looks deep into my eyes. 'Everything is fine, Samantha. You mustn't worry about anything.'

'I only really worry about Edward.'

'You don't need to worry about Edward either. He has everything he needs here, right here. He has you and me and his brothers and his friend and that is quite enough for one small boy.'

'Yes, you're right.'

'And,' continues John, 'who knows whether his father will keep in touch with him, but there's nothing we can do about that. That is up to John the First and his own conscience.'

'Do you think he and Santa will work out?'

John laughs. 'Absolutely not.'

'Oh dear.'

'Oh don't "oh dear" about Santa. She's a practical girl. She'll survive.' Then he looks back into my eyes again. 'And we have survived, Samantha. We've more than survived.'

Then we hear Edward and Stanley go back down the stairs.

'Let's go and surprise Bennie!' they are saying. 'Let's go and waggle our willies at Wally!'

'Oh God,' I say, now trying to hoik myself off the bed. 'John, we'd better go downstairs.'

'Not before you kiss me.' And John takes me into his arms and kisses me long and deeply. 'Do you think anyone would notice if we . . .'

'If we what?' I say, kissing him back.

'If we . . . you know . . .'

'Made another baby?'

'Yes, that's one way of putting it,' he says and now he's lifting off my dress and running his hands up and down my body, and the long, white linen curtains at our bedroom window are blowing back in the breeze and I feel as light and airy as that breeze itself . . . then I hear the unmistakable sound of shuffling.

John stops kissing me. 'What's that noise?'

We look towards the door. There, balancing precariously on both his stubby, one-year-old legs, is Jamie.

'Jamie, you're standing up!'

'Erggh, blerp, ga!' says Jamie.

'Jamie, come to Daddy!' says John and Jamie looks at his father and gives a little wobble and a little giggle and then, with a look of pure determination on his face, he puts one still furled and curled baby foot in front of the other and takes a step.

'Ma-ma-ma!' he says, waving his arms in the air then slumping back down with a jolt onto his bottom.

'Jamie, you walked!' says John, sounding utterly amazed.

'Oh the wonder of it,' I say as John rises to pick his last-born son off the floor. 'The wonder of it all.'

Acknowledgements

I would like to thank Polly and David for all their support and generosity and the use of their house. I would also like to thank Charles and Sylvia and Cherry and Brian, and Helen Turton for helping me write in peace.

I could not have done this book without the unwavering support of my agent Kate Jones and editor Louise Moore at Penguin, who showed such inspiring faith in me. I am indebted to Claire Bord and Clare Parkinson for their meticulous editing and Louise Allen Jones and Bridget Hancock for their enthusiasm and advice.

Thanks also to all my family and friends and, of course, my crazy children. And, to Michael, thank you, my love.

Read on for more about the
Smythe family from

Lucy Cavendish's new novel

coming in Autumn 2008

1. A Stormy Day

For the first time in his life, Edward is wearing clothes on the beach. I am watching him from where I am perched on a sand dune. I am trying to pretend I'm not looking at him as I know Edward is will get cross if he thinks I am observing him, for now, aged ten (or 'nearly eleven' as he puts it), Edward has finally become aware of his body. I've seen him looking at himself in the bathroom mirror. He has huge long legs and dangling arms. Sometimes he smells a bit and I have to remind him that he needs to use soap on his body.

'Why do I have to use soap?' he'll say truculently.

'Because when you start getting older and you play more sport, you start to sweat and when you sweat you –'

'But you don't need to use soap for sweat,' Edward usually chips in. 'I asked my cousin Robert about that once and he told me that actually if you leave your body alone, it looks after itself.'

'Who told him that?'

'I think Auntie Julia did.'

'Well, I think maybe Auntie Julia was referring to hair. Some people do say that if you leave your hair long enough it will replenish its own oils and –'

'No, Robert said Auntie Julia told him that your whole body can clean itself so I'm not going to use soap and that's final.'

'Right, Edward,' I'll say firmly. 'If you don't use soap,

you will not be able to play on your computer at the weekend.'

Edward will then glower at me a bit.

'Where is the soap, then?' he'll say accusingly, as if I have deliberately taken all the soap in the house and hidden it. 'There isn't any soap!'

'Yes there is.' I'll point to his younger brothers' soap dispenser, a plastic frog that squirts out something liquid smelling of a chemical version of strawberries.

'Not that soap,' Edward will say. 'That's for babies. Where's the type of soap big boys use?'

Over the past few months we have had many encounters like this and I have had to accept the fact that, on top of hating having a bath, Edward no longer feels that freedom about his body that he used to. When he was a young child, he would happily discard his clothes everywhere and anywhere. Here are some of the places where Edward has taken his clothes off: London Zoo on a hot summer's afternoon, when it occurred to him, aged three, that he would like to be as free and unfettered as the monkeys looping from tree to tree chattering on about this and that.

'I wanna be free like a monkey, Mama,' he said to me as he pulled his tee shirt off over his head.

'Yes, Edward,' I said, 'but you are not a monkey. You are a small boy and small boys keep their clothes on.'

'But monkeys are naked, Mama,' he replied.

'Yes,' I said, 'but they are not really, are they? They have *fur* so, in the world of monkeys, they are actually fully clothed.'

'But I can see their winkies,' said Edward, now pulling down his pants. 'They have *huge* winkies.' It took me two

392

ninety-nine ice creams to persuade him to put his clothes back on and then he was sick down his trousers and ended up having to take them off anyway.

Then, about a year later, on his first day at school, he tried to take his clothes off before he'd even got through the gates. I'll never forget him standing in his rather over-large uniform with his serious owl face looking at me.

'I don't like this,' he said, ripping at the buttons. He was half excited, half terrified. He pulled faces as I took photographs of him. Then he locked himself in the loo and divested himself of his clothes. That time, it took a promise to take him to the ice cream parlour directly after school to persuade him to put them back on.

After that incident, Edward got very adept at locking himself in loos and taking his clothes off. He once had a very exciting time in TGI Friday's. The toilets in there apparently had some spraying mechanism so not only did Edward come back in to the restaurant soaking wet, but, I discovered, he'd also managed to soak absolutely everything else including all the loo rolls and the hand towels.

'Sorry,' said Edward, looking very sorrowful. 'I just can't help it.'

He also said 'I can't help it' when he took all his clothes off in the middle of Tuscan village and jumped into their obviously sacred waterfall. 'I'm so hot!' he said as he launched himself in, ignoring the shouting of the locals who ran out of their houses to remonstrate with him. 'Sì, sì!' yelled Edward who now, aged six, had learnt a few words of Italian. 'Gelato, gelato!' he yelled as they wagged their fingers at him. I just hid behind my guidebook leaving John the Second, my lovely wonderful husband, to sort it out.

*

So nudity is not something alien to Edward. His brothers, little Bennie and baby Jamie, are happy to be naked. I always think of them as like cherubs in the sky, looking down on us tooting their horns and held aloft by their golden wings. Maybe that's what cherubs are, babies waiting to come to earth, watching us from above and picking out the mothers and families they like although God knows why anyone would pick me. I remember when Edward was very tiny and he cried all the time, especially when I was trying to give him a bath. (See? Thinking about it now, he's never really liked having a bath.) One day, my mother came round to find me crying along with Edward.

'What on earth is the matter?' she said. 'Why are you and that baby crying?'

'He doesn't like me,' I wailed. 'Everything I do is wrong. I tried to give him a bath and he threw his little arms out and he looked terrified and –' I wailed some more '– he *hates* me!'

My mother made me a cup of tea and sat me down. She then picked up Edward and held him for a while.

'You need to support his head when you bath him,' she said, wedging Edward firmly into the crook of her arm. 'Maybe he doesn't feel properly supported. That's why most babies panic, you see.' Then she took him over to the bath and swooshed him around in the water and he cooed with happiness.

'You see?' she said. 'He's a perfectly affable little chap.' Then she looked at me and said, 'Babies choose their parents you know, so, believe it or not, Edward chose you so if I were you I'd get on with it and stop feeling sorry for yourself.'

*

Now I know two things: I know that Edward isn't really an affable chap. He is amazing and magnificent and probably the love of my life but he is not affable. He is odd and scratchy and sensitive. He knows this and I think it concerns him. I see him furrow his brow when children in the playground tell him he is weird which, according to him, they do quite often.

'Am I weird?' he will say to me and I'll do that thing my mother always used to do – which actually irritated me beyond all measure – and say to him, 'Well Edward, it takes all sorts of people to make a world.'

Edward will think about this and then his face will clear and he'll say, 'Yes, it does, doesn't it, Mummy?'

I also know that Edward and I probably did choose each other. We are two units that have become a whole. I like being with him possibly more than I like being with anyone else.

Today, on the beach, Edward is going to extreme lengths not to be seen. I can see him carefully wrapping himself in a towel. He takes his tee shirt off, clutching the towel round his waist, and then tries to wriggle out of his underpants.

'Do you want some help, Edward?' I call out to him. Edward glowers at me. 'Do you want me to hold the towel?' I say.

'No,' says Edward, trying to ignore me. He looks around for his swimming trunks. He can't see them. Of course he can't see them because I have them. The reason I have them is because I have everything. I always have everything. I have packed the entire boot of the hire car with all the things we might need and in amongst all the things we might need, in the bags I have brought down to the beach, are Edward's swimming trunks. Now I can see that Edward is getting a little panicked. He looks confused for a minute then he turns to me and it's as if sunlight has shone across his face and he smiles endearingly at me as he always used to do.

'Mummy,' he says, raising his big blue eyes to look at me, 'do you know where my swimming trunks are?'

For a brief moment the thought comes into my mind that I should say, 'No, I don't know where your swimming trunks are. Did you not pack them?' for do I not spend hour upon hour moaning to my husband John that I feel taken for granted and that my children are too dependent on me and why can't they pack their own bags and make their own tea and clean their own teeth and John will point out very patiently that yes, that's all very well for Edward, but what about Bennie who is four and Jamie who is two? But then I wonder why John can't do the packing. Why is it my job? Then again, he did try to help pack for this holiday and I found him stuffing raincoats into side pockets and packing some tiny nappies that Jamie hasn't worn for at least a year.

'It's April,' I said to him. 'We are going to Crete. Crete is one of the hottest places known to mankind, even this early on in the year.'

'Great,' said John smiling.

'So why are you packing the raincoats?'

'Because it's not the summer holidays, is it? It's Easter and maybe Crete is cold at Easter,' he said and then he wandered off and I had to unpack all the bags and start over again because I was not sure that anything John had packed was suitable for a holiday – even if it was only an Easter holiday – at all.

*

So, here we are, on the beach. I am about to delve into one of my bags and find Edward's swimming trunks when I feel Jamie tugging the bottom of the long linen dress I am wearing. I had deposited him next to me on a beach towel and the last time I looked at him, all of thirty seconds ago, he was happily playing with his bucket and spade but now he is trying to climb up my leg and on to my shoulder. He is shrieking, hopping from foot to foot. He has somehow managed to manoeuvre himself off the towel and is standing on the sand looking desperate. Jamie, it has to be said, hates sand, especially on his feet. I have taken him to countless sandpits and encouraged him to play, but all he does is cry. The first time I rolled his little baby trousers up and took his tiny shoes off and helped him toddle into the sand play area, he reacted with horror. As soon as his feet hit the sand, he let out a high-pitched squeal, and then did a bizarre dance of irate disgust before he turned, buried his face in my skirt and tried to climb up me, his podgy little fingers clawing away at my clothes. Since then, I have tried everything. I have taken him to play parks and shown him lots of other children having a good time. Last summer, when it was deliciously hot, I found a park with a sandpit and a large paddling pool. I packed Bennie and Jamie in the car and then Jamie and I watched Bennie take off all his clothes and wriggle right down into the warm sand like a snake. But it made no difference to Jamie. He just watched Bennie and then squealed every time I took him near the sand. In fact, now I think about it, he was no more enthusiastic about the water.

'Oh Jamie,' I say to him. 'Is it the sand? Is it too hot?'
Jamie just looks at me rather sadly.
'Is Jamie ever going to speak?' Edward says, shuffling

towards me with his towel still clasped round his waist. 'God, this sand's hot.'

'Of course Jamie's going to speak,' I say, picking Jamie up before he starts crying. 'He's just a baby, Edward. You didn't speak for years, you know. I had to get you speech therapy and –'

'Oh forget it, Mum,' says Edward. 'Look after Jamie.'

Edward turns his back on me. In one motion, I deposit Jamie on my hip, his little feet all curled up, and hurl Edward's swimming trunks towards him. He puts them on and mooches off towards the sea.

'I love you, Edward,' I say to his back.

'Yeah right,' he replies, not turning around.

I sit and stare at Jamie, who I have plonked back down on my towel.

'Jamie,' I say. 'What is the matter with you?'

Jamie sits wiggling his toes and burbling away.

'Jamie!' I say more sternly. 'Why don't you like the sand?'

'Dada,' Jamie says to me, with a doleful look.

'No, Jamie,' I say, 'I am not your daddy. I am your mummy.'

Jamie gives me one of his heart-melting smiles then he reaches out, hauls himself on to my lap and cuddles right into me.

'Dada,' he says happily and pops his thumb into his mouth.

We sit there for a while – him and me. I look out at the glistening sea and the sand and the sun. I suddenly feel rather exultant. I can imagine how I look; long tousled hair pushed back by the sunglasses resting on my head, tanned arms, tanned face, wearing a floaty white linen dress, beautiful blond baby cuddled into me. God, I feel good. This is a wondrous place. Even though it is only April, the sun is warm, the sand is golden, there are only a handful of people here. I like watching the sea and the gulls and the flocks of birds that wheel around overhead. I have our picnic hidden in the cool shade of a rock; there are sandwiches and fruit and a salad plus some water for the boys and a bottle of chilled white wine for me and John.

We are having a good time here, John and me. So much of our lives are spent passing each other in a rushed, chaotic muddle. He goes off to work. I look after the children. Sometimes we swap lives and I do some work and he runs around like a headless chicken trying to get the children ready to go to school/nursery/anywhere but stay in the house. 'Where are your socks?' he'll ask Bennie.

'My socks?' Bennie will say. 'They are here,' and then he'll grab a pair of Edward's that I have left out in the vague hope that Edward might find them and not put on the smelly ones from the day before. Then Bennie will run outside into the garden at great speed brandishing the socks above his head.

'Those are my socks!' Edward will yell, running after him, and then Jamie will put his own socks in his mouth and, five minutes later, John will come in wild-eyed and find me getting ready in the bathroom and say, 'I can't seem to get the children dressed,' and then I will go outside and persuade them to behave.

Then I'll try to find the car keys – usually in the dog basket – and then I'll hang out the washing and then I'll come back inside and find that still none of the children have their socks on and that, in fact, John is now playing a version of a game Edward calls 'Conquerors' with them, which involves John hiding behind the sofa while the children creep up on him until he finally roars and chases them back out into the garden.

'Bye,' I'll say, heading towards the front door. Everyone will ignore me. Later, on my way home, I'll get a call from John who by now is exhausted. 'When on earth are you coming home?' he'll say.

So our minds are always befuddled which is why I write everything down. I make endless lists and then I insist that John also makes his own endless lists and, sometimes, our lives seem run by these bits of paper inserted in our diaries. We spend evenings staring at dates and pages and booking in time – time for Edward to go on a sailing course, time for Bennie to get used to the idea of starting school this September, time to persuade Jamie to start speaking.

'You're spending a couple of weeks going to Edward's school in the mornings before the beginning of the summer holidays,' I tell Bennie.

'Why?' Bennie will ask.

'To get used to it,' I say. 'It'll be fun!'

Then John tells Edward that he must take the time to speak c-l-e-a-r-l-y to Jamie so that his brother can learn to speak properly.

'I d-o speak c-l-e-a-r-l-y,' Edward will say.

John and I try to have time for us. Sometimes we go out for dinner. Sometimes we see friends. Often, we just like hanging out together. Yet somehow on this holiday I feel that here we have found each other again. I didn't know we had lost touch but here, well, we have been happy. Here we have found what we have always known, what has never really gone away but somehow faded into the background: that we love each other.

Every night we have made a fire on the beach and then John and I have told the children stories and watched them as they have drifted off to sleep happy, tanned and tired. Then we have taken them back to our hotel room, tucked them in and spent time with just the two of us, drinking wine and laughing and making love like teenagers, quietly and surreptitiously in the dark.

Why, even Edward, truculent Edward, is happy. Look! There he is. I can see him lunging into the waves now. He is diving through them, like a seal pup with his wet brown hair flattened on to his head. I put my hands over my eyes and squint. I see John and Bennie in the waves near Edward. Is that John and Bennie? I think so. Yes, that's John. I can make out his body. Lord, how I know that body. I can tell it by its outline – tall but with that stuck-out middle, like a bear. 'It's my curve of pleasure,' John always says when he points to his stomach. Sometimes, when I am feeling particularly witty, I ask him when he is having the baby. 'Next spring,' he'll say laughing, but it is true that the buttons are popping off his shirts and his jackets don't do up any more. Ah, and there with him is Bennie. Bennie is a mini-John. He has exactly the same figure, even the same bottom – cute and round but flat at the sides. Bennie has taken his clothes off, as per usual. I can see his blond curls, long and straggly over his shoulders. I can see his rosebud mouth opening as he screams in delight as John swooshes him up and then in and out of the waves. Look at Bennie! He is laughing so much he is almost hysterical. And John is throwing him higher and higher and maybe a little bit too high I think and Edward is leaping into and through the waves now alongside John. The waves come big and rolling and John grabs Bennie and hurls him forwards into them. Hurl. Splash. Crash go the waves as they plummet down and smash on to the beach.

'Oh Jamie,' I say, as Jamie snuggles further down into my arms. Don't you want to go into the water? Why don't you want to go into the water? It's so delightful and cold and refreshing.'

Jamie gazes up at me.

'Oh I love being on holiday,' I say to him.

I look down at him and kiss him. I kiss his little snubby nose and he wrinkles his nose up in pleasure and I kiss his little pink mouth and . . .

Suddenly I hear a noise. The wind catches it and brings it across the beach towards me. I strain forwards to hear it for, somehow, I know it is important. Someone is shouting. I look around. Who is shouting? Then I see a long-limbed figure running across the beach towards me. It is Edward. It is he who is shouting. Oh God. What has happened? I leap up, depositing Jamie in the sand. Jamie starts crying. Christ, what is going on? Edward is yelling now. I can see his mouth yawning open. '*Muuuum!*' he is shouting and then I can see he is shouting something else but I cannot hear what for his words keep getting caught up and snatched away by the wind. He sounds panicked. What is it? Has he stepped on a sea urchin? No, he is not limping. I hear Jamie crying. I do nothing about it. I cannot concentrate on him right now. I know something has happened. I look for John but I can't see him. '*Muuuum!*' yells Edward, still struggling up the beach towards me. I look for John again.

I still can't see him. I run towards Edward. I can see the panic in his face. He has gone totally white. I can still hear Jamie crying behind me. I keep going. I look for Bennie. Where is Bennie? There is John. Thank God. I can see him in the water. He is up and looking around. I can see his head swivelling around like a crazed dog looking for a stick. He has lost something in the water. I look for Bennie.

Oh God. Where is Bennie? I can't see him. Why can I not see Bennie? I can see John looking this way and that, this way and that, yet I cannot see Bennie. I start to panic. I see John looking frantically at the sea and then suddenly he dives down. But when he comes up he is still alone and there is still no Bennie and now all I can see is John, only John, silhouetted in the sea against the sun and Edward thrashing across the sand towards me, now breathless and half crying, half yelling. I can hear Jamie wailing behind me and then, finally, I hear it. I hear a roar. It is not the sea. It is not a flock of seabirds with their wings beating heavily through the air. It is John. '*Bennniiee!*' he yells and the sound of his voice breaking, cracking, is carried across the water and ends up echoing all around the perfect inlet of Elafonisi beach.

And that was it. In that very moment, before John dived down one more time, before John beat his arms against the waves and, somewhere, somehow, found Bennie at the bottom of the sea and pulled him up all cold and seemingly lifeless and dragged him away from the wave that was tugging at him once again to take him back out to sea forever. Before the Greek doctor we had never met before, who just happened to be on the beach with his family that day, bent his head down to inflate Bennie's lungs and bring him back to life. Before I knew whether Bennie was dead or alive, I knew something very important. I knew that it was me and me alone who had this ability to create these children and love them and keep them. It was an incredible feeling. It seemed to be the only thing that made any sense. Bennie was mine and only I could make the decision to lose him. No one else had the right to take my child away from me. In the moment it took for that doctor to force air into Bennie's body, that breath that wrenched Bennie back to life, I knew something else. I wanted another baby. And that knowledge made me put my hand fleetingly on my belly and, once Bennie was breathing regularly, I let myself smile a secret smile.

Lucy Cavendish

1. Becoming a novelist

2. Samantha Smythe
   and her family

3. Life as a writer

4. What's next . . .

Photograph © Harry Borden

Becoming a novelist

Samantha Smythe took a while to come about. I have spent most of my working life in journalism and, like most journalists, would dream of writing a book while I edited copy. I used to sit wondering what I could write a book about. I longed to turn my usual one-thousand word articles into something longer and more thoughtful but life kept getting in the way. I got married. I had children. I got tired. I just about managed to hold onto my job but life was changing. Pretty quickly I realised an office life wasn't going to work for me. I missed my children like an ache. Everything was so manic. With my eldest son, I'd drive to Canary Wharf where I was working, drop him at his nursery, tear into the office (probably with my skirt tucked into my knickers), grab a coffee and then sit down and try to pretend I was a cool, calm and collected editor.

> **'Life kept getting in the way. I got married. I had children. I got tired.'**

At 5.30pm, I'd start sneaking frantic peeks at the clock. I had to pick my son up by 6pm or meet with an understandable chorus of disapproval from the nursery staff. At 5.45pm, just as I'd be gathering my coat, my boss would come over with some intricate query that needed sorting out that second. I'd sit there gawping like a goldfish with no air and then try to answer the problem in a nanosecond when it probably needed a good hour's thought, and then I'd run madly back to the nursery to drive a fractious, over-tired baby home.

'My work was suffering, my child was suffering and my marriage.'

In truth, my life wasn't working. Like many women I felt I wasn't doing either job properly. I was just about holding it all together but my work was suffering, my child was suffering and my marriage - well, I barely saw my husband. It was obvious something had to change. This is where Samantha Smythe came in. She started life, not that I knew it then, as a character in a set of columns I did first for the *Sunday Telegraph* magazine and then for the *Evening Standard*. In these columns I'd write about my own life as a working mother. Somewhere along the line, these columns morphed into a semi-fictitious state so that the 'I' character could comment quite freely on what she saw mothers actually going through. The 'I' person went on play dates, took her children on holiday, went off to see cranial osteopaths, etc. She started having a life above and beyond my own in her search to experience every facet of being a wife, a mother - the ultimate juggling machine. The columns generated a lot of response. I always knew there were tons of women out there juggling their lives. I just didn't know that so many of them felt the same way I did. Something in the columns obviously resonated so when an agent approached me about writing a book, I could see it was a very exciting prospect. At first I thought I'd do a guide - or a sort of polemic really - on how to bring up children. I started off by writing five thousand words on what happens in my family life every day but as the book went on and I wrote further, it became obvious to me that I wasn't writing a guide at all but a novel with the 'I' character at the centre of it.

Samantha Smythe and her family

People ask me every day if Samantha is me. She certainly started out as me. I used her as a mouthpiece to explore my life, a life that I felt was pretty representative of many other women's lives. But gradually, as the book changed from fact to fiction, Samantha started having a life of her own. She became a better person than me. She is kind. She is always there to listen. She is very supportive. She tries not to be judgemental. She is a very good person. She is also supposed to symbolise every woman. Like every woman, she tries to do the best by her husband and children. She is the one who makes the packed lunches and reads bedtime stories and knows what day swimming lessons occur. She feeds the dog and strokes the cat and

'She certainly started out as me. I used her as a mouthpiece to explore my life.'

washes the socks and cleans the kitchen. She helps out her friend Dougie who has got divorced. She tries to balance her abandoned sister. She loves her husband. In fact, Samantha really does love John and this relationship turned out, eventually, to be of much importance in the books. I always wanted

John to be a real character, not a cardboard cut-out. It was absolutely vital that he wasn't the typical two-dimensional, useless man often portrayed in fiction. John loves his children as much as Samantha does.

'Edward makes a very significant and important choice about whom he feels his father is.'

He tries to help, to be supportive. He too can cook and clean and hold his children when they cry and read them bedtime stories. In fact, Samantha and John's relationship has a real, loving base to it. Like any couple, John and Samantha argue but they know how strong their relationship is, how much it works. They are each other's greatest supporter and defender but they are also honest with each other. They can dare, within this strong marriage, to challenge each other, to say things that are hurtful but sometimes necessary.

The other main characters are, of course, the children. When I first started writing this book, I had no idea how strong a character Edward would become. I just love Edward so much. I can see him in my mind's eye and he makes me laugh and cry at the same time. For me, Edward is at the heart of this book. He is Samantha's son by another man.

He is a part of her past that neither John the Second
nor Bennie and Jamie can ever really know about.
There is a very strong bond between Samantha and
Edward but, again, this is not a traditional and
obvious tale of a boy rejecting a new man who is
trying to be his father. John the Second has become
Edward's father and, at the end of the book

'I get asked if the children are based on my children and to a certain extent they are.'

Edward makes a very significant and important
choice about whom he feels his father is. I hope that
readers can experience Edward as I do. I wanted the
children to be real, fleshed-out characters. I read
so many books where the children are almost in
the way but this is a book about a family and that
family includes children. As it turns out, this book
is only the first of a trilogy. The next two books will
slightly change in emphasis. Book two will focus
more on Bennie, book three on Jamie, as they both
grow into their characters. Edward will still be very
present though! I think it's impossible for him not
to be. Again, I get asked if the children are based
on my children and to a certain extent they are
but, yet again, their characters have become their
own and what happens to them certainly does not

happen in my own children's lives. My eldest son, I have to say, loves me reading the book out to him. I think he feels flattered that he is the inspiration for Edward. He is very happy that I write really.

Sometimes people ask me why Samantha doesn't have a job. She does have a job of sorts but she doesn't have an office life. Once again, I didn't really choose it that way for Samantha. When I first thought about her, she had a job but as I begun to write about her, the nuances of her life with her children and John the Second became more interesting than any office relationship could be. I began to like the fact that she wasn't interested in designer clothes and the glass ceiling. I love the fact that she embraces her life. She has wobbles -

> ## 'Life may overtake her sometimes but she is the kingpin in the home that everyone revolves around.'

we all have wobbles - but she always tries to help people. She may be frantic and life may overtake her sometimes but she is the kingpin in the home that everyone revolves around. She is the consummate warm-hearted wife and mother. Sometimes I wonder if I have done her a disservice by not giving her a working life. Yet I look around me and see many mothers who have given up their jobs to stay at home with their children. They all seem happy. They all seem fulfilled. They are intelligent women and these are the choices they have made. It is these women and their lives - successes and failures - that I want to represent in my novels.

'Samantha's former mother-in-law, Janet, can't bring herself to meet Samantha's children by John the Second.'

Samantha has, in many ways, inadvertently chosen the stay-at-home route but this has left her free to be a very useful canvas. She can, as a character, express what we are all feeling. In *Samantha Smythe's Modern Family Journal*, she is in the same position of many of us - that of not having a traditional, nuclear family. She must balance the needs of her eldest son with those of her second husband and her other two children. This book deals with what it means to be a mother to all these children with all their individual needs. It also looks at a particularly modern phenomenon of the non-nuclear family. Nowadays, many children come from families that are made up of more than one mother or father as relationships separate and parents remarry. I have always been fascinated by how these relationships work out. Who is called 'dad'? What role do grandparents have to play? In this book, Samantha's former mother-in-law, Janet, can't bring herself to meet Samantha's children by John the Second because she finds the break up of Samantha's marriage to her son John the First very hard to deal with. She seems to want to maintain an illusion whereby Samantha never remarried or had any more children. It is a decision she regrets in the end and one she apologises for. I also wanted to look at Edward's relationship with both his fathers. The Johns both seem very relaxed about it at first. It is Samantha who is left worrying about her son but, as the book progresses, Edward gets embroiled in an emotional battle between his two fathers. It is he, I think, the reader wants to protect as Samantha herself becomes increasingly emotionally confused.

Life as a writer

Sometimes I have no idea how I manage to write. My daily routine seems so full of everything else: there's the breakfast to get ready and the children to get to school. They go in three different directions because of their age. By the time I get home there's the house to clean and the washing up to do and the laundry and the bedrooms to tidy. And then there are the animals, for I have realised I am an animal freak. In fact, the older I get, the more animals I seem to acquire. We started off with a cat we were given by our next-door neighbour when her relationship broke up. My eldest son had casually said one day, 'oh I do like your cat', and the next thing we knew, the cat came over the fence, our neighbour drove off in the opposite direction and the cat was ours. He is a big tomcat and rather aggressive and we are all terrified of him. Then one Christmas, I saw some puppies advertised in the local paper. The children had been begging for a puppy for years so I went to see them and they were all black and tumbling over each other and they smelled divine and so ... one girl puppy became ours. She is, of course, Beady in the books and she is as lovely as Beady. My best friend actually said, 'you've put your dog in the book!' and I told her I was happy to as I have immortalised her for us and I'm very happy about that. Currently we have some fish (won at a fair and growing bigger and bigger by the day) and some chickens who strut about our garden and don't lay eggs for some reason, and also a horse. We are in the process of getting two kittens and another puppy, and my husband keeps talking about pigs in a loving fashion and eyeing the field behind our house. So, once I have done the animals, fed them and groomed them and, if I am very lucky, ridden the horse occasionally, I sit down to write.

'I had children crawling underneath me and pulling at me and asking me to get them juice every five minutes.'

When I first started writing the book (this book!) rather than a set of columns strung together, I found it incredibly enjoyable but also incredibly difficult. I wasn't really sure where I was going with it and what I was trying to say and so everything got very convoluted. I'd have one character in two places at the same time. Then I got into a rut of making them explain *absolutely everything* which became rather annoying for me and, I was sure, for any potential readers. I realised quite quickly that my piecemeal way of writing, squeezing in an hour here and an hour there, wasn't really going to work. I was also writing in the house which meant I had children crawling underneath me and pulling at me and asking me to get them juice every five minutes. At this point two things happened: my husband downsized his job to spend three days a week at home and I was offered a peaceful Portakabin by the river in which to write. Suddenly I had time and space so I became very disciplined and I abandoned my husband for huge tranches of time while I went and created Samantha and her world whilst looking at swans drifting down the Thames. It was an incredibly lovely thing to do. I immersed myself in her. I am still immersed in her. I began to realise what fun you could have with characters, how they each become their own person. This is why I am not Samantha. She is her own person.

What's next…

There will definitely be more of Samantha. I am not done with her yet! Every person I know who read the first book wanted more. They wanted to see where Samantha's life would go next so it ended up feeling a natural thing to progress her life further. The second book heralds in a new cast of characters, bar Dougie and Julia. It starts with an incident that rocks the harmony of the Smythe family. It is this event that underlies the rest of what happens in the book as Samantha finds herself spending the summer trying to sort out everyone's lives again.

> **'It starts with an incident that rocks the harmony of the Smythe family.'**

On top of this, in walks Samantha's oldest school friend Naomi. They were very close as children. They spent their childhood pretending to be the characters from *Black Beauty* and carving their initials into a tree but then Naomi moved away and she and Samantha barely kept in touch. Now Naomi is back, with her somewhat disturbed daughter Lexie in tow, and somehow Samantha ends up with Lexie for a time while Naomi goes out to look for work. On top of all this, Samantha is dealing with the comic attentions of the nude-sunbathing and former footballer Gary White ... Not even Samantha can cope with all this.

This second book really deals with what it means to be a mother and the effect on Lexie in particular of not being mothered very well. At the same time, Samantha is desperately trying to get pregnant with a girl and John is off working in London. In many ways, this book looks at how families survive life-changing events. Samantha has to pull on every reserve she has to keep everyone afloat and she also has to realise that she cannot save everyone.

Visit www.mumsnet.com,
the home of Samantha Smythe online.

Feeling desperate, baby waking every two hours at night Any recommendations for ballet-themed novels for an 8 year old? **Single and pregnant – tips needed** Calling Coronation Street watchers **Would you send your kids to private school if money were no option?** Any IVFers out there? **Where can I buy large quantities of plaster of Paris?** Ever wonder how life got like this? **Separating – how do you explain it to a three year old?** Are school secretaries all jobsworths? **Alexander McCall Smith: Is he pure genius?** My four month old doesn't like Grandma **Need a saucy read... I am rubbish at expressing – tips please?** What does a contraction actually feel like (kinda urgent)?! Can I cook a shepherd's pie from frozen? **Things to do in South Wales** Feeling broody – should I try for baby number three? **Best treatment for nits?** Personal trainers – do they work? **Does your child know the f word?** Pooing in the bath...

...another day on **www.mumsnet.com**

by parents, for parents

He just wanted a decent book to read ...

Not too much to ask, is it? It was in 1935 when Allen Lane, Managing Director of Bodley Head Publishers, stood on a platform at Exeter railway station looking for something good to read on his journey back to London. His choice was limited to popular magazines and poor-quality paperbacks – the same choice faced every day by the vast majority of readers, few of whom could afford hardbacks. Lane's disappointment and subsequent anger at the range of books generally available led him to found a company – and change the world.

'We believed in the existence in this country of a vast reading public for intelligent books at a low price, and staked everything on it'
Sir Allen Lane, 1902–1970, founder of Penguin Books

The quality paperback had arrived – and not just in bookshops. Lane was adamant that his Penguins should appear in chain stores and tobacconists, and should cost no more than a packet of cigarettes.

Reading habits (and cigarette prices) have changed since 1935, but Penguin still believes in publishing the best books for everybody to enjoy. We still believe that good design costs no more than bad design, and we still believe that quality books published passionately and responsibly make the world a better place.

So wherever you see the little bird – whether it's on a piece of prize-winning literary fiction or a celebrity autobiography, political tour de force or historical masterpiece, a serial-killer thriller, reference book, world classic or a piece of pure escapism – you can bet that it represents the very best that the genre has to offer.

Whatever you like to read – trust Penguin.